THE TIME FOR LOVE

A CYNSTER NEXT GENERATION NOVEL

STEPHANIE LAURENS

ABOUT THE TIME FOR LOVE

#1 New York Times *bestselling author Stephanie Laurens explores what happens when a gentleman intent on acquiring a business meets the unconventional lady-owner, only to discover that she is not the biggest or the most lethal hurdle they and the business face.*

Martin Cynster arrives at Carmichael Steelworks set on acquiring the business as the jewel in his industrialist's crown, only to discover that the lady owner is not at all what he expected.

Miss Sophia Carmichael learned about steelmaking at her father's knee and, having inherited the major shareholding, sees no reason not to continue exactly as she is—running the steelworks and steadily becoming an expert in steel alloys. When Martin Cynster tracks her down, she has no option but to listen to his offer—until impending disaster on the steelworks floor interrupts.

Consequently, she tries to dismiss Martin, but he's persistent, and as he has now saved her life, gratitude compels her to hear him out. And day by day, as his understanding of her and the works grows, what he offers grows increasingly tempting, until a merger, both business-wise and personal, is very much on their cards.

But a series of ever-escalating incidents makes it clear someone else has an eye on the steelworks. The quest to learn who and why leads Martin and Sophy into ever greater danger as, layer by layer, they uncover a diabolical scheme that, ultimately, will drain the lifeblood not just from the steelworks but from the city of Sheffield as well.

A classic historical romance, incorporating adventure and intrigue, set in Sheffield. A Cynster Next Generation novel. A full-length historical romance of 100,000 words.

Praise for the works of Stephanie Laurens

"Stephanie Laurens' heroines are marvelous tributes to Georgette Heyer: feisty and strong." *Cathy Kelly*

"Stephanie Laurens never fails to entertain and charm her readers with vibrant plots, snappy dialogue, and unforgettable characters." *Historical Romance Reviews*

"Stephanie Laurens plays into readers' fantasies like a master and claims their hearts time and again." *Romantic Times Magazine*

Praise for The Time For Love

"Sophy Carmichael is expertly managing the family steelworks in Sheffield when businessman Martin Cynster comes calling with an offer to buy. His visit coincides with an attack on the plant, and when his and Sophy's lives are threatened, they join forces to find out who is plotting against Carmichael Steelworks. Fans of Regency romance with exceptionally strong female leads are sure to relish this tale." *Angela M., Copy Editor, Red Adept Editing*

"When Martin Cynster approaches Sophy Carmichael about buying Carmichael Steelworks, his life takes an unexpected turn. Fans of romance will enjoy this great story and its intriguing historical setting!" *Kristina B., Proofreader, Red Adept Editing*

"Martin Cynster is interested in buying Carmichael Steelworks, but quickly finds himself with more than just a business deal on his hands. He's intrigued by a series of suspicious accidents at the works and even more so by the company's majority shareholder, the astute, unconventional, and beautiful Sophia Carmichael. By the time the pair unmasks the culprit behind the sabotage, their entanglement has expanded beyond business to encompass some very personal pursuits indeed." *Kim H., Proofreader, Red Adept Editing*

OTHER TITLES BY STEPHANIE LAURENS

Cynster Novels

Devil's Bride

A Rake's Vow

Scandal's Bride

A Rogue's Proposal

A Secret Love

All About Love

All About Passion

On A Wild Night

On A Wicked Dawn

The Perfect Lover

The Ideal Bride

The Truth About Love

What Price Love?

The Taste of Innocence

Temptation and Surrender

Cynster Sisters Trilogy

Viscount Breckenridge to the Rescue

In Pursuit of Eliza Cynster

The Capture of the Earl of Glencrae

Cynster Sisters Duo

And Then She Fell

The Taming of Ryder Cavanaugh

Cynster Specials

The Promise in a Kiss

By Winter's Light

Cynster Next Generation Novels

The Tempting of Thomas Carrick

A Match for Marcus Cynster

The Lady By His Side

An Irresistible Alliance

The Greatest Challenge of Them All

A Conquest Impossible to Resist

The Inevitable Fall of Christopher Cynster

The Games Lovers Play

The Secrets of Lord Grayson Child

Foes, Friends and Lovers

The Time for Love

The Barbarian and Miss Flibbertigibbet (March, 2023)

Lady Osbaldestone's Christmas Chronicles

Lady Osbaldestone's Christmas Goose

Lady Osbaldestone and the Missing Christmas Carols

Lady Osbaldestone's Plum Puddings

Lady Osbaldestone's Christmas Intrigue

The Meaning of Love

The Casebook of Barnaby Adair Novels

Where the Heart Leads

The Peculiar Case of Lord Finsbury's Diamonds

The Masterful Mr. Montague

The Curious Case of Lady Latimer's Shoes

Loving Rose: The Redemption of Malcolm Sinclair

The Confounding Case of the Carisbrook Emeralds

The Murder at Mandeville Hall

Bastion Club Novels

Captain Jack's Woman (Prequel)

The Lady Chosen

A Gentleman's Honor

A Lady of His Own

A Fine Passion

To Distraction

Beyond Seduction

The Edge of Desire

Mastered by Love

Black Cobra Quartet

The Untamed Bride

The Elusive Bride

The Brazen Bride

The Reckless Bride

The Adventurers Quartet

The Lady's Command

A Buccaneer at Heart

The Daredevil Snared

Lord of the Privateers

The Cavanaughs

The Designs of Lord Randolph Cavanaugh

The Pursuits of Lord Kit Cavanaugh

The Beguilement of Lady Eustacia Cavanaugh

The Obsessions of Lord Godfrey Cavanaugh

Other Novels

The Lady Risks All

The Legend of Nimway Hall – 1750: Jacqueline

Medieval (As M.S.Laurens)

Desire's Prize

Novellas

Melting Ice – from the anthologies *Rough Around the Edges* and *Scandalous*

Brides

Rose in Bloom – from the anthology *Scottish Brides*

Scandalous Lord Dere – from the anthology *Secrets of a Perfect Night*

Lost and Found – from the anthology *Hero, Come Back*

The Fall of Rogue Gerrard – from the anthology *It Happened One Night*

The Seduction of Sebastian Trantor – from the anthology *It Happened One Season*

Short Stories

The Wedding Planner – from the anthology *Royal Weddings*

A Return Engagement – from the anthology *Royal Bridesmaids*

UK-Style Regency Romances

Tangled Reins

Four in Hand

Impetuous Innocent

Fair Juno

The Reasons for Marriage

A Lady of Expectations An Unwilling Conquest

A Comfortable Wife

THE TIME FOR LOVE

This is a work of fiction. Names, characters, places, and incidents are either products of the writer's imagination or are used fictitiously and are not to be construed as real. Any resemblance to actual events, locales, organizations, or persons, living or dead, is entirely coincidental.

FOES, FRIENDS AND LOVERS

Copyright © 2022 by Savdek Management Proprietary Limited

ISBN: 978-1-925559-54-5

Cover design by Savdek Management Pty. Ltd.

Cover couple photography by Period Images © 2022

ALL RIGHTS RESERVED.

No part of this work may be used, reproduced, or transmitted in any form or by any means, electronic or mechanical, without prior permission in writing from the publisher, except in the case of brief quotations embodied in critical articles or reviews.

First print publication: August, 2022

Savdek Management Proprietary Limited, Melbourne, Australia.

www.stephanielaurens.com

Email: admin@stephanielaurens.com

The names Stephanie Laurens and the Cynsters and the SL Logo are registered trademarks of Savdek Management Proprietary Ltd.

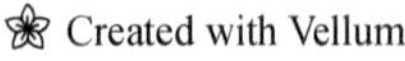

CHAPTER 1

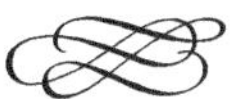

SATURDAY, MAY 9, 1863. SHEFFIELD, SOUTH YORKSHIRE.

Impressive.

Perfect.

This *is what I need to complete my dreams.*

With one hand resting on the silver head of his cane, Martin Cynster stood on the pavement of Rockingham Street and allowed his gaze to roam the lines of the buildings that comprised Carmichael Steelworks.

He'd been hunting for just such a business for more than five years. Acquiring a medium-sized enterprise that specialized in producing high-quality steel in a variety of alloys had always been crucial to bringing to fruition his long-term vision for his investments in the burgeoning iron and steel industries. He already owned a foundry that would supply pig iron to the steelworks and manufactories that would take the steel produced and make it into various products; all he needed was the right steelworks to provide the critical lynchpin, and his vision would be complete.

Focused and diligent inquiries had led him to Carmichael Steelworks. His investigations suggested that the Carmichael works had the ability to produce the sorts of steel his other businesses required, now and into the future. That the works were located in Sheffield, within easy reach of the iron foundry he already owned in neighboring Rotherham, was an added attraction, as was the works' established and stable workforce.

The steelworks occupied the entire block bounded by Rockingham Street on the west, Trippet Lane on the south, Bailey Lane to the east, and

Boden Lane to the north. The Carmichael works were much smaller than the massive steelworks located to the northeast of the town, but significantly larger than the nearby foundries and furnaces that dotted this area west of the town center.

Martin had studied the municipal plans of the site. Now, he stood on the pavement opposite the southwest corner and took in the reality.

The steelworks' shed, a huge edifice of redbrick walls and iron panels, covered much of the site, its pitched roof rising above the surrounding structures. Taking up the full width, east to west, of the site, the shed extended from the northern boundary on Boden Lane to thirty yards or so from the steelworks' frontage on Trippet Lane. Consequently, most of the long Rockingham Street and Bailey Lane boundaries and the shorter Boden Lane boundary were marked by the shed's redbrick wall.

The remainder of the site—the area between the front of the shed and Trippet Lane—played host to several single-story buildings, also in red brick, the majority of which lined Trippet Lane. Wrought-iron railings and gates secured the site's perimeter, filling the gaps between the corners of the shed and the other buildings. The gates, one on Rockingham Street and the other on Bailey Lane, gave access to the cobbled yard that lay between the main shed and the row of buildings on Trippet Lane.

Martin scanned the Rockingham Street façade. The shed's brick wall rose to several feet above a man's head, and above that, vertical iron panels extended to a height of more than twenty feet, as high as a two-story building. A narrow strip of iron-framed windows ran above the panels, letting daylight into the shed. The roof, also iron, angled upward to a long, central spine, broken by a succession of large brick chimneys, most of which were puffing gray smoke into the equally gray sky.

The brick wall continued along Rockingham Street for ten yards past the front of the shed, forming one side of a smaller, single-story building, before the wall gave way to wrought-iron railings and a wide double gate with a single-man gatehouse just inside. The activity in the yard beyond the gate suggested that entrance was used by the heavy wagons bringing in pig iron, the raw material for the works, which Martin had learned was presently sourced from the massive Atlas Works on the other side of town. Once received, the pig iron was carted into the smaller building abutting the shed, no doubt to allow ready access to the iron for the workers to feed the furnaces inside.

South of the gates and filling the southwest corner of the site stood the receiving office. The plain door, bearing a discreet sign, fronted Rockingham Street, almost directly across from where Martin stood.

He'd been observing the steady trickle of people in and out of the office and the wagons trundling up to the gates. He'd learned to approach businesses from the rear, as it were. A neat and efficient-seeming front office could hide a plethora of ills, while activity around the rear gate often told the real tale.

Thus far, everything he'd seen of Carmichael Steelworks spoke of competence, efficiency, and sound upkeep, all attributes he appreciated.

I've seen enough. He looked up and down the street, then crossed and entered Trippet Lane. Cane swinging, he strolled along the steelworks' southern boundary. The Trippet Lane frontage was comprised of adjoining redbrick buildings. Beyond the side of the receiving office, he passed what he suspected was the rear wall of a store for the works' final products, steel bars or rolled plates of the various sizes and compositions currently used in an increasing number of industries, including wire and cable making, the forging of knives and all manner of implements, and more recently, button making; Martin already had an interest in those industries, and there were many more besides.

Steel was the future, and he was determined to secure a well-designed slice of it.

Ahead, the steelworks' main office squatted on the southeast corner of the site, fronting Bailey Lane. Martin rounded the corner, and the main entrance—a pair of wrought-iron gates more ornate than at the rear—came into view; together with a stretch of railings, the gates filled the gap between the office and the southeast corner of the shed. As on Rockingham Street, the wall of the shed formed the rest of the Bailey Lane façade.

He halted outside the office door and, through the main gates—the ones that admitted customers with drays to take away the works' products—looked across the yard to the massive double frontage of the main shed. It seemed that the shed was divided into two lengthwise, with each half sporting huge doors that rolled aside. Both doors were currently fully open, and an ear-assaulting cacophony of machinery pounding and furnaces roaring, punctuated by shouts and curses, rolled out. Even at that distance, Martin could feel the wash of hotter air carrying with it the unmistakable tang of molten metal and burning coal. Through both doors, he could see men and equipment moving, but the relative dimness inside the shed veiled all details.

Martin turned to the office door. The glass panel was etched with the name and logo of Carmichael Steelworks. He reached for the knob, opened the door, and walked in.

He seized the moment of shutting the door to scan the office. A polished wooden counter faced him, and the area behind it contained two desks. The rear wall boasted three doors; he suspected the central door—largest and most impressive—was the one he wanted. The door to his right was half glazed, and through the glass, he could see the yard inside the main gates.

A clerk—a solid-looking middle-aged man in a neat suit—rose from behind one of the desks. "Can I help you, sir?"

Seated at the second desk, a middle-aged woman, neatly garbed, with her graying hair secured in a severe bun, glanced up from the orders she was sorting. On seeing Martin, she blinked, then her gaze grew suspicious.

Martin summoned his most innocently charming smile, trained it on the woman, then switched his attention to the clerk. "I hope so. I'm here to see Miss Carmichael." He waved westward. "I called at her house in Portobello Street and was told I would find her here, at the works."

The clerk was eying him every bit as suspiciously as the woman. "Is Miss Carmichael expecting you?"

Martin kept his mask of relaxed confidence firmly in place. "Yes, I believe she is." Given she'd ignored his letters, she certainly ought to be.

The clerk—possibly secretary—frowned and glanced at the woman. "She didn't mention any meeting…"

The woman—who seemed to have revised her earlier judgment enough to accept Martin's assertion—gestured dismissively. "You know how she is. She gets some idea and comes rushing in and goes straight up to the laboratory, forgetting anything and everything else."

Is that so?

Martin hid his surprise. He hadn't been able to learn much about Miss Sophia Carmichael, majority shareholder of Carmichael Steelworks. He'd asked, but apparently, she didn't move in the social circles for which he had sound intelligence. Until he'd knocked on the door of her Portobello home and been told that she was at the works—in a manner that suggested he should have known that—he'd fully expected to find her filling her morning doing the usual things ladies of quality did.

"So she's in the laboratory in the shed?" He hadn't seen any other building that might reasonably house a laboratory, and many works had their laboratories close to the action. Smiling confidently, he moved to round the counter, making for the door to the yard.

"I'm not sure…?" The secretary—Martin had decided he was probably that—hurried to come out from behind his desk.

Martin waved the man back. "I can find my way. Given the subject of our discussion, we would have ended in the shed anyway." One way or another, he would have ensured that.

He reached the side door, opened it, and stepped through. Leaving the harried secretary to close the door, Martin set off, striding across the yard. He didn't glance back but heard no further remonstrations, and after a moment, the office door quietly shut.

Smiling to himself, he slowed his pace and looked about him, drinking in all he could see. His suspicion that the long building between the receiving office and the main office served as a store for the works' products proved correct; large doors were currently wedged open, providing access to well-stocked bays within.

Several carts had come through the main gates and were loading up with steel sheets. Judging by the sheets' thickness, the load was destined for one of the city's numerous cutlery manufacturers. Meanwhile, trolleys laden with slim steel bars were being hauled out through the shed's nearer door. Judging by the steady *thump-whump* and the clanging rattles emanating from that half of the shed, it housed the steam-powered hammers that beat the steel into the desired shapes, the rolling mills that produced the steel sheets, and no doubt other machinery to work and mold the still-malleable steel.

The farther side of the huge shed, with its noise, heat, and peculiar smell, drew him on. He walked up to and through the huge open door and stepped into a setting that some wag had recently dubbed an early circle of Hell.

Heat enveloped him. Nearby, a furnace roared, spewing red light across the shed. A head-high brick wall ran down the center of the shed, directly beneath the ridge of the roof, and various furnaces were built into that wall, their chimneys rising like massive brick pillars up to and through the roof far above.

Three huge, black Bessemer converters sat along the central wall, each backed into its own brick alcove with a chimney flue opening like a maw above the converter's mouth. The nearest converter was being loaded with pig iron in preparation for a blow—the process during which hot air was bubbled through the molten iron to remove impurities and convert the iron to steel. The middle converter was being tapped, molten steel being drawn off to one side and slag pushed in the other direction, while the third converter was in the middle of its blow, with crushed additive ores—necessary to form whichever alloy was desired—starting to be fed into the converter to mix with the molten iron in the rounded belly of the beast.

Martin halted and took in the scene with one slow, sweeping glance. The staccato sounds from the forging area on the other side of the shed punctuated the sullen roar of the furnaces and the constant hiss of steam.

One comprehensive look was all it took to verify that Carmichael Steelworks had been constructed and organized to maximize efficiency. Quite aside from the steel it produced, this was definitely the steelworks he ought to acquire to complete his portfolio.

Several workmen, leaning on their long-handled implements and waiting for their moment, saw him and stared curiously, then one handed his tool to his mate and approached.

By then, Martin had spotted the set of metal stairs running up the outer wall to a long, narrow room of many windows, set at mezzanine level. The sturdy glass-and-metal-walled and wood-floored room was supported by massive iron pillars bolted to the concrete floor.

As the workman neared, Martin, his expression easy and unconcerned, pointed to the stairs. "I've been told Miss Carmichael is in the laboratory. I take it it's up there?"

The man's features eased, and he nodded. "Aye, sir. Through the door at the top of the stairs."

Martin saluted and, cane swinging, headed for the stairs. He went up quickly, paused on the narrow landing at the top, opened the half-glazed door, and stepped through.

The laboratory stretched the entire length of the narrow room, with a long bench against the outer wall hosting numerous apparatuses while a raised table with papers and rocks littering its surface ran down the room's center. Cupboards and cabinets lined the inner wall, sitting beneath and between the wide windows that provided an unobstructed view of the furnaces and converters below.

The area closest to the door was, relatively speaking, less crowded, as the bench and table didn't reach that far. Three people were in the room, all with their noses, metaphorically speaking, pressed to the glass. Their gazes were trained on the third Bessemer converter, the one where the additive mixture was being combined with the purified molten iron.

Two men in gray laboratory coats stood farther down the room. Both wore wire-rimmed spectacles and were somewhere in their thirties, one brown haired, the other ginger haired. Neither glanced Martin's way.

Equally oblivious was the slender lady with pale-blond hair, twisted into a knot and anchored at the back of her head, who was standing at the window nearest the door. She was dressed in a plain gown of charcoal twill. Noting the absence of any other female, Martin assumed she was his quarry.

Her attention remained unwaveringly fixed on the scene below. "What is it?"

Martin closed the door.

The noise level in the room abruptly fell, and the lady glanced his way.

Her eyes flew wide.

That's better, Martin thought, then her startled gaze rose, and she met his eyes.

The punch of visceral awareness was disorienting.

Turquoise. Her eyes were a most unusual turquoise blue.

Beyond that…his brain was swamped by the impression of a lithe figure, slim, svelte, subtly yet alluringly curved. Her complexion was alabaster pale, and finely arched brown brows and long, thick lashes framed those large and distracting eyes. Her face was heart-shaped, but the set of her lips and chin bore witness to willfulness and determination even while her lush rose-tinted lips, slightly parted in surprise, evoked thoughts he'd never before entertained in the pursuit of business.

Business, some part of his brain insisted. *This is supposed to be about business.*

Sadly, the majority of his mind was already otherwise engaged.

Sophy stared at the man—the gentleman—standing just inside her laboratory as her wits reeled disconcertingly and her senses all but swooned.

The latter shocked her to her toes.

She was *not* a susceptible female—she never had been—yet her eyes simply would not look away, and her attention remained riveted on him while she drank in each and every visual detail.

He was tall—somewhere over six feet of long, rangy, well-built male. He was wearing a black top hat; as she watched, he tipped his head and removed the hat. His hair was dark with the faintest of waves and long enough to brush the collar at his nape. He was carrying an ebony cane with a finely wrought silver head, and his black wool overcoat hung from his broad shoulders in a way that only the most expensive garments did. Every item of clothing she could see—black suit, ivory shirt, gray-patterned waistcoat, neatly arranged stock of a paler gray, and well-polished boots—fitted the image of a wealthy gentleman, and the diamond that flashed in the gold ring on the little finger of his right hand completed the picture.

Yet it wasn't his figure that captivated her and held her speechless, breathless, and close to mindless.

His face was that of a fallen angel, with broad brow, black slanted eyebrows, and deep yet well-set eyes of a shade that reminded her of rich burnt caramel. Those eyes were framed by black lashes that had no business being so thick and lush, and his heavy lids, combined with his lean cheeks, patrician nose, thin, mobile lips, and sculpted chin, contributed to an expression of lazy, good-natured, faintly amused, confidently relaxed benevolence.

She was perfectly certain that whoever he was, he was not benign, much less benevolent.

His gaze held hers—effortlessly, commandingly.

Everything about him screamed danger, yet all she wanted was to move closer and learn more.

Like a moth to a flame.

The thought jarred her. Her wits jerked back into the ascendancy, and she registered the oddity of him being there.

She managed a frown and, with suitably imperious crispness, demanded, "Who the devil are you?"

His eyes didn't leave her face. "Cynster. Martin Cynster."

She blinked and remembered… "Oh. Yes. You wrote."

"Four times."

She remembered his letters quite well. She'd read all of them. Several times each. She forced herself to nod. "I apologize for not replying. Yet."

She should have known better than to let such a persistently eloquent—and curiosity-engaging—offer to buy the steelworks slide, yet while she'd told herself to respond with her standard rejection, she simply hadn't.

Yet.

She met his eyes and tipped up her chin. "I fear I've been distracted."

From the corner of her eye, she caught a flicker—a subtle change in the color of the flame shooting upward from the mouth of the third converter, the one she'd been monitoring. She turned her head and squinted, senses and wits redirected. "I'm not interested in selling the steelworks…"

Something's wrong.

"Damn!" She dove for the speaking-trumpet attached to the wall beneath the window. She seized the instrument, raised it, and yelled, "Hinckley! Shut Betsy down! Stop the feed and throttle the blow!"

She waited only to see her foreman racing toward the controls, then rehung the trumpet and ran for the door.

The gentleman—Cynster—had the sense to smoothly step out of her way. "You name your converters?"

As she rushed past, despite them not touching, a frisson of awareness swept over her, simply because she'd got too close to his flame. Setting her jaw, she pushed through the door and, over her shoulder, flung him an arrogant look. "Of course."

Then she hurried down the steep metal stairs, disturbingly aware that he followed close behind. She didn't have time to bother with him. On reaching the floor, she strode rapidly to where Hinckley and his men were turning the heavy valve to close down the stream of heated air that had been feeding the fire in Betsy's belly.

Hinckley glanced at her. "Off entirely or…?"

"Hold it to a simmer." She continued past Betsy, making for the other side of the massive converter. "I'm hoping I've caught it in time to be salvageable."

Hinckley gave his men their orders and followed. "I saw the flame didn't look quite right."

"There's something wrong with the additives." She yanked her work gloves from her pocket and pulled them on, then climbed the short ladder so she could look into the bucket containing the mix of additive ores. She peered inside.

Hinckley climbed up on the conveyor belt's other side.

Sophy raised her head and looked at the ore lying on the conveyor belt, then reached out, picked up a handful, and examined it closely before letting the rough mixture slide back through her fingers. "Something is missing—namely, the spiegeleisen."

Hinckley frowned. "But how can that be? I watched it being loaded into the feed bucket."

Quickly, Sophy descended the ladder and hurried past the three smaller conveyor belts that fed the crushed ores into the mixer bucket, her goal the ladders that led to the three feed buckets fixed on the wall.

She hurried up the ladder beside the first bucket, the one reserved for spiegeleisen given it was an essential ingredient for all the steel Carmichael's produced. She looked into the bucket. "Huh! It's still full."

Frowning, she followed the trail the ore should have taken and saw... "Aha!" Lips setting grimly, she reached into the narrow chute through which the crumbled rock needed to pass and gripped and wiggled and finally pulled out—

Spiegeleisen rattled down the chute and onto the smaller conveyor belt as she held up the lump she'd pulled free. "A piece of coal. It was blocking the chute."

Hinckley frowned.

Before he could say it, she did. "It couldn't have got there on its own."

While there was plenty of coal around the shed—it fueled the boilers that produced the steam used throughout the works—the lump simply could not have got wedged in the chute without the help of human agency. Holding the lump in her fingers, grimly furious, she glared at it.

"So what do you want to do now?"

Hinckley's question jerked her back to the issue at hand. She thought, then ordered, "Open up the valve again and let the blow run, but keep the feed going until all the spiegeleisen is in and fired. Essentially, extend the blow until everything that should have gone in is in and has been incorporated. As long as everything that should go in does go in, the resulting steel will be the same." Still clutching the lump of coal, she descended the ladder as Hinckley called instructions to his crew.

On reaching the works' floor, Sophy backed away from the converter, then halted. With her head tipped, she watched the blow fire up and studied the flame that, once again, shot up from the converter's mouth. Eventually satisfied that all was as it should be, she handed Hinckley the lump of coal, then dusted off her gloves, pulled them off, and stuffed them into her pocket.

After one last look at the flame, she caught Hinckley's eye. "You were about ten minutes into the additive run when I called a halt, so it'll be about another ten minutes or so of extra time that will be needed."

Like all the men in sight, Hinckley had taken note of the looming presence beside her, the one she was doing her damnedest to ignore, and was understandably curious. Nevertheless, her foreman merely nodded respectfully. "I'll keep an eye on it."

Correctly interpreting her consequent nod as a dismissal, Hinckley lumbered back to his crew, who were standing to one side of the now-firing converter.

She folded her arms and, as soon as Hinckley was out of earshot, without deigning to glance Cynster's way, inquired, "Why are you still here?"

Despite not looking, she heard the amusement lacing his voice as he replied, "Because I'm persistent."

Martin paused, then in a lower tone, added, "Especially when pursuing something I want." As of a few moments ago, that something included her. He resettled his hat on his head and shot her a glance. "Am I to take it that you're the resident metallurgist?"

She was frowning at the converter flame and answered absentmindedly, "Yes. I was always interested in the process, so Colonel Tom taught me."

"Vickers?" He couldn't keep the surprise from his voice. Although still young, Colonel Tom Vickers was well on his way to becoming a legend in steelmaking.

"Hmm. We more or less grew up together. He's like a big brother to me."

The converter was once more in full blow, yet with a faint frown knotting her fine eyebrows, she continued to study the flame.

Martin shifted his gaze to the converter as well.

After a moment, without glancing at her, he quietly asked, "Am I right in thinking that, had you not noticed the anomaly in the flame and the batch of steel had progressed through forging and on to product, then when your customer subsequently used that steel, it might well have failed?"

She remained silent and unmoving for nearly a minute, then replied, "I'm not sure it would have passed through forging, but if it had…yes."

He glanced at her; although she continued to stare at the converter, her lips—those exceedingly luscious and distracting lips—had thinned. "I imagine," he murmured, "that such an outcome would have adversely impacted Carmichael Steelworks' reputation."

Her gaze shifted to him in a narrow-eyed glare, then she lowered her arms and faced him. "And I have to wonder whether there's any connection between a piece of coal wedged into the spiegeleisen chute and you turning up to press your offer to buy the works."

The accusation took him by surprise, and before he could mask his reaction, he'd narrowed his eyes back. "If you'd actually read my letters, you would know that I want to buy the steelworks as a going concern to act as the central cog in my portfolio of steel industries, which rather obviously means with its reputation intact. Damaging Carmichael Steelworks' reputation is the very last thing I would do."

She held his gaze, but her own grew uncertain. Then huffily, she stated, "I did read your letters. That's why I haven't yet replied."

She swung on her heel and stalked off down the shed.

For a second, he watched her walk away, taking in the distracting sway of her hips, then, lips compressing, went after her. "What do you mean?"

He had a sister and many female cousins; he knew better than to imagine he, a mere male, could unravel the workings of a female mind. Lengthening his stride, he caught up with her. "Why did reading my letters stop you from replying?"

She was glancing around, nodding to men as they looked up, smiled, and touched their caps to her. Given the overwhelming noise of the furnaces and the continuing *thump-whump* from the forge, although she and he had to shout, they could converse with little real chance of being overheard. "I found the ideas you outlined interesting. *Not* your offer. As I said, I have no interest in selling the steelworks. My father founded the business and bequeathed it to me. Keeping the works running is in my blood, and I have no interest whatsoever in giving up my legacy."

"But you were interested?"

"In the concept. In your approach to future expansion." Briefly, she met his eyes. "Thank you for giving me some new notions to ponder, but I'm not going to sell Carmichael Steelworks. Not to you or to anyone else."

"I see." He rather thought he did, and somewhat to his surprise, what he saw wasn't disheartening. Not in the least.

Apparently alerted by something in his tone, she threw him a suspicious look, then presumably reverting to ignoring him, she marched on, progressing farther down the shed while running her eyes over the activity occurring all around.

The men clearly knew what they were doing. Some were subforemen, in charge of one area or another. Most of the workers looked up with a brief smile or nod; many took note of Martin, but he detected curiosity rather than hostility in their gazes.

The molten steel tapped from the second converter was being ferried down the shed, and she and he fell in behind four men transferring two of the huge cauldrons of molten metal to the casting area, which lay across the rear of the shed. The central dividing wall ended some thirty yards from the rear wall, and the casting troughs were neatly arranged across the ends of both halves of the massive shed.

Several of the subforemen came up to speak with his hostess. Martin shamelessly eavesdropped as the men asked what the steel from the latest pour—the one from the second converter, which, at that very moment, was being tipped into molds—was destined to make, and she explained the particular properties of the alloy the steelworks had been commissioned to produce. "The plate will form part of the Atlas Works' supply to the government for the latest batch of naval vessels. We—none of us—have been told which type of ship the plate is destined for."

Martin pricked up his ears at that.

From the casting area, he strolled beside her into the other half of the shed. Steam hammers thudded and pounded, and the resultant sheets were fed into rolling mills to be pressed to the required thickness. Again, she stopped to speak with various workers.

Again, Martin listened and, again, was impressed. Not only by the detailed and experienced knowledge she demonstrated of every aspect of the steelmaking process but even more by the transparent respect she commanded from each and every man. Most notable of all, not one iota of resistance did they evince to a woman being in charge.

The observations left him rethinking his offer on several counts.

When she continued on, he fell in alongside her.

"In case you haven't noticed," she muttered, "I'm ignoring you. So why are you still here?"

He felt her gaze fleetingly touch his face, but kept his eyes directed forward. "I told you. I don't give up, and frankly"—he glanced around—"Carmichael Steelworks is proving to be everything I'd hoped it would be." With a tip of his head, he added, "Indeed, it's proving to be a great deal more."

Sophy told herself she wasn't any green girl to be bamboozled by a smooth tongue, yet she heard the sincerity in his voice—both over not giving up and also about his appreciation of the works.

She truly didn't want to be curious—or at least not let her curiosity show—yet she heard herself ask, "What had you hoped for?"

"For a steelworks that has the potential to operate as the critical link between my other steel-based businesses." His gaze flicked her way, and he slowed his stroll, and she matched his pace; she wanted to hear what more he might say.

"I have a foundry to produce pig iron, and I've set it on course to ramp up output, which needs to be made into steel. On the other side of the equation, I have a knife factory outside London and a part share in another here in Sheffield, and I own a wire and cable factory in Nottingham, all of which require steel. More, I want to acquire a steelworks with an interest in producing different grades of steel. Steel with specific properties or rather to better match the properties of steel to the use to which it will be put. Stiffer cable or more malleable cable. That sort of thing. I believe there are lots of uses for steel that have yet to be properly developed. And there are other types of steel-based manufacturing I would like to explore."

Listening to him reminded her of why she hadn't written to refuse his offer—because the picture he conjured was fascinating and rather intriguing, at least to her. She focused on another aspect of his approach that had tweaked her curiosity. "You knew I was female, yet you wrote asking for a meeting to discuss your offer."

The look he threw her was faintly wary. "Yes… And here I am."

"Indeed." And refusing to be dismissed.

Hearing his ideas in person had rendered his proposal even more attractive, yet she couldn't help but wonder if she was being influenced by considerations that had nothing to do with business.

She frowned. She was actually considering discussing matters further with him, yet she needed to remember that the odd accidents that had plagued the works started just after she'd received his third letter, and now he'd turned up right on the heels of yet another odd happening, another potential "accident."

An odd whistling caught her attention.

"Look out!"

She got no chance to look anywhere. A steely arm wrapped about her waist, cinching her against a rock-hard body, and she—they—dove to the ground before landing on the concrete floor in the space between two rolling mills.

Not that *she* landed on the floor; he'd flung them sideways in such a way that she landed mostly on him.

The jolt of their landing knocked the air from her lungs, and the sensation of her body slamming into his all along her length shot through her, scrambling and scattering her wits.

She lay in his arms and struggled to breathe. For the first time in her life, her mind was so awash with tactile stimulation, she couldn't think.

Disconcertingly, she felt utterly safe.

Her head rested on his upper chest, cushioned by firm, warm muscle, and the steely strength of him, of his arms wrapped around her, for some mystical reason left her prey to a burgeoning impulse to press herself even more deeply against him, to sink further into his embrace.

Her heart was pounding in rapid time, and a flush was spreading beneath her skin.

With a massive effort, she hauled in a breath and felt him tense beneath her.

Then he shifted. His hands gently gripped her shoulders, and he lifted her enough to peer into her face. "Are you all right?"

No. You've broken my brain.

She cleared her throat and croaked, "Yes." She tried to scramble off him, and he winced, then helped her up. Only once she was upright and he was, too, did she meet his eyes.

The awareness that swam in the burnt-caramel depths left her in no doubt that he'd sensed the impact the unanticipated embrace had had on her… She blinked as it dawned on her that he'd been affected, too.

She didn't get even a second to dwell on that revelation. As if a bubble popped, sound—which until that second had been distant and muted—erupted and rushed in, and pandemonium enveloped them.

Men rushed up from all sides, while others, she saw, were leaping and grappling with the huge hook swinging from one of the gantry cranes.

That's what made the whistling noise.

The massive iron hook was one of several attached to the overhead cranes used to hoist cauldrons and buckets and even move converters. The overhead cranes, mounted on gantries high above, were a necessary part of any steel-works. But the hooks—big enough and heavy enough to brain anyone they struck—were normally hoisted on their chains high above and secured.

The hooks were never left with enough loose chain to allow them to swing almost to ground level, as that one had.

Even less frequently were hooks positioned directly over the aisle, not when they weren't in use.

Oh, God. If it had struck us…

She felt the blood drain from her face.

Instantly, hands—hard, long-fingered, their touch almost familiar—locked about her waist and steadied her.

She glanced over her shoulder, met Martin Cynster's eyes, and read in them the same realization. If he hadn't reacted as he had, they would both be dead.

She looked about at the continuing chaos. It wouldn't have been just them, either. Four workers had been in the aisle, two ahead of her and him and two behind. All would have been collected by the swinging hook.

He'd heard the odd sound, turned, seen, and had yelled to warn everyone, not just her. Thanks to his excellent reflexes, catastrophe had been averted.

Hinckley, white-faced and frantic, rushed up, as did several of the older crew.

She looked again at Martin Cynster. Death had come so very close to claiming her, him, and four others, too.

CHAPTER 2

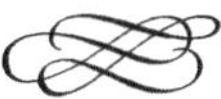

The realization of what had almost happened left her mentally reeling, but the clamorous questions and shocked faces crowding around her demanded an immediate response. Determinedly, she drew breath and set about reassuring everyone that she was entirely unharmed. After several minutes of patient repetition, she managed to calm everyone sufficiently to confirm that the four workers who'd been forced to scatter hadn't taken any hurt.

Everyone seemed more concerned about her, but she'd been so cushioned she didn't even feel jarred. Shocked, yes. Jarred, no.

The memory of those moments made her breath hitch. Reminded of the cause, she glanced at him. "Are *you* all right?"

No one had asked him.

He straightened from retrieving his hat and cane, and his expressionless look somehow managed to convey male affront. "Yes." The unspoken "Of course" rang loud and clear.

She turned back to Hinckley and the rest of the men and instantly saw that their attitude to Cynster had changed. Previously, they'd been as curious but also as suspicious as she. Now, he was a savior, of her and some of them, too.

Although still shaken, the four who'd escaped death courtesy of his warning pressed forward to tender their thanks.

His expression serious, he accepted the overtures, but sought to downplay his actions. "Your hearing is probably deadened through working in all this noise." He looked at Hinckley. "I heard the clink of metal hitting the floor, followed by the rattle of chains and the whistling as the hook swung."

Frowning, Martin took in the heavy winch hook—as tall as a man and almost as wide—that the workers had finally brought to a standstill. The hook was suspended on heavy chains, and the lower curve hung a foot or so above the ground. It had come to rest in the middle of the central aisle, about a third of the way from the rear wall.

He looked toward the rear of the shed. "I wonder what fell to the floor."

Turning away from Miss Carmichael—whom he needed to haul his senses from—he stepped into the aisle. Tension still rode him; the impulse to lay waste to whatever had threatened pressed on him. The workers—also curious—parted and let him through, then fell in behind him. Hinckley came up on his right, and everyone scanned the floor as they walked slowly toward the shed's rear.

"Here!" A worker darted to the left. He reached beneath the edge of a steam hammer's platform and pulled out a large, heavy metal clamp. He carried it to Hinckley.

The foreman took the clamp and held it up where all could see.

Someone in the crowd behind Martin said, "That's one of the clamps we use to hold the winch hooks to the gantry."

"Aye." Grim-faced, Hinckley pointed to the long, thick, iron bolt that was obviously only half the length it should have been. "And it's been sawn through."

Martin felt the men behind him part and, without looking, knew it was to let Miss Carmichael through. Some part of him—some combination of his senses—had become immutably fixed on her.

Forcing his mind to the matter at hand, he took the clamp and examined the bolt. "This was sawn partway through. Whoever did it left enough for the bolt to hold for a while, but eventually, under the weight of the hook, it snapped and released the chain."

A younger voice piped up, "But we don't leave the winches rolled out like that, above the aisle. That winch should've been hard by the wall."

"It was!" An older man—one of the subforemen—turned to Hinckley. "I swear, me and Sam, we rolled that beast"—he pointed up at the winch from which the hook hung—"back against the wall last night, before we went home. We had it out yesterday to load that pallet of steel bars, remember?"

Hinckley nodded. "Aye. I remember. The rail tracks that went out."

Another older man—presumably Sam—confirmed that the winch and its heavy hook had been properly stowed the previous night. "Besides, we never let out the chain like that, so the hook nearly touches the ground. We always let out just enough for the job, then haul it back up, and we did that last night as well."

Excruciatingly aware that Miss Carmichael had halted beside him, Martin glanced her way and saw that she was staring in a disturbingly blank fashion at the sawn-off bolt. "So," he concluded, "it seems this act of sabotage was carried out sometime last night, after the works closed, but it wasn't designed to harm any specific person." He looked at Miss Carmichael, as did Hinckley and most of the men. "There was no way whoever rigged this could have known who they would harm, but by moving the winch to above the aisle and lengthening the chain, they were clearly intent on hurting someone."

A dark murmur rose from the assembled men, but Miss Carmichael didn't seem to notice. Instead, she blinked those huge turquoise eyes and, in a curiously detached tone, murmured, "Sabotage. Just like the coal wedged into the spiegeleisen chute."

Sophy's wits weren't whirling quite as badly as they had been; she could see the sense in what he'd deduced. Still, she wasn't really thinking clearly when she added, "Just like the other accidents."

Cynster faced her; she felt his gaze lock on her face. "What other accidents?"

She wouldn't have chosen to tell him, but given his tone and the focused intent she could sense pouring from him, obliging seemed easier than trying to resist. She raised a finger and rubbed her temple. "Well, the first might not have been sabotage. The hoist used to lift the pig iron to the mouth of the converters failed. A cable had frayed, and it snapped. Luckily, no one was hurt."

Hinckley growled, "It seemed odd—suspicious, even—but still, it might have been just a bad cable."

"Next," Jeb, a subforeman, said, "it was a gasket between one of our Cowper generators and the converter springing a leak. The bolts were loose, but they weren't the day before."

"No one was hurt." Hinckley grimaced. "We just thought it was one of those things."

Sophy drew in a breath and took up the tale. "But then, about a week later, a steam pipe blocked and nearly exploded." She glanced around at the men. "Young Patrick got burned that time."

"Only a little, miss!" Patrick called from the rear of the group.

She summoned a weak smile. "Yes, but those bolts…" She looked at Hinckley. "Thinking back, I really can't see how they could have come loose without someone deliberately undoing them. All six were loose, yet we run the generators for most of the day, every day."

Gravely, Hinckley nodded. "I agree. In hindsight, that's impossible to explain as anything other than sabotage."

Sabotage. After today, she had to accept that someone was…

Hard fingers gripped her elbow. "Perhaps, Miss Carmichael, we might return to the office. A cup of tea might be wise."

Hinckley, Jeb, and many others, their faces creased with worry, nodded encouragingly.

"Good idea," Hinckley said. To Sophy, he added, "You go and have a sit-down and a cuppa." He glanced at the men. "We'll find another clamp and take a closer look at the winch and get that hook properly stowed again."

Sophy felt she should argue, but she was feeling rather strange. Aside from all else, she found herself leaning into Cynster's strength, imparted through his hold on her arm. She was acutely aware of his grip, but wasn't inclined to free herself, which was ludicrously unlike her.

A chair and a cup of tea did seem called for.

Cynster caught Hinckley's eye. "You might want to start checking over the works every morning, to make sure no fresh accidents have been staged." He glanced questioningly at her. "At least until this is sorted out."

She nodded. "Yes. We should take what steps we can to keep everyone safe, until we learn who's behind this and put a stop to it."

Hinckley, Jeb, and all the men looked relieved and also determined.

A kernel of anger flared inside her. How dare whoever it was do this to her and her workers!

She clung to that burgeoning anger and used it to stiffen her spine. The men started to disperse, and with her head high, she allowed Cynster to steer her down the aisle and out of the shed.

Once she was in the yard, her thoughts claimed her, and before she fully registered what was happening, she found herself settled in her chair behind the desk in her office, with a concerned Harvey and Mildred serving her and Cynster tea and ginger biscuits.

He'd steered her through the office and to her seat, then set aside his hat and cane and claimed the visitor's chair, and curiously, neither Harvey nor Mildred seemed moved to question his right to be there.

Sophy vaguely recalled a low-voiced conversation in the outer office. Tommy, one of the lads who acted as messengers for Hinckley, had been in the office when she and Cynster had reached it. Tommy had already imparted the shocking news, sending Harvey into a tizzy. Luckily, her secretary was tethered to reality by the infinitely stoic Mildred, the company's bookkeeper.

Sophy sipped and felt revivifying warmth slide down her throat and start to thaw the lump of cold dread that had taken up residence inside her. Her nerves calmed further. She looked up and saw Harvey dithering in the doorway. Over his shoulder, she caught Mildred's eye. "Thank you. That will be all."

Harvey looked doubtful, but Mildred tugged, and he reluctantly retreated and shut the door.

Sophy took another sip, her gaze unfocused. She couldn't let the situation just roll on. She had to think and decide what to do. She drew breath and stated, "Someone is attacking Carmichael Steelworks."

"Indeed."

She met Cynster's caramel eyes; they no longer looked the least bit warm but as cool and hard as agate.

"The question," he went on in an even, anchoring, authoritative voice, "is why." He raised his cup and sipped, but his attention remained locked on her.

She grimaced and focused on her cup. "I really have no idea."

In silence, she sipped until she'd imbibed enough tea. By that time, he'd drained his cup and replaced cup and saucer on the tray. She set down her own, buzzed for Harvey, and straightened in her chair. "Thank you for your help, Mr. Cynster. We—all of us at Carmichael Steelworks—are in your debt. I can't imagine"—*I don't want to imagine*—"what might have occurred had you not been present and acted so swiftly. However"—she stressed the word—"I must get on." She rose, bringing him to his feet. "As I informed you earlier, I will not be pursuing your offer to buy the works."

The door opened, and Harvey came in, and she waved him to the tray. Returning her gaze to Cynster, she held out her hand. "Again, thank you for your help today. I hope you enjoy your stay in Sheffield."

His gaze locked on her face, he made no move to take her hand.

Ignoring Harvey, he calmly stated, "You haven't been listening. I still want to buy the business, and I haven't lost hope of changing your mind. However, I want to buy a going concern, not one struggling to hire men because the rumor mill—which I'm sure operates in Sheffield as well as it does in other towns—paints Carmichael Steelworks as jinxed. That would be bad enough, but given my interests, the last thing I would want to see is this steelworks, with its sterling reputation for alloys, losing that reputation because of an incident such as occurred earlier today that you and your men fail to catch."

He hadn't altered his tone throughout that speech, but the unrelenting power behind his words made her—and Harvey, too—blink and regard him with new eyes.

What the devil am I to do with him if he won't go away?

Martin knew better than to glare or to approach a female of the likes of Sophia Carmichael with anything other than cold logic. Showing his frustration and irritation would get him nowhere; he had to convince her to let him help her deal with whatever danger threatened. He had multiple reasons for doing so. Not only did he want Carmichael Steelworks to continue thriving and developing, he also wanted—*needed*—to protect her.

He wasn't interested in wasting time questioning that overriding instinct. Aside from any personal element, there was the undeniable fact that, in terms of completing his business empire, Carmichael Steelworks was better than perfect, and he'd already seen more than enough of how the business operated to grasp that she was an integral part of it.

Indeed, given his ultimate aims, she was a critical feature, one he would move heaven and earth to retain.

Concealing his annoyance at her attempt to dismiss him, he evenly asked, "As today is Saturday, I assume the works operates for only half the day."

She eyed him levelly for several long moments, but eventually deigned to answer. "Yes." She glanced at the clock on the wall. "The whistle will sound in a few minutes, at one o'clock, and the works will close until Monday morning. We open at seven."

Glancing from one to the other, Harvey added, "There will be a handful of men on duty tomorrow, to keep the furnaces stoked."

Martin inclined his head. That was standard procedure for any decent-sized works.

On cue, the whistle shrieked—three short blasts.

Harvey still dithered, the tray in his hands.

She nodded to the secretary. "That will be all for today, Harvey." She glanced sidelong at Martin. "I believe I'll head home."

"Indeed, miss." Harvey turned to the open doorway. "After all the excitement, you should take things easy."

Watching Miss Carmichael's face, Martin saw her lips tighten as she suppressed a no doubt pithy retort. Taking things easy after being threatened wasn't her style.

It wasn't—most definitely wasn't—his, either.

He picked up his hat and cane and patiently waited while, pointedly ignoring him, she tidied her desk and drew her bag and gloves from a desk drawer. When she straightened, he waved to the door. "I'll escort you home."

She rounded the desk—on the far side from him—and met his gaze with a bland, rather distant expression. "No need." She silenced all protest by adding, "My groom will be waiting to accompany me home."

He allowed his brows to rise fractionally and followed her into the office's foyer. Sure enough, a solid-looking individual in a neat and unremarkable suit waited beside the outer door.

The older woman was just leaving. She nodded to Miss Carmichael, including Martin in the gesture, then looked meaningfully at the groom as he moved to hold open the door. "Good afternoon, Hector."

Martin would have sworn some unvoiced communication passed between the pair, then the older woman stepped out and walked off.

Harvey was busy putting away the tea things. "I'll lock up, Miss C."

Miss Carmichael nodded. "Very well. I'll see you on Monday." With that, she walked to the door and stepped out, onto the pavement.

Martin followed at her heels. As he passed Hector, he wasn't entirely surprised to receive a respectful nod; he suspected the older woman, and possibly Harvey, too, had already told Hector what had happened that morning.

Good.

Martin settled his hat on his head and, with two long strides, caught up with Miss Carmichael. In silence, they walked down Bailey Lane toward the corner of Portobello Street.

They'd almost reached the corner when she glanced at him. "This really isn't necessary."

A half smile on his lips, he swung his cane. "We're heading in the same direction. Why not walk together?"

Her eyes narrowed on his face. "Where are you staying?"

"At the Kings Head."

"In that case"—she halted at the corner—"we part company here." She held out her hand. "Once again, thank you for your assistance today."

He grasped her gloved fingers and felt the frisson of reaction that streaked through her, setting his senses slavering. Keeping his relaxed mask in place, he returned, "I'm glad I was there to help."

He forced himself to ease his hold, and she swiftly retrieved her hand.

Regally polite, she nodded. "I hope you enjoy your stay in our town, sir."

"From all I've learned today, I'm sure I will, Miss Carmichael." He tipped his hat to her. "I'll see you on Monday."

Her eyes flashed bright fire, and her lips tightened ominously, but after a second's pause, she turned and walked away.

Martin watched her go, then Hector bowed to him and followed her, cutting off the enticing view.

Martin turned and strolled toward the town center. The Kings Head stood on the corner of Church and Orchard Streets, far enough away to allow him to revisit the events of the morning.

He was immeasurably glad that he'd surrendered to the impulse to come to Sheffield, to Carmichael Steelworks, and plead his case in person. The curious fact that the major shareholder in the business was female had, admittedly, piqued his interest, but purely in the sense that, such being the case, he'd believed he would have an even-money chance of persuading her to sell to him. While he rarely bothered with social charm, charm in pursuit of business was another matter entirely. He'd entertained visions of dazzling Miss Carmichael into selling the business to him.

Then he'd met Sophia Carmichael and had jettisoned all thoughts of charming her into parting with her company. Over the years, he'd grown to be an excellent judge of business character, and she was too level-headed, too clear-sighted, and far too wedded to the steelworks to happily consign it into another's hands, no matter how talented those hands might be.

If he wanted to acquire Carmichael Steelworks—and he most definitely did, even more so now than he had earlier that day—he was going to have to rework his approach.

Yet if he hadn't traveled to Sheffield, hadn't imposed his presence on her, and stuck with her in going around the shed… Lord only knew what the situation might have been then.

The one lesson the morning had taught him was that if he wanted to reap the full benefit of acquiring Carmichael Steelworks, he would need to ensure that Sophia Carmichael and her very real talents were a part of the deal.

He reached the hotel, went in through the door for private guests, and climbed the stairs to the uppermost suite. He was met by his man, Roland, and after surrendering his hat, cane, and overcoat, he sat down to consume the luncheon Roland had waiting.

Martin ate in silence, and familiar with his moods, Roland left him undisturbed.

Once Martin had finished the steak-and-kidney pie and washed the whole down with a pint of local ale, he called Roland and sent him to fetch Figgs, Martin's groom, and Tunstall, Martin's secretary.

After the three men joined him and, at his invitation, filled mugs of ale for themselves, Martin described the happenings of the morning. The three—all experienced in his ways—listened without interruption.

At the conclusion of his recitation, he eyed the trio. "I want you to go out and see what you can learn about any others—anyone at all—who has evinced an interest in Carmichael Steelworks. Quietly." He stressed the qualification. "Don't stir up any dust, and don't let on that we have any interest in the place, either. That's one tidbit I definitely want kept under our collective hat."

All three grinned. They lived for such assignments.

"Aye, sir." Figgs saluted. "They're a hardworking lot hereabouts. Hard drinking, too, it seems, which should make our task much easier."

Martin dipped his head and waved them off. "I won't need you for the rest of the day or the evening. See what you can learn."

The following morning, alongside her widowed aunt, Mrs. Julia Canterbury, Sophy sat through the service at St. George's Parish Church and tried to keep her mind on the vicar's words. Sadly, she had little success.

The prospect of some unknown enemy trying to ruin Carmichael Steelworks had kept her up half the night.

Dwelling on her unexpected reaction to Martin Cynster had kept her awake for the rest.

Bad enough that he'd shredded her comfortable belief that she lacked all susceptibility to handsome men. Courtesy of rescuing her, he'd cemented an entree into her business and, judging by his statement when they'd parted, he wasn't of a mind to step back.

What she should—or could—do about that, she didn't know.

After her disastrous first and only London season, when she'd made her come-out under her grandmother's wing, she'd jettisoned all thoughts of finding a husband and had devoted herself, entirely contentedly, to working alongside her father in managing the steelworks. Since childhood, she'd spent as much time as possible there, and when her father passed from an infection of the lungs a little over fifteen months ago, her continuing to manage the business was viewed by everyone as a natural progression. To her, the steelworks was another sort of home.

All of that fed into how much, to her, the threat to the works mattered.

In the small hours of the night, she'd accepted that she could no longer equivocate over the accidents at the works being anything other than deliberate sabotage. Even more pertinently, they were *dangerous* sabotage, targeting her, all who worked there, and the business itself. She had to do something to defend against them and, ultimately, ensure they stopped.

That much, she saw clearly.

What to do about Martin Cynster and his offer for the steelworks was a great deal murkier. The truth was she wanted to hear more about his vision for the steelworks' future. Not because she was in any way interested in selling the works but in order to gain a better perspective of what was possible. Of what the future potential of the business might be. Judging by the comments in his letters, he was well grounded in the various businesses that took the finished material produced by a steelworks and converted it into more profitable goods.

She'd heard sources she trusted declare that steel was the future, which intrigued her to no end. She wanted to know exactly in what way, so she could work out what alloys might be most profitable in the years to come.

Such knowledge would be key to steering Carmichael Steelworks into a prosperous future.

Her thoughts far away, she rose with the rest of the congregation for the benediction.

"Come along." Julia glanced fondly at her. "You've been woolgathering all service. You didn't even hear the sermon, did you?"

Sophy sent her aunt a sheepish look. "I heard the vicar's voice. I know he gave a sermon. I just didn't hear the words."

Julia chuckled. Long accustomed to Sophy's daydreaming, she merely shook her head and, linking her arm with Sophy's, led her up the aisle.

Sophy duly smiled at the vicar, shook his hand, and murmured an appropriate response to his comment regarding the fine morning, then followed Julia onto the expansive lawns that ringed the church.

Mrs. Pritchard and Mrs. Hughes, two old dears who lived nearby, were waiting to waylay them and chat, and Julia and Sophy obliged. The older ladies prided themselves on being up with the latest social news, and Julia made an effort to stay up to date in that sphere.

Sophy smiled and nodded, but otherwise let the chatter wash over her; she rarely found anything in the social sphere worthy of notice.

Portobello Street ran along the southern boundary of the green expanse surrounding the church, and the Carmichael residence, a three-storied town house, stood in the middle of the block on the street's other side. While Sophy and Julia chatted with the ladies, from the corner of her eye, Sophy could see her front door.

By the time she and Julia took their leave of Mrs. Pritchard and Mrs. Hughes, Sophy's mind had fastened on the what-should-I-do question. Hoping to avoid further unproductive chatting and steer Julia directly home, Sophy turned in that direction, only to find herself confronting a black wall.

She recognized the overcoat first; it was better cut than most and made of an exceedingly soft and commensurately expensive wool-and-cashmere blend that her senses remembered very well, courtesy of being all but wrapped in it the day before.

When she raised her gaze to Martin Cynster's face, he was smiling—devastatingly—at her.

Her heart started to beat faster. Her mouth dried.

She forced herself to nod politely and extend her hand. "Mr. Cynster. We meet again."

He grasped her fingers lightly, and holding his hat and cane in his other hand, the epitome of elegance, he half bowed. "Miss Carmichael. A happy encounter. I hoped to reassure myself that you'd taken no hurt after the excitements of yesterday."

The gently teasing look in his eyes—warm, delectable, melted caramel at that moment—suggested that he knew perfectly well that to her, he himself qualified as one of yesterday's excitements.

She really should want to dent such unshakable confidence. Instead, she fought to smother the butterflies erupting in her stomach and quell her senses' overreaction to the perfectly gauged, perfectly gentlemanly grip of his fingers on hers.

He released her hand, and she felt that deeply, too.

Don't fret. His impact will surely fade with time.

Even as the thought formed, she acknowledged the prediction might well prove false.

She glanced at Julia. Her aunt had, of course, noticed Cynster—his wasn't a presence any sane female could overlook—and one glance at Julia's eager expression told Sophy that Hector had embellished Sophy's own report of the troubles at the works and given her aunt chapter and verse about the gentleman who had rescued her.

Martin noted the eagerness in the older lady's eyes and, from his research, limited though that had been, guessed that she was the widowed aunt who filled the role of Miss Carmichael's chaperon, even though, doubtless, Miss Carmichael no longer believed she needed one.

He smiled politely at the older lady and flicked an inquiring and faintly challenging glance at his quarry. "Won't you introduce me to your companion?"

He saw her lips tighten, then resignation swept her features; he could almost hear her smothered sigh.

She gestured to him. "Mr. Martin Cynster, allow me to present my aunt, Mrs. Canterbury."

Increasing the intensity of his smile, he grasped the gloved fingers Mrs. Canterbury readily offered. He bowed, then released her. "A pleasure, ma'am. I had the honor of meeting your niece yesterday."

"So I heard." Mrs. Canterbury glanced at said niece. "I understand, Mr. Cynster, that the family and I owe you our most fervent thanks for your quick actions in protecting dear Sophy yesterday." She returned her gaze to him and beamed. "I'm exceedingly glad to make your acquaintance, sir, and to be able to tender the family's gratitude in person."

He summoned his most bashful look. "It was nothing any other gentleman wouldn't have done had they been there. I was happy to be of assistance." Smoothly, he transferred his gaze to Miss Carmichael. "And I'm doubly glad to have confirmed that Miss Carmichael took no lasting hurt."

She studied him as if surprised to hear the sincerity in his words.

Her aunt was looking back and forth between them, a shrewd glint in her eye. "Mr. Cynster." When he looked at her, she smiled benevolently. "Am I correct in assuming that you're residing in town?"

"Indeed, ma'am. I have rooms at the Kings Head."

She nodded. "A very worthy establishment. However, I doubt the quality of their table can compete with ours. You must allow us to host you for luncheon." Without looking at her niece—who, from the corner of his eye, he could see was shooting daggers at her—Mrs. Canterbury fixed a guileless gaze on him. "Unless you have some prior engagement?"

Well, that was easier than I expected.

He inclined his head gracefully. "Thank you, ma'am. I must admit that as I've been at the Kings Head for several days, a change in fare would be welcome."

"Well, then. That's settled!" Beaming, Mrs. Canterbury glanced around as if checking for others approaching. Finding no one, she turned back to Martin. "I believe we can head home." She waved down the path that led to Portobello Street. "It's just this way."

Martin promptly offered his arm, and pleased with the courtesy, Mrs. Canterbury claimed it.

After directing a suspicious—not to say dark—look his way, Sophy Carmichael fell in on her aunt's other side.

Somewhat to Martin's surprise, his men hadn't turned up any whispers about others with an active interest in Carmichael Steelworks. Feeling restless over not knowing more and guessing that his quarry would attend church that morning, given there was a parish church directly opposite her home, he'd deemed attending service there a potentially useful excursion.

And so it had proved.

Because of his family's social prominence, he'd been forced from an early age to cultivate the facility for social patter, and he deployed that talent now, much to Mrs. Canterbury's delight.

Even as he did, he remained acutely aware of the slender female presence who glided on his hostess's other side.

By the time they reached the pavement outside the Carmichael town house, he and Mrs. Canterbury were on excellent terms.

He couldn't say the same for her niece. Sophy Carmichael continued to regard him with considerable suspicion, although she cloaked it well.

When Mrs. Canterbury released his arm and stepped forward to ring the bell, Martin met Sophy's gaze and arched a questioning brow, inviting her comment.

She studied him for several silent seconds, then the front door opened, and she turned and, with distant hauteur, walked inside in her aunt's wake, leaving him to follow.

Hiding a smile, he did, and was soon handing over his hat, cane, and overcoat to a very correct butler.

Mrs. Canterbury gestured at Martin. "This is Mr. Cynster, Richards. The gentleman who so dashingly came to Sophy's aid at the works yesterday. I've persuaded him to take luncheon with us."

"Indeed, ma'am." Richards bowed to Martin, and Martin caught a glimpse of gratitude and respect in the butler's eyes. "I will set an extra place at once."

"Thank you. We'll be in the drawing room." Mrs. Canterbury led the way, and Martin waved Sophy ahead of him and followed.

Sophy trailed Julia to the sofa and sat on the other end. Her aunt waved Cynster to the armchair opposite, and he subsided with an ineffable grace that, along with his earlier patter, screamed of significant social experience.

That, she had to admit, surprised her. She'd assumed he would be all about business to the exclusion of society. Apparently not. She listened as he entertained Julia by continuing a story he'd commenced during the short walk from the church.

He had a glib tongue; she had to give him that. She made a mental note to be wary of that, then realized the thought assumed she would see more of him in the future.

After a second's resistance, she acknowledged that, given his demonstrated doggedness, she most likely would, and it would be just as well to be prepared. Consequently, she watched and observed and drank in all he let fall.

The more she listened, the more she was forced to accept that his appearance today wasn't by way of pressing his case regarding the steelworks. Or at least not directly.

He seemed genuinely devoted to entertaining Julia and, by extension, Sophy, and wholly focused on spending a pleasant Sunday luncheon with two ladies he'd only recently met.

She felt exceedingly wary over accepting that as the truth, but when Richards arrived and announced that luncheon awaited, and they rose and strolled to the dining room, she couldn't fault Cynster's—Martin's

—performance.

He'd navigated the change to first names, so he was now Martin, and she was Sophy. Julia, of course, remained Mrs. Canterbury to him, a distinction that suggested he was accustomed to dealing with older ladies.

He saw Julia to her seat at the foot of the table. Sophy quickly slipped into her chair at the table's head before he could return to assist her. He claimed the seat between them and sat, and Richards commenced serving.

Sophy seized the moment to redirect the conversation, which, to her mind, had strayed too close to her. "You mentioned traveling in America. Were you there for long?"

He met her gaze. "Several years."

"Oh? How many?"

"Eight." He hesitated, then with a glance at Julia, added, "I went direct from Eton and learned much about business through my associations there." He looked at Sophy. "I returned in '51."

"You mentioned various businesses you own. Did you acquire them on your return?"

"Not immediately. I spent several years consolidating the wealth I'd accumulated in America. Over those years, I spent much of my time investigating the prospects of various industries."

"And you settled on the steel industry?"

"Iron and steel, although these days, my interest lies primarily in steel-based manufacturing."

"Do you own other businesses outside iron and steel?"

He nodded and patted his lips with his napkin. "I have stakes in cotton mills and also in the railways." His lips twisted in wry self-deprecation. "My brother-in-law is the Earl of Alverton, so the latter was almost a family requirement. Certainly, it was necessary to induce him to turn his mind to the other businesses in which I wished to take an interest. His ability to value existing businesses meshes well with mine in looking ahead and foreseeing the areas in which significant expansion is likely."

"Is that a skill you've specifically cultivated?"

"I would say it was one that was inculcated in me during my years in America. Industry-wise, they have a more rapidly evolving landscape over there, so gauging what will be successful and profitable becomes a necessary survival skill for businessmen and investors."

Unwilling or not, she was fascinated. "What do you think of—"

"Mr. Cynster." Julia interrupted rather forcefully, then softened her intervention with a smile. "Martin. I believe you mentioned you were up from London?"

"Indeed, ma'am."

Sophy watched as, literally in a blink, he switched from discussing the fraught business of evaluating industries for future growth to describing the latest styles in ladies' hats.

Indeed, she was rather envious of his facile tongue and the brain that drove it. She wasn't half as glib as he was.

She'd now heard enough to have some notion of the social standing of his family, namely, that they were of the haut ton, yet from all she'd seen and learned of him, he was a far cry from the archetypal scion of a noble house.

He might dress in suits from Savile Row and bear accoutrements of understated wealth, yet the impression she was receiving, building fact by fact, was of a man who might once have been a typically reckless, hedonistic youth, but whom experience had seasoned, matured, and honed into the man presently seated at her table.

She suspected he was older than the thirty-five she'd initially thought him; he had a certain weight of years about him. He was very much the sort of man who was, quietly and calmly, in complete control of himself and all he owned and commanded and was unswervingly determined to achieve his goals.

That he'd effortlessly held her attention for the past hour and more spoke volumes.

Martin kept his gaze and his relaxed and amiable focus on Mrs. Canterbury, yet his senses remained transfixed by the lady on his other side. Sophy Carmichael remained something of an enigma. She definitely did not follow the accepted social rules for young ladies of her class.

Even the way she spoke with him—be it about business or the latest design of carriage to grace London's streets—was distinctly unusual; she was direct and forthright, with no flummery or airy qualifications. She was entirely without any false social façade.

Many ladies of comparable ability or facility with business would have cultivated a fake social persona to screen their intelligence—commonly held to be off-putting to eligible partis—but Sophy Carmichael employed no such veil. She reminded him of Felicia Cavanaugh, wife of his investing mentor, Lord Randolph Cavanaugh. Felicia was a talented mechanical inventor. Once, when Martin had called at the Cavanaughs' house, Felicia had handed him a cog and a pair of goggles and asked him to hold a screwdriver while she tightened a bolt.

Yes, she's like Felicia, only more in control and more in command of her own destiny.

The realization that she didn't actually need his help in shaping that destiny was food for thought. Looking beyond dealing with the recent accidents and whatever was behind them, he would have to persuade her of the benefits of changing her current path to the one he now wished to steer them both down.

Thanks to this unexpected luncheon, he had a much better notion of how to proceed.

The meal progressed through three courses, and the conversation rolled on, weaving through aspects of the social scene, both in Sheffield and in London. He made no effort to guide the discussion to business matters. That could come later and, in truth, wasn't his immediate focus. At that moment, he was infinitely more interested in learning all he could about Sophy Carmichael. She was unquestionably the single most crucial person he had to win to his side; the more he learned of her, the better.

He was careful not to overstay his welcome, and as soon as the meal was over and they rose from the table, he signaled his intention of taking his leave. After bowing over Mrs. Canterbury's hand and thanking her for her hospitality, he turned to find Sophy waiting to accompany him to the front door.

He fell in beside her and tendered his thanks to her as well. She acknowledged the standard phrases with a regal tip of her head, but no unnecessary expressions of delight.

The lingering watchfulness he glimpsed in her eyes made him inwardly smile. She wasn't going to be any easy conquest.

After he'd donned his overcoat and collected his hat and cane from the butler, he followed Sophy to the door. When she opened it, he stepped onto the porch, then paused and, looking back, met her eyes and smiled with rather more amused understanding than he'd allowed to show to that point. "Just so you know, I'm rethinking my offer."

"Good. I can assure you that you won't get anywhere on that front." Her gaze remained steady, and her chin firmed. "Regardless of any inducements, I have no intention of selling my inheritance, much less giving up my independence." Her nose tipped up, and she very deliberately added, "Not even for a face as handsome as yours."

He almost laughed—she was so refreshingly direct—and seized the moment of putting on his hat to subdue his mirth. Nevertheless, he was smiling more deeply when, again, he met her gaze. "Saying I'm 'rethinking my offer' doesn't mean I've given up the idea of adding Carmichael Steelworks to my portfolio of businesses."

She blinked.

Smoothly, he continued, "I meant that I've accepted that whatever deal I strike with you will need to have different parameters to those I originally envisaged and intended to suggest. Obviously, my initial proposal was formulated before I met you. Having done so, I can see that significant rejigging of the structure of my offer will be required."

Specifically, it was now transparently obvious that any successful offer would need to include her and her talents as part of the deal.

She frowned, but it was a vague affair that suggested he'd surprised her, puzzled her, and she was still working out how to react.

He tapped his hat straight. "Wait until you hear my reworked proposal before making up your mind."

With that, he turned and went down the steps. On the pavement, he glanced back and saluted her, then strode off toward the center of town and his hotel.

His lips remained curved. He'd achieved much more than he'd expected to that day.

Still standing in the doorway, Sophy watched their visitor stride away, cane swinging and black overcoat billowing about his long legs. After a moment, she snorted softly and shut the door.

She turned to face the hall, but remained where she was, staring blindly toward the stairs as she replayed their recent exchange.

There'd been something underlying his words—some intent, some sense of purpose—that had captured her attention and lured…

The strength of her reaction to whatever that something was was unnerving.

And disturbing, because she definitely wanted to know more.

After several minutes of trying to fathom what his reworked proposal might include, she grimaced in defeat. "No doubt I'll eventually learn what he intends to suggest." Clearly, he wasn't going to vanish back to London anytime soon.

She looked around, then shook herself and headed for the stairs. She had better things to do than waste her time trying to work out what a gentleman was thinking.

CHAPTER 3

The following morning, Sophy was seated behind the desk in her office, reviewing the orders fulfilled over the previous week, when she heard a deep male voice in the outer office, then her door opened, and unhindered and unannounced, Martin Cynster walked in.

Sophy narrowed her eyes at him, then, exasperated, looked past him at Harvey. “Why didn’t you stop him?”

Harvey’s eyes rounded in shock. “But…” He cut a glance at Martin’s dark head. “He saved you on Saturday.”

Martin’s flashing smile dragged her gaze to his face. His laughing eyes met hers. “It’s no use—I’m the hero of the hour. Well, of Saturday, but apparently, the aura lingers.”

She fought to keep her lips straight. *I will* not *smile!*

Harvey, eyes still wide, promptly shut the door.

After two seconds of internal struggle, Sophy managed a creditable grumble. “Regardless, I’m not going to waste any of my time discussing a putative sale.”

“Entirely understandable.” With negligent ease, he sat in her visitor’s chair and, when she looked his way, met her eyes. “That’s not what I’m here to discuss.”

Martin saw her debate whether to encourage him or not, but eventually, she arched a brow. “Oh?”

He smiled in a manner he hoped was reassuring. “After the incidents on Saturday, given my interest in acquiring the works, it’s clear my first priority should be to determine who wants to damage the business and why."

She frowned, patently considering the logic of that statement. Before she could question it, he asked, "Those previous accidents. How many were there?"

She focused on him. "Just the three we told you about." She grimaced. "Before the two on Saturday, so that brings the count to five."

"When were they? Do you remember?"

The look she cast him informed him that of course she did. "The first was on Saturday, just over two weeks ago. That was the time when the cable on the hoist lifting one of the cauldrons of molten pig iron snapped."

He nodded. "And the second incident?"

"That was the following Saturday, when the gasket on the Cowper generator leaked."

"So that was Saturday a week back?"

"Hmm. The third incident was last Wednesday. That was the blocked steam pipe, which could not possibly have been an accident. Someone had disconnected the pipe, forced a lump of rubber into it, then connected it again."

"And Young Patrick got scalded—a little."

"Yes. And then came Saturday's efforts." She met his eyes. "The accidents are increasing in frequency."

"Indeed. Whoever is behind it, they're determined." He held her gaze. "They're not going to give up."

He saw anxiety seep into her expression. When she looked away, he leaned forward, clasping his hands between his knees, the movement refocusing her attention on him. "Tell me what you know of the details of each accident. Start with the first."

She studied him for a moment, then complied.

He quickly realized that, other than for the two incidents on Saturday, she hadn't been present at the time but had been summoned after the fact. Her description of the earlier accidents was therefore secondhand and, consequently, short on detail.

She concluded, "And you saw for yourself what happened on Saturday."

He inclined his head. "Would it bother you if I spoke with the workers involved? For instance, Patrick with the blocked steam pipe?" When she frowned, trying to see what he was about, he added, "I wondered if talking to the men and getting the details firsthand might shed some light on who is behind this campaign."

Her expression cleared, and she pushed back from the desk. "I'll come with you."

He rose as she did, entirely content to have her beside him.

They walked out of the office, across the yard, and into the shed. The combination of his newfound status at the works combined with Sophy's presence made questioning the men that much easier; they were as eager as anyone to get to the bottom of the accidents and put a stop to them.

His years of working in America enabled him to set aside his birth and step past the barriers of class; he knew what to ask and how to ask it, and as he'd hoped, the men responded.

By the time they left Young Patrick and walked out into the sunshine now bathing the yard, one fact was crystal clear.

He halted and, when Sophy faced him, stated, "All the accidents occurred in the morning, the first time each machine was used. So someone had to have broken into the works during the previous night and tampered with the equipment."

Lips setting, Sophy folded her arms and nodded. "There's no other explanation."

"Hinckley and the subforemen also made an excellent point in that the nature of the sabotage suggests the person or persons involved know how the equipment operates. In none of the five accidents to date were the tamperings evident before the machine was used."

"I agree."

The lunch whistle sounded, two sharp blasts. She glanced up at the steam whistle, mounted on the ridge of the shed's roof, then lowered her arms. "The men break for a full hour, although most of them remain inside the fence."

Martin waved toward the gate. "I'll walk you home."

With worry eating at her, she replied, "Hector will be waiting in the office." She looked at Martin. With him, the shield she invariably maintained, fully deployed, against all males of marriageable age was well and truly down. She studied his expression for a second more, then explained, "I don't normally go home for luncheon. I go to the Crofton Arms, farther down Rockingham Street." She drew in a breath and said, "If you would accompany me, perhaps we could"—she gestured—"discuss things and see what we might do."

Martin managed not to beam, but his smile was irrepressible. "An excellent notion." He had absolutely no doubt of how honored he should feel to be invited to join her. "I assume we should collect Hector on the way?"

She nodded, and they walked to the office.

While she fetched her coat and bag, Martin waited with Hector and Harvey in the outer office. When Sophy joined them, her coat already on and her bag on her arm, Martin held the door for her, then followed her onto the street, with Hector several yards behind.

There were too many people walking the pavements to allow them to safely converse, and the Crofton Arms, Martin discovered, was only one and a half blocks away, on the other side of the intersection with Portobello Street.

He'd wondered if they would encounter any of the men from the works, but when they entered the low-ceilinged public house, he saw only a smattering of clerkish types hunched over tables as they ate.

Sophy raised a gloved hand to the barman. "Hello, Saul. I'll just go through. This gentleman's with me."

"Of course, Miss Carmichael." Saul smiled and moved to lift a flap in the long bar, allowing Sophy, with Martin at her heels, to pass and walk on, through a narrow doorway and down three steps, into a neat snug.

Sophy slid behind one of the two long tables inside the small room, set her bag beside her, and waved Martin to sit opposite. As he did, she summoned a smile and aimed it at Saul, who was hovering in the doorway. "What does Gemma have for us today?"

Saul grinned. "Game pie, which isn't half bad if I say so myself."

Sophy nodded. "I'll have a small slice." She looked inquiringly at Martin.

He caught Saul's eye. "A not-so-small slice."

His grin widening, the barman tipped him a salute. "I'll have Gemma bring that out right away." He glanced at Sophy. "Your usual?"

She nodded, and when Saul arched a brow at Martin, he asked for a pint of the local ale.

As soon as Saul withdrew, Sophy said, "Hector refuses to eat with me. He'll be settled in the main room."

Martin nodded his understanding. "About these accidents." Immediately, he had her full attention. "There has to be a reason that someone is targeting the Carmichael works. Have any other steelworks suffered odd accidents?"

She paused, clearly pondering, and a bright-cheeked woman bearing two plates appeared in the doorway.

"Good day to you, miss," she cheerily announced, "and here are your game pies."

She served them and pulled cutlery from a capacious apron pocket, then stepped back as Saul appeared with their drinks and set them down. "Anything else you need, Miss C, you just ask."

With nods to Sophy and more reserved ones to Martin, Saul and Gemma withdrew.

Martin and Sophy picked up their glasses. From the color of the liquid in hers, Martin guessed Sophy's "usual" was the local cider.

She sipped, then set the glass down and started on her meal. After swallowing her first mouthful, she looked at Martin and shook her head. "I'm sure I would have heard if any other works was having this sort of trouble. Or if not me directly, then Hinckley or one of the other older men. They have friends at all the other steelworks around town." Her lips twisted wryly, and she met his eyes. "And they're the biggest gossips you'll ever meet. They put Aunt Julia to shame."

"Hmm." He swallowed a mouthful of what was, indeed, an excellent game pie. "All right. Let's take it that it's purely the Carmichael works being targeted." He trapped her gaze. "Why? If we can establish the why, that will likely suggest the who, and vice versa."

Her expression turned frustrated, and she waved her fork in a helpless gesture. "I have no idea on either count. There really is nothing that I'm aware of that would explain someone taking such action against the business."

He tipped his head in acceptance, and they ate and thought. The atmosphere, he realized, felt much the same as the times he'd sat in a pub somewhere, discussing some issue with one of his cousins. Or often, some investigation with his cousin Toby.

The observation underscored that they were, indeed, embarking on an investigation.

Eventually, he asked, "What about competitors?"

She wrinkled her nose. "Theoretically, that's possible, I suppose, but not in this town."

"Why do you say that?"

She proceeded to explain that the steelworks in Sheffield weren't truly in competition with each other. "The demand is so high that there's always a market for whatever any of us produce." She pushed away her empty plate and folded her hands on the table. "And in Carmichael's case, the alloys we produce are most often custom runs. What we make is specific to an order, and the reason we get that order is that larger steelworks find it uneconomical to make the adjustments to produce a relatively small run of such alloys."

"So the works' size plus your facility in switching to different alloys sets Carmichael's apart?"

She nodded. "And between such jobs, we fill in by subcontracting to the larger steelworks, like Atlas and Naylor and Vickers, to help fill their larger orders of more routine steels."

"I see." He thought, then said, "If this was some other sort of business, I might have wondered if the sabotage was due to someone wishing to buy the works and wanting to drive the value down before making a rock-bottom offer, but as I pointed out earlier, when a business relies so heavily on reputation and standing—"

"And our ability to meet orders on time."

He nodded. "That, too. Your reliability as well as your reputation is a critical plank of the business, so destroying those things prior to buying doesn't make sense."

"So," she said, "if it's not a competitor or a potential buyer, who does that leave?"

They fell silent—a companionable moment in which both thought over the possibilities—then Martin stirred. "Let's leave that angle for now and concentrate on the accidents themselves." He met her gaze. "How is someone sneaking into the steelworks at night to engineer these accidents? I take it the place is locked?"

She nodded. "All the gates and the doors are securely locked every night. Hinckley always checks before he leaves."

"No reports of damage to the locks or the gates and doors?"

"No. Nothing that would suggest a break-in..." She paused, then added, "At least not that I've heard."

He arched his brows. "It might be time we asked specifically. Someone may have noticed something, but considered it too minor to report."

Her lips firmed, and she collected her bag and stood. "Let's go and ask the men."

He followed her from the snug and forestalled her by paying their shot, which earned him a respectful nod from Saul and an approving look from Hector.

The groom-cum-guard fell in behind Martin and Sophy as they walked briskly up the street to the steelworks. She went into her office only long enough to doff her coat and set down her bag, then she was back and, determination in every line of her face, made for the yard door, plainly intending to go to the shed.

"Perhaps," Martin said as he started in her wake, "as our questions are regarding security, it might be wise to include Hector."

She paused and glanced back at him, then looked at Hector. "Indeed. Please join us, Hector."

They quit the office, leaving Harvey and the older lady wondering what was afoot.

In the middle of the yard, Martin slowed. "Sophy."

Frowning, she glanced at him, and he halted and waited for her to turn and join him.

When, clearly not happy with the delay, she did, he refrained from smiling understandingly and evenly said, "As much as we all would prefer not to think it, it's possible one of your men is involved. It might be better to talk to Hinckley—and the subforemen, if you're comfortable with that—out here."

She stared at him for several seconds, then nodded. "You're right." She looked at Hector, who had halted a respectful yard away. "Hector, can you please fetch Hinckley and the four subforemen from the shed?" Her gaze shifted to the receiving office. "Meanwhile, Mr. Cynster and I will collect Oakshot and"—she flicked a glance at the main gates—"Phillips."

Hector saluted. "At once, miss."

Martin trailed Sophy as she summoned the receiving clerk and the gatekeeper. As he and she returned to the center of the yard, she whispered, "With Hinckley and the four others from the shed, these are our oldest and most reliable men."

"The most devoted," he murmured and received an acknowledging nod.

Once the group had gathered, forming a circle that included Martin, Sophy, and Hector, Sophy briskly outlined their reasoning regarding the accidents and asked if any of them had seen or heard of damage that might indicate a break-in.

None had.

More, after further consultation, all were very certain no such damage had occurred.

"I haven't seen anything," Hinckley said, "and I lock up every night, so I would notice any tampering with the locks."

Frowning, Sophy folded her arms and drummed one finger on her elbow. "Whoever is doing this has to have a key."

The men dipped their heads in agreement, but said nothing more, leaving Martin to ask, "So who has keys to the works?"

To his dismay, every man in the group pulled out a key. Martin glanced around the circle, confirming that every man in it was holding one key. Including Hinckley, who held out his meaty palm with only one key on it, yet locked all the doors and gates every night.

Martin glanced at Sophy. He managed to keep his voice level. "Only one key?"

She nodded. "Papa lost patience with having different keys to the various gates and doors, so he had them all made the same."

He smothered his reaction. "How many copies of the key were made?"

She arched a brow at Hinckley, but the foreman shook his head. "Your father took care of handing out the keys. I don't know how many he had cut or who he gave them to. Well, beyond us here, of course, and Mildred and Harvey in the office."

Martin swallowed a sigh and caught Sophy's eye. "Regardless of anyone having kept a record, and it sounds as if no one has, the first thing you need to do is change all the locks."

She grimaced. "It hadn't occurred to me, but yes. We'll change the locks."

"And get different keys for each," Hector put in, and everyone nodded.

Given the circumstances, no one was going to argue that point.

"The locksmiths we use—Moreton and Sons, down the street—is a sound firm," Hinckley said.

Sophy nodded. "We'll go there immediately."

When she looked at Martin, he said, "I'll accompany you." To ensure they got different locks and keys for every last door and gate. "Do you have a tally of how many locks you need?"

She waved toward the office. "Harvey can make one. Hector"—she glanced at her groom-cum-guard—"please ask Harvey to make up a list immediately. We'll go to the locksmith's as soon as it's ready."

"Yes, miss." Hector bobbed and headed for the office.

Sophy looked around the rest of the group. "Thank you for your help.

I'll organize for the new locks to be installed as soon as possible and, of course, will hand out the keys."

Hinckley caught Martin's eye, and Martin fractionally nodded in reply. He would go with her and make sure everything possible was done to guarantee the security of the site.

After organizing with the locksmith to have all the locks changed—a process that had taken more than an hour—Sophy headed back to the works. Martin walked beside her, and as usual, Hector trailed behind.

Purple shadows were lengthening and the temperature was falling as the sun dipped toward the moorland to the west of the town, and evening approached on gentle feet.

Looking toward the works, she said, "This business of the accidents—the threat they pose—has become much more real over the past days."

She sensed rather than saw Martin nod.

"That's because the accidents have escalated in seriousness and are coming more frequently, and you and the men have recognized them for the attacks they are and are taking action."

Largely thanks to you.

Even at the locksmith's, she doubted she, alone, would have achieved the right outcome—the best type of lock for each location and the correct number of keys for each—had he not been standing beside her, asking what had proved to be just the right questions to steer her and the locksmith to the optimal decisions.

He'd been subtle about it, but she'd noticed and had been far too grateful to refuse his help.

Freely offered help. No matter his rationalization regarding his continuing interest in offering for the works, she got the impression his assistance had no limits, that she could rely on him and his agile brain to remain at her service until the threat was properly dealt with and, indeed, eradicated.

Quite where that certainty came from, she couldn't have said, but it was there, quite solid and clear in her mind.

"Do you have any plans for the evening?" A bold question, but she was past standing on any sort of ceremony with him. Being seized and wrapped in his arms had, apparently, vaporized all the usual social barriers; increasingly, she'd been treating him—and thinking of him—as someone she'd known for years.

As someone she'd trusted for years, which, on reflection, was truly strange.

"No plans as such. Just dinner at the Kings Head."

"In that case"—she didn't stop to think—"come and dine informally with Aunt Julia and me in Portobello Street." She flicked him a glance. "Come as you are. We don't dress for dinner when it's just us. After all your exertions on my and the works' behalf today, the least I can do is treat you to a good dinner."

He smiled and inclined his head. "Thank you. I accept." His eyes met hers, an amused twinkle in the caramel depths. "Besides, something might occur to one of us, and it would be useful to be able to discuss it in more relaxed surroundings."

He can't read minds, can he? She narrowed her eyes on his, then humphed and looked ahead.

They returned to the office just as the whistle sounded its three short blasts, signaling the end of the working day. Harvey confirmed that there was nothing urgent awaiting her attention, and she and Martin followed Harvey and Mildred out of the door and onto the pavement.

After farewelling the other two, she and Martin walked to Rockingham Street, then down to Portobello Street.

As they neared her door, Martin murmured, "Your aunt strikes me as the sort to grow anxious, regardless of reassurances. It might be wise to save any discussion of the current situation at the works until after dinner, when hopefully, she'll be less inclined to pay unrelenting attention."

"Indeed. I truly would prefer not to unnecessarily exercise Julia's worrying tendencies."

With that decided, the following hours passed much as she'd hoped. On entering the house with her and Hector, Martin set himself to beguile Julia with his ready charm, and he, she, and her aunt enjoyed a pleasant, cordial, and surprisingly relaxed meal.

After Martin denied any wish for spirits, they returned to the drawing room, and as Sophy had hoped, Julia settled in her favorite armchair by the fire and picked up her tatting. Knowing that, once her aunt was absorbed with her craft, she had to be specifically called should her attention be required, Sophy shared a conspiratorial look with Martin, then claimed one of a pair of armchairs set back from the hearth and waved him to the other.

If they kept their voices low, they could converse in reasonable privacy.

"I've been wracking my brains," she murmured by way of opening the discussion, "over who might be behind all this. You mentioned competitors."

He arched a brow. "You've thought of someone?"

"Not specifically. As I said, while we have no local competitors—something no doubt you've already verified from your research into steel-works, especially if you've been focusing on those works that produce custom alloys..." She paused, a question in her eyes, and he dipped his head.

"Yes. In this region, Carmichael Steelworks stood out."

She nodded. "So we have no real competitors locally, but from farther afield, I know there are several works around Birmingham and also about Newcastle that are envious of some of the contracts we currently hold." She frowned. "I might hypothesize that one of those firms, desperate for the work—and as we're talking of government contracts, there's a certain element of prestige attached—have decided to compromise Carmichael's ability to deliver so that we'll fail, and they can step in." She met Martin's eyes. "The puzzle is why they either wouldn't approach me first with an offer to take over the contract, which they could do, or alternatively, simply underbid me when the contracts come up for renewal."

She pulled a face. "Hobbling another steelworks seems a rather desperate tack for any respectable firm, and of course, to be considered for government contracts, you need to be a respectable firm."

"It's hard to imagine any reputable business going to such lengths." Martin paused, then added, "Over the past days, my men have been haunting the pubs and taverns, chatting and asking around, searching for any hint of unexpected others, especially from outside the locality, who've shown an interest in Carmichael Steelworks. My men are good at what they do, yet they haven't stumbled across anyone."

"Exactly." Sophy raised her hands in a helpless gesture, then allowing them to fall to the chair's arms, she stared across the room. "I literally cannot think of who it might be, let alone why anyone would do such a thing. It makes no sense."

Martin studied her frustrated expression, then looked at Julia, who remained absorbed with her tatting. "The timing of the accidents. You said they started over two weeks ago?"

Sophy nodded. "Saturday, two weeks back, to be precise."

"Think of the preceding month or even two months." He leaned forward, clasping his hands between his knees and fixing his gaze on her face. "Over that time, did anyone contact you regarding buying the steelworks or even about some specific contract?"

She wrinkled her nose, her gaze growing distant as she thought. "We receive inquiries fairly regularly, but not so frequently as that. But thinking back, over the past two months, aside from your letters, I did receive one other inquiry regarding buying the works." She narrowed her eyes. "About five weeks ago, I think. About a week before your first letter."

"Did you refuse the offer in writing?"

She met his eyes and faintly colored. She hadn't replied to him. "I did. Quite promptly."

"So they would have received your letter rejecting the offer several weeks ago, before the accidents started."

She nodded.

"So timing-wise, it's possible they—for whatever convoluted reason—might be behind the attacks." A thought occurred, and he went on, "It's possible the accidents are intended to simply make life sufficiently difficult for you—a well-born female—so that you throw up your hands and entertain their offer." He held her gaze. "Not many people outside Sheffield would know you're not just the majority owner—that's easily learned—but that you are actively involved in running the steelworks. I didn't know that until I arrived here."

She returned his gaze, her own steady. "The other offer was from a group in London."

"Who?"

"Coulter Enterprises."

He blinked.

She studied his expression. "You know them."

He grimaced. "I should have guessed." He met her eyes. "Oliver Coulter and I are…competitors of sorts. We went to Eton together, but thereafter, our paths diverged. More recently, I discovered he's been gradually expanding into the same areas in which I'm involved." He tipped his head. "At present, our business interests run roughly parallel. That said, my plans in this particular sector are rather more advanced than his. While the Carmichael works would provide the final piece in my overall structure, the works would be Oliver's first foray into steel."

"I see." She searched his eyes. "Could Mr. Coulter be behind the accidents?"

Martin considered that, then grimaced. "I don't know him that well. Not these days. Has he visited the works?"

"No. He wrote from London, and as far as I know, he hasn't visited Sheffield and certainly not our works. From the tone of his letter, like you, his interest was driven by our size and also our ability with alloys. One can learn of those things from a distance, as you did."

Martin nodded. "If Oliver didn't know that you were actively involved with the works, then the reasoning I mentioned earlier—of making life uncomfortable for you—might have occurred to him." He paused, then shook his head. "I wouldn't have thought he would have resorted to accidents, though. That's too underhanded for the man I once knew, but I haven't spoken to him other than socially for years." He lightly shrugged. "He might have changed." He met her eyes. "I really can't say either way."

The door opened, and Richards rolled the tea trolley in, and Julia looked up and laid aside her tatting.

Martin rose and dutifully handed Sophy her cup, then took his own and resumed his seat.

Unsurprisingly, while sipping her tea, Julia engaged them in the usual discussion of their plans for the next day. Soon after, with the tea consumed, Martin rose and took his leave.

Sophy accompanied him to the door. They were both pensive when they parted.

He paused on the porch and threw her a glance. "I'll be around tomorrow."

She nodded absentmindedly, and he set his hat on his head and turned away. Smiling to himself, he set off along the pavement and, behind him, heard the door close.

He'd rarely met a female who was oblivious to him, who could become so wrapped up in her own thoughts that she treated him as…well, not as a gentleman of his ilk should be treated. It was a novel experience and just a tad amusing.

And heartening, too.

Courtesy of the situation at the works, drawing closer to Sophy was proving remarkably easy. Seeing her drop all resistance where he was concerned was definitely encouraging.

Not so encouraging was the possible involvement of Oliver Coulter.

As he strolled toward the town's center and into areas more populated by gentlemen like him—walking the streets, passing between houses, or returning to the major hotels—Martin scanned the pavements. If Oliver Coulter was behind the accidents—or even if he wasn't—if he saw Martin in town, Oliver was certain to turn up in short order at the steelworks to press his offer.

If the accidents were part of a scheme to pressure Sophy to sell, then Oliver would be somewhere near. Possibly not actually in town, as Martin's men had discovered no sign of him.

Martin paused outside the Kings Head and looked around one last time. Then he turned and went inside.

If Oliver was behind the accidents, Martin truly hoped he turned up soon.

CHAPTER 4

Martin walked into the steelworks' office at nine o'clock the next morning and found that the locksmith had just arrived with the ordered locks and his tools.

Debating his options, Martin paused in the doorway of Sophy's office. She was ensconced behind her desk and, with Mildred the bookkeeper, was apparently engrossed in reconciling orders and invoices.

Smiling at the sight, he rapped on the door frame. When Sophy looked up, he tipped his head toward the yard door. "The locksmith's here. If you like, I'll go with him and Hector while they install the new locks."

Sophy blinked at him, then waved him away. "Please. By all means."

Interpreting that—he was sure correctly—as meaning "just don't interrupt me," Martin grinned and followed the locksmith and Hector, who was helping the man get his barrow, piled with equipment and locks, through the door into the yard.

The locksmith eyed the shed's massive doors and elected to start with the westernmost one. "These'll take the longest."

With Hector, Martin stood back and watched. When the locksmith finished replacing the lock on the first door and moved to work on the second, Martin and Hector inspected the newly installed lock.

Hector grunted in approval. "Good quality. Nice and heavy."

Satisfied with what he saw, Martin nodded. "No one's going to be able to easily pick or force their way through that."

After the locksmith installed the lock on the second door, they circled the yard, replacing the locks on all the doors inside the works, including the door to the laboratory, then the locksmith progressed to the Rockingham Street gate. Once that was done, as a trio, they walked around the southern end of the site, putting new locks on the external doors to the receiving office, the main office, and finally, the main gates.

Martin knew enough about locks to verify that the locksmith knew his trade. Not only were the locks he'd supplied high quality, but he also set them into the doors and gates in such a way as to make it difficult for anyone to pry them loose. It would be easier to break down the doors or the gates than to force those locks.

When the man rose from tightening the last bolt on the lock on the main gates and started putting away his tools, Martin commended his work and tipped him generously.

The locksmith looked startled, but grateful. "Thank ye, sir." He pocketed the money and touched the brim of his cap. "If you ever want any locks done yourself, I'll be happy to oblige."

Martin smiled. "Thank you. I'll remember that."

"Aye, well, I'd better remember these an' all." The locksmith reached into his barrow and pulled out a leather pouch. He opened it, thrust in a hand, and drew it out, displaying a bunch of keys on rings with tags attached. "I've put labels on so the lady will know which key goes with which lock."

He tipped the keys back into the bag, closed it, and held it out to Martin.

He kept his hands in his overcoat pockets. "I'm just a visitor." He glanced at Hector. "Best give the keys to Hector to deliver to Miss Carmichael."

The locksmith handed over the keys, then with a salute to Martin and Hector, hoisted his now-much-lighter barrow and trundled it off down the street.

Hector hefted the clinking bag. "I, for one, will be happy to know these keys are going only to people who need to have them."

Martin nodded, turned, and started across the yard for the office.

Sophy was pushing aside her completed correspondence when he and Hector walked in.

"All done." Hector placed the clinking pouch on the desk. "A good job he made of it, too."

"Excellent!" Sophy fell on the pouch's ties and pulled out sets of keys. She arranged them on the desk, studying the labels as she did. "Now to hand them out."

"Make a list this time," Martin advised. When she glanced at him, he added, "Please."

She arched a haughty brow. "Of course." Looking back at the keys, she added, "Luckily, I'm not my father. I'm not at all inclined to have everyone associated with the place be able to waltz into whatever area they choose." She looked at Hector. "Please tell Harvey to bring his list of locks so we can make a note of who should have which key."

Hector nodded and left.

Martin sat in one of the visitors' chairs and watched as Harvey breezed in and he and Sophy went over the list and noted who should get a key to what.

That done, Sophy rose and picked up the list and the pouch of keys. Unbidden but, he noted, also not dismissed, Martin ambled in her wake as, starting in the main office with Harvey and Mildred, Sophy did the rounds of the works, handing out the necessary keys to the relevant people.

Him being present when she handed out each key wasn't without design; he watched to see if any of the men were taken aback to be given only the keys they were deemed to need to perform their duties. However, if anything, every man looked relieved to have responsibility for only the keys he needed. Other than Hinckley, who received keys to all the new locks, none of the crew who worked in the shed received keys to the main office or the receiving office, and only some got keys to the warehouse or the store.

Feeling vindicated in his reading of the men—none had struck him as bad apples—Martin followed Sophy up the steep metal stairs to the laboratory, their last stop on their key-delivering journey.

He hadn't been into the laboratory since his visit that first day. The same gray-coated, bespectacled individuals he'd seen on that occasion looked up from their instruments and charts and greeted Sophy with smiles and assurances that everything was behaving as it ought.

She asked several questions about the recent blows, then, plainly satisfied, handed out the new keys and explained their limitations. Neither man seemed the least bothered by the restriction of their access to other parts of the works. They pocketed the keys and, with polite nods to Sophy and curious glances at him, returned to their work.

As if drawn by some enchantment, Sophy drifted to the wide

windows and halted there, looking out at the second converter that was currently building toward a blow.

Both she and Martin, standing, waiting, just inside the door, heard the rapid patter of boots rushing up the metal stairs.

Martin stepped away from the door. It was thrust open, and the lad he'd seen working in the office under Mildred's eye came barreling in.

The youth's wide gaze swept the area and landed on Sophy. "Miss Carmichael, miss! Mr. Harvey sent me to tell you there's a gentleman in the office says he needs to speak with the owner."

"Oh?" Quitting the window, Sophy made for the door. "Did Mr. Harvey mention the gentleman's name, Timmy?"

Timmy nodded. "A Mr. Coulter, miss."

Martin caught the startled look Sophy, halting, sent him and fought to temper his smile into a less-feral expression. "Perhaps," he suggested, "Timmy could tell Harvey to show the gentleman into your office and inform him that you'll be along shortly."

Sophy considered that, then looked at Timmy. "Please tell Mr. Harvey what Mr. Cynster just suggested, but don't mention Mr. Cynster's name." From the corner of her eye, she saw Martin smile in appreciation of her stipulation.

Timmy frowned. "You want me to say it like this, miss?"

He repeated the order as if it had come from her, and she nodded approvingly. "Just like that."

She pointed to the door, and Timmy spun around and rushed off, clattering back down the stairs. She looked at Martin. "Coulter turning up at this moment is surely suspicious."

To her surprise, he looked equivocal. "Possibly." He waved her to the door. "There's one way to find out. Let's see what he has to say."

She led the way out of the laboratory. At the bottom of the stairs, she waited for Martin to join her, then started for the shed door. "It would be helpful—to me at least—were you to join us." She glanced at him. "Will Coulter recognize you?"

"Oh yes." He met her gaze. "We belong to the same clubs, and as competitors of sorts, we're very much aware of the other's existence."

She tipped her head and increased her pace. She wanted to throw Coulter off his stride and, she judged, finding Martin in her company would accomplish that. As, no doubt, he intended to accompany her regardless, she might as well make best use of him.

She was itching with curiosity by the time they reached the main office. Martin held open the door, then followed her inside. Harvey spotted them and semaphored madly, indicating that, as instructed, Coulter was waiting in her office, the door to which was helpfully shut.

She glanced at Martin. He met her gaze and waved her on, and she led the way past the counter, opened the door, and swept inside.

At the sight of her, Coulter, who'd been sitting, apparently impatiently, in one of the visitors' chairs, leapt to his feet. "Miss Carmichael." His gaze swept over her, and his eyes lit, and his smile bloomed—only to immediately and rather comically fade as he saw Martin in her wake.

Coulter was brown haired, brown eyed, not quite as tall as Martin but of similar build. His attire was equally precise and expensive, although he favored browns rather than the blacks, charcoals, and grays Martin favored. Stiffening, Coulter stared past her. "Cynster."

Coulter's jaw clenched. Sophy suspected he was grinding his teeth.

"Mr. Coulter." When he looked at her, she nodded equably and walked behind her desk. "Good morning. I understand you and Mr. Cynster are acquainted." She waved Coulter to the chair he'd vacated. "Please, won't you sit and tell me what brings you here?"

Stiff and distinctly prickly, Coulter remained standing and looked at Martin.

Outwardly calm and unruffled, Martin closed the door. Despite his appearance, Sophy sensed he was less relaxed than he had been. He nodded at Coulter. "Oliver."

His eyes narrowing, Coulter looked from Martin to Sophy.

She smiled, sat, and clasped her hands on her blotter; this was rather amusing. "You and Mr. Cynster are acquainted, are you not? Do I have that right?" The pair reminded her of two bantam cocks placed in the same coop.

Coulter glanced at Martin and grumbled, "Acquainted? Yes, you might say that."

She looked from one to the other; despite their wariness, she sensed no actual animosity between them but rather uncertainty. They might not be friends, but they weren't enemies, either.

Coulter returned his gaze to her. "I was hoping to meet with you and discuss a possible business venture."

She arched her brows and, again, waved to the chair. "Further to your earlier communication?"

He sat. "Indeed."

Instead of claiming the second visitor's chair—possibly too close to

Coulter for his liking—Martin ambled to lounge against the cabinets that lined the wall behind and to the right of Sophy's desk, both position and posture indicating he was there in support, but didn't intend to participate in the discussion.

Regardless, Coulter's gaze locked on him.

Sophy inwardly sighed; yes, Martin Cynster was a transfixing presence, but Coulter would have to get over it. "Your business venture, Mr. Coulter. I take it you still wish to buy Carmichael Steelworks?"

Her question had Coulter focusing on her. Then he frowned. "While I had learned that you were the majority shareholder, I hadn't realized you took an active interest in the business. If I had, I would have come in person sooner."

She widened her eyes. "Why? Do you imagine that, as a female, I'll prove easier to sway in person?"

"No!" He flushed and glanced at Martin. "I..." He swallowed. "That is, if I could speak with you in private?"

His faintly pained expression suggested that he realized how that sounded. For a lady such as she to meet privately with a gentleman...

She decided to put him out of his misery. "I seriously doubt Mr. Cynster will agree to that, and I know of no way to eject him, forcibly or otherwise, and I would strongly suggest you don't try. Not in my office at any rate." She shot Martin a warning glance, then returned her attention to Coulter. "However, I have no qualms about him hearing firsthand what you wish to say to me. That will simply mean I don't have to tell him later and will save time all around. Regardless, he does not make decisions pertaining to Carmichael Steelworks. I do. So"—she gestured to Coulter—"please, proceed."

His lips tight, Coulter studied her for several seconds.

With her hands clasped on her blotter, she stared back.

Finally, he began, "As I stated in my letter, I would like to discuss..."

She listened attentively as he outlined his proposal to buy Carmichael Steelworks, and indeed, he did a better job of making his case in person than he had in writing. Sadly for him, his proposal—which amounted to a straightforward purchase, with Carmichael Steelworks becoming the first steel-associated business Coulter Enterprises owned, with no wider vision in place—was nowhere near as compelling as Martin's fully fledged, well-thought-out, and virtually complete portfolio of connected businesses, with real potential to expand even further.

In terms of ideas and solid future prospects, Martin's offer beat Coulter's hands down.

If she was to accept any offer, it would be Martin Cynster's.

Not that she intended to sell to either man.

One pertinent aspect that listening to and evaluating Coulter's offer and comparing it to Martin's emphasized was that Martin was in significantly greater need of the steelworks—of securing just such a steelworks as Carmichael's—to complete the line of his connected businesses. Without the steelworks, the foundry in Rotherham couldn't connect with the knife factory, the wire-and-cable factory, or any other potential manufactory. He *needed* to purchase Carmichael Steelworks, while Coulter merely *wanted* to purchase it.

Martin had a lot more riding on the acquisition—more to lose and, commensurately, a lot more to gain.

Hmm.

Coulter continued, "I can assure you that Coulter Enterprises would…"

Sophy glanced at Martin, but he was presently doing an excellent imitation of a marble statue. His expression was utterly unreadable.

Another point this interview was clarifying was that she was actively considering doing some sort of deal with him. She wasn't so blind that she didn't appreciate that Carmichael Steelworks might never receive a better offer, one that promised to keep her father's business not just continuing but expanding and evolving into the future.

Hmm, indeed.

Eventually, Coulter reached his summation. With a dark look at Martin, he declared, "And I'm prepared to better whatever offer Cynster has made."

Plainly, the pair entertained an open rivalry. She caught Coulter's gaze and evenly stated, "I will tell you what I've told Mr. Cynster. I am not, at present, interested in entertaining offers to purchase Carmichael Steelworks. However, I do have several questions for you."

"Yes?" He looked hopeful.

"When did you arrive in Sheffield?"

He frowned and flicked a glance at Martin. "Yesterday, late afternoon. I came up by train."

"I see. And is this your first visit? Or have you connections with the town?"

His frown deepened. "I..." His jaw firmed. "No. I don't. I've never been here before." He looked challengingly at Martin. "Have you?"

"Yes," Martin replied. "I own a foundry in Rotherham. But that's not why Miss Carmichael asked."

Confused and willing to show it, Coulter looked from Martin to Sophy. "What's going on?"

Martin watched Sophy smile at Coulter; she was all sweetness on the outside and steel within. "We were wondering, Mr. Coulter, if you knew anything about the series of accidents that, over the past weeks, have plagued Carmichael Steelworks."

"Accidents?" Oliver looked again at Martin, then returned his gaze to Sophy. "What sort of accidents?"

Martin studied Oliver's face as Sophy ran down the list of incidents. Oliver had never had much of a poker face, and that hadn't changed with the years. He was shocked, but also intrigued by the details; Martin could almost see Oliver putting the information together in his head as to what each accident would have meant for the steelworks.

By the time Sophy was describing the last incident, he was convinced Oliver knew nothing about any of them. He was so patently thinking through each happening that it was obvious he hadn't thought of them before.

Oliver wasn't the villain behind the attacks.

Martin glanced at Sophy and, from the slump of her shoulders, concluded she'd seen that, too.

She reached the end of her recitation and, with her gaze on Oliver's face, sighed. "You have no connection with these accidents, do you?"

It finally occurred to Oliver why she'd asked. "No!" Incipiently offended, he looked at Martin. "You can't possibly think—"

Bang!

The crash in the outer office had Martin straightening and brought Oliver and Sophy to their feet.

"What now?" she demanded and rushed to the door.

Martin was at her heels, with Oliver at his.

They spilled into the outer office to find Harvey attempting to calm a wild-eyed lad. Martin recognized the youth as one of the receiving clerk's helpers. The lad was gasping like a fish out of water, his lungs heaving, but clearly had some message he was desperate to impart.

"Take a deep breath," Harvey instructed, "and then just tell us."

The lad did his best to comply with the first part of that order. The second part resulted in a torrent of words. "A dray. Piled with pig iron from Atlas. Coming to us." The lad paused to haul in another breath. "A wheel fell off as they were coming around the corner of West and Rockingham, and the load shifted and came off!"

Sophy paled. "Good Lord!" She started for the front door, then stopped and whirled. "We need to get Oakshot. And Hinckley, too." She rushed for the door into the yard.

Martin followed as she went out of the door and ran to the receiving office, calling for Hinckley as she went.

Men came out of the shed, then Hinckley was lumbering their way.

Sophy reached the receiving office and raced through the open yard door.

Grim-faced, Oakshot met her. "I heard." He held open the front door, then followed her onto Rockingham Street.

With Hinckley and Oliver and several of the men from the main shed as well as two of the older receiving clerks, Martin was right behind Sophy and Oakshot as they ran down the street toward a scene of pandemonium several blocks away.

Essentially, the situation was as the lad had described it. What he hadn't mentioned were the hundred or so people gathered all around due to the fact that the busy intersection, on one of the main roads leading into the town center, was now blocked.

Along with Oliver, Hinckley, Oakshot, and the men from the works, Martin helped clear the heavy bars of pig iron from the main thoroughfare. One of the receiving clerks ran back to the works and drove one of the works' drays down to pick up the bars.

Sophy had taken charge of seeing the shaken driver and his mate settled on a stoop and supplied with mugs of tea, brought out by a local shopkeeper eager to do his part in dealing with the catastrophe.

Working alongside Oliver, Martin helped free the pair of heavy Clydesdales from the wreckage and handed them into the care of the steelworks' crew. Then, again with Oliver, Martin used his charm to calm and reassure those travelers and locals inconvenienced and inclined to be tetchy. Eventually, Hinckley and Oakshot had the roadway clear again, with the pig iron rumbling up Rockingham Street and the half-wrecked dray drawn up onto the pavement, as out of the way as it could be.

Sophy went into the nearby shop to return the mugs. Martin seized the moment to speak with the dray driver and his mate, then Sophy returned and urged the shaken pair into Hinckley and Oakshot's care.

With the rest of the men from the steelworks going ahead, striding back to their work, and Hinckley, Oakshot, and the driver and his mate trailing more slowly behind, Martin walked beside Sophy up Rockingham Street. Oliver kept pace on Sophy's other side.

Martin glanced across at Oliver and noted his pensive expression.

They returned to the main office, and Sophy gave Harvey and Mildred a pared-down account of what had occurred and asked Harvey to send a messenger to notify the Atlas Works of the accident. Then Sophy requested tea. She glanced at Martin and Oliver and ordered three cups and, after Mildred assured her she'd have it ready in two winks, led the way into her office.

Oliver met Martin's gaze rather challengingly. Martin's lips quirked, and he waved Oliver ahead of him into the room.

Oliver entered and made for the chair he'd previously occupied.

Martin shut the door and, this time, claimed the second armchair before the desk as, behind it, Sophy slumped into her chair.

They all sat for a second, thinking of what had just occurred, then Oliver blew out a breath. He looked at Sophy. "Was that another of these 'accidents' you mentioned earlier?"

Sophy glanced at Martin, but he gave her no direction. It was up to her to decide whether or not to include Oliver, although he hoped she did. Oliver had different contacts than Martin and might also have a different perspective on the situation. At this point, they needed all the help they could get.

Sophy returned her gaze to Oliver and slowly, reluctantly, nodded. "I suspect it was."

Martin stirred. "I had a look at the Atlas dray—at the wheel that came off—and had a quiet word with the driver and his mate. The long and short of it is that both they and I believe the forward offside wheel nut had been deliberately loosened. It stayed on well enough for them to drive the dray into town, but they told me that corner—at West and Rockingham—is the sharpest and tightest they have to get around, so the pressure on the offside wheel as they make the turn is greatest as they go around there, and that's where the nut came off, and the wheel shattered, the dray tipped, and the load came off."

"So this was planned by someone who knew what they were doing," Oliver said. "Someone who knew about heavily laden drays and the route the men took." He looked at Sophy. "Where did the dray come from?"

"The Atlas Works. That's out to the northeast of the town."

"More to the point," Martin said, "this accident, while a shock and an inconvenience as it is, could have been a disaster. Someone could have been walking along the street when the load came off."

"Someone might have been killed." Sophy's sober and serious expression suggested she'd already grasped that. "That would have been dreadful for the Atlas Works and for us as well."

Oliver shook himself. "Just thinking of that is appalling. Who would do such a thing?" He appealed to Martin. "Who would take such a cavalier risk? And for what? Why?"

Grimly, Martin nodded. "That's what we've been trying to figure out." He paused, then added, "These inexplicable accidents have been occurring for over two weeks."

"And clearly"—Sophy gestured—"whoever it is doesn't plan to stop."

Oliver frowned. "Have you received any demands?" He looked from Sophy to Martin. "I mean, it's intimidation, isn't it?"

"It is," Martin replied. "I hadn't thought of it like that, but you're right." He grimaced. "The problem is that the only two people who've made any sort of demand regarding Carmichael Steelworks are you and me."

Oliver huffed. "And it's not us, so…who?"

There was no answer to that, not yet. However…

Martin looked at Sophy. "Today, your luck held, and disaster didn't eventuate. But your luck isn't going to hold forever. The next accident or the next is liable to be deadly. You—we—need to put an end to this."

Oliver raised his hand. "Count me in. I was a witness today, and I didn't like what I saw. This sort of thing…no matter what industry is being affected, it can't be allowed to go on." He looked at Martin, then at Sophy. "Consider me another pair of reasonably intelligent eyes and ears, another brain, a different perspective. I would like to help."

Sophy looked at Martin, who looked steadily back at her. The decision had to be hers.

She returned her gaze to Oliver and, transparently suspicious, arched her brows, wordlessly questioning his altruism.

He reluctantly smiled and dipped his head. "I do have an ulterior motive." He shot an assessing glance at Martin. "I want to make a counteroffer for the steelworks, but this situation needs to be resolved first. So you might say that me helping you put an end to these accidents is furthering my own aims."

Martin wryly grinned; he wasn't the least surprised by Oliver's refusal to back away. Regardless, he remained confident of winning in any eventual competition for Sophy's favor.

When she turned her gaze on him, her turquoise eyes plainly asking if he was willing to accept Oliver even though he was determined to cast himself as a rival over purchasing the steelworks if she ever contemplated selling, he nodded. "The more people we can trust to work with us on this, the better, and the sooner we'll get to the bottom of whatever is going on." He arched a brow. "If you're willing for Oliver to join us?"

She studied Oliver again, then nodded decisively. "Thank you, Mr. Coulter. Your help will be welcome."

He smiled. "Please, just Oliver."

Sophy inclined her head just as the works' whistle screeched to announce the midday break. She glanced at Martin, then looked at Oliver. "If you're free, Oliver, perhaps you would join Martin and me at the Crofton Arms. They have a useful snug in the privacy of which we can go over all the incidents, consider the possible perpetrators, and discuss what we should do."

Oliver grinned; as Sophy pushed to her feet, he and Martin rose. "I would be delighted to join you, Miss Carmichael."

"Sophy, please." With a wry smile for Martin, she led the way to the door. "We're all in this together, it seems."

Martin followed Sophy into the snug and waited while she sat on the bench against the wall, as she had before. When she glanced up at him, he looked steadily at her, and with the faintest of blushes, she gathered her skirts and shuffled farther along. Hiding a smile, he sat beside her.

Oliver glanced around, noting that they were the only ones in the small room, then slid onto the bench on the other side of the table.

Saul appeared and took their orders. Today's special was rabbit stew, and after Martin recommended the ale, he and Oliver ordered pints of that while Sophy stuck to her cider.

They settled and exchanged desultory comments until their drinks and meals arrived. Tempted by the delicious aroma, they all started on the stew.

After savoring two mouthfuls, Oliver leaned forward and, voice low, said, "Those accidents you mentioned, the ones that occurred inside the works. Is there anything that connects them?"

Sophy glanced at Martin, deflecting the question to him. She ate and listened as he outlined the evidence that suggested the perpetrator had visited the works the night before each accident, apparently using a key.

She cut in to explain why there'd been only one key to all the locks and that no one had kept a record of who held a key. "So this morning, we had the locksmith around and had all the locks changed."

"Now, the various people have only the keys that are pertinent to their job." Martin glanced at Sophy. "Of course, attacking Carmichael's by sabotaging the delivery from Atlas required no key. At least not to the Carmichael site." He frowned. "I've never been to the Atlas Works' site. Would it have been easy to reach their delivery drays?"

She thought, then waggled her head. "If whoever did it was willing to scale a tall fence, then it wouldn't have been difficult. The drays are lined up in the open yard, not shut away. Mind you, I'm not sure how they knew which dray would have carried our pig iron—" She broke off, then grimaced. "Most likely, the Atlas crew loaded our dray yesterday, ready to leave this morning, and left the ticket for the delivery driver on the load. We always get that delivery today—it's a standing order."

"So no way forward there," Martin said.

Oliver observed, "It'll be interesting to see if you have any further accidents now that you've changed the locks."

Sophy nodded.

Silence fell as they ate and thought. Eventually, Martin said, "I keep tripping over the motive. Why would anyone want to damage a business such as the steelworks? What possible benefit could it yield?"

After a moment, Oliver said, "If one were wanting to buy Carmichael Steelworks as an ongoing business"—with his knife, he indicated Martin and himself—"as you and I wish to, then attacking it in this manner makes no sense at all. But what if someone wants to buy the business and absorb it into their own ongoing enterprise, renaming it and making it into something similar but different?"

Martin stared at Oliver, then huffed. "I knew there was some reason I thought we should include you in our deliberations. That's an entirely valid point." He looked at Sophy. "If someone wants to transform the business into something that's no longer identified as Carmichael Steelworks, then attacking the business in what are, ultimately, minor ways makes sense. Nothing they've done has damaged any of the major machinery."

"That's true." She frowned. "But they must want the steel for something." She looked at Martin, then across the table at Oliver. "Have either of you heard of anyone currently wanting to move into the steel industry in some way other than as a straightforward steel producer?"

Oliver shook his head. "I haven't, but I should have guessed Martin would be interested in Carmichael Steelworks."

"And I should have guessed you might be, too," Martin said, "but both of us are interested in continuing Carmichael's as a steelworks, albeit as one of a string of associated businesses. I haven't heard of and can't immediately think of anyone else—any other investor of the right caliber who might be looking this way."

"Nor I." Oliver paused, then added, "In fact, other than you and me, I can't think of anyone with the money to invest and an interest in Sheffield steel. At present, those interested in investing in steel are focusing on other towns."

Martin nodded. "That sums it up. I also can't think of any established company beyond yours and mine for whom such an acquisition would make commercial sense at this time."

Oliver murmured agreement, and they fell silent again.

After a moment, Sophy ventured, "Given all that, perhaps we shouldn't be looking for a commercial motive."

Oliver frowned. "What other motive could there be?"

Martin shifted to face her. "Do you or your family—or, indeed, the steelworks itself—have any enemies? Any ill-wishers of any kind?"

She blinked at him. "No. The steelworks are well respected, and we've never had even a disagreement with anyone."

"Not a neighbor?" Martin asked. "Not a competitor? No fatal accidents in the past?"

Adamantly, she shook her head. "No disagreements of any kind, and that extends to myself and, as far as I'm aware, the family as a whole."

"What about disgruntled suitors?" Oliver suggested. "Surely you must have some of those?"

Martin hid a smile as Sophy directed a look of haughty disdain across the table, but he was listening avidly when she repressively replied, "No. Nothing of that sort. I've never had any interest in society or the Marriage Mart. I've always made it clear I'm devoted to the steelworks, so no. We need to look elsewhere for our villain."

"All right." Martin caught her eye. "Let's try another tack. Who else has a financial interest in the steelworks?"

She readily replied, "My paternal cousins Edward and Charlie

Carmichael, my late uncle's sons, each have a fifteen-percent shareholding, but neither has ever shown any interest in the steelworks. Both are entirely content to pocket the distributions that come their way and otherwise ignore the business."

Martin exchanged a look with Oliver; neither could imagine such disinterest, not if one had a stake in a business, even if only fifteen percent. Martin returned his gaze to Sophy. "Can you describe them for us? What interests they have, what type of gentlemen they are."

Sophy huffed; judging by her attitude, she didn't approve of her cousins' disinterest, either. "Edward is the elder. He's thirty-three. He inherited his father's house in Sycamore Street and lives a bachelor existence there. He hasn't any real interests as such, no passionate hobbies, at least none that I know of. He's a stuffy sort, stiff and starchy and, if one allows it, overbearing."

Martin surmised Sophy didn't allow Edward any opportunity to indulge his overbearing tendencies.

"As for Charlie… He's twenty-seven, a year younger than me, and is widely considered to be a profligate hedonist who cares only for the latest reckless challenge. He gambles, although I know nothing of any details. He spends much of his time in London, in lodgings, and when in Sheffield—where I suspect he only comes to rusticate and avoid his creditors—he often stays with Edward, but sometimes Edward makes that unbearable, so Charlie will put up at one of the local inns."

She paused, then shook her head. "I can't imagine either being involved in these accidents. Neither has ever evinced the slightest interest in the steelworks."

Martin exchanged a look with Oliver. Neither of them, Martin felt sure, was quite so ready to discount either cousin. It sounded as if Charlie might have debts, and no man could possibly be as disinterested in life as she'd made her cousin Edward out to be.

Sophy glanced at the watch-brooch pinned to her bodice and sighed. "I have to get back. I have orders to check and authorize."

The three of them rose, and Oliver paid their shot. They left the pub and walked to the steelworks, Martin on Sophy's right and Oliver on her left.

On the pavement outside the office door, Martin and Oliver made their farewells.

With Oliver there, Martin refrained from taking Sophy's hand or paying her any particular attention. But before she turned away, he held her gaze for just a second longer than called for, and she returned his regard.

Feeling just a touch happier—more content—he watched as the office door closed behind her, then Oliver gestured along the street and set off, and Martin fell in alongside.

For several minutes, he and Oliver strolled along, side by side, just two gentlemen idly ambling toward the town center.

Canes swinging, they were pacing up Bow Street when Oliver said, "I don't know about you, but I have difficulty believing Sophy's cousins are totally disinterested in a valuable asset such as the steelworks."

His gaze, like Oliver's, on the streetscape ahead of them, Martin replied, "Even if they have no interest in managing the business, that doesn't equate to not being interested in the works in terms of the value of their shareholding."

"Exactly."

They skirted two nannies pushing prams, and as they resumed their steady perambulation, Oliver asked, "Where are you putting up?"

Martin told him. "And you?"

"The King James in Campo Lane. It's a block or so north of the Kings Head." After a fractional pause, Oliver asked, "Do you know where Sycamore Street is?"

Martin grinned. "As it happens, I do. We're heading in the right direction."

"Fancy an amble that way?"

Martin's grin widened. "Why not?"

CHAPTER 5

Half an hour later, Martin and Oliver ambled through the rooms of the Iron and Steel Club. Located on Church Street, in an older building adjacent to the town's famous Cutlers Hall, the club premises were only a short distance from Martin's hotel.

Gaining entry to the august establishment had merely been a matter of identifying themselves as investors from London, visiting the town on business. Their names had helped. Like Martin, Oliver hailed from one of the better-known families in the ton.

They'd called at Edward's house in Sycamore Street and had been informed by the starchy butler that at that hour, his master would be at the club.

Keeping their eyes peeled for anyone they knew, they worked their way through the club's extensive lounge, but most of those occupying the armchairs were too old by a decade to be Edward Carmichael. On returning to the corridor, Martin stopped a footman and asked for their quarry and was directed to the smoking room's far right corner.

They found the smoking room and discovered that the stipulated corner played host to a grouping of four armchairs arranged in a square around a low oval table. Three of the chairs were empty, while the one deepest in the corner was occupied by a large barrel-chested man in a brown tweed suit who was flicking through a newspaper.

Edward Carmichael had a fleshy face; he would have jowls when he was older. His features were heavy yet austere, with a broad nose, firm lips, and thick eyebrows. His curly hair was brown, the same color as his suit, and his complexion suggested he would readily color with anger, frustration, or embarrassment. His hands were large, thick-fingered, and his waistcoat was a trifle snug around his stomach. He sat stiffly in the chair, his attention on the contents of the paper.

Martin glanced around the room. Enough of the chairs were occupied to excuse him and Oliver claiming the empty chairs in the corner grouping.

Martin exchanged a look with Oliver, then with Oliver at his shoulder, he strolled down the room, paused beside the chair opposite Edward's, and in an arrogantly languid tone, inquired, "Do you mind?"

"Heh?" Edward looked up.

Gracefully, Martin waved to the chairs. "We were wondering if we might avail ourselves of these seats, old son."

His guess regarding Edward's tendency to color up was borne out. Under Martin's heavy-lidded gaze, Edward's face turned pink. He shuffled the newspaper and sat even straighter. "Oh. Yes. Of course."

Edward's widening gaze took in Martin's and Oliver's elegance, and more welcomingly, he added, "By all means."

Martin smiled sweetly, as did Oliver, and they sat, lounging in the chairs.

Oliver reached into his coat pocket and drew out a silver case. Opening it with a practiced flick, he offered it to Martin. "Cheroot?"

Martin didn't normally smoke but would in pursuit of a worthy cause. "Thank you." He picked up one of the thin rolls of fine tobacco. Oliver stuck one between his lips, then as if just noticing Edward, leaned forward and held the case out to him. "Would you like to join us?"

Edward beamed. "Thank you. I will." He helped himself to a cheroot, then Oliver slid the case away, drew out a pack of lucifers, lit one, and held the flame around until they were all puffing contentedly.

A footman rushed up with an ashtray, which Oliver accepted and set on the low table between them.

Martin blew out a thin stream of smoke, then focused on Edward, who was puffing appreciatively. "Martin Cynster." He waved a languid hand at Oliver. "And this is Oliver Coulter."

"Edward Carmichael," Edward returned.

"Carmichael?" Oliver frowned slightly. "Do you live in town?"

"Indeed, I do," Edward replied.

"Carmichael?" Martin echoed. "I say, you aren't by any chance connected to Carmichael Steelworks?"

Edward smiled. "I'm a part owner."

"Is that so?" Martin exchanged a faux-meaningful look with Oliver, then leaned forward and lowered his voice. "In that case, perhaps you can help us. We're here to look into the local steelworks with a view to purchasing one, and the Carmichael works was suggested to us as a possibility."

"Really?" Edward's bushy brows rose. "I must admit that surprises me. Although my brother and I own a significant percentage of the stock—and I daresay, given the right offer, both of us might see our way to accepting—the company is controlled by my cousin, and trust me, I entertain no illusions that she would ever be persuaded to sell."

"She?" Oliver managed to look creditably shocked. "You can't possibly mean that a woman runs the business?"

Edward looked grave. "I do, indeed, and I assure you, I'm no more in agreement with that than the next man. But"—he shrugged—"my uncle founded the company and held the controlling interest, and he encouraged his daughter, Sophia, to become involved and, ultimately, to take the reins when he passed. She still runs the steelworks on a day-to-day basis—makes all the decisions and what have you." Edward gestured and drew deeply on his cheroot. After he exhaled, he added, "In truth, I've never had any interest in the industry myself, so for my part—and my brother Charlie's, too—Sophy is welcome to her inheritance. It seems to keep her busy."

Martin frowned. "I thought you said earlier that you weren't in agreement with her running the business?"

Edward primmed his lips. "I have no quibble with Sophy's ability to manage the steelworks. If the distributions and profits are any guide, she does that very well. However, I cannot bring myself to condone a female acting in such a capacity. It's unnatural, and I wish she would...well, get married and go off and have children and leave running the business to some suitably qualified man."

Martin couldn't help but wonder what Carmichael family dinners were like. Then again, he could imagine that Sophy had long ago cowed her cousins into not airing such views within her hearing. Yet... "You have no ambition to manage the reins yourself?"

His expression supercilious, Edward declared, "None whatsoever.

I've never had the slightest inclination to involve myself in what, in truth, is only one step up from being in trade."

There was more than enough snobbish arrogance in those words to assure Martin and Oliver that Edward was speaking from the heart. He truly wanted nothing to do with running the steelworks, but clearly enjoyed the fruits of Sophy's labors and was in no hurry to interfere with that. "What about your brother, then?" Oliver asked. "If your cousin was induced to give up the position, would he—Charlie, was it—step in?"

Edward barked a laugh. "Not likely. My brother is more at home at the gaming tables—preferably those in London—than behind a desk. Indeed, I suspect he would know even less than I about the steelmaking business. Charlie, I fear, is a reckless profligate and will likely come to a bad end. Sophy, however, has a soft spot for him, and in return, I seriously doubt it would even occur to him to suggest she step aside."

Edward fell silent, his darkening expression suggesting he was brooding on Sophy's closeness to his younger brother.

Martin caught Oliver's eye as he responded, "Pity. Do you know of any other steelworks in this town similar to Carmichael's?" They didn't want Edward to think their interest was specific to the Carmichael works.

"No. Sorry." Edward shook his head. "As I said, that's not my area of expertise."

"I don't suppose," Oliver said, "you can point us to anyone here who might know more?"

"Hmm. O'Connor, if he's here, would be the one to ask." Edward peered up the room. "Can't see him, but he might be in later."

"Thank you." Martin leaned forward to stub out his cheroot in the ashtray, and Oliver did the same.

With a nod to Edward, Martin rose. "Thank you for your company."

"A pleasure," Edward returned, then his eyes widened. "Oh, I say. If you want to scout out the state of the steel industry in Sheffield, then the best thing you could do is to attend the charity ball tomorrow night. It's an annual affair, and everyone who's anyone in town will be there, including all the steel magnates—every last one. It's tradition and virtually obligatory that they show their faces, so they'll definitely be present."

"Where is it held?" Oliver asked.

"At the Assembly Rooms," Edward replied. "Any hackney driver will get you there. Anyone can purchase entry, and if you want to make contacts with a view to doing business in this town, that'll be the perfect place to advance your cause."

"Thank you," Martin said, entirely sincerely.

He tipped Edward a salute, then he and Oliver moved off, slowly walking down the room.

"Where to now?" Oliver looked about them.

"The bar," Martin replied. "I think we should seek corroboration of Edward's views, and at this hour, there should be at least a few gentlemen there."

There was, indeed, a smattering of six likely gentlemen in the cozy room, and while Martin and Oliver circled the tables, covertly seeking information on Edward and his brother, more thirsty souls arrived.

Oliver nudged Martin's elbow. "Isn't that Mellow, sitting at the bar?"

Martin looked and smiled. "It is. How fortuitous."

Mellow was an old acquaintance, a gentleman of similar background and age to Martin and Oliver and, like them, most often found in London.

"If memory serves," Oliver murmured as he and Martin headed Mellow's way, "his family lives in the district."

Mellow hadn't noticed them; he appeared wholly focused on the almost-empty glass of whiskey before him. Martin fronted the bar on one side, while Oliver did the same on the other.

"What-ho, Mellow?" Martin asked. "Rusticating again?"

Mellow cut him a sidelong look. "Cynster. And sadly, you're correct." He noticed Oliver. "You here as well, Coulter?" Mellow looked from Oliver to Martin. "Didn't know you two were close. Can't imagine you're gracing this lovely town for the same reason I am."

"We're old school friends," Oliver replied. "And no, we're here for other reasons."

"In pursuit of those reasons"—Martin leaned on the bar and signaled the barman to repeat Mellow's order and provide the same to him and Oliver—"we bumped into a gentleman, a member of this club. He's in the smoking room at present. Edward Carmichael." The barman placed the three glasses of whiskey on the counter before them. Martin reached for one and nudged the second Mellow's way. "You wouldn't happen to know anything about him, would you? Anything at all—personal, business, whatever."

Mellow drained the glass he was holding, set it down, and reached for the one Martin had provided. "Don't know him well. He's standoffish and, I would say, a loner. I've rarely seen him in anyone else's company, although I gather he's well known in town. Possibly a family thing. The Carmichaels have been here since the year dot."

Sipping his drink, Mellow turned, scanning the room, then his features lightened. He nodded toward two gentlemen of similar age, farther down the bar. "Casey'll likely know more. He's the biggest gossip in town."

Mellow caught the pair's attention and beckoned.

Patently curious as to who Martin and Oliver were, Casey and his friend eagerly joined them. Mellow made the introductions and explained Martin and Oliver's desire to know more about Edward Carmichael.

"Oh, very much a man who prefers his own company," Casey said. "More than that, he's a stiff customer and quite a wet blanket. He doesn't belong to any group—has no interest in the dinner club or the wine club and definitely not anything to do with gambling. Not even bridge! As far as I know, he has no close friends. No one makes the effort with him anymore."

"Hmm." Pritchard—the other gentleman who'd joined them—nodded sagely. "I'd agree with every word, but perhaps Edward has interests that connect with others farther afield. I saw him bring in a guest a few weeks ago—a hard-looking man in a very nice coat. He and Edward seemed quite chummy, which, of course, is why I noticed so particularly. I've never known Edward to be the chatty sort, yet the pair were quite animated and very absorbed in whatever they were talking about." Clearly caught up in the memory, Pritchard added, "Never seen anything like it, actually—Edward animated. Quite a sight."

Casey snorted. "Now, if you'd been asking after the younger Carmichael—Charlie—that would have been a different story."

"Oh?" Martin prompted.

Casey and Pritchard both nodded wisely.

"A game one, is young Charlie," Casey said. "Always up for a lark and a laugh and good company, too. Couldn't imagine a bigger contrast to his older brother."

"A pity Charlie spends so much of his time these days in London," Pritchard said. "We could use some of his liveliness in this place."

"He probably heads to London to escape Edward," Casey sapiently remarked. "And really, who could blame him?"

That seemed to be the extent of what Martin and Oliver were destined to learn, at least without more pointed questioning. After wordlessly agreeing there was no benefit in highlighting their interest further, they finished their drinks, bade farewell to Mellow, Casey, and Pritchard, and made their way out of the club.

As they stepped onto the pavement, Oliver said, "We might not have learned much, but at least we learned something."

"Hmm." Martin swung his cane as they started along the street. "I suggest we need to digest what we heard, decide if it sheds any light on the accidents, then define what more we need to know and how we might learn it."

They accomplished the first of their self-appointed tasks over a satisfying dinner in the Kings Head dining room. Reviewing what they'd heard didn't take that long, but they decided to leave more detailed discussion until later, when they weren't in such a public place.

Since their initial meeting in Sophy's office, they hadn't mentioned their competing bids for Carmichael Steelworks. Now, with the clink of cutlery and the hum of conversations all around them, Oliver asked about Martin's other steel-based businesses.

Martin answered without reservation and could almost see the wheels turning in Oliver's head.

By the time they reached the end of the meal, it was clear Oliver had worked out how the land lay. He set down his napkin and, across the table, met Martin's eyes. "Carmichael Steelworks is far more critical to you than it is to me."

Martin inclined his head. "It's the final and central piece I need to complete my steel portfolio."

Oliver nodded. "You're ahead of me in this area, and you started acquiring at the rim of the wheel, so to speak, while I intend to start at the center."

"That wasn't by design," Martin admitted. "It was simply the way the businesses became available for purchase, and they were all the right businesses—the right structure, the right product—to fit my plan. I wasn't going to pass up acquiring them, but that left me lacking the critical link, namely a steelworks of the capacity of Carmichael's."

Oliver studied Martin's face. "You're not going to let me have Carmichael Steelworks, are you?"

Martin smiled entirely sincerely and shook his head. "It's the perfect lynchpin for me and, therefore, has greater value to me than it could possibly have for you, at least at this time."

Oliver grimaced. "There's no benefit to me in forcing you to pay more than the business is worth. Luckily, I'm not restricted by any previous purchases. I can look for some other steelworks to start my steel portfolio."

"True. And if you back off from Carmichael's, I might be moved to help."

Oliver grinned and held out his hand. "Deal. I want your research into steelworks for a start."

Martin laughed and shook hands, and they rose. "Come up to my suite. My whiskey's better than that available here. We can enjoy a dram and decide what's next regarding the Carmichael situation." Martin paused and arched a brow at Oliver. "Unless you've lost interest now that you're no longer actively pursuing the business?"

"No. I haven't lost interest." Oliver fell in beside Martin, and they made their way from the dining room. "Not being set on buying the business frees me of considerations driven by that and, instead, allows me to indulge my curiosity, and I'm definitely curious about what's going on."

Martin led the way up the stairs. "It's certainly not the sort of thing one would want happening to other businesses in other industrial spheres."

"Exactly. And we both have several of those."

On reaching Martin's suite, they settled in the comfortable armchairs angled before the fireplace.

Roland—pleased to have something appropriate to his station to do—provided them with glasses of whiskey, then withdrew into the shadows.

Oliver sipped, then, startled, held up the glass to study the amber liquid. "This is very nice. What is it?"

"Glencrae Special Reserve."

Oliver sipped again and closed his eyes in appreciation. "I didn't know they produced a special reserve."

Martin grinned, sipped, then said, "Only for family."

Oliver looked at Martin, then Oliver's expression cleared. "Ah yes. I had heard of the connection." He looked at his glass. "A nice one to have."

"Indeed." After sipping again, Martin lowered his glass. "Putting together all we've learned about Sophy's cousins, what are the chances one or the other is behind the accidents?"

Oliver cradled his glass. "We haven't heard much about the younger one, Charlie, but from the sounds of it, it wouldn't be hard to imagine him getting into serious debt."

Martin nodded. "The sort that might make a man desperate. But if so, then how do the accidents benefit him?"

"Perhaps he's being pressured to ruin the steelworks by some cent-per-cent."

Martin frowned. "What interest would a cent-per-cent have in ruining a steelworks?"

Oliver grimaced. "Therein lies the rub. I can't see the connection."

They fell silent for several moments, each trying to find the right pieces to link together to form a believable motive. After getting nowhere with that, Martin pondered, then said, "If you think about it, when we asked about Edward and Charlie, we were looking for anything unusual."

Oliver nodded. "Given their well-established disinterest in the steelworks, something that pointed to a change in their view of it."

"Or their view of other things, meaning something that might have prodded them into acting against the family business. But the only thing odd that anyone mentioned was Edward's unusual interaction with the hard-looking man. Could he—that man—be relevant?"

Oliver frowned, then shrugged. "Who's to say? Unless we learn what they were talking so animatedly about, there's nothing we can follow up. Ten to one, the man was some old acquaintance from Edward's school days, passing through town."

Martin dipped his head in acknowledgment. "That no one in the club knew who he was—that he was a stranger to them—fits that scenario." He sighed. "We have to allow that Edward might have interests that lie beyond Sheffield, and perhaps the man was connected with that."

Oliver humphed. After a moment of staring at his leather-shod toes, he said, "We learned a little about each of Sophy's cousins, but nothing that gets us any further."

"Sadly, no." Martin drained his glass, waited while Oliver did the same, then met Oliver's eyes. "That said, I'm not yet ready to strike either of them off our list of potential suspects."

"No, indeed. Just because we haven't found anything to suggest a motive doesn't mean they don't have one."

"This ball Edward mentioned," Martin said. "While I habitually avoid all social events possible, I rather think this is one charity ball it might be worth my while to attend."

Oliver nodded. "It might be a profitable excursion in more ways than one."

Martin responded with a sharklike smile. "Precisely my thoughts.

Especially as you and I can legitimately claim to be interested in investment opportunities in the town."

"It does seem the sort of event tailor-made for us at this time." Oliver grinned. "While pursuing any whispers about Carmichael Steelworks, we can both further our own ends."

"Indeed."

The clock on the mantelpiece whirred, then softly *bonged* ten times.

Oliver set down his empty glass on the side table beside his chair. "And now I must be on my way, especially if we're going to this ball tomorrow night." He rose, and Martin stood as well.

As they walked toward the door, Oliver said, "Tomorrow, I plan to spend the day scouting around town on other business. While I do, I'll keep my eyes and ears open for any mention of Carmichael Steelworks."

"Do." Martin halted before the door. "I'll call in there tomorrow morning. I want to know if changing the locks has put a halt to the accidents."

Oliver tipped his head. "That might be revealing."

"We can but hope." Martin opened the door.

Oliver grinned, saluted him, and walked out. "I'll see you tomorrow evening at the Assembly Rooms."

Martin grunted a reply, then shut the door. He stood staring at the panels for a full minute, acknowledging the restlessness that rode his nerves, the edgy tension, all due to the sense that he should be doing something more active and tangible to protect Sophy and her steelworks. It was a strangely powerful feeling, more a compulsion than a mere inclination.

He turned to face the room. Roland appeared, and on impulse, Martin said, "I have a different job for you, Figgs, and Tunstall."

Roland brightened; he lived for moments when his "duties" took him beyond those activities normally associated with a gentleman's gentleman. "I'll fetch them." He turned and vanished through the unobtrusive door used by the servants.

Martin walked back to the chair by the fire and subsided into its depths. He was sitting there, cogitating, when his three most-trusted staff arrived and formed a line before him.

Leaning back in the chair, Martin studied the three. Figgs was his groom and readily identifiable as such, while Tunstall—his secretary—was visually much harder to pigeonhole. In his neat, well-made, but not expensive clothes, he was more of a chameleon, a trait he—and Martin—

used to their advantage. In this instance, however, little subterfuge would be required.

"I want the three of you to set up an effective overnight watch on the Carmichael steelworks."

"That place in Rockingham Street that you're looking to buy?" Tunstall clarified.

"Exactly." Martin considered, then said, "Every morning Monday to Saturday, the foreman, Hinckley, opens the works' gate at seven o'clock or just before. The works shut down at five, and it'll be Hinckley again who locks the main gate. I'm not sure when those working in the offices arrive, but they depart at that time. I'm interested in the hours between five in the evening and seven in the morning, Monday to Friday, and from one o'clock on Saturday afternoon through to seven o'clock the following Monday."

Figgs nodded. "So all day Sunday."

It was Tuesday. "If it comes to that," Martin confirmed. "I suggest you hire enough others—men you feel you can trust to do the job for a reasonable fee—to cover all four streets surrounding the works, but obviously, the entrances, which are on Rockingham Street and Bailey Lane, are the principal points of interest. I want at least one of you there at all times to oversee those you hire."

"You can count on us," Roland informed him, and indeed, the eagerness in all three faces was marked. They hated living a quiet life every bit as much as Martin did.

Hiding a grin at their enthusiasm, he went on, "If anyone tries to break in, regardless of the time or what I might be doing, notify me immediately. Keep watch, but don't interfere, and track them if they leave. Otherwise, report every morning."

"Very good, sir," they chorused.

Martin let his grin show and waved them off, then rose and headed for his bed. For tonight, he'd done all he could, and tomorrow would bring a new day.

CHAPTER 6

Sophy was sitting at the breakfast table, absentmindedly nibbling a slice of toast and rather trepidatiously wondering what the day would bring, when Richards entered and announced, "Lady Bracknell, miss. Ma'am."

"Oh!" Immediately, Julia, seated opposite Sophy, put a hand to her hair, checking that her chignon was tidy.

Sophy's grandmama swept in like a galleon under full sail, utterly unstoppable.

Sophy blinked as she registered that, even though it was barely eight o'clock, her grandmother was dressed for a day about town, with her improbably dark hair fetchingly secured beneath a fashionably feathered hat, and her robust figure tightly encased in a new carriage gown of plum silk.

She rose. "Is something wrong, Grandmama?"

"Wrong?" Lady Bracknell fixed her slightly protuberant eyes on Sophy. "Of course not, my love. Can't I visit my favorite granddaughter at breakfast time?"

"Yes, of course, Grandmama." Sophy forbore to point out that she was her ladyship's only granddaughter and dutifully came around the table to plant a kiss on her grandmother's lined cheek. "It's just… I didn't know you were back in town."

Lady Bracknell waved. "The Season is all but over, so I came up to see how you and everyone else is getting on." She beamed at Richards as he held a chair for her. "Thank you, Richards."

Sophy returned to her seat. She waved to the toast rack and pots of jam. "Can we offer you anything?"

"Just a cup of tea, dear." While Sophy duly poured a cup, her ladyship turned to Julia. "How are you faring, Julia?"

Julia uttered the usual assurances of her continuing good health and asked after Lady Bracknell's famously more-robust constitution.

Sophy surrendered the cup and saucer to Richards to deliver and listened as the pair opposite settled to discuss several local acquaintances, with Julia bringing her ladyship up to date with the latest gossip.

"Well, that's all very much as I expected. Gladys should never have countenanced that match." Lady Bracknell set down her cup and turned her attention to Sophy. "The other reason I called was to remind you, my dear Sophy, of the charity ball that will be held tonight."

Sophy smothered a grimace before it showed.

Her grandmother fixed her with a knowing look. "You are going, of course."

That was a statement—a definite statement with no room left for any other answer.

"I…hadn't forgotten." She'd just hoped she would be able to ignore it.

Her grandmother nodded decisively. "Of course not. As the head of Carmichael Steelworks, you have no option but to attend. Everyone—literally everyone who is anyone in this town—will be there, as you're perfectly well aware. I daresay I'm fussing over nothing, but I wanted to ensure that you looked your best. I've brought you a new gown from London. I had it from a modiste who's the latest thing and made sure she fashioned it out of silk in your favorite shade of aqua blue." Lady Bracknell beamed at Sophy. "I gave it to Richards to hand on to your maid."

Sophy inwardly sighed. Outwardly, she smiled gratefully. "Thank you, Grandmama. Of course, I'll wear the new gown tonight."

"How very fortuitous, Sophy!" Julia's eyes were bright. "A new gown always gives one confidence, and perhaps Mr. Cynster will be there."

"Cynster?" Lady Bracknell looked stunned. "Here?" She looked from Julia to Sophy and demanded, "Which Cynster?"

Resigned to the inevitable, Sophy replied, "Mr. Martin Cynster. He's interested in Carmichael Steelworks and has been assisting me with a bit of bother we've been having at the works."

Lady Bracknell stared at Sophy. Silently, for quite some time.

Sophy braced for some sort of overreaction, but eventually, her ladyship blinked, twice, then in a faintly strangled voice, said, "Well, that's…interesting."

It was Sophy's turn to blink. Since when didn't her grandmother leap on any scent of an eligible gentleman?

She was quite sure Martin Cynster qualified.

But after staring unseeing across the table, apparently lost in thought —or contemplating some vision only she could see—Lady Bracknell turned to Julia. "I take it you plan to attend as well, Julia?"

"Oh yes! I wouldn't miss it for the world."

"Excellent!" Lady Bracknell beamed. "I'll call for you and Sophy in my carriage at eight o'clock." She shot a glance at Sophy. "Don't keep me waiting, child. You know I like to get in before the crush."

"Yes, Grandmama."

Her grandmother rose, and Sophy followed suit and dutifully saw her ofttimes-trying relative to the door.

Although her grandmother looked energized and quite desperately eager, she said nothing more—demanded nothing more—but just parted from Sophy with a pat on her wrist and an unwaveringly delighted smile.

Sophy struggled not to narrow her eyes as she watched her grandmother being handed into her carriage. After the carriage door shut, Sophy closed the front door and returned to the breakfast parlor, where Julia was still sipping her tea.

Sophy rounded the table and sank into her chair. Then she looked across and caught Julia's gaze. "What is she up to?"

Julia smiled. "I have no idea, but clearly, we'll need to be ready at eight—you know what she's like about punctuality—and then, no doubt, we'll see."

Sophy wasn't sure she wanted to learn what plans her grandmother was hatching for the evening, but sadly, she wasn't going to have any choice.

Martin walked into the main office of Carmichael Steelworks at just past nine o'clock.

He'd already learned from his staff that there'd been no attempts to gain entry to the premises during the past night. Nevertheless, after exchanging good mornings with Mildred and Harvey, he inquired, "Have there been any accidents reported this morning?"

"No, thank heavens!" Harvey looked hugely relieved. "With any luck, those new locks will put a stop to such things."

The door leading to Sophy's office stood open, and Harvey turned as Sophy, having heard Martin's voice, appeared.

She smiled at him, and Martin felt something in his chest swell.

"Good morning," she said, still smiling. "And yes, changing the locks seems to have given our persecutors pause. All appears to be running smoothly. Hinckley and the subforemen came in early and checked over the equipment thoroughly before opening the gates. Thus far, nothing's broken or stuck."

"Good." Martin hesitated, then confessed, "I have several staff with me, and at the moment, they have little to do. So I set them the task of keeping watch over the steelworks through the night. They reported that no one had tried to get in. Given that, there shouldn't be any accidents today, but nevertheless, it's comforting to know there haven't been any thus far."

Because that means that none of the workers were themselves involved in causing said accidents.

Sophy understood what Martin didn't say and, sobering, tipped her head in acknowledgment. He was right, and it was reassuring to have that confirmed.

Indeed, she was sufficiently grateful for that reassurance to overlook his overstepping all reasonable bounds and putting a watch on the place without consulting her. At that moment, she had more pressing matters on her plate. She glanced at Harvey. "I'm going to the laboratory. I want to start work on the alloy for the new contract for Osborn."

Harvey saluted. "Right, miss. We'll hold the fort here."

Smothering a smile, Sophy turned toward the door leading into the yard. She was fairly certain Martin would dog her heels, especially now that he knew she was off to create a new alloy.

Sure enough, he followed her.

She was almost at the door when it opened to reveal Oakshot. He stood in the doorway, blinking, then bobbed his head. "Miss Carmichael. I was wondering if I could have a word?"

Sophy stepped back and waved him into the office.

Oakshot came in and shut the door, but looked uncertain. He saw Martin and bobbed his head to him.

"What is it?" Sophy asked.

"Well, miss, I don't rightly know whether this is any of my business, but I was wondering about us canceling our order for pig iron from Atlas. If we're not going to be getting it from them, where should I expect the deliveries to come from?"

Sophy wondered if she'd heard aright. She frowned. "But..." She glanced at Harvey, who appeared as mystified as she, then looked back at Oakshot. "Why do you think we've canceled our order with Atlas?"

Oakshot looked confused. "Well, miss...because *they* think we've canceled the order."

"But we haven't!" Sophy said.

Behind her, Martin shifted. "Perhaps, Oakshot, you could tell us what led you to think the order has been canceled."

Oakshot's expression cleared, and he readily explained, "I got chatting with the driver of the load that came off yesterday. While I was doing the paperwork with him, he said as how it was just his luck that the very last delivery he'd be making to us—the last time he'd be taking a laden dray around that corner—it was *that* time the load would come off. At first, I thought he meant he'd been let go, for some reason, but he'd only be in his forties, so that didn't seem right. So yesterday evening down the pub, I got to thinking that maybe he'd meant the drivers were changing rosters, and as one of my mates works in the Atlas dispatch office, I asked him, quiet-like, what he'd heard about the delivery of Carmichael's regular order, and he said they was all that surprised that you, miss, had canceled it."

"I haven't." Sophy felt like she'd been clubbed over the head. Without the steady supply of pig iron, the furnaces and converters would have to be shut down...and steelmaking at Carmichael's would stop. To start the furnaces up again would be hugely costly, both in time and money...

"Aargh! It's another accident, just of a different type." She focused on Oakshot. "Thank you, Oakshot. If you hadn't checked with your friend and then come to tell me, it would be dark days for Carmichael's." She shot a glance at the clock. "I'll go to the Atlas Works immediately and get this sorted out." The new alloy could wait.

Determination welling, she nodded to Oakshot, spun on her heel, and stalked to her office. Passing Harvey, she said, "I'll get this sorted out, but I'll likely be several hours."

"Yes, miss," Harvey returned. "We'll manage."

After shrugging into her coat and grabbing her bag, she returned to the outer office. She wasn't surprised to find Martin waiting. He held the door for her and followed her out.

She strode quickly along the pavement toward Broad Lane; finding a hackney would be easier on the busier street.

Martin kept pace easily. "I take it this is urgent."

"Yes," she bit out. "We get pig iron delivered three times a week, but Atlas's runs are always close to fully committed, and if I don't rectify this mix-up in time, they might not be able to supply us again until later in the week."

They reached Broad Lane, and he whistled up a hackney; another reason to take him with her. He grasped her hand and helped her in, then followed and called to the jarvey to get them to the Atlas Works as fast as humanly possible.

The jarvey took him at his word, which was something of a relief. As they rocketed along, weaving in and out of traffic, her heart was racing, although whether in reaction to the situation—surely fraught enough—or from sitting in such close proximity to Martin, she couldn't have said. Yet over and above everything, even her unrelenting awareness of him, she was glad he was with her.

The hackney swerved, and her shoulder pressed hard into his arm. As she righted herself, she prayed she wasn't blushing furiously.

"If the worst comes to be," he said, and she heard nothing but single-minded focus in his voice, which greatly assisted her to find the same, "and Atlas can't fill your order, I could divert some supply from my Rotherham foundry."

She glanced at him. "But your runs must be close to fully committed, too."

His features hardened, and he met her eyes. "There are some benefits to being an owner. If I tell them to divert, they will."

And he would. She read as much in his eyes. He was prepared to risk creating problems with his foundry's contracted customers in order to help her and Carmichael's.

She summoned a weak smile and lightly gripped his arm. "Thank you. But with any luck, it won't come to that."

Just as long as she reached the Atlas Works in time.

The hackney rocketed around a corner and onto Lady's Bridge.

"How long have Carmichael's been ordering their pig iron from Atlas?" Martin had to shout to be heard over the rattling of the wheels.

"Since my father's day," Sophy yelled back.

"And they're your sole supplier?"

"Yes."

"So everyone in town knows that Carmichael's is entirely dependent on Atlas deliveries."

The hackney shot off the bridge and headed up The Wicker.

Sophy looked at Martin. "What are you thinking?"

His expression was decidedly grim. "That the accidents didn't work as our villain had hoped, so he's turned to sabotaging your essential supply line. That's what the dray was about. It wasn't a Carmichael dray. It was Atlas's."

"So the dray accident was actually a part of this new tack?"

"Had the accident been worse, as it could have been, it would have caused trouble—friction at least—between Carmichael's and Atlas. Atlas might not have wanted to continue dealing with Carmichael's. I think making Atlas believe you've canceled a long-standing order is another part of this new attempt to undermine Carmichael's."

She frowned. "If they thought that a dray accident, however bad, would cause Atlas to step away from dealing with Carmichael's…that suggests they don't know the connections in this town all that well."

From the corner of her eye, she saw Martin frown at that, but before he could ask for clarification, the hackney drew up outside the massive gates of the even more massive Atlas Works.

"Thank you!" she called to the jarvey and all but tumbled from the hackney as it rocked to a halt.

Leaving Martin to pay the jarvey, she hurried to the gatehouse.

The gatekeeper saw her and beamed. "Miss Carmichael! It does my old eyes good to see you, miss. It's been too long." He raised the bar he manned and waved her through.

"It's not been that long, Ben, but I need to see the old man immediately. Is he in?"

Martin neared as Ben replied, "I believe he is, miss. In the office still, I think."

"Thank you!" She waved at Martin. "Mr. Cynster is with me."

With that, she hurried across the open yard in front of the huge works.

With his longer legs, Martin quickly caught up. He peered at her face. "The old man?"

"John Brown, the owner of Atlas." She spared a quick glance at Martin's face, along with a very swift grin. "He's my godfather."

"Ah." Martin nodded. "You really are a child of this town."

That, Sophy thought, was a gross understatement. She reached the main office, hauled open the door, and rushed in.

Following at Sophy's heels, over her head, Martin scanned the office. His gaze landed on a female secretary who kept guard behind a raised counter.

The woman's stern expression softened at the sight of Sophy. "Miss Carmichael. It's a pleasure to see you."

"Good morning, Agnes. Is Mr. Brown available? It's a matter of some urgency." Sophy halted before the counter. "Actually, regarding that, you might be able to help me. Apparently, there's been some sort of mix-up, and Atlas might be under the impression that I've canceled Carmichael's standing order for pig iron."

Agnes's expression grew serious. "I understood—"

"Sophy, my girl!" a jovial voice called through the open doorway of an adjoining office. "Just the person I most wanted to see."

A second later, a large middle-aged man with a presence to match his voice loomed in the doorway. He beamed at Sophy as she turned to him with obvious relief. He strode up, holding out his hands to take hers. "I was just wondering if I should come down and see you, my dear, and instead, here you are."

"Uncle John." Sophy gripped his hands and looked into his face, her expression one of worry and concern. "First, let me say how sorry I am about that dray."

Brown's smile didn't waver. "That was hardly your fault, my dear." A hard gleam appeared in Brown's eyes. "However, it did prompt me to increase our nighttime patrols. I'm not convinced that was an accident, and if so"—he squeezed Sophy's fingers—"I can only be glad we had nothing worse to deal with than a shaken driver and his mate."

"Yes, well, unfortunately, that's not the only accident that's been occurring around and about Carmichael's."

Surprised, Brown eased his grip, and Sophy retrieved her fingers.

"Indeed, it's another of those happenings that's brought us here." She stared into Brown's face. "I heard that Atlas might be laboring under the misapprehension that I've canceled our order."

Brown's expression sobered. "I did wonder why, after all these years, you'd decided to stop ordering from us. That was what I was wanting to see you about."

"But I haven't canceled anything!" Sophy all but wailed.

"Actually…"

Along with Sophy and Brown, Martin glanced at Agnes; it was she who had spoken.

She held up a sheet of paper. "I have the letter canceling the order here, Miss Carmichael."

Lips setting, Sophy hurried to the counter. "Let me see that." She brushed past Martin, then paused and looked at Brown. "My apologies. I should have introduced you. This is Mr. Martin Cynster. He's been helping me with all the accidents we've been having."

She glanced briefly at Martin, and the line of her lips softened. "And this"—she waved at Brown—"is, indeed, John Brown, commonly known as the Father of the Sheffield Iron and Steel Trade and owner of the Atlas Works." To Brown, she added, "As you'll hear if you come to Carmichael's, Martin saved my life—mine and several of our workmen's—last Saturday. And as you'll no doubt discover, he's also interested in your favorite subject, steel."

With that brief but effective introduction, she turned to Agnes.

Brown had been eyeing Martin curiously from the first. Now, he thrust out his hand. "Anyone who saves Sophy's life is always welcome at Atlas."

Valiantly trying to conceal his eagerness, Martin shook hands. "I'm thrilled to meet you, sir." He glanced at Sophy. "I'm only just discovering how much a part of the Sheffield iron and steel trade Sophy is."

"Indeed, she's very much one of us, as the saying goes. But speaking of belonging"—Brown narrowed his eyes on Martin's face—"unless I miss my guess, you're the Cynster who's taken over the old foundry at Rotherham."

Martin admitted he was.

"Well, sir, I'm just as pleased to meet you. You've done an excellent job of turning the place around. When I heard you'd taken it on, I was doubtful you'd be able to haul the business out of the mire into which the previous owners had sunk it, but in just a few years, you've proved me wrong." Brown eyed Martin in a shrewdly assessing fashion. "It might never come to it, but if we ever run low on pig iron, I wouldn't mind turning to you. I've heard very good reports about the quality of your product."

Martin called on every ounce of his hard-won control to keep his delight within bounds and managed to coolly incline his head. "We would be honored to contract to Atlas. We're still ramping up production, but expect to be in full swing by the end of summer."

Brown humphed. "And does that have anything to do with your appearance at Carmichael's, I wonder?"

Martin smiled. "It does. I made an offer and came to Sheffield thinking to persuade Sophy to sell to me, but now I've seen how central she is to the business, I'm reviewing my approach."

Brown nodded. "A wise move. In all the ways that matter to a business, she *is* Carmichael Steelworks. Without her input, the place is worth only a fraction of what it otherwise would be."

"So I've realized." Martin judged that being candid was worth the risk. "I'm specifically interested in acquiring a steelworks that specializes in custom alloys or at least has that capacity. That's what prompted my interest in Carmichael's. I already own several downstream businesses—knives, wire—and I'm looking to expand into manufacturing steel safes. Making the steel plate for such items requires a solid understanding of the right sort of alloys." He met Brown's eyes. "I gather you have significant experience in producing armor plate for the navy. I would be keen to hear your thoughts on such uses of steel at some time."

Brown was plainly intrigued. "Safes, heh? Interesting idea."

"Well!"

The exclamation from Sophy had both men swiveling to look at her.

She turned from the counter and Agnes and, with her face a mask of anger, waved the letter at them. "This is a forgery!"

Brown nodded, obviously not entirely surprised. "I wondered if it might be. The wording didn't sound like you at all. But the signature, Sophy…it seemed right or at least close enough so that I couldn't be sure."

Martin watched Sophy study the signature, then she grimaced. "It's not a bad attempt. The *S* isn't quite right, and nor is the capital *C*. But otherwise…"

"That means," Martin said, "that someone must have had an example of your signature to work from."

She stared at him, then grimaced again. "I sign all the major orders, so there would be hundreds of copies of my signature in lots of different offices all around town."

Martin sighed and thrust his hands into his pockets. "So we're stymied on that front."

From behind the counter, Agnes had been looking from one to the other. "Should I ignore this letter, then?"

"Please!" Sophy looked at Brown, who nodded to her and to Agnes.

"See it gets sorted out, Agnes."

"Yes, sir. I'll send a boy to Dispatch to make sure they understand that the Carmichael order is continuing and that the next regular delivery should go out as usual."

"Thank you!" Sophy was plainly hugely relieved.

"Well, my dear"—Brown grinned at her—"I expect I'll see you at the ball this evening."

Sophy's expression fell into one of hapless dejection, and Brown laughed. "I heard your grandmother's back in town, so I know you'll be there."

"I will be." Her tone suggested she found no pleasure in contemplating the event.

Brown turned inquiring eyes on Martin. "Have you heard of our charity ball, Cynster?"

His gaze on Sophy's face, Martin nodded. "I have, and I plan to attend."

Sophy looked up, her expression lightening to one of consideration.

"Excellent!" Brown clapped Martin on the shoulder. "You can tell me more about your ideas there. I wouldn't mind investing in a venture like that."

"I'll look forward to it, sir." Martin half bowed, and Sophy bustled up to hug Brown and buss his cheek.

"I'll see you tonight, then." Sophy stepped back. "As Grandmama is fetching Julia and me, I can guarantee we won't be late."

Brown laughed again and waved them off.

While he strode beside Sophy to the works' gate, Martin reviewed all he'd heard.

They passed through the gate, and he hailed a hackney. Once they were bowling back to Carmichael's, he murmured, "So you will be at the ball tonight?" He'd assumed she would be; it hadn't occurred to him that she might avoid the occasion.

She sighed deeply. "My grandmama is a force of nature and not to be denied."

Abruptly wary, he asked, "And your grandmother is…?"

"Lady Bracknell. My mother's mother."

"Ah." Enlightenment dawned.

Sophy glanced at him, then studied his face. "I take it that means you're acquainted with her. She recognized your name when Julia let it fall."

He sighed, much as she had done. "Your grandmother is a friend—a close friend—of my grandmother, Lady Horatia Cynster."

Sophy read his expression and laughed. Then she patted his hand where it rested on his thigh. "Don't worry. Courtesy of my advanced years, I've cured—or perhaps more accurately exhausted—Grandmama's matchmaking tendencies."

"Ladies like your grandmother *never* lose their matchmaking tendencies."

"Well"—still grinning, she faced forward—"I assure you such machinations no longer work on me."

They might, however, work on Martin. In fact, the more he considered the prospect, he wondered if, perhaps, Lady Bracknell might not prove to be an ally in the not-too-distant future.

Hmm. A curious notion, but not one he was inclined to reject out of hand.

A second later, Sophy turned to him, a puzzled expression on her face. "Where did you hear about the ball?"

He looked into her turquoise eyes and decided that, given the direction of his plans vis-à-vis her, candor and the simple truth was his only real option. "After we left you yesterday, Oliver and I decided to see what we could learn about town. We thought to look up your cousin Edward, and we ran him to ground at the Iron and Steel Club."

She widened her eyes. "And…? What did you make of him? Could you see him as the villain behind the accidents?"

Martin grimaced. "He was as pompous and stuffy as you'd described, and while Oliver and I agree he seems an unlikely fit for the role of villain, neither of us is as yet willing to strike him off our list of suspects. But to answer your question, it was Edward who encouraged us to attend the ball. We'd introduced ourselves essentially as who we are—investors looking to engage in the iron and steel trade. He said if we wanted to meet everyone who was anyone in iron and steel in Sheffield, the ball was the place to be."

He paused, then added, "We also heard from Edward and several others about Charlie, again confirming all you'd told us. From what we gathered, he's in London."

She nodded. "As I said, I can't see either of them being involved."

There was considerable traffic on the bridge, and their progress slowed. Relaxing against the seat, Martin said, "Tell me about those I'll meet at this ball."

Sophy arched her brows, then admitted, "Edward was correct. If you want to extend your contacts in the Sheffield iron and steel trade, our Annual Charity Ball is guaranteed to afford you the best opportunities."

She went on to list the various magnates and luminaries of the trade who were certain to make an appearance. "Sad to say, my grandmother was also correct in saying that, as the head of Carmichael Steelworks, I really have to attend."

The hackney finally reached the town end of the bridge and turned west, toward the Carmichael works. Once they were bowling along again, Sophy slanted an assessing glance at Martin. "Are your and Oliver's interest in the evening purely due to your personal agendas, or are you imagining that we might learn something pertinent regarding our accidents?"

"Both." He met her gaze. "If we assume that whoever's behind the accidents and the attempts to damage Carmichael Steelworks has the ultimate aim, for whatever reason, of having the steelworks fail, then there's every chance we might learn something useful at the ball."

She leaned against the padded seat and considered that prospect.

Eventually, distinctly wryly, she admitted, "For the first time in my life, I find I'm looking forward to a social event."

From the corner of her eye, she saw Martin smile.

CHAPTER 7

Having remembered Sophy's comment to John Brown that she wouldn't be late to the ball, Martin walked into the Assembly Rooms shortly after the doors had opened.

Immediately, he realized his mistake. As neither Sophy nor Lady Bracknell had yet arrived, he fell victim to the most senior hostess, a Lady Ponsonby, who was acquainted with his great-aunt Helena. Holding his social mask firmly in place, he concentrated on remaining free of other young ladies' clutches until Sophy and her grandmama appeared.

Being keen to set eyes on Lady Bracknell was a wish he'd never thought to entertain.

He was fending off the advances of a pair of determined matrons with daughters in tow—luckily, they appeared to be competitors, which allowed him to maintain the upper hand—when a stunning figure in a pale-turquoise gown walked into the room and effortlessly captured his attention.

She captured his awareness and every one of his senses.

With real effort, he forced his gaze back to the besieging matrons and smiled his most charming smile, causing the one who was speaking to break off and regard him hopefully. He seized the moment. "Ladies, thank you for making a newcomer to your lovely town so welcome. However, I've just seen someone to whom I must pay my respects. Please excuse me." Giving them no chance to protest, he half bowed, stepped around them, and made for the gathering of hostesses just inside the door.

He was loitering with intent when Lady Bracknell, with Julia and Sophy trailing behind, parted from the last of the hostesses. He stepped into her ladyship's path and bowed. "Lady Bracknell, I'm delighted to see you. It's been far too long since we met."

Her ladyship leveled a disbelieving look on him. "Martin Cynster, please don't think I'm anything but immune to such flummery. I understand you've already found your way to Portobello Street."

"I have, indeed, and Mrs. Canterbury and your granddaughter have been nothing but kind."

"I daresay. So"—her ladyship's gimlet gaze locked on his face—"how are your parents?"

Martin readily surrendered to the inquisition he'd known would come. In between her inevitable questions about his siblings and their families and his own recent doings, her ladyship appropriated his arm and commanded him to steer her to a sofa by the wall. Julia and Sophy followed, Julia looking anxious while Sophy appeared amused.

After seating her ladyship on one corner of the sofa and assisting Julia to the spot alongside, Martin stood patiently before her ladyship and consented to be interrogated as to why he was there.

His candid admission that he'd come to Sheffield with a view to acquiring Carmichael Steelworks had her ladyship's gaze sharpening and swinging to Sophy, who had halted beside him.

"And what reply did you give to Martin's offer, my dear?" Lady Bracknell inquired.

Sophy smiled sweetly. "Exactly what you would expect, Grandmama. I told him I wasn't interested in selling."

"I see." Lady Bracknell regarded her granddaughter for a long moment.

As far as Martin could tell, the prolonged and intense scrutiny had no effect whatsoever on Sophy.

Eventually, her ladyship looked back at Martin. "And yet, here you are."

Sophy quickly explained, "Mr. Cynster—Martin—has been helping me resolve some issues at the steelworks. There've been a spate of accidents, and we're attempting to get to the bottom of them."

Her ladyship's eyes widened. "Is that so?"

Before she could demand further enlightenment, the musicians, stationed in a gallery above the main floor, set bow to string, and the strains of a waltz wafted over the heads of the now-considerable crowd.

Martin turned to Sophy and half bowed. "Miss Carmichael, will you grant me the honor of this dance?"

Sophy smiled, partly, he felt sure, in relief. "Thank you, sir. I would be delighted." When he extended his hand, she clutched it and smiled at her grandmother and aunt. "If you'll excuse us?"

Lady Bracknell looked to be fighting a grin. Lips prim, she waved dismissively. "By all means. Go, go!"

With a brief bow to the older ladies, Martin turned and, much relieved himself, led Sophy into the crowd.

"Phew!" She met his eyes. "That was considerably more detailed than her usual inquisitions."

He shrugged. "She knows my family root and branch. I assumed she would want to know everything I could tell her so came suitably prepared."

"Just as well." Sophy had been quietly fascinated by all he'd let fall; his revelations had painted an intriguing picture of his plainly extensive family and their current exploits. Her own family was limited, and that Martin knew so much of not just his siblings' but also his cousins' lives proved that he was in contact with many of them, that they were all close in a family way, and she'd found that alluring. While growing up, she'd often fantasized about being a part of a large, affectionate, and supportive family.

The sensation of his hand wrapped around her fingers slowly permeated her brain and refocused her thoughts. They were about to dance. She was about to step into his arms for the first time since landing in them within the first hour of meeting him. The realization had her girding her senses, steeling them against the inevitable jolt.

They reached the area being cleared for the dancers.

In truth, she didn't enjoy dancing and had no fond memories of any waltz; her previous experiences had left her bored and strangely dissatisfied, feeling as if she'd missed out on something that her conscious mind couldn't define. However, consenting to waltz with Martin had been the fastest way to escape her grandmother, and after her earlier experience of being in his arms, some wanton part of her wanted to discover whether waltzing with him would be different.

Whether the activity would satisfy that part of her that waltzing with others had left unfulfilled.

He halted at the edge of the dance floor, and with an expectant smile on her lips, she swept her skirts around and stepped boldly into his arms.

His grip on her fingers had shifted; now, it firmed, and his other hand splayed over her back. Neither contact was overly forceful, yet the pressure was definite and impossible to ignore. He smiled into her eyes as the music swelled, then he stepped out and swept her into the circle of whirling couples.

Instinctively, she moved with him, fluidly, without thought, as if her body had been made for this. Just as well, because all thought had deserted her.

Trapped in fascination, she delighted as they whirled smoothly, effortlessly traversing the floor, and it was as if she'd been freed of tethers that, to that point, unbeknown to her, had been anchoring her to drab earth.

Caught on a wave of sensation, her wits drifted away while her senses exulted and swirled. A delicious tension infused her, gripped her. Excitement, tantalizing and novel, beckoned, and eager and curious, she followed his lead into this new unknown.

From the first instant, their gazes had locked, the rich caramel of his eyes warm and enticing. She felt as if, hand in hand, palm to palm, they were sinking into the moment, into the experience, that she and he had stepped onto some other plane.

A plane inhabited solely by them—one on which the physical ruled, yet where every sweeping movement, every subtle pressure, and every bold step was infused with feelings beyond the tactile. In that private world, desire bloomed, and passion welled and swelled, and need slowly, steadily burgeoned until her nerves sparked with a heightened awareness, and she felt more alive than she ever had before.

This is what it feels like to be alive in every sense. To want and need and hunger.

To live as I'm meant to live.

Those realizations hammered at her as she stared into his gorgeous eyes, and the magic of the moment surrounded her.

For magic it was. She'd never felt the like, where her breath caught and her senses whirled and drew her inexorably on. The sensations wreathing through her mind were a flagrant sensual invitation to indulge in so much more; their temptation was blatant and provocative, yet also concealed, cloaked by the conventional and accepted rhythm and sway of the dance.

She drew in a much-needed breath, and her breasts swelled beneath the silken bodice of her new gown, and she understood beyond all question that—over the past short minutes—her life had taken a drastic turn.

She couldn't drag her eyes from the promise in his.

She wanted him, and he wanted her. It took effort not to move closer, to press closer than the dance allowed.

They waltzed under the eyes of all of Sheffield, and that dictated a certain circumspection, yet she didn't doubt what she felt, couldn't close her eyes to what she now wanted.

Nor did she doubt that he felt and wanted the same.

And the magic of that was the most potent of all.

Acting on instinct, guided by habit and experience, Martin whirled them down the room. Lost in her eyes, in her turquoise gaze, he felt captured and cast adrift on a sea of swelling, roiling, turbulent passion he hadn't in any way anticipated.

Never in all his many years spent in the haut ton, sampling the delights of the legion of ladies who had invited him to share their beds, had he ever felt such a powerful, overwhelming, all-consuming need.

A need that encompassed so much more than physical lust and carnal hunger that he hadn't yet glimpsed the full extent of its reach.

Before stepping out with her in this waltz—this totally unexpected, unprecedented journey of revelation—he'd recognized and accepted that she was the one for him. That Sophy Carmichael was the lady above all others he needed by his side, working with him to forge a full, satisfying, and complete-in-all-aspects life.

That much had been obvious from their first meeting, and all that had happened between them since had only added to his certainty, but whirling down the floor with her in his arms, supple and giving and so temptingly close, stripped the last veils from his eyes. When it came to her, the power that drove him, that guided, pressed, and compelled him, was…immense, intense, and utterly undeniable.

Irresistible.

It was that and more. No other woman had ever sparked this particular fire within him.

No other lady ever would, of that he was certain.

She was his one and only, and his life would mean nothing if she wasn't there, the lynchpin around which he revolved.

That she was and forever would be his ultimate weakness yet simultaneously his greatest strength came as a shocking, visceral realization. On one level, the understanding was frightening. He was a man who had always seized life's chances and made them work for him; to know that his ultimate success in life now depended on another—and he could do nothing about that because, somehow, it had already been decided—was difficult to process, to absorb and accept.

He'd embarked on the waltz with complete confidence that, as usual, he was in control, not only of the immediate situation but also of the evolution of what would, he'd assumed, grow between him and her.

Yet the feel of her in his arms, the subtle sway of her distinctly feminine figure as she followed his lead without the slightest hesitation, the *shush* of her gown as her skirts brushed his trousered legs—indeed, each and every minor sensation combined to provoke a searing hunger that had him battling a nearly overpowering urge to seize, to haul her closer, lock her to him, and plunder.

As the music reached its apogee, then slowed and faded, and the dance drew to an end and he strove to hold his demons in check, while he remained ever more certain of his direction, he was no longer sure who—or what—held the reins.

Their feet halted.

Her gaze still locked with his, Sophy blinked at him; the dazed expression in her turquoise eyes assured him that she was as affected as he.

He forced himself to release her, and that was no mean feat. He bowed and was aware the gesture, while perfectly correct, was far stiffer than his usual, gracefully accomplished act.

He raised her from her curtsy, and she wobbled. He held her hand until she'd steadied, then slowly—plainly reluctantly—she drew her fingers from his clasp.

Her eyes held his. "That was…" She paused to sweep the tip of her tongue over her lower lip, and he fought not to close his eyes and groan.

"Enjoyable," she concluded. She gave a little nod, then flicked open the fan dangling from her wrist and plied it as she looked about them as if noticing the other dancers for the first time.

He drew in a deep breath, filling his lungs in the hope more air would steady his wits, then looked around as well. More by luck than design, they were at the opposite end of the large room from where they'd started—from where her grandmother and Julia were sitting.

He didn't want to but felt compelled to wave in that direction and ask, "Shall we?"

Sophy didn't want her aunt, much less her grandmother, to see her in such a mental tizzy. Others might not be able to tell, but they assuredly would, and then she'd never hear the end of it.

She dithered, something she rarely did and hated being reduced to. "Perhaps…"

As if in answer to her unformed hope, Oliver appeared through the increasing crush.

"I say!" He greeted Sophy and Martin with exuberant eagerness, then settled the sleeves of his evening coat. "This is clearly the place to be for those with any interest in steel." He grinned at Martin. "Purely while making my way across the room, I've stumbled over more czars of the industry than I'd ever hoped to meet."

Martin nodded; to Sophy's eyes, he appeared a touch relieved. "Courtesy of accompanying Sophy while she followed up another odd occurrence at the steelworks, I got to meet John Brown this morning. He assured me that everyone in the business would be here."

Oliver looked from Martin to Sophy. "That's excellent news for us personally and also for addressing Sophy's problem, but what 'odd occurrence' did I miss?"

Sophy duly explained, and by the time she had, the stilted stiffness that, in the wake of the waltz, had afflicted Martin and, indeed, her had faded. She was about to suggest they work out some sort of plan for pursuing their various interests when the musicians again interrupted with the prelude to another waltz.

Oliver smiled delightedly and bowed with extravagant grace before her. "Miss Carmichael, would you do me the honor of granting me this dance?"

His eyes were laughing, his expression the epitome of encouraging.

Normally, she would have politely declined, citing her aversion to dancing, but with Martin standing beside her and Oliver having seen Martin and her waltzing, that wasn't an option.

Besides, she should investigate whether her unprecedented response to waltzing in Martin's arms was due to something that had changed within her rather than anything peculiar to him. And being a gentleman of similar age and background, Oliver was the perfect choice for that experiment. She smiled and gave him her hand. "I would be delighted, Mr. Coulter."

Beside her, Martin shifted, but he merely inclined his head to them both and stepped back—away.

Sophy nearly frowned; it felt as if some of her senses remained stubbornly locked on Martin even while Oliver led her through the crowd to the dance floor.

They reached the cleared space, and smiling easily, Oliver turned to her, and she stepped into his arms.

Holding her confidently yet correctly, he whirled them into the swirling throng, confirming that he was, indeed, a very good dancer—perhaps not quite as smooth or understatedly expert as Martin, but experienced nonetheless—yet within three revolutions, Sophy had established that, at least for her, magic flared only when she was in Martin's arms.

So. Now I know.

Quite what it meant… She doubted that the middle of a ball was a wise place to ponder that.

Setting the issue aside, she gave herself up to taking what enjoyment she could from the waltz. At least Oliver didn't stand on her toes or steer her into anyone else.

At the end of the dance, he bowed, and she curtsied, then he offered his arm. "I suggest we return to Cynster. We should formulate some sort of plan or at least list our priorities as to what we'd like to achieve tonight."

"I couldn't agree more." She was relieved to see that Martin had waited for them more or less where they'd left him.

He, too, was ready to discuss what they wanted to gain from the evening.

She was genuinely interested in learning what contacts each of them already possessed and who they wanted to meet among the local industrialists. With respect to the latter, she declared herself entirely willing to oblige with introductions.

The three of them agreed that the same people—all those involved in managing the Sheffield iron and steel trade—would also be the most likely sources of information about anyone who might have developed an unhealthy interest in Carmichael Steelworks.

"I think," Martin said, "that we should also keep our ears peeled for any mention of the man Edward spoke with at his club."

Sophy frowned. "What man is that?"

Between them, Martin and Oliver explained.

"Hmm. A hard-looking man in a good coat. That's not much of a description," she pointed out, "but if he was in the Iron and Steel Club, then there's a decent chance someone here will know him."

"Right, then." Oliver waved at the crowd now packing the room. "Shall we?"

With two tall men flanking her—moreover, ones who were plainly used to locating people in crowded ballrooms—Sophy found that effectively quartering the room wasn't as hard as it would have been had she been alone. Looking over the crowd's heads, Martin and Oliver singled out people among those standing and chatting and directed her attention their way, then she confirmed identities, and they decided whether to approach or pass those people by.

They concentrated on the upper echelons of Sheffield industry, assiduously avoiding those of purely social status.

That suited Sophy to the ground; she was much more comfortable with the local captains of industry than she was with the mavens of Sheffield society. Luckily, the wives of said captains weren't members of the latter group.

As they wended their way through the crush of bodies, she grew increasingly aware of Martin's presence beside her, of the light brush of his hand on her back as he guided her this way or that. Curiously, rather than leap at every touch, as her senses previously had, now they quietly purred.

Between them, they charted a course through the crowd, meeting and chatting with every steelworks or foundry owner they came across. The Vickers family was there in strength, along with their cousins, the Naylors, both families as entrenched in Sheffield iron and steel as the Carmichaels. Likewise the Osborns, Hadfields, Firths, and Sandersons; Sophy greeted them all and made Martin and Oliver known to everyone.

She was impressed by how readily Martin, and Oliver, too, although to a lesser degree, interacted with the steel men; it was as if Martin spoke the same language as they… In fact, she decided, that was it, exactly. He was a businessman who demonstrably cared nothing for class, and Sheffield's steelmakers were cut from the same cloth; they were fundamentally the same sort of character and quickly relaxed in each other's company.

In addition, however, both Martin and Oliver had been raised within the ton. They had the experience and the glib tongues to be able to lead the various conversations in the directions they wished. Through the exercise of that particular talent, they learned that no other steelworks had found themselves plagued by strange accidents, and although the others had—of course—heard rumors of the accidents that had been occurring at the Carmichael works, no one had any notion of who might be behind such attacks. No one had heard of anyone, other than Martin and Oliver, expressing interest in any steelworks, much less Carmichael's.

"Besides," Thomas Firth said with a smile for Sophy, "everyone around here and his dog knows you'll never sell."

She laughed and agreed. After exchanging a pointed look with her, Martin turned the conversation to other matters, namely Edward's unknown man. But, as they'd found again and again, no one knew anything about the fellow, although one of the Naylors confirmed seeing him with Edward at the club.

"Never seen him before, here or elsewhere." Naylor shrugged. "Reserved-looking chap with a craggy face, not the sort you'd choose to amble up to and chat with. Mind you, whoever he is, he has excellent taste in overcoats, but other than that." He shook his head and grimaced at Sophy. "Sorry I can't be more help."

She assured him the man wasn't particularly important, and they moved on.

A few steps on, Oliver halted and stared across the room. "I might just leave you two to your own devices for a while. There's someone over there I want a word with—about iron, rather than steel."

They parted, and Sophy and Martin continued their perambulation through the town's industrialists. They came upon Tom Vickers in the crowd, and it transpired he'd already heard of Martin's interest in new steel alloys. As the chief metallurgist of Naylor, Vickers, and Company, Tom had taught Sophy her skills and was unsurprisingly interested in Martin's ideas.

The three chatted animatedly for some time, then recalling that they were at a ball and couldn't simply stand talking alloys for hours, reluctantly, they parted.

Soon afterward, Sophy heard herself hailed. By then, Martin had offered her his arm, and without hesitation or, indeed, much thought, she'd wound her arm with his, shifting that much closer into his protective aura. She drew him to a halt and turned and beheld her godfather making his way through the crowd.

She smiled delightedly and waited for him to join them.

His face telegraphing his delight, he halted and sketched her a bow. "You're pretty as a picture, Sophy, m'dear. I remember that color on your mama—it suited her, too."

She beamed. "Thank you."

He nodded at Martin. "Cynster."

"Mr. Brown." Martin half bowed. "We meet again."

"Indeed." Her godfather's eyes twinkled. "I warned you we would. I'm here to pick your brains about this idea of yours about armor-plating safes."

"Not precisely armor-plating."

Every bit as interested as her godfather, Sophy listened avidly as he drew details from Martin, and in turn, Martin probed her godfather's long experience in steelmaking as they discussed the possibilities. As the exchange continued, with Martin easily holding his own, she could tell her godfather was impressed.

To impress the Father of the Sheffield Iron and Steel Trade with one's insights into the future of steel wasn't a task easily accomplished. Indeed, she doubted many could manage it.

"Huh." Her godfather finally fell silent, then leveled an incisive look at Martin. "You've given me a great deal to think about, Mr. Cynster. I would like to speak with you further, but m'wife'll be searching for me by now. I'd better go and be found."

Sophy laughed and sent her best wishes to the long-suffering Mrs. Brown.

"One last thing," Martin said, and her godfather paused. "Sophy mentioned that her cousins, Edward and Charlie, have no real interest in the Carmichael business. I wondered if that lack of interest extended to all such enterprises or was specific to the Carmichael holdings."

Her godfather readily replied, "Oh, their aversion is general in every sense. Indeed, their attitude might be said to be against all forms of work—administration, management, all such exertions." He shook his head. "Never understood it, myself. Their father, Hubert Carmichael, at least tried, mostly to placate his older brother, Sophy's father, but really, Hubert wasn't much better, so I suppose you might say Hubert's apples fell close to his tree."

"Thank you." Martin nodded, and with a salute and a smile, her uncle John turned to forge a path up the room.

Sophy caught Martin's eye and arched a brow.

He smiled. "Your godfather knows absolutely everything about the iron and steel industry in this town, and he would certainly know of anyone with even the vaguest involvement. If he says Edward and Charlie have no interest in any such business, I think we can be sure that's still the case."

She studied his eyes. "You wondered if one of them had changed his mind and recently developed an interest in the industry?"

"It seemed a possibility, but clearly is one we can safely discount." He met her eyes and smiled wryly. "That's one possible suspect-and-motive combination struck off our list."

She frowned and was about to grumble about how little they'd learned that evening when the musicians started playing the introduction to another waltz.

While they'd been investigating, they'd ignored several opportunities to dance, but Martin had noticed her frown, and he caught her hand and tugged. "Come and dance."

He didn't have to ask twice.

She told herself her eagerness was understandable; she needed to see if the magic would flare and ensnare her again.

She stepped into his arms, and as soon as they took the first sweeping steps, the enchantment returned in a rush, and she stopped thinking.

Martin watched the delight of the dance take hold and sweep their current difficulties from Sophy's mind and felt an unexpected contentment warm him.

Once again, the exercise affected him—afflicted him—as it never had before.

This was so very different—so new and novel and engrossing.

The subtle movements of the dance—their closeness in the turns, the powerful revolutions as they went up the room—combined with the giddy joy in her face, the same joy the sight sent bubbling through his veins, to tighten a vise about his chest and render him almost breathless.

Expectation and anticipation had already sunk their claws deep. The compulsion to go further—to pull her nearer so her soft, slender body was flush against his—pricked and prodded.

Since their first dance, he'd found himself struggling to hold the line against a fascination driven by lust—by rabid wanting—more than anything else. Lust did not mix well with business, and given the company they'd been keeping, he'd needed all his wits about him.

The waltz was confirmation, if any was needed, of just where he now stood, namely, on the other side of a line he'd never thought he would cross.

In his mind, he could hear his sister, Therese, cackling in I-told-you-so delight.

For many long years, he'd been wholly engrossed in building his business empire, and to keep his female relatives at bay, he'd taken to insisting that he simply didn't have time for this.

And indeed, he'd spoken truly. He hadn't had time for love.

Apparently, love had given up waiting.

He was too experienced and too wary of the emotion's inherent power not to name it accurately, as what he knew it to be.

He knew in his heart—and deep in his bones—what this feeling, this giddy rush of lust, desire, possessiveness, and protectiveness, was.

He knew what it was that, when he looked at Sophy's face, with her lips curved and her lashes low as the sensations of the shared dance swept her wits away, left him feeling so deeply contented.

The musicians reached the final chords, and the music faded. The dance ended, and patently reluctantly, they halted and stepped apart.

He bowed, and when he raised her from her curtsy, their eyes met, and their gazes held.

In that moment, he saw her desire with crystal clarity and knew she saw his answering need.

Quite what he or she might have said next, they never learned.

Oliver appeared beside them and, while glancing around, stated, "I've learned precious little about our mystery man, but I did hear more about Edward and Charlie."

Finally, he looked at Martin and Sophy. By then, they'd recovered their composures and redonned their social masks.

Oliver grimaced. "I also learned several useful tidbits about a business I might be interested in purchasing, but sadly, that doesn't advance our collective aims—" He broke off as they noticed movement in the crowd. "Ah—suppertime." He looked at Sophy and Martin and arched a brow. "Shall we? We might be able to snaffle a table sufficiently removed that we can talk freely."

Sophy agreed, as did Martin, and they filed into the supper room along with a goodly percentage of the other attendees.

Sophy squeezed Martin's arm. "I'll go ahead. I know of two nooks over there"—she pointed to the far end of the room—"that should have small tables in them. I'll go and claim one—"

"And meanwhile, I'll fetch you a plate," Martin said.

She flung him a smile and dove into the crowd.

Alongside Oliver, Martin grinned and charmed his way to the extensive buffet table. Between them, they quickly filled three plates with the most succulent of the offerings, then went to find Sophy.

She was seated at a small round table in an alcove tucked away in an adjoining anteroom. She'd managed to attract one of the footmen circulating with flutes of champagne and had three glasses waiting on the table.

Martin handed her a plate, then set his down and sat in the chair alongside her.

Oliver claimed the chair on Sophy's other side and reached for one of the glasses. "I'm parched after all that talking." He took a healthy swallow.

Martin picked up one of the remaining glasses and tipped it so that the rim clinked with the last—Sophy's. "Here's to our collective aims, frustrated though they may presently be."

"Indeed." Sophy picked up the glass, sipped, then looked at Oliver. "So what did you hear about Edward and Charlie?"

Oliver set down his glass and considered the morsels on his plate. "Firstly, everyone unanimously agrees that neither Edward nor Charlie has any interest—of any stripe, at any level whatsoever—in the steel industry, much less in Carmichael Steelworks."

Martin nodded. "Everything we heard confirmed that as well."

"More," Oliver continued, "while Edward has remained in Sheffield and rarely travels anywhere else, Charlie normally haunts London's streets and has for several years."

Sophy frowned. "We already knew that."

"However," Oliver rolled on, ignoring the interruption, "last night, Charlie was seen in a local gambling den."

"He was?" Sophy looked surprised.

Oliver nodded. "Not for long—he didn't stay and play—but he was there, and the two who saw him have known him for years, well enough to be absolutely certain it was him."

"Well, well." Martin popped another oyster tart into his mouth and chewed. He swallowed and voiced what all three of them were doubtless thinking. "I wonder what's brought him home?"

"And," Oliver added portentously, "although Edward is here tonight —I saw him on my trek through the masses—apparently, Charlie isn't. I even checked, very discreetly, with the hostesses—brave of me, I know—but it seems Charlie hasn't been sighted, so it looks like he's lying low."

Eyes narrowing in thought, Martin said, "'Tis the season for rustication."

Sophy studied his expression. "You mean he might be in debt?"

He focused on her face. "That's usually the reason game cocks like Charlie flee London for the country. And May—at the end of the London Season—is often a time when impecunious young gentlemen find themselves without a penny to their name."

He looked at Oliver. "We didn't find anyone who had any idea who the man Edward met with might be, nor did we turn up any hint of who might be behind the accidents or any clue as to a possible motive. Did you learn anything pertinent about the man, the accidents, or a motive?"

Oliver grimaced. "Sadly, no. Nothing at all." Frowning, he shook his head. "I'm starting to wonder if there's anything to be found, at least in this"—he circled his fork—"sphere."

Martin ate, thought, then confessed, "I, too, am starting to wonder if we're looking in the right places. To have unearthed not the slightest whisper, even though, as we learned, everyone who's anyone in Sheffield steel has heard about the accidents, suggests that the source of the attacks isn't known to those here."

"Or at least," Oliver added, "they're not aware of any connection."

Sophy looked from one to the other. "What do you mean by that?"

Martin pushed aside his empty plate. "We mean that we've assumed our villain—for want of a more accurate term—is somehow connected with steelmaking. That they're some other outfit wanting to take over Carmichael Steelworks."

Oliver grimaced. "We probably leapt to that conclusion because *we* came here, to Sheffield, thinking to acquire Carmichael Steelworks ourselves."

Martin shrugged. "It was a reasonable assumption, at least at the start, but what if it's not correct?"

Sophy glanced from him to Oliver. "If that's not the case…where does that leave us?"

Frowning, Martin admitted, "I'm not sure."

Movement at the edge of his vision drew his attention. He turned his head and saw a footman shifting impatiently from foot to foot while scanning the tables.

The footman's gaze reached their table, and recognition lit the man's face. Plainly relieved to have sighted his quarry, he hurried over and halted, facing Sophy. "Miss Carmichael. I've been sent to find a Mr. Cynster and was told he would most likely be with you."

Excitement shot through Martin, and he shifted to face the footman. "I'm Cynster. What is it?"

"There's a man at the door who's asking for you, sir. He says he works for you—a Mr. Roland."

Martin nodded and rose. "I'll come immediately." He gestured to the footman to lead the way. As soon as the man was out of earshot, Martin looked at Sophy and Oliver, who had also come to their feet. "I've had my men keeping an overnight watch at the steelworks. Roland's one of them."

Sophy's eyes flared wide. "Someone's trying to break in?"

"Possibly. I reasoned that whoever had been using a key to gain access wouldn't necessarily hear about us changing the locks and would therefore try again at some point." Martin waved at the retreating footman. "Let's find out what's happened."

The three of them hurried in the footman's wake, ignoring the curious looks of those they passed. Most of the guests were still in the supper room or standing chatting and nibbling just outside.

Sophy clattered down the main stairs directly behind Martin. They reached the Assembly Rooms' foyer to find the senior footman in his town livery waiting beside a tallish man, rather thin, dressed in a scrupulously neat black suit.

Martin walked up to the pair and nodded to the senior footman. "Thank you."

The man bowed and retreated to stand by the door.

Martin looked at his man. "Roland. What's happened?"

Roland had been looking at Sophy and Oliver, but at the command in Martin's voice, he straightened to attention. "As usual, we've been keeping watch at the steelworks, and a short time ago, a man—well, by his bearing and clothes, I would say he was a gentleman—walked up, bold as brass, to the main office door and tried to use a key to open it. When the key didn't work, the man swore and kicked the door. He stood and stared at the door for a minute or more, then turned around and strode off."

"You followed?"

Roland nodded. "All of us. The man walked down Rockingham Street to a small hotel called the Waterloo Arms. Not the most salubrious of inns but not dreadful, either. He went in, and Tunstall followed. He quickly came back out and said the man had hired a horse and gone upstairs, we assumed to pack. Figgs and his crew rushed off to get our horses while Tunstall and I kept watch. The man eventually came out with a carpet bag, tied it to the saddle, mounted, and rode off.

"Figgs returned on horseback at that moment—he passed the man in the street, but the man didn't seem to notice. Figgs's boys were hanging back, and they knew to set off after the man and did, strung out so he wouldn't spot them and get the wind up. Figgs had brought mounts for me and Tunstall, and the three of us followed the lads."

"Did you lose him?" Oliver asked.

Roland blinked at him. "No. We picked him up easily enough and continued on his trail." Roland returned his gaze to Martin and continued, "He went out along Broad Lane, then took the road up over Crookesmoor. At that point, we agreed that I should come and report while the others continued following him, leaving either a man or a message at each change of direction, like we'd planned."

Martin nodded. "Good work."

Sophy had listened without interruption while her heart sank to her slippers. She cleared her throat. "Crookesmoor. You're sure this man, the gentleman who tried to break into the steelworks, took the road over the moor?"

Roland looked at her curiously, but nodded without hesitation. "Quite sure, miss."

Martin and Oliver had both turned to look at her. Martin caught her eyes and arched a brow.

She drew in a breath, then looked at Roland. "This gentleman, did you see him well enough to describe him?"

"Yes, miss. I was the one closest to the main office door. The man was wearing a hacking jacket of good quality and cut, over tan twill breeches and top boots that were likely from Courtauld's in Bow Street. He had brown hair, a trifle long at the collar and slightly wavy. He was clean-shaven and of medium build."

Sophy's heart sank even further. She met Martin's eyes and simply said, "Charlie."

Martin's expression was a mixture of intentness and concern. "Edward's brother? Your cousin?"

When she nodded, Oliver asked, "Are you sure?"

Lips tightening, she nodded decisively. "That's him. I know he had a key to the works—my father gave him one long ago, when trying to get

Charlie and Edward interested in working in the business." Suspicions, speculation, and a host of questions filled her mind. She shoved them aside, forced herself to draw a tight breath, and said, "And I know where he's going."

"Where?" Martin asked.

She met his gaze. "He's taken the road to Mistymoor Manor. My country home, out by Stacey Bank. Charlie has always treated it as his bolt-hole whenever he needed to escape his father, Edward, or town in general."

Martin nodded and turned to Roland.

With thoughts and conjecture winging through her head, Sophy stood silently beside Martin while he gave orders for Roland to fetch his curricle. That snapped her to attention. "I'm coming, too."

Martin met her eyes, opened his mouth, then shut it.

She nodded curtly. "He's my cousin, it's my steelworks, and it's my house."

Martin studied her for a moment, then glanced at Oliver. "You'll come as well?"

"I wasn't planning otherwise."

She realized that Martin was ensuring the proprieties were met; even now, he'd thought of that… She grimaced. "I'll need to send a message to Aunt Julia and Grandmama."

They decided on the wording, enough to inform the two older ladies what was afoot and reassure them without revealing their ultimate destination—because they knew that, if she could, Lady Bracknell would follow. Provided with pen, ink, and paper by the senior footman, Sophy quickly wrote the note. By the time she finished, Martin's man had returned with his curricle and pair.

Sophy thrust the folded note into the senior footman's hand with instructions to see it delivered to her ladyship as soon as they were away, then accepted her evening cloak that Martin held for her, drew it around her, and when he grasped her hand, hurried beside him down the steps and into the street.

The curricle was a work of art, and the padded leather seats were wonderfully comfortable. As for the horses, they were unquestionably superb; in the light of the streetlamps, Sophy could see their glossy hides gleaming over sleek muscle.

After handing her up, Martin took the reins and climbed onto the seat beside her.

Oliver buttoned his overcoat and swung onto the box seat.

Roland came hurrying from the rear of the carriage. He flicked out a luxurious carriage blanket and expertly draped it over Sophy's lap. "There!" He smiled at her and stepped back.

Despite everything, she smiled back. "Thank you."

She clutched the blanket as Martin flicked the reins. The horses surged, and they rattled off, heading for Mistymoor Manor.

CHAPTER 8

Clouds had swept in over the moors. It was after midnight and cold and dark when Martin tooled his horses carefully along the graveled drive that led to Mistymoor Manor.

They crested a low rise, and the manor house came into view. Surrounded by clipped lawns, initially, the old house loomed like a crouching beast wreathed in shadows and mist, then the clouds drifted, and the moon sailed free and lit the scene in silvery light, revealing a two-story house built of local stone with dormers set into the attics here and there, a substantial yet comfortable and welcoming home.

Diamond-paned windows glinted in the moonlight, and flickering golden light gleamed through the gap between the curtains in a ground-floor room at the far left of the house.

Sophy nodded at the sight. "He's here. He's in the library. There wouldn't be a light in there if he wasn't."

They already knew that Charlie Carmichael—assuming the man who'd tried to gain access to the main office at the steelworks was, indeed, he—had ridden directly to the manor. Martin's men, as well as those Figgs had hired, had been stationed along the road from Sheffield to direct Martin, Sophy, and Oliver onward. Roland had ridden behind on a jobbing nag and, at Martin's direction, had paid off the hired men along the way.

The fewer locals who learned that the man they were following was Sophy's cousin, the better.

Martin slowed his horses even more and glanced at the chimneys punctuating the manor's roofline. The one on the far left was smoking. "They've lit the fire in there."

Sophy pointed in the other direction. "Follow the drive around to the stables."

Martin obliged, keeping the horses to a walk to minimize the sound of the wheels on the gravel and the clop of the horses' hooves. He saw no reason to advertise their arrival. Without having to be told, the three horsemen following—Roland, Figgs, and Tunstall—veered onto the verge, muffling their horses' hoofbeats.

They rounded the house, and Martin followed Sophy's direction past a screening line of trees to the long, low stable block that lay nestled in a dip beyond. There was a lamp burning in the stable, and an old man, rather short but broad of beam and heavy fisted, came rolling out of the open stable door. He watched as Martin steered the horses into the yard and halted the curricle before the stable.

Sophy pushed back the hood of her cloak and quickly climbed down. "It's me, Old Joe."

"Miss Sophy!" The man's undeniably old face creased into a beaming smile. "You're a fair sight for sore eyes an' all."

The man's smile faded as he took in Martin and Oliver, descending from the curricle, and Figgs, Roland, and Tunstall, who had followed the curricle into the yard and were dismounting. The old man looked at Sophy and volunteered, "Young Charlie's here, in case you don't know. He didn't say aught about you coming up."

"We followed him, but he doesn't know that." Affectionately, Sophy gripped the old man's arm. "These"—she waved at Martin and Oliver—"are friends of mine. Mr. Cynster and Mr. Coulter. They've been helping me with difficulties at the works."

"Oh, aye." Old Joe nodded deferentially to Martin and Oliver, but his gaze quickly shifted to Martin's horses, which Figgs had hurried to take charge of. Old Joe looked at the horses approvingly. Almost covetously. "Nice beasts, those. Nothing like the nag Young Charlie rode in on."

Sophy introduced Figgs, Roland, and Tunstall as Martin's men.

Martin instructed the three to help Old Joe stable the horses, and grateful, Old Joe said he'd take the three men up to the house afterward. "I'll see they get a bite to eat and get bedded down for the rest of the night." He looked at Sophy. "But you'd best get up to the house yerself.

The Elliots will have heard the wheels and be out looking to see who's come."

Sophy patted Old Joe's arm, then waved Martin and Oliver toward the house. They fell in on either side of her as she led them along a path through the trees.

They stepped out of the trees' shadows into a neatly tended kitchen garden. Farther ahead, beyond the garden bed closest to the house, a tall, thin man in butler's garb stood holding a lighted lamp and squinting toward them.

Sophy waved and hurried on. "It's me, Elliot."

"Miss Sophy!" The relief in the man's voice carried clearly.

"Oh, miss!" The exclamation drew their gazes to a round, buxom woman who, hands tightly clasped, had been peering out from the kitchen step. "We're so very glad to see you."

There was a smile in Sophy's voice as she called, "I've brought you some gentlemen to feed, Mrs. Elliot. Not for supper, but for breakfast tomorrow."

"That's lovely, miss." With reassurance at hand, Mrs. Elliot drew herself up and wrapped herself in dignity. "But in case you didn't know, we've already got your cousin Charlie here, and he's staying, so he'll want to be fed as well."

"Yes, I know. It's Charlie I've come to have a word with. But first." Sophy waved at Martin and Oliver and introduced them to Elliot, the butler-cum-caretaker, and Mrs. Elliot, the housekeeper.

Sophy described Martin and Oliver as friends who were helping her with the business, which resulted in them being enthusiastically welcomed.

"Mr. Charlie's in the library, miss," Elliot said. "I just lit the fire in there, and what with its popping and crackling, I doubt he would have heard the carriage arrive. He seems in something of a funk."

"Does he, indeed?" Determination gleamed in Sophy's eyes as she glanced at Martin. "I believe we should go and inquire of my dear cousin what's so troubling him."

Martin hadn't previously seen her so aggressively intent. He waved into the house. "Lead on."

Mrs. Elliot stepped out of the way, and Sophy led them inside. She walked briskly through a large country kitchen and along a tiled corridor, but paused before pushing through the swinging door at the corridor's end. She glanced past Martin and Oliver at Elliot, who had followed close behind. "If we need anything, we'll ring."

"Yes, miss." Elliot turned and drifted back.

Sophy faced forward and, with a militant set to her chin, pushed open the door and walked on into a pleasant, tiled front hall. She led the way around the base of the main stairs and down another long corridor that ran the length of that wing. A thick runner muffled their footsteps.

On reaching the door at the corridor's end, she paused, drew in a deep breath, then opened the door and swept in.

Martin followed at her heels, and Oliver was just behind him. They crossed the threshold in time to see a younger gentleman, with a glass of brandy held loosely in one hand, lounging at his ease in a chair angled before the recently lit fire, look toward the door in sudden trepidation—nay, in fear.

He saw Sophy bearing down on him, and surprise and confusion overwrote the fear. "Sophy!" He set the glass down on a side table and rose, gaining his feet just as Sophy reached him.

"Don't you 'Sophy' me!" She jabbed a finger into his chest. "What were you doing trying to get into the steelworks' main office?" She folded her arms and rapped out, "Answer me, Charlie! Now!"

Charlie jerked as if she'd physically struck him. "Ah…" He glanced at Martin and Oliver, who were coming up to flank Sophy, but Charlie quickly refocused on the more dangerous personage directly before him. He eyed her warily.

Sophy glowered back.

Charlie moistened his lips. "I…ah, wanted to check something."

"At midnight?" Incredulity rang in her voice. "What the devil would you be checking? You know nothing about the business."

His expression impassive, Martin halted on Sophy's left, while Oliver drifted right, effectively flanking the pair.

Charlie had no option but to face his highly irate cousin and answer her questions. His gaze flicked to Martin, then to Oliver; he comprehended his position well enough.

Sophy lost what little patience she possessed. Narrowing her eyes on her cousin's face, she said, "Is it you, Charlie? Are you the one who's been causing accidents at the steelworks?"

Charlie blinked, then frowned. "What?"

"There've been accidents at the steelworks," she said. "One after another after another. Accidents that couldn't possibly be accidental! Someone has been attacking the steelworks by engineering increasingly dangerous incidents, and what I want to know is"—she unfolded her arms and stepped closer; his eyes flaring at whatever he saw in her face, Charlie edged back—"are *you* the one behind the attack that almost killed me?"

Charlie's instinctive recoil and the horror in his face told their own story. "No!" Then his brain caught up with the enormity of what she'd said. "Wait…*what*?" He stared at her, stunned, shocked, and totally confused. "Sophy, what the devil's going on?"

Martin looked at Sophy and watched the steely strength that had infused her leach away. She'd seen Charlie's confusion and accepted it as genuine.

She studied his face for an instant more, then sighed. "What's going on? That's what we'd hoped you would be able to tell us."

"Me?" After a second of studying her dejected expression, Charlie raised his gaze to Martin, then looked at Oliver. "Us?"

Sophy waved a hand and introduced Martin and Oliver.

Martin nodded briefly, as did Oliver. Warily, Charlie nodded back, understanding the silent message that they didn't yet trust him.

Sophy studied Charlie for a moment more, then walked to the armchair facing the one he'd been occupying. She waved Martin and Oliver to the other armchairs in the group. "Sit down, Charlie." She sank into the armchair. She watched as he obeyed, then fixed him with a commanding look. "If you haven't been trying to ruin Carmichael Steelworks, then what were you doing there tonight, trying to get into the office?"

Sitting upright in the chair, no longer lounging as he had been, Charlie looked back at her; she knew the instant he decided to tell the truth. He grimaced. "I'm being hounded by the local gang leader. Or rather by his bully-boy of a younger brother. Murchison Junior—Vince—is pressuring me to repay a stack of IOUs that I ran up in London."

Sophy saw Martin frown slightly, but focusing on his knees, Charlie didn't notice and went on, "That's why I came home—to lie low until I figured out a way to repay the debts. Only somehow, Murchison got his hands on the notes, and he told me I had to get the money, enough for a down payment at least. I told him I didn't have the funds, and he said a little bird had told him that I had a key to the steelworks. He told me I had to use the key to get into the office and take all the money I could lay my hands on and bring it to him."

Charlie spread his hands in a helpless gesture. "I told him I doubted there would be much there, but he said he didn't care how much it was, just that I took it all and brought it to him, along with some document he wanted me to sign." Charlie frowned. "That seemed rather rum to me, but that's what Vince insisted I had to do. He said if the money was enough and I handed over the signed document as well, he might consider handing back my IOUs—all of them."

Bemused, Charlie glanced at Martin and Oliver. "I know! It sounded too good to be true, but...well, I was desperate. If Vince took the notes to Edward, I'd never hear the end of it, and regardless, after the last time, Edward swore he wouldn't bail me out again, so who knows what Vince might have done next. He's a vicious sort who loves to cause trouble and pain for others simply because he can."

Charlie shot an apologetic look at Sophy. "I know I shouldn't have agreed, but...I thought if there was a reasonable amount in the office, I would take it and leave you a note, then once I'd got my IOUs back, I could see about repaying you."

She shook her head at him. "You would have told me to take it out of your next distribution."

Charlie grimaced. "Yes, that's what I most likely would have done. But the locks have been changed, and my key didn't work, so I couldn't get into the office in the first place." He shrank down in the chair. "I panicked at that point."

Sophy studied him. Charlie was only a year younger than she was, but often, he seemed much younger.

Certainly less mature.

Directing his words to the tips of his boots, he went on, "I thought I would lie low here long enough for Vince and his henchmen to lose interest. Or at least lose interest in beating me to a pulp, which is the least of what he threatened to do."

After a moment, plainly puzzled, Charlie raised his gaze to her face. "That lock—the one on the office door—was brand new. You've only recently changed it. Why?"

Before Sophy could decide what to say, Martin asked, "When did you arrive in Sheffield?"

Charlie looked at Martin and decided to reply. Carefully. "Yesterday." He glanced at the clock. "No, the day before yesterday. Tuesday, late afternoon. I came up on the train."

"And?" Martin prompted.

Charlie grasped his glass and drained it, then lowered it and went on, "I decided against going to Sycamore Street. Edward would interrogate me over why I'd come home, so I dropped my bags with Smithers at the Waterloo Arms, had a bite to eat, then went to one of the local dens."

"Gambling?" Sophy asked, incredulous again.

Shamefaced, Charlie grimaced. "I thought I might have better luck here and be able to win back at least some of what I owed, but I didn't even make it to the tables. Vince's boys grabbed me and hauled me into Vince's office. Vince's older brother, Walter, owns the place, and Vince manages it. His boys forced me into the chair in front of his desk, and Vince slapped the stack of my IOUs down in front of me and proceeded to make his demands."

Oliver leaned forward. "So this Murchison—Vince—was on the lookout for you. He already had your notes."

Charlie nodded. "And before you ask, I have absolutely no idea how he got them." He glanced from Oliver to Martin. "As far as I know, neither of the Murchisons, or for that matter, anyone else here, has any connection with the London crews. That's why I thought this was a safe place to rusticate."

After a moment, Martin asked, "Did you examine the notes Vince had?"

Charlie nodded. "I insisted on verifying they were mine. As I said, I couldn't imagine how he got them. I refused to believe he had until he showed me. He lined them up on the desk, and yes, they were mine."

"How old was the most recent?" Martin asked.

Charlie frowned, clearly thinking, then his face cleared. "A little over a month old. Vince had them all, and that was the most recent." He refocused on Martin. "I didn't quit London until the gentlemen started knocking on my door."

Martin leaned back in the chair and caught Sophy's gaze. "I suspect your cousin is being used as a pawn. Or at least that's what this latest incident has been about."

A frown in her eyes, she regarded him steadily, thinking it through.

Charlie looked from Martin to Sophy, then back again. "Well, I certainly feel that I'm being used. I don't have a clue what's going on."

When no one leapt to enlighten him, Charlie fell silent, obviously reviewing what he'd heard, then he looked at Sophy. "Why do you think someone tried to kill you?"

She met his gaze. "Because someone nearly did."

Concern flared in Charlie's face—a very easy-to-read face.

Sophy waved it away. "The accident wasn't aimed at me, but if it hadn't been for Martin, I would have been one of several who died."

Charlie's expression grew serious, and he looked at Martin and Oliver. "I say, what's actually going on here?" He transferred his gaze to Sophy. "How is what I've done connected to accidents at the steelworks and people nearly dying?" He frowned. "Why would you think I had anything to do with that?" He glanced at Martin and Oliver again, then, entirely sober, looked at Sophy. "I think you'd better tell me."

Sophy sighed and proceeded to do so, assisted by Martin and Oliver.

To say that Charlie was shocked was an understatement. Martin had no difficulty reading the younger man's reactions; it was no wonder he lost at the gaming tables.

Relisting the incidents clarified the relentless sequence in Martin's mind. When they reached the end and had reduced Charlie to stunned silence, Martin added, "And now we have an attempt to rob the steel-works via you." He focused on Charlie. "Quite aside from the monetary inconvenience, news of the robbery would have further undermined morale among the workers."

Sophy nodded. "And if it ever came out that it was Charlie—a Carmichael—behind the theft? That would only make matters worse."

"What I can't understand," Oliver put in, "is where this Vince Murchison person comes in. How and why is he even involved?" Oliver met Martin's gaze. "It can't be him wanting to wreck the steelworks with a view to buying a bargain. That makes no sense."

Martin narrowed his eyes. "Not Murchison, no. But I wonder if someone hired him."

"That's more Vince's style," Charlie said. "He runs thugs for hire, no awkward questions asked."

Martin tipped his head assessingly. "In that case, there might be a way forward for us via Murchison if, through him, we can identify and also implicate the man who hired him. But we'll need to go carefully, or we'll alert our quarry and get nowhere."

Charlie eyed Martin doubtfully. "Trust me when I say Murchison is not the sort of man sane people want to meet."

Seeing the unease in Charlie's eyes, Martin shrugged. "Let's sleep on it and see what we can work out tomorrow, but at the moment, learning who hired Murchison seems our only viable route forward."

Charlie still looked unnerved by the prospect, something both Sophy and Oliver also saw.

Sophy pushed to her feet. "It's late. I'm sure Mrs. Elliot will have rooms prepared by now."

The men rose and followed her out of the library and back to the front hall, where they found Elliot hovering.

Lamps had been lit, and wall sconces shed a soft glow, lighting the stairs and the gallery above.

"I'll turn everything off as usual, miss," Elliot said, "after I've done my rounds."

Sophy smiled. "Thank you, Elliot. Which rooms has Mrs. Elliot prepared for Mr. Cynster and Mr. Coulter?"

Elliot rattled off the rooms and, turning to Martin, added the information that his men had retired to servants' rooms in the attic. "We only have a skeleton staff at present—just the four of us—so there's plenty of room."

"Thank you." Martin smiled at Elliot. "I'm sure they'll appreciate the beds and the country quiet as well."

Sophy turned to Charlie. "Can you show Oliver to his room? It's closer to yours than mine."

"Of course." Charlie waved Oliver up the stairs and, after murmuring goodnights to Sophy and Martin, the pair started up.

Martin looked at her and arched a brow.

She waved at the stairs. "I'll show you to your room. It's just along the gallery." To Elliot, she added, "Given the current hour, I suspect we should move breakfast back a trifle. Perhaps half past eight?"

Elliot bowed. "Mrs. Elliot will, I'm sure, have dishes ready at whatever time you and the gentlemen come down."

Sophy smiled. "Of course. Goodnight, Elliot."

"Goodnight, miss. Sir."

Martin nodded and fell in beside her as she set an unhurried pace up the stairs.

By the time they reached the head of the stairs, Oliver and Charlie had vanished. The quiet of the night enveloped them, then at some distance, two doors shut, one after the other, assuring them they were entirely alone.

Unbidden, memories of the waltz replayed in Sophy's mind. As she walked silently beside Martin, leading him into the long gallery, she realized that, despite the excitement of the chase and the ensuing drama of the confrontation with Charlie, the strange tension the waltz had left wound within her—incited by the first dance and inexorably heightened by the second—hadn't dissipated in the least.

She was still tense. Tense in that new and novel way that left her senses skittering, aware of Martin as she'd never been aware of any other man before, with her nerves taut, tight and quivering but in a deliciously expectant way, as if waiting for some touch to set them pleasurably twanging.

She was waiting—waiting to take the next step.

Anticipation gripped, and she halted. Just stopped. In the middle of the long gallery, with portraits of her long-dead ancestors looking down upon them.

Trying to find sleep while her nerves were in such knots and her skin felt so tight, all but prickling with desire, would be an exercise in futility.

Realizing she'd stopped, Martin halted a step farther on and glanced back, and she looked into his face.

He scanned her features, met her gaze, then slowly turned to face her, one dark slash of an eyebrow rising in wordless question.

She didn't stop to think. She was perfectly certain what the next step ought to be.

This is inevitable.

She stepped forward and halted breast to chest with him, reached up with both hands and framed his lean cheeks, then stretched up on her toes and, lids falling, set her lips to his.

She'd never kissed a man before—never taken the initiative like this—but she'd wanted to kiss him for days, and she wasn't about to squander her moment. Curious and eager and intentionally tempting, she caressed his lips with hers and felt his chest swell as he drew in a slow, impossibly deep breath, then he kissed her back.

One hard hand rose to frame her jaw and tip her face upward a fraction more.

She slid her hands from his cheeks to spear her fingers through his dark hair, glorying in the silky texture as the locks fell over the backs of her hands.

His lips firmed on hers, teasing, luring, and between one heartbeat and the next, he smoothly seized the reins.

She willingly sank into the enthrallment as his lips artfully played on her senses.

More.

Whether the thought, the demand, was hers or his, she couldn't have said, but the compulsion to part her lips swelled and grew, and anticipation built, and she surrendered.

Her senses leapt, then whirled as his tongue threaded past her lips, and with blatant expertise, he laid claim. Not forcefully but beguilingly. When he wished, he deployed a ready and potent charm in his speech and expressions, but when brought to bear in this sphere, the attraction was devastating.

Hunger bloomed, deep in her belly. Need tripped along her nerves and left them sparking.

In languid fashion, he supped and sipped at her lips and, with his tongue, caressed hers, and every subtle beckoning spurred her on as she kissed him back ever more confidently, ever more demandingly.

Heat flared and spread beneath her skin, and desire and passion—feelings she'd never previously felt—combined and rose in a dizzying wave.

I want him.

She pressed closer, deeper into his embrace, fitting her slender form to his harder, larger frame.

She felt the evidence of his desire, a hard, rigid rod pressing against the soft swell of her belly, and her senses swooned, and hunger and need and ever more compulsive greed surged.

Martin was as captured by the kiss as she. He hadn't imagined kissing her would be fundamentally different to kissing any of the other women he'd indulged with over the past twenty years.

But the lure of her lips was a hundred times—a thousand times—more potent, and the satisfaction of sampling those luscious lips, of sinking into the succulent softness of her mouth, was commensurately greater as well.

Kissing Sophy was all pleasure laced with unexpected, unprecedented joy.

It was, he was also discovering, addictive. Having started, he didn't want to stop.

He didn't want to step back from the engagement, and some part of him had already seized on the promise of what lay beyond and was avidly clamoring for appropriate action to ensure that ultimate satisfaction.

The awareness that they stood mere yards from a bed battered at his mind and tugged at him.

No, it's her tugging.

She'd fisted her hands in his lapels and was trying to shift him. To waltz him to a room—hers or his, he had no idea—and the insistent compulsion to fall in with her wishes was growing to clamorous heights.

He knew the signs; they were racing full tilt toward intimacy. She might be an innocent, but she was making her passionate demands crystal clear. And while most of him had absolutely no issue with her direction, some part of his brain still functioned, and that part was screaming *Danger!*

Through the fog of lust wreathing his faculties, he perceived the threat, the very real pit of doom toward which she and he were waltzing.

If they fell…

Momentary satisfaction was not what he was after, not with her.

They were moving too fast. Far too fast. Not for him, but for her—or more precisely, for what he wanted of her. With her.

Despite his experience, his oh-so-many lovers, he'd never been in this position before. He was sophisticated, an acknowledged expert, yet she and what she meant to him had thrust him onto an unknown stage.

In his mind, he could hear Therese laughing.

Hysterically.

It took immense effort to fill his lungs and find sufficient willpower to draw back from the kiss. To pull his lips from hers enough to say, "No. Wait."

From close quarters, her lips rosy and gleaming in the soft light, she blinked at him. "Wait?" Her voice was strained. "Why?"

He looked into her face, lit by the glow of the wall sconces, and all but fell into her turquoise eyes, huge and luminous and shining with blatant desire…

On a smothered groan, he closed his eyes.

That didn't help. The sight was etched on his brain.

He raised his lids and, lips thinning, met her gaze. After a second of marshaling his wits and corralling his wayward impulses, he managed, "Have you thought this through?"

His voice was the definition of gravelly.

She stared at him. "I have to think?"

He clenched his jaw against the temptation to simply kiss her again and be damned. "Unless I miss my guess, this would be your first time with a man?"

She stiffened slightly, then her chin tipped up. "One has to start sometime, and in case you haven't realized, I am twenty-eight. Even my grandmother would probably approve."

"I seriously doubt that," he muttered. Voice strengthening, determined to cling to his purpose, he went on, "Regardless, between you and me, there's more to it than just a night of passion."

Her gaze grew faintly wary. "There is?"

He nodded as definitely as he could. "If we go on from here and fall into bed together, then as far as I'm concerned, that will be the equivalent of you accepting my offer of marriage."

She stared at him, blinked, then stared again. "I'm sure you didn't say that to all the ladies who came before."

He could see nascent anger in the aqua depths of her eyes and realized that would help his cause. "Obviously not."

"So why me?"

He clung to his purpose. "That—they—were different. You are you, I am me, and as far as I'm concerned, that puts any liaison between us on a completely different footing."

She wasn't convinced. She narrowed her eyes. "Is this because I'm my grandmother's granddaughter?"

He paused, then admitted, "Actually, that hadn't featured in my reasoning."

Not that he was all that clear on what his "reasoning" was; all he knew was that in the instant he'd laid eyes on her, some fundamental part of him had been ineradicably convinced that she was the wife he hadn't known he was looking for.

That fundamental part of him was, ultimately, dominant; in the end, that inner core defined him and dictated all he did, at least when it came to anything important, and he knew beyond question that she was critical to his future in oh-so-many ways.

Thinking of her grandmother, he added, "Now you mention it, however, being your grandmother's granddaughter is probably a contributory element."

Her eyes only grew narrower. "Is this sudden decision to marry me your way of gaining control of the steelworks so you can complete your portfolio of steel industries? Is this"—she waved one hand between them—"an attempt to provoke uncontrollable lust and use it to persuade me to marry you?"

He frowned. "No." But he could see why she'd leapt to that conclusion. He gritted his teeth and informed her, "And for your information, my decision regarding you is anything but sudden. I realized I wanted to marry you within ten minutes of meeting you."

Her eyes widened, and she tipped her head, studying him as if seeing him for the first time.

Thinking of the steelworks, he gave a short laugh. "Besides, while I definitely want to acquire the steelworks, it's obvious that you and your talents need to be a part of the deal and willingly, too. So no. Wanting to marry you isn't a roundabout strategy to gain control of your business."

He searched her face, taking in the calculation in her eyes, then huffed. "And you're not so lacking in self-confidence that you truly believed that."

After a second, her lips quirked wryly. "Still, the question had to be asked."

Sophy paused, then sighed. "And you're right, damn it. I haven't thought through the potential ramifications." She hauled in a deeper breath and fixed her eyes on his. He'd been honest with her… "To be perfectly truthful, I hadn't thought beyond the next ten minutes."

His black brows flew. "*Ten* minutes? Only ten?"

She frowned. "Don't tease. Obviously, I have no idea how long such matters take." She primmed her lips, then parted them to say, "But obviously, I'm not going to gain any experience of that tonight." She looked at him. "Am I?"

A thread of hope—of desperate desire—thrummed within her, hovering as she watched his jaw clench. But while she sensed he was battling his own inclinations, the muscles in his jaw set like iron, and he confirmed, "Nothing beyond a kiss or two is going to happen *until* you've thought things through—considered all the ramifications—and have made up your mind to marry me." His voice had lowered, the tone deep but also dogged. Determination shone in his eyes and etched his face. "There is no other way—not for us."

She held his gaze. Anyone in her social circle—Julia, for certain—would be thrilled with that declaration and his obvious battle to hold to his line. In their terms, he was being "honorable" and was intent on being so despite…

Despite the temptation I pose.

That thought—that fact—acted like a balm to her questioning soul, to the uncertain virgin locked inside her.

She drew in a breath; her pulse was still pounding in her veins, an insistent tattoo, urging her to push him, to argue and seize… She forced herself to take a step back.

His arms—those warm, steely bands that had seized her, held her, surrounded, and supported her—fell away.

"In that case"—she pointed to the door behind him—"that's your room."

His gaze roved her face, reading her expression—the complex mix of emotions that she was sure was there to see. "Thank you," he murmured, his lips curving in a small wry smile. "And on that note, I'll bid you goodnight." He stepped back, his lips quirking, his eyes still locked with hers. "Sleep well." He saluted her and turned away.

She watched as he strode to the door she'd indicated, opened it, and without looking back, stepped inside and quietly shut the door.

She stared at the wooden panel.

Her restless, reckless inner self railed, urging her to walk to that door and go inside. If she was bold and brazen, she was fairly sure he wouldn't deny her, not a second time.

"But that wouldn't be fair," she murmured to the darkness.

Not to him or, indeed, to her.

Because he was right. She needed to think, to make a definite and fully considered decision, and to get to that point, she needed to be away from him.

She breathed in, then pushed out a breath and walked on to her room.

On reaching her door, she opened it and went inside; obviously, she needed to think, and she most definitely would.

CHAPTER 9

At nine o'clock the next morning, Sophy paused in the doorway of the breakfast parlor and smiled appreciatively. Martin, Oliver, and Charlie were already seated around the oval table. While Charlie was dressed for the country, Martin and Oliver, perforce, were clad in the evening clothes they'd worn the previous night. Despite the incongruity, both managed to look rakishly handsome in an attractively disheveled way.

Luckily for Sophy, she'd had the wardrobe she maintained at the manor to choose from, and she'd elected to wear a dark-blue twill dress with turquoise piping adorning the collar and certain seams.

She took in the plethora of dishes lined up along the sideboard. Clearly, Mrs. Elliot had risen to the challenge of having three gentlemen to feed. Judging by the mounds of food on the men's plates, their appetites were sufficiently hearty to satisfy even the Elliots. The couple loved to have people to serve and had clearly been starved of the chance for too long.

As if sensing her presence, Martin glanced at the doorway, saw her, and met her gaze. Interest and an unvoiced question shone in his eyes.

She let her smile deepen and walked in; when the men made to rise, she waved them back. "Good morning," she said, and they returned the greeting and her smile.

She claimed her accustomed place at one end of the table. Apparently having guessed which chair was hers—or more likely, having asked Elliot

—Martin was on her right, with Oliver beside him and Charlie opposite Oliver.

Elliot rushed in with a fresh pot of tea and made a production of pouring her first cup exactly as she liked it.

She nodded her thanks, picked up the cup, and sipped, then set down the cup and reached for the toast rack. "I hope everyone slept well."

From beneath her lashes, she glanced at Martin, but it was Charlie who grumbled, "I might have slept, but I'm still having trouble trying to sort out what the devil's going on."

"You and all of us," Oliver returned.

Although he briefly met her gaze, Martin refused to rise to her bait and returned to demolishing a mound of kedgeree. "Perhaps we should review what we think has happened to this point and see how Vince Murchison and his men fit into our picture."

She nodded. "For instance, are all the accidents within this Vince person's ability to arrange?"

"Also," Oliver pointed out, "Charlie had a key, but he still has his and, presumably, hasn't lent it to the Murchisons."

Charlie shook his head. "Not likely."

"Well, then," Oliver continued, "who else has a key—the old key to the steelworks? Because whoever arranged the earlier accidents had to have one."

Martin glanced at Sophy, then looked across the table at Charlie. "I assume your brother also has a key."

"He does," Charlie confirmed. "But I wouldn't like the chances of anyone talking him into lending it to them. Very upright and correct, is Edward. He would want to know chapter and verse about why they wanted it, and even then, I honestly can't see him doing it—letting someone other than family borrow the key—regardless of their reasons."

Martin let the point lie and, with Sophy and Oliver assisting, ran through the list of accidents in order, this time describing each in sufficient detail to allow them to consider how it was engineered.

Charlie listened attentively and asked several pertinent questions. After Martin outlined what had happened with the Atlas dray, Charlie said, "The type of accidents means that whoever actually did the deeds knows their way around a steelworks, and I can confirm that several of Vince's favorite men were once to be found working the floor at some of the larger steelworks about town."

Martin nodded. "So the Murchisons could have been responsible."

After a moment of mentally slotting everything together, he summarized, "As matters stand, it's possible the accidents at the steelworks were ordered by Vince Murchison with the actual sabotage carried out by some of his thugs. And presumably, Vince is operating under the orders of his older brother, Walter, who in turn is acting for whoever has hired them." He looked at Charlie. "Are those statements accurate?"

Slowly, Charlie nodded. "As far as they go. But the stumbling block for me is that I can't understand why anyone would want to ruin Carmichael Steelworks."

"We can't imagine the reason," Sophy said, "because we don't yet know who hired the Murchisons to make trouble for us."

"And until we know who," Oliver put in, "we're just guessing at his motive."

"We could waste a lot of time trying to find a motive," Martin said, "so at present, our best way forward looks to be via identifying the person who hired the Murchisons."

Sophy wondered aloud, "Could it be some company rather than an individual?"

"I can't see it," Charlie replied. "The Murchisons are not the sort of helpers any company would think to hire." Across the table, he met Martin's eyes. "My money would be on someone to whom using the likes of the Murchisons would come naturally."

Martin arched his brows. "Any ideas?"

Charlie grimaced. "None at all. It comes back to what I said before—I can't think of anyone who would want to damage Carmichael Steelworks."

Oliver glanced at Martin. "What about Edward's mysterious friend?"

Charlie frowned. "What friend?"

Oliver recounted what he and Martin had learned at the Iron and Steel Club. "Unfortunately, no one knew the man's name, and the only description is distinctly vague—a hard-faced man in an excellent coat that everyone seems to notice. The coat, I mean, not the man. For some reason, everyone remembers his very nice coat."

Charlie's expression cleared. "That sounds like the man I saw in Sycamore Street."

Oliver straightened. "At Edward's house?"

Charlie nodded.

"When was this?" Martin asked.

"Several weeks ago," Charlie said. "The last time I came home. I often stay at the house—at least when I don't have debt collectors after me—and I came in one afternoon and realized Edward had someone with him in the library. The library door was open, and I could hear them talking. I didn't want to intrude, so I crept past, but I couldn't resist peeking in as I did. I was curious because Edward doesn't have many friends, not of the type he invites into the library, which he considers his sanctum. Your man was seated, relaxed and cozy, by the fire—and yes, his coat is something one would notice. It was black and, even from a distance, looked extremely expensive. It was one of those long coats that can be worn inside or outside—as an overcoat or as a general coat—and it suited him. He wasn't a small man. I also agree that his face is hard—very craggy and hewn. He and Edward were chatting away in friendly fashion, all very comfortable."

Sophy leaned forward. "Do you know the man's name?"

Charlie shook his head. "I never heard it." Frowning, he added, "And Calwell, the butler, didn't know it, either, which is rather odd. I was curious, so I drew Calwell out, but he honestly didn't know."

"You didn't hear Edward use the man's name?" Martin pressed.

"Not while I was listening, which wasn't for long. I didn't want Edward to catch me eavesdropping. I wasn't, not intentionally, but he would have interpreted it that way." Charlie glanced at Sophy. "You know what he's like."

Resigned, Sophy nodded.

Oliver said, "You only heard Edward and this man speaking briefly, but think back. Were they talking in a focused way? Was it about something in particular, or was it more along the lines of the usual rambling social conversation with not much point to it?"

Martin glanced at Oliver. That was an insightful question; clearly, the man wasn't just a pretty face.

Charlie stared at Oliver, then frowned. "You're right. They were discussing some subject, but unfortunately, I didn't hear what."

Sophy grimaced, and they all fell silent.

After a moment, Martin glanced around the table. From the pensive expressions the others wore, it seemed they'd reached the end of their immediate deliberations.

They'd also finished their breakfasts.

Elliot noticed and asked if he could clear the dishes. Sophy glanced around, then assented.

Martin pushed back his chair. "I'm going to send my men back to town." He looked at Sophy. "Do you want them to take a message to your aunt and grandmother? I imagine they'll be wondering what's happened."

"And the last thing we need," Sophy said, "is for Grandmama to send out a search party." She met Martin's eyes. "We told them we were chasing Charlie out of town. If I write that we arrived here safely, have spoken with Charlie, and all is well, that should keep them at bay."

Martin smiled. "You'd better tell them when we intend to return." He glanced at the other two. "If we wait until this afternoon, that will give my horses a decent rest, given they pulled all three of us here."

Sophy, Oliver, and Charlie readily agreed.

Martin rose and pulled out Sophy's chair, and Charlie and Oliver came to their feet.

Charlie glanced at Oliver. "There'll be newspapers in the library, including some from London. A day or so old, but still. I like to keep up with what's going on down there."

"I wouldn't mind doing the same." Oliver waved toward the door. "Lead the way."

The pair stood back and let Sophy and Martin leave first.

Sophy made for the morning room, supremely conscious of Martin prowling at her heels. His gaze lingered on her back; she could feel its banked heat. It took effort not to react by adding a little extra sway to her gait.

She walked into the morning room and crossed to the escritoire set against the wall between the wide windows. "This won't take long."

Martin halted before the window to her right. Clasping his hands behind his back, he stood looking out while she wrote a brief note—as brief as she could safely make it—reassuring her aunt and grandmother that they'd found Charlie at the manor and that all was well, and they would be returning to town…

She raised her nib and slanted a glance Martin's way.

As if he felt her gaze, without turning from the view, he murmured, "This is very pleasant countryside. Do you ride?"

"Not as much as I would like, but in summer, I often go rambling on the moors. Charlie sometimes comes with me. We've been doing that since we were children."

"Not Edward?"

She made a rude sound. "Too much exercise for him to stomach." Her gaze on Martin, she tipped her head. "I assumed you'd grown up in London."

He flashed her a grin. "No. In Kent, on a farming estate. Mostly orchards, hops, and grains. Like you, I spent a lot of my summers rambling, although in my case, it was over the Weald."

"I've heard that's very pretty country, too."

"It is, but this"—he gestured to the moorland—"is…grander. More dramatic."

She studied him for a moment more, then dipped her nib in the inkwell and swiftly wrote that they expected to return to town either later that day or the next.

After signing the note, she blotted it, folded the sheet, and set about inscribing her grandmother's name as well as her aunt's on the face.

During the night, she'd spent hours thinking and weighing the possibilities and had concluded that she needed to learn more of what he had in mind before she agreed to marry him. She wanted to pursue her thoughts and his so she could make up her mind and declare her decision and seize the moment and all that would follow, and there—now, at the manor—was the perfect time and opportunity to further her goal.

She was determined to follow the path she and he had embarked on to its end; in truth, she seriously doubted anything she learned from him or about him would alter their ultimate destination.

A destination she was anticipating reaching with a keenness she couldn't remember feeling for anything before.

But she would do the responsible thing and ask and learn and decide and declare.

"There!" She set down the pen, shut the inkwell, swiveled on the seat, and held out the note.

He took it and crossed to the bellpull. When Elliot answered, Martin asked for his men to meet him in the front hall.

Sophy rose and followed him into the hall. Roland, Figgs, and Tunstall soon joined them. The trio appeared ready to leave.

Martin handed the note to Tunstall with instructions to deliver it to Portobello Street, then thanked the three for their help the previous night. When Figgs inquired whether they should continue to watch the steelworks every night, Martin glanced at Sophy and arched his brows.

She lightly shrugged. "If you think there's value in that, by all means continue."

He inclined his head. "Better to be certain." He confirmed his orders regarding the surveillance, then dismissed the three men, who bowed to Sophy before striding off.

As their footsteps faded, she looked at Martin. "I'm going to take a turn about the gardens. I like to see how things are growing whenever I come home." Innocently, she added, "Do you fancy a stroll?"

Martin considered the gleam in Sophy's eyes and wondered what she was planning. The fastest way to learn the answer was to fall in with her suggestion. "Why not?" He waved her on. "Lead on, and I'll follow."

~

Sophy led Martin out of the side door. They stepped onto the path to find Oliver and Charlie just ahead of them.

The pair looked over their shoulders, and Charlie called, "We're off to ride over the moors. Want to join us?"

She put a restraining hand on Martin's arm. "No, thank you. We're going to walk the gardens."

Oliver took note of her hand. He shot Martin a knowing look, then he and Charlie waved in acknowledgment and continued toward the stable.

Grateful the pair would be safely out of the way and unable to interrupt, she lowered her hand, turned, and made for the formal parterre. "My great-grandmother laid out the gardens."

Strolling beside her, Martin looked around. "They look well tended."

"That's down to Old Joe and his brother, Reggie. They love gardening and take great pride in keeping the place up to the mark."

Martin nodded at the walled rose garden to one side of the parterre. "Those roses must be immense to be visible over those walls."

"Reggie swears the material they muck out from the stable does wonders for his blooms."

"The weather up here must help. You're out from under the smoke of the town." He glanced around, looking back toward the house. "What with the views as well as the gardens, this place is remarkably picturesque."

She grinned. "And you haven't seen the lake yet."

"Is there a boathouse?"

She nodded. "And rowboats."

His appreciation of the manor afforded her an opening to segue into the discussion she wished to have; she glanced at him and caught his eye. "Given what you've seen of my responsibilities, not just at the steelworks but here as well, you must see that I can't simply"—she faced forward and kept walking—"succumb to the lure of the heat between us, throw my cap over the windmill, and marry you. I'm the anchor for too many people's lives and livelihoods to make any rash decision."

"I wouldn't expect you to." His words were a deep murmur just behind her ear.

She ruthlessly suppressed a delicious shiver and cast a swift glance at him, only to meet a raised eyebrow and a too-knowing look.

She narrowed her eyes. "Yes, I've thought further—indeed, long and hard—about your…proposition." She looked ahead and continued strolling. "And for me, one major issue is the impact that marrying—you or anyone else—will have on so many people. The staff here"—she waved toward the house—"the staff in town, and of course, the workers at the steelworks."

"Albeit on a smaller scale, you're a bit like our queen. Yet nevertheless, she married Albert."

She blinked, then countered, "That's not a bad analogy. So"—she shot an assessing look his way—"if we married, would you behave as Albert did?"

He'd clasped his hands behind his back. As they strolled on, he studied the ground before his boots.

She waited as the silence stretched, then he nodded and raised his head.

"Yes." He met her eyes. "I would support you in your duties and endeavors and, beyond that, pursue my own ideas and businesses that fall outside our joint enterprise."

Inside, hope skipped, then rose; although prompted by the unexpected comparison, that was very much what she needed to hear. She inclined her head. "I see."

They walked on for several steps, then he said, "Your position and the dependency of others on you is self-evident and undeniable. To me, that is simply a part of you. An integral part of you, one that contributes in a fairly major way to making you the lady I want as my wife." He glanced at her. "What more do you need to know?"

She considered the question and eventually replied, "What I want to know is, in practical terms, how a marriage between us would work." She glanced around. "For instance, take this place." She waved widely, encompassing the gardens and the house. "Would this be our principal residence, or do you have somewhere else in mind?" She met his eyes. "Do you have some other house you would expect to live in?"

His features eased, and he smiled. "No. I have a house in Mayfair, but

I use that purely as my London base. I'm not all that fond of the capital and don't foresee us living there on any permanent basis. My house there is more a business office than anything else."

"And in the country?"

He grinned. "One good thing about being a third son is that I didn't inherit any estate. And I haven't bothered to acquire a country residence. Until I stumbled on Carmichael Steelworks and set my heart on buying it, I couldn't be sure where in the country my physical focus would be."

"Whether Sheffield or London?"

"Or Nottingham or some other town. There was no point in settling on a locality until I'd completed my critical acquisitions." He glanced around, then met her gaze. "When we wed, I'll be perfectly content living here."

Ignoring his unrelenting confidence, she imagined them living together and arched her brows. "At the manor or in Portobello Street or both?"

"Both." Martin studied her profile, seeking insight into what she needed to know. They ambled on, and he faced forward. Given he wanted her to join her life with his, it was, transparently, time to reveal his plans. Possibly all of them, which went very much against his grain; exposing any vulnerability never came easily to men like him, and he'd learned from long experience to keep his deepest desires close to his chest, to keep his most precious dreams hidden, protected and shielded from interference.

Negotiating a marriage is different from landing a business deal.

He drew a deeper breath and said, "Until I met you, my vision of what I most wished my future life to be—the entirety of it, personal and social as well as business—was largely opaque. I had most of the business elements in place, but the rest was hazy and essentially undefined. Then I met you, and the vision cleared, more or less instantly." Remembering that moment, he glanced at her. "I saw you, and everything fell into place, and the entire picture was complete and sharp and clear."

That instant of stunning clarity flared vividly in his mind and underscored how much he had riding on the conversation. "Seeing you—meeting you—was a revelation. You filled the gaps in my mental picture. In terms of creating my most-desired life, you are the essential central focus, the vital element."

He needed to make her see the future he envisioned so clearly. He needed to make her want it as much as he did. "I've been constructing my life, brick by brick, piece by piece, for all my adult life. I started when I went to America. Even before that, I'd accepted that my life was mine to make or break, that it was up to me to craft the interesting, engaging, exciting existence I craved." He glanced briefly at her; as he'd hoped, she was listening intently. Looking ahead, he continued, "I walked into Carmichael Steelworks still lacking a critical piece of my personal edifice—the central element required to link the other pieces into a cohesive whole. And there you were. I knew the instant I saw you that the last piece I needed for my most-desired life was right in front of me and that creating the perfect whole was, finally, possible."

He reviewed what he'd said and, lips twisting wryly, admitted, "That sounds as if I'm speaking of my business interests and how Carmichael Steelworks will complete my chain of businesses, but that's..." He paused, then went on, "I was going to say that's only a part of it, but it would be more accurate to say that, in this, what's right for me business-wise aligns perfectly with what I most want and need on a personal level."

He looked at her and, when she glanced his way, met her eyes. "While, with you, my business and personal needs intertwine, it's the personal side that dominates. Until now, business has largely filled my life, but I don't want that to be the case going forward. If I fail to secure Carmichael Steelworks as the centerpiece of my steel portfolio, I'll find some other business that, while it might not be such a perfect fit, will nevertheless work well enough."

He filled his lungs, conscious of an unaccustomed tightness about his chest, and forced himself to say, "But if I fail to secure you as my wife..." He felt his face harden, and he looked ahead. "That will leave a bigger, possibly unfillable and ineradicable hole in the structure of my most-desired life."

With her attention wholly fixed on him, until then, she'd paced silently beside him. Now, she nodded and murmured, "Hence your insistence on marriage. On gaining my agreement to marry you."

He dipped his head to her. "Exactly." He paused, then voice lowering, said, "I can't entirely explain it, even to myself, but lying with you without marrying you, or at least having that agreed between us, just won't work. Not for me. Not with you. It's almost as if something inside me would view that as betraying my vision." He hesitated, then put the true label on it. "Betraying my most-precious dream."

Speaking the words brought the reality into sharp focus, and understanding and insight into his own motivation swelled. “It’s about commitment.” Immediately, he sensed that was correct. “Through all the adventures I’ve experienced and the travails I’ve faced—and there’ve been many—I’ve learned one universal, inviolable truth, namely that, even though so little in life is certain, genuine commitment to an ideal and devotion to making it a reality will steer a person to achieve both happiness and success.”

Voice firming, he went on, “Committing to a vision and staying the course almost always delivers that most elusive of things, happiness. After all my efforts over the past twenty years, I want happiness. I want to be content.”

He met her eyes. “I want you as my wife. All the rest is either incidental or will fall into place.”

Sophy searched his eyes and saw conviction and resolution shining strongly. The tones and cadence of his voice made clear that establishing a home and family was the core of the milestone he hoped to find at the end of a journey he’d embarked on a long time ago. She dipped her head in understanding. “You want me as your wife because I fit into and fill the empty space in your life.”

“Completely. To achieve my dream, I need nothing more than you.”

She was starting to appreciate that, and it was an alluring and tempting realization. But she had to—needed to—consider her own wants and needs.

Their slow perambulation had taken them across the parterre. They reached the far edge, and she continued onto the lawn beyond. Her gaze on the grass, she said, “Given that, what I need to decide is whether you fit into and properly complete *my* life—my life as I want it to be.”

From the corner of her eye, she saw his black brows rise, but then he inclined his head. “Yes. That’s true.”

The entrance to the shrubbery beckoned, and she angled in that direction. He paced by her side, shortening his stride to match hers.

As the archway in the hedge neared, she drew breath, raised her head, and determined, plunged in. “*If* we married, would you expect me to cease working at the steelworks?”

“Good God, no!” He stared at her, shock vying with disbelief and mild horror in his face. “That is…” He swallowed and faced forward. “Is that what you want? To cease your activities at the steelworks?”

She hid a smile; he was still trying to be honorable. “No, of course not. I would expect to remain in the role I currently fill, including overseeing the alloys on the floor. Indeed, that especially."

He let out the breath he'd been holding and nodded earnestly. "Good. That's exactly as I'd hoped." A second later, he cast her a shrewd glance. "And just so we're clear, I view your talents with alloys as one of the principal assets of the steelworks. I wouldn't want to lose that."

She would have smiled broadly, but quashed the impulse; they were still some way from defining an acceptable arrangement. She thought further, then observed, "You're clearly not envisioning a conventional marriage."

He snorted. "Of course not. That was never on the cards. Not for me"—he shot her a glance—"and not for you, either." She acknowledged that with a dip of her head, and he went on, "I'm thirty-seven, yet far from beating a path to any altar, I actively avoid all matrimonial snares by assiduously limiting my time in society. I've three older siblings, and all are married and have been for some time." A fond smile touched his lips. "I have a small army of nephews and nieces who claim me as their favorite uncle."

She was intrigued, but before she could ask for details, he concluded, "So I've no pressing need to marry."

She couldn't resist wryly observing, "Yet here you are, set on marrying me."

His brows lowered. "That's something I can't entirely explain, not even to myself."

She smothered a snort of her own, yet at least he was admitting that much—that he didn't fully understand how they had reached this point.

They turned the first corner and started down the central alley of the shrubbery. Now they were enclosed within the high hedges, the mild sunshine no longer reached them.

Suppressing a shiver brought on by the cooling touch of the shadows, she focused on what she needed to know. "For argument's sake, let's say we marry. Obviously, I'll be largely fixed here, in Sheffield, at the steelworks, while you have businesses scattered around the country and, as you've mentioned, a base in London." She glanced at him. "How would you see that playing out?"

His reply came immediately. "With respect to the steelworks, I thought we could get in people you trust as your seconds there. Someone competent to manage the day-to-day ordering and administration, plus someone you have confidence in to oversee your instructions regarding the alloys. While I envision us spending most of our time in Sheffield, I hope you'll accompany me when I visit my other businesses, especially those that, in the future, will work with Carmichael steel." He caught and held her gaze. "I would value your insights into the Rotherham Foundry, Nottingham Wires and Cabling, and Bloomfield's Knives. And I would like you to work with me on the new factory and production line I want to build here for making steel-plated safes."

She couldn't stop her enthusiasm from showing. Tipping her head, she held his gaze. "So you see us working as, essentially, partners?"

He nodded decisively. "Yes. Exactly that." He grinned charmingly. "Partners in business and in life."

She looked ahead, thinking of the scope of all he'd proposed, the magnitude of it. She wanted to believe it—wanted to reach for it.

"Can you see the vision?"

His voice was a seductive murmur by her ear.

She could—and she wanted to make that vision into her reality.

The next corner loomed, and as they made the turn, she opened her lips—

Thump!

Martin groaned and collapsed at her feet.

Stunned, Sophy stared at him, then a large man pocketing a cosh stepped up to stand over Martin.

Sophy hauled in a breath to scream, but another man pushed past the first and thrust her roughly along the alley.

"Keep your lips shut!" the second thug ordered.

Furious, she whirled. Her gaze fell on Martin, and her breath seized.

The first thug had crouched over him, wrapped a meaty hand under Martin's jaw, lifted his head, and was holding the edge of a wicked-looking knife against Martin's throat. "Better do as he says," the thug with the knife advised, "leastways if you want this fine gent to survive."

A medley of emotions erupted and surged through her—horror, rage, fury, fear, and others equally potent and powerful. But if they were threatening Martin's life… At least he was alive.

She took in his lifeless face. Clearly, it was up to her to keep him alive and ensure that their now-mutual dream had a chance to become reality.

Pushing her tumultuous feelings deep, she swallowed and pressed her lips tightly shut.

Heavily built, bald, and beady eyed, the thug holding the knife had been watching her closely. He nodded approvingly. "Good decision." He shifted his gaze to his friend, who was hovering beside her, and tipped his head at Sophy. "You bring her, and I'll lug pretty boy here."

The second thug—a wiry individual with small eyes, a weaselly-looking face, and lank brown hair—gripped her arm. "No struggling," he growled. "Not if you want your beau there to keep his pretty face intact."

Lips tight, jaw clenched, she allowed the man to pull her around and tow her on through the shrubbery.

Rapidly, she canvassed her options. The shrubbery was neat and tidy, and she seriously doubted Old Joe and Reggie would be anywhere near. Martin's men had left for Sheffield, and Oliver and Charlie would be far distant by now.

The heavyset thug lumbered after them with Martin draped over his shoulder. Martin's arms swung limply; he was clearly still unconscious.

Worry for him tugged at her mind, but she pushed it aside. For both their sakes, she had to keep her wits about her.

The wiry man led her to and through the rear arch of the shrubbery and across the verge of the back lane—not much more than a rough track—that skirted the rear of the gardens.

She was surprised they'd known the track was there, but a farm cart waited. The wiry man led her to the cart's open back.

He released her arm only to seize her waist and hoist her up to sit on the cart's straw-strewn bed. "Up you go."

The instant he released her, Sophy scrambled away from him, toward the front of the cart.

His expression mean and malevolent, the wiry man caught her eye. "Remember—keep your trap shut, and the gent won't get hurt." The man glanced across as his companion staggered to the side of the cart and tipped and heaved Martin over the side.

On a gasp, Sophy lunged across and caught Martin's head. The weight of his shoulders nearly flattened her, but she wriggled and managed to sit upright with his head in her lap.

The wiry man had watched her antics and chuckled evilly. "Well, more hurt than he already is."

"Come on." The heavyset thug shrugged his coat straight and climbed up to the cart's front bench. "We've got what we were sent to fetch. Let's get moving."

The wiry man joined him. As his friend flicked the reins and the cart started rolling, the wiry one turned and fixed Sophy with a flat stare.

"Keep your mouth shut and don't try to scramble off or attract anyone's attention. Not if you want him"—he nodded at Martin—"to live."

Coldly furious, Sophy returned the man's stare levelly until he sniffed and turned his back on her.

Immediately, she returned her attention to Martin. The first thing she'd done was slide her fingertips beneath the folds of his ivory-silk stock. She could feel his pulse beating strongly and steadily in his throat.

He's alive, just deeply unconscious.

The heavyset thug had hit him hard. Possibly hard enough to crack his skull.

She'd worry about that later. Martin lay in a sprawl on the hard wood of the cart's bed, half on his side with his long limbs tangled. She settled her thighs under his head, but he was far too heavy—even his shoulders were too heavy—for her to shift him enough to straighten his limbs. All she could do was cushion his head from the worst of the bumps.

She brushed the tumbled locks of dark, silky hair from his forehead, and as the cart rolled away from the manor, she set her wits to the task of working out what she could do.

CHAPTER 10

There were benefits to being kidnapped by those with little imagination. The thugs were so oblivious to Sophy's abilities that they didn't bother tying her up and, most importantly, didn't blindfold her. Consequently, she knew exactly where they were when the cart horses slowed.

After leaving the manor estate, they'd followed several old tracks over the moors to a shepherd's hut, perched high on the flank of Loadbrook Moor. It wasn't that far from the manor, yet very much out of anyone's way, and she knew the hut was rarely used these days.

Despite the rocking and occasional jolting, Martin hadn't stirred. She'd carefully felt around his head, fingertips gently probing through his thick hair, and had discovered a hideous lump the size of a goose egg on the back of his head. The heavyset thug had, indeed, hit him hard, but the wound hadn't split his scalp. She'd given thanks for that and offered up several silent prayers that he would wake soon, with his wits intact.

She had a strong suspicion that she and he were going to need as much mental acuity as they could muster to deal with whatever this situation was. She had to assume it was an extension—an escalation—of the accidents that had been plaguing the steelworks.

Perhaps they were closer to discovering who was behind the attacks than they'd realized.

The cart rocked to a halt directly before the hut.

The wiry man swung down from the bench and came to the back of the cart. Impatiently, he waved to her. "Come along, Goldie—let's get you inside."

And that was enough. She narrowed her eyes on the weaselly man. "My name," she informed him, doing a more-than-passable imitation of her grandmother, "is Miss Carmichael." She leveled a censorious stare at the fellow. "What's yours, Wiry?"

The man blinked.

The heavyset thug guffawed and elbowed his mate out of the way. "Don't answer, but she's got you there." He clambered into the cart, then glanced back at Wiry. "Don't forget. The master told us to take all due care and not harm a hair and all that, so just help her down and into the hut while I get the gent."

"Be careful," Sophy ordered as the heavy man bent and, with difficulty, hoisted Martin up. She scrambled to her feet and watched, but the man knew what he was doing when it came to lifting inanimate men. When she was sure Martin wasn't about to sustain any additional hurt, she followed the heavy man with his burden to the rear of the cart and, without acknowledging Wiry, gave him her hand and allowed him to steady her as she jumped to the ground.

Immediately, she retrieved her hand and hurried after Martin. She ducked around the heavy thug, who, weighed down by his unwieldy burden, was doggedly clumping up the path, and reached the hut ahead of him. She pulled open the door, walked in, and paused to look around the rectangular space. It was much as she remembered it from her childhood, rough and rudimentary but not without the essential comforts.

With its head against the rear wall, a bed jutted into the room. It possessed a mattress in reasonable repair, covered with an old blanket. There was a small hearth in one rear corner and a washstand in the other. A rickety cupboard stood against the wall by the door, and a rough table, with a wooden chair on one side and a bench on the other, occupied the middle of the remaining clear space.

Sophy swung to watch as the heavy thug maneuvered his awkward burden through the door. She swallowed a protest when he just missed knocking Martin's poor head on the doorframe.

She rounded the bed and stood ready as the heavyset thug halted on the other side, then jostled Martin off his shoulder, half dropping him onto the mattress. She leapt in to support his head and gently lower it to the lumpy pillow.

The heavyset thug stepped back. "You two wait in here. The master'll be along shortly."

"Who?" Sophy whirled, but the heavyset man was lumbering through the doorway where Wiry had remained, hovering outside. The door swung snugly shut. She heard a bar rattle into holders outside and softly swore as she remembered that the hut's door opened outward.

Even the shutters on the two small windows set in the front wall latched on the outside.

She dismissed any thought of immediate escape and returned her gaze to the large, worryingly unmoving and silent figure on the bed.

What can I do to make him more comfortable?

She eyed his shoes, but thought better of taking them off; they needed to be ready to run at short notice. She hoped very much that he would regain consciousness soon; it had to be at least half an hour since he'd been struck, and she was growing seriously concerned.

Thinking of him waking, she looked round. Surely the thugs had left them some water. She could use it to cool his brow; that might help.

She searched the room, even looking in the cupboard. She found bowls and a jug, but no water.

Irritated, she thumped on the door. "We need water!" When no reply came, she thumped harder.

After a moment, a muffled voice reached her. "Calm down. The master'll be here soon, and we'll see what he says."

They kept talking of a "master." Was she about to meet the mastermind behind the accidents as well as their abduction?

Who knew? She might finally learn what this incomprehensible situation was about.

With nothing else to do, she sank onto a stool beside the bed, stared at Martin's face, and willed him to wake up. He didn't stir. After a moment, she reached out and lifted one of his long-fingered hands, cradling it between hers.

Wake up—I need you.

And when had she ever thought that of any man?

But she needed to look into his melted-caramel eyes and know that in facing whatever was to come, he would be with her.

Determined to do something useful, she turned her mind to evaluating the likelihood of rescue. Oliver and Charlie knew she and Martin had gone for a walk in the gardens, but realistically, it wouldn't be until she and Martin failed to come in for luncheon that questions would be asked and people would start searching.

The tracks had been dry, and anyway, why would anyone think of looking there? Even less likely was that someone would venture to the old shepherd's hut.

She grimaced and, for Martin as much as for herself, murmured, "We need to rescue ourselves."

Outside, a stir followed by a scraping sound heralded the door being hauled open. A man, younger and better dressed than the thugs, stood haloed in the doorway, feet braced apart, his hands on his hips, then he sauntered inside.

That was supposed to be a dramatic entrance, designed to throw me into a fluster.

The observation told her something of the newcomer, and indeed, as she focused on his face, her first thought was that he was far too young to be anyone's "master." She would have sworn he was no older than she and probably not even that age. Mid-twenties, she guessed, as his swaggering walk took him to the table, and he halted there, facing her.

His small eyes had fastened on her; he studied her as if he wasn't sure what he'd expected to see. He was of average height and stocky build, and his features were doughy, somewhat unformed. He sported what looked to be a strawberry birthmark on his chin; it stood out against his pasty complexion and almost reached his thick lips. All in all, he was an unlovely specimen of youthful manhood, yet judging by the quality of his clothes, he wasn't a workman of any stripe. His suit was a definite step up from those worn by his henchmen; to her eyes, his attire was that of a clerk.

The impression she received was that he was trying to appear more—and socially better—than he was.

She remained seated and, her expression impassive, regarded him steadily; she wasn't about to help him by asking questions. Not yet. Let him open the conversation; she was curious to see where he led.

He studied her for a moment more, then smiled in an oily fashion and drew a folded document from his pocket. "Here." He tossed the document on the table. "I'm told you can read."

Sophy glanced at the document, but made no move to take it.

Watching her, the "master" reached into his other pocket and pulled out a small vial and a pen. He paused to inspect the pen's nib, then grunted, "Good enough," and set both pen and the vial, which contained ink, on the desk.

He caught her eyes. "All you need do, dearie, is sign this paper. There's a place on the last page, and you're supposed to make your mark on the bottom corner of each page as well. Full signature on the dotted line, mind. Soon as you do that, you and the gent"—his gaze drifted to Martin, and for an instant, his expression grew wary—"can be on your way."

Sophy looked at the document; it appeared to be some sort of legal instrument. Curious, she reached out and lifted it from the table. She straightened it from the curl it had assumed in the man's pocket, then swiftly scanned the four closely written pages.

As she'd thought, it was a legal instrument of some kind, specifying something about Carmichael Steelworks. Beyond that, the legalese obscured its purpose. "What is this?" She looked up at the man.

He frowned and shrugged. "Don't know. And I don't care."

She regarded him steadily and arched her brows. "Then why are we here?"

He shot her a don't-be-stupid look. "Because your signature on that paper is what the gaffer wants, ain't it?"

"Your gaffer?" That normally meant a superior.

"The man what hired me and m'boys." He nodded at the document. "He wants you to sign, so you'll sign the blessed thing, hand it to me, then you two and us can go our separate ways."

She considered stating that she wouldn't sign, but that might not buy her—and more importantly, Martin—sufficient time for him to recover, and there was another tack she could pursue that was more likely to drag things out.

She heaved a sigh, rose from the stool, and moved to sit in the chair on her side of the table. She laid the document on the scarred wooden surface and pretended to read it through.

After several minutes of flicking pages back and forth, she frowned and shook her head. Then she glanced up at the waiting man. "In case you hadn't noticed, I'm a lady. I never sign any legal papers without first having my solicitor read them and explain to me what they mean—what will happen if I sign." She pushed the document to the middle of the table. "No sane lady would simply sign a document without understanding what it says. I certainly wouldn't. I can't make head or tail of this, so unless you can…?"

The man looked stumped. He met her gaze and shook his head.

She hid a smile and continued with her earnest explanation, "Then you can't possibly expect me to sign it." Inspired, she added, "Indeed, no one would believe it if I did, not without first consulting someone who could explain it to me. In such circumstances, I could claim I'd been forced to sign under duress, which would make the document, signed or not, not worth the paper it's written on."

Her captor's expression grew thoroughly confused.

Good.

Eventually, after a full minute of apparently painful cogitation resulting in an increasingly black scowl, he shifted his gaze to Martin, still lying immobile on the bed. "Well, we don't happen to have any fancy solicitor skulking about the place but"—he tipped his head Martin's way—"Sleeping Beauty there will wake up soon, and he looks the sort to understand documents like that well enough. You can get him to explain it to you."

Sophy looked at Martin. He still appeared to be unconscious, but was that a gleam of a caramel eye beneath the thick fringe of his lashes?

Her heart leapt, and she quickly turned to their captor, drawing his gaze back to her. She waved at the bed. "Obviously, we'll have to wait for him to recover enough to read anything."

And whether he could read or not couldn't be judged by anyone else.

She expected the man to argue—to say that they could pretend that Martin had read and explained the document and she should sign it immediately—but to her surprise, the man's scowl evaporated, and he nodded. "You can have an hour or two." He glanced at the open doorway. "I have somewhere I need to go, people I need to see. But"—he looked at her, and his features hardened into a pugnacious mask—"when I get back, I'll expect you to sign on the dotted line."

She arched her brows. "And if I won't?" At that point, there was no reason not to ask.

The pugnacious expression transformed into a nasty smile. "Then we'll just keep you here until you do. No food, no water, no help for the gent." His gaze shifted to Martin. "Who knows? He might even suffer another accident. Or two or three." The man looked at her, and his eyes narrowed. "Or perhaps there'll be another accident at the steelworks."

Sophy's thoughts stilled. She studied the man's knowing smirk. "You're the one responsible for the accidents at the steelworks." A statement, not a question.

He grinned—actually grinned. "Easiest money I've ever made. All I had to do was send in m'boys to fiddle with things. They've all spent time on the floor at one or other works, so they know how to cause a nice amount of havoc." Satisfaction glowed in his expression. "Worked, too, didn't it?"

She refused to be deflected. "You had a key to the works. Where, I wonder, did you get that?"

"From the gaffer what hired us, o'course." He nodded at the document. "Now, just be a good girl and sign that, and with luck, you'll be back home before anyone knows you've been taken. No need to have your reputation besmirched, is there? I'm told that sort of thing matters to ladies like you, or so the gaffer said."

Sophy stared at him while her mind raced, but she couldn't think of anything more to ask. She reached for the document, drew it toward her, then picked it up and flapped it. "This is pages long. We'll need time to go through it"—she glanced at Martin—"once he wakes up and can think."

Their captor snorted. "Like I said, you can have an hour or so. Once I get back after talking with the rest of my men, you'd better be ready to sign."

She made no reply, just sat and watched as the man turned and walked out. The door swung shut, and a second later, the sound of the bar rattling into place reached her.

She strained her ears and heard the rumble of male voices, too low for her to make out what was said.

Then she looked at Martin and gazed into his very-much-open eyes.

Her heart soared, but he held a warning finger to his lips. Then, moving slowly, he sat up.

She rushed to help him.

Martin sat and swung his legs over the side of the bed. The back of his head ached fiercely, but the pain was bearable. He caught and gripped one of Sophy's small hands and held it while he checked that his wits and senses were functional.

It seemed they were. Through the thick planks of the door came sounds he interpreted as two men settling to play a card game immediately outside the hut.

Reassured, he squeezed Sophy's hand, then released it, pointed to the document lying on the table, and gestured for her to bring it to him.

She seized it and handed it over.

He scanned the first page, then quickly flipped through the subsequent pages. Then he grunted, folded the document, and shoved it into his coat pocket.

Slowly, allowing Sophy to steady him, he got to his feet, checking for any lingering weakness. He was relieved to find none of any consequence. Then he looped an arm around Sophy, drew her close, bent his head, and with his lips near her ear, whispered, "Now we search—in complete silence—for a way out."

Her heart in her throat, Sophy watched as Martin hoisted himself up and out of the hole they'd created in the rear corner of the hut's roof.

The old roof tiles had been fixed with nails that had rusted long ago, but lifting each tile free without making any noise had been a painstaking effort. They'd been alert and on edge throughout the exercise, knowing that the thugs could open the door at any point and there was nothing they could do to protect against that.

The hut had been built backing onto a rise, and luckily, there was a section of the roof at the rear where the battens were sufficiently far apart for Martin to angle his shoulders through, allowing him to climb out without creating any appreciable sound.

As Martin's shoes disappeared through the hole, Sophy realized she was holding her breath. She rectified the omission, then crept to the door and pressed her ear to the solid planks.

By listening at the door and the shuttered windows, they'd established that the thugs who'd brought them to the hut were sitting—they assumed on upturned logs—directly in front of the door and that the pair were deeply engrossed in a game of cards.

Sophy glanced back and up at the gaping hole, and uncertainty welled. When she'd asked how Martin expected to subdue not one but two thugs, he'd just smiled in piratical fashion and whispered that he had several tricks up his sleeves.

That had hardly been reassuring, yet he'd seemed utterly confident, and as she hadn't had any alternate strategy to suggest, she'd had to let him go.

After planting a desperate kiss on his lips and insisting he take care.

The truly sweet smile he'd left her with had wrapped about her heart.

Now, of course, she felt frustrated and helpless and worried.

The faintest *creak* from directly above her head was the only warning she had that he was there.

She looked up, a prayer on her lips, then a heavy *thump* sounded outside, followed by an inarticulate cry that was immediately cut off.

Several dull thuds ensued, then silence fell.

Sophy gripped her hands tightly. What was happening? Who had cried out? Had it been—

The scraping as the bar across the door was lifted cut off her frantic thoughts, then the door swung outward, and Martin stood there, a triumphant smile on his lips.

Her breath left her in a *whoosh*, and when he beckoned her out, she flew into his arms.

He laughed and caught her and, for a fleeting instant, hugged her to him, but as he set her back on her feet, she sensed the hardness in his body and the urgency with which he looked around.

She looked, too, and saw both thugs—Wiry and his heavyset mate—sprawled, inanimate, on the rough ground.

She turned to Martin, who was resettling his coat. He appeared unruffled and calm and still ridiculously elegant. "How?" She waved at the unconscious pair. "There were two of them and one of you."

His swift smile was faintly feral and distinctly predatory. "Not just a handsome face."

She huffed and shook her head, then followed his lead in surveying their surroundings.

Martin cudgeled his brains, then glanced at Sophy. "I vaguely remember being jostled in the rear of a cart." He reached a hand to the back of his head and gingerly felt the lump there. It was painfully tender, but the ache in his head had lessened now that he was upright and in the open air.

Sophy was turning in a circle, looking all around. "They had a cart waiting on a track at the rear of the gardens. They brought us here in it, but it's not here now."

"That 'master' of theirs must have taken it." Martin planted his hands on his hips and scanned the rolling moorland all around, then glanced at the pair sprawled before the hut. "Their skulls are thick. They won't be out for much longer."

"Never mind." When he looked at her, Sophy smiled. "I know where we are. We can walk out easily enough."

He frowned. "People get lost tramping over moors."

"Indeed, they do. But not people who grew up rambling all over said moors." Her expression was all confidence as she waved past the hut. "Come on. The sooner we start, the sooner we'll get back."

He looked at the thugs. "And the sooner we'll be out of their sight. Still…"

As if reading his mind, Sophy said, "I doubt they'll follow. From their accents, they're town lads, and it's not easy to track over moorland."

From hunting with his cousins in Scotland, he knew that was true. With no better option offering, when Sophy headed around the side of the hut, he followed.

Marching on, she called back, "Remind me to send someone to repair that roof."

He grunted and glanced up at the sky. "At least there's no sign of rain."

"Not at the moment," she replied, the implication being that could change at any time.

Martin swallowed another grunt and trudged on. He had other matters on his mind, such as the document burning a hole in his pocket.

Uncounted minutes later, Martin was still trudging in Sophy's wake. They'd put sufficient distance between them and the hut that he was no longer concerned that the thugs he'd ruthlessly knocked out would come chasing after them. Thus far, the pair hadn't appeared, suggesting that they hadn't been able to pick up his and Sophy's trail.

Reassured, he turned his mind to the route Sophy was taking. She'd struck more or less southward, in the opposite direction to the track that led to the hut.

He frowned. "Are we heading away from the manor?"

She nodded. "On foot, this is the easiest way down and also means we won't risk running into our late captor as he returns to the hut."

"Good thinking."

He heard the smile in her voice as she replied, "I thought so."

He held back for as long as he could before asking, "How much longer?"

"About an hour. Perhaps less."

At least the crisp air and the exertion were helping to clear his head.

He found himself staring at Sophy's back. The ease of her gait, her steady pace, and, even more, her cheery disposition proclaimed that she was not the least bothered by the prospect of an hour-long hike.

He smiled to himself. She was, very obviously, not your average young lady. Clearly, she had stamina…

His mind drifted into thoughts he really didn't need to indulge in at that moment; they were definitely not helpful. With a mental wrench, he hauled his wits back and refocused on their journey—on trudging along in Sophy's wake as they steadily descended the flank of the moors.

A decent-sized road snaked along the floor of the valley into which they were descending. They were almost on the flat again when Sophy pointed to a collection of buildings that lay between them and the road. "That's Westerfield Farm. It's owned by the local squire, also Westerfield." Although she'd been confident of her direction, she was rather relieved that they hadn't, in fact, been followed.

A few minutes more saw them approaching the farmyard gate.

Martin was scanning the buildings. "It might be wise not to mention that we were kidnapped."

She widened her eyes at him. "And what possible story could I tell to account for us wandering down off the moor?" She let her gaze drift over him. "On foot and with you dressed as you are."

After several moments of staring ahead, he grimaced. "I can't think of anything."

Smiling, she faced forward. "Squire Westerfield is an old friend and a trusted neighbor. We can rely on his discretion."

As they neared the gate, Martin murmured, "All right. I'll follow your lead."

His acceptance of her judgment put a spring in her step as they crossed the yard, and Blackie, the collie, sent up a bark in welcome.

Sophy paused to greet the black-and-white dog, then leaving her to welcome Martin, straightened and went to meet the squire, who had appeared in the farmhouse's doorway.

A stout man with a shock of white hair, he smiled delightedly and came to meet her. "Sophy, my dear! It's always good to see you." He took her hands and squeezed them, then glanced at Martin as he rose from petting Blackie.

Sophy quickly made the introductions.

Martin nodded respectfully. "Please overlook my rather crumpled and less-than-appropriate attire."

Squire Westerfield considered Martin assessingly. "Well, m'dog likes you, and she's an excellent judge of character, so welcome to Westerfield Farm, sir." Westerfield had noticed their lack of a conveyance and turned a questioning look Sophy's way. "Don't say you walked over?"

"Not entirely." Briefly, Sophy told the story of their abduction from the manor gardens and their incarceration in and escape from the shepherd's hut.

Westerfield was instantly solicitous. "Shocking! Utterly shocking." He patted Sophy's hand. "Anything I can do, my dear, just ask, and I'll see it done."

Sophy glanced at Martin. "If we could borrow a gig to get us home?"

Martin nodded, and Westerfield assured her that of course they could. He sent up a shout for his stable lad, and when the youth poked his head out of the barn, sent him to harness a horse to the farm's gig. "I'll send Johnny with you to bring back the gig. He's young, but reliable."

Sophy mentioned the tiles they'd been forced to remove from the hut's roof.

"Don't you worry about that," Westerfield said. "I'll send two of my workers up to set the tiles back in place."

"Given we've left two thugs with sore heads at the hut"—Martin glanced at the western sky—"and it doesn't look like there'll be rain overnight, you might want to leave repairs until tomorrow."

Westerfield met Martin's eyes and nodded. "Aye. I'll do that."

The clop of hooves on the cobbles had them turning to see Johnny leading out a dappled mare harnessed between the shafts of a simple gig.

"Thank you." Sophy pressed Westerfield's arm.

"My pleasure, my dear." Westerfield patted her hand, then waved her to the gig.

Martin went forward and accepted the reins. He waited while Westerfield helped Sophy to the seat, then Martin joined her. As Johnny scrambled up behind, Martin nodded to Westerfield. "My thanks as well, sir. I plan to remain in the area, so I look forward to seeing you again."

Westerfield smiled and inclined his head, and with a flick of the reins, Martin set the horse trotting out of the yard and on down the short drive to the road.

Once they were bowling along the macadam, he said, "I've been thinking. Our recently acquired acquaintances and presumably the man who hired them are targeting you. They knew you were at the manor. Now that they've lost you, the first place they'll look for you will be at the manor."

Sophy wrinkled her nose. "So we shouldn't go back there."

"No. And the second place they'll look is in Portobello Street, and they'll also keep watch on the steelworks." When she glanced at him, he caught her eye. "I was wondering whether your grandmother's house might not be the best bolt-hole, at least for the moment."

She thought about that, then nodded. "She's not in town all that often, so I rarely visit her house. She usually drops in at Portobello Street, rather than the other way around."

"So they might not know about her house at all. Where is it?"

"St. James' Street, not far from St. James's Church."

Martin consulted his mental map of Sheffield. "That's just north of Church Street, correct?"

"Yes." Wryly, she added, "And of course, Grandmama will be delighted to have us seek refuge with her."

Martin asked Sophy to direct him to the mews behind the Bracknell town house.

After descending from the gig and helping Sophy down, Martin handed the reins to Johnny, along with a generous tip.

"Take your time driving back," Sophy told Johnny. "No need to rush."

"Yes, miss." After offering them a jaunty salute and a wide grin, Johnny drove the gig sedately up the mews and turned out into the street.

Sophy glanced at Martin. "Right, then. Let's go and beard the dragon."

She led the way into the kitchen, surprising her grandmother's butler, Higginbotham, and Mrs. Queerly, the housekeeper and cook.

After greeting both, Sophy inquired, "Is my grandmother in?"

"You'll find her ladyship in the morning room, miss," Higginbotham replied.

Sighting the prospect of people to feed, Mrs. Queerly beamed encouragingly. "You go right in, miss, and please tell her ladyship I'll send in some tea just as soon as I can set the tray."

Sophy hid a smile and, with Martin at her back, followed Higginbotham into the front hall. She dismissed his half-hearted offer to announce them. She had a fair idea what they would find in the morning room, and sure enough, when Higginbotham opened the door and she and

Martin walked in, it was to discover the curtains half drawn and her grandmother reclining on the sofa.

"Higginbotham…" her grandmother murmured in tones of dire warning. She cracked open one eye and peered toward the doorway.

On seeing Sophy, her grandmother sprang to life. She swung upright, raising a hand to resettle the beaded widow's cap she invariably wore.

"Sophy! What are you doing here"—her grandmother squinted at the windows—"in the middle of the afternoon?" Her gaze moved on. "And Martin, too…" Abruptly sharpening, her gaze shot back to Sophy, and in a much stronger voice, she demanded, "What's going on?"

Sophy diverted to the windows and opened the curtains, then went to sit on the matching sofa facing her grandmother. She beckoned Martin to join her, which he did, and over the promised tea—with fruit scones and cake—they delivered a bare-bones account of their adventures from the time they'd left the Assembly Rooms to the present, scrupulously omitting any mention of their personal interactions.

To give her grandmother her due, she held back her questions and let them recount the events all the way to their arrival at her back door. Then she drew breath, but before she could launch into her inquisition, Martin said, "Before we elaborate further, might I suggest that we inform those who, as we speak, are likely searching for us?" He caught Sophy's eye. "We should send word to the manor, to Oliver and Charlie as well as the household. And we need to warn your aunt and Hector that the Portobello Street house might be being watched, which is why we've sought refuge here."

She nodded. "And we should send word to your men at the Kings Head. They'll be expecting you to return, and if Murchison and his men have been watching me over recent weeks, for all we know, they might be watching you as well—or at least watching the Kings Head."

Martin conceded the point with a tip of his head.

Sophy's grandmother wholeheartedly agreed. She had Martin tug the bellpull and, when Higginbotham appeared, instructed him to send a groom riding to the manor, and footmen to the Portobello Street house and to the Kings Head, bearing the relevant messages.

With that done, Lady Bracknell sat back and regarded Sophy and Martin. Then she grimaced. "There's no point going over everything twice, so let's leave any further explanations until Julia arrives. Meanwhile, perhaps we can go over what you've learned about this situation and formulate the most urgent questions that lie before us."

Martin noted the use of "we" and "us," but knew better than to imagine things might be any other way. He shot a glance at Sophy. "Let's list the questions that have already occurred to us."

She nodded. "First question. Who is the man who brought the document to the hut?" She looked at Lady Bracknell. "He admitted that he and his men were responsible for the accidents at the steelworks."

"And who is his 'gaffer'?" To her ladyship, Martin explained, "By that, he meant the man who'd hired him to engineer the accidents at the steelworks and, more recently, kidnap Sophy and force her to sign the document."

"Third question," Sophy went on. "Why does that man—the gaffer—want to damage Carmichael Steelworks?"

"And how did he come by a key to the place?" Martin added.

Sophy's eyes widened. "I'd forgotten about the key."

"And lastly"—Martin drew the folded document from his pocket—"what would Sophy signing this mean?" He looked at the rolled pages. "What would it achieve?"

"Let me see that." Imperiously, Lady Bracknell held out a hand.

Martin glanced questioningly at Sophy, and at her nod, he stretched over the low table and handed the document to her ladyship.

Lady Bracknell accepted it with a humph. She glanced over the first page, flicked through the rest, and sniffed disparagingly. "Legal stuff. I never could make heads or tails of it. Why they write everything in language that no one but one of their own can understand is beyond me." She handed the document back to Martin. "We'll have to get some legal eagle to decipher it for us."

Martin nodded. "It's the typical sort of company instrument, so weighed down with convoluted phrasing that no ordinary person could possibly comprehend it." He looked at Sophy and arched a brow. "Who is your solicitor?"

She pulled a discouraging face. "Mr. Cromerford is old and stuffy and is never exactly helpful when dealing with me. He's one of the brigade who think ladies shouldn't bother their heads with legal matters and, more, that our heads simply aren't equipped to understand the complexities of a solicitor's art."

Martin managed not to laugh. Her tone suggested that last sentence was a direct quote.

Lady Bracknell snorted and dismissed Mr. Cromerford with a haughty wave. "You should get rid of him. He's clearly a dodo and, as such, is of no use whatsoever to you or the steelworks." Her ladyship frowned. "Unfortunately, my man—whom I trust and who knows his place—is in London."

Both she and Sophy looked at Martin.

Sophy asked, "Do you consult with someone in Sheffield?"

He hadn't wanted to suggest his solicitor, but given the circumstances… He nodded. "I use Mr. Edgar Brumidge. He came highly recommended, and to date, my dealings with him have been entirely satisfactory." He met Sophy's gaze. "Would you consider speaking with him?"

She nodded decisively. "We need to learn the purpose of this document as soon as we possibly can."

They all looked at the clock on the mantelpiece. The hands stood at ten minutes to four o'clock.

Martin glanced at Sophy. "If we go now, we might catch Brumidge before he leaves for the day."

"I'm coming, too." Lady Bracknell pushed up from the sofa. She waved Martin to the bellpull. "Ring for Higginbotham, and let's get going."

To Martin's relief, Roland had arrived with a bag. While the carriage was being prepared, Higginbotham showed Martin to a room, and he quickly washed and changed. He hadn't been thrilled by the idea of appearing at his local solicitor's offices looking as if he'd spent the night carousing and hadn't bothered to make himself presentable.

Feeling much more the part in a fresh overcoat, coat, waistcoat, and trousers, he descended the stairs just in time to hear Higginbotham report that the carriage was ready.

A minute later, in the mews, Martin helped Lady Bracknell into the small closed carriage, then assisted Sophy up the steps and followed.

A groom shut the door, and the coachman set the horses trotting.

Martin sat opposite Sophy and her ladyship, the pair of whom occupied the forward-facing seat. He'd given the coachman directions to Brumidge's chambers in the High Street; as the carriage turned out of the mews, Martin hoped they'd be in time to catch the man.

CHAPTER 11

They reached Brumidge's chambers in good time and were assured by his secretary that the solicitor was still there. They waited impatiently in the outer office while the secretary took in Martin's card and his request for a few minutes of the man's time.

Almost immediately, Brumidge himself threw open his office door. He was a tall, well-built, rather burly presence, today kitted out in a suit of brown tweed. His alert blue gaze swept over them, and a beaming smile split his face.

"Mr. Cynster!" Brumidge advanced, hand outstretched, allowing his secretary to slip back to his desk.

Martin gripped Brumidge's hand, and the solicitor assured him, "It's an honor to be called on, sir, whatever the time. I believe I've mentioned that I'm happy to be of service in any way whatsoever."

"Indeed. And here I am." Martin released the solicitor's hand, and Brumidge turned his beaming countenance on Sophy and her grandmother.

"And who are these lovely ladies?" Brumidge asked.

Amused by the gleam in Brumidge's eye, Martin made the introductions.

Brumidge was a self-made man who'd had the wits and good fortune to be well-educated and the sense to then read law, a career path to which his agile brain had proved well suited. He'd chosen Sheffield in which to hang his shingle specifically because it was a town of growing industrial might, and he was steadily expanding his practice among the town's elite.

"Do come in, ladies, Mr. Cynster." Brumidge ushered them into his inner sanctum. "Please, sit and tell me how I may assist you."

Once they were seated in the comfortable chairs set before the desk and Brumidge had subsided into his chair on the other side of the impressive expanse, Martin drew the document from his pocket.

He glanced at Sophy and, at a nod from her, said to Brumidge, "Miss Carmichael is a part owner of Carmichael Steelworks, located here in town. Earlier today, she was given this document, and a demand was made that she sign it. As part of your services to me, I would like your advice on what the purpose of the document is and your opinion of the likely outcome were Miss Carmichael to sign it."

His eyes on the document, Brumidge nodded. "Only too happy to oblige."

Martin handed the document over the desk. Eagerly, Brumidge took the sheets, smoothed them out, placed them on his blotter, and started to read.

He reached the end of the first page and, frowning, glanced across the desk. "This will take a moment. I'm fairly sure I know the answers to your questions, but I would like to study the entire document before tendering my opinion."

Martin, Sophy, and Lady Bracknell nodded their understanding and encouragement. They watched as Brumidge bent over the document, poring over each page, then flipping back to check earlier clauses, all the while muttering under his breath.

Finally, he nodded to himself—one satisfied nod—then he looked up, folded his hands on the document, and fixed his gaze not on Martin but on Sophy. "Miss Carmichael, your ladyship, as to the question of purpose, this document is occasionally—possibly even frequently—used when a family-owned company has, over several generations, had their shareholding split and split and split again until there are a very large number of part owners, each holding a few voting shares. Such a situation renders making the decisions necessary to manage the company—those executive decisions that generally require a majority vote of shareholders—extremely difficult. Consequently"—he tapped the papers—"this type of document is enacted, usually between the members of a branch of the original founding family."

He continued, "For instance, let's hypothesize that a company is founded by one man who has four children, sixteen grandchildren, and sixty-four great-grandchildren, and in each generation, the shares are equally split among the offspring. Once the four children and the sixteen grandchildren have passed, that leaves the company in the hands of sixty-four individuals, all with equal voting rights."

Brumidge spread his hands. "Obviously, a company board with sixty-four people seated around the boardroom table, each with equal say, would have a difficult time coming to a decision on any issue. To solve the problem and make the company voting structure manageable again, the great-grandchildren might consolidate their voting rights by using this instrument." He tapped the document again. "In our hypothetical case, the descendants of each of the sixteen grandchildren might use this document to transfer the voting rights of their shares to one of their number—say one sibling in each group—so that there would be only sixteen people around the boardroom table again. It might even be that some of those sixteen agree to transfer the rights they hold to maybe six final individuals. All those transfers would be made legal through enacting a document such as this one."

Martin glanced at Sophy.

With her brow lightly furrowed and her gaze locked on the document, she slowly nodded. "I see." Frowning more definitely, she met Brumidge's eyes. "But having a large number of shareholders isn't a problem at Carmichael Steelworks. There are only three shareholders. Myself and my two cousins."

Brumidge frowned. After a moment, he asked, "If I might inquire, of the three of you, who holds the controlling interest? Who is the majority shareholder?"

"I am. It was my father who founded the company, and I hold seventy percent of the shares."

"Ah." Brumidge's expression grew a lot more serious. He glanced at Martin, then looked back at Sophy. "Miss Carmichael, if you had signed this document, your shares would have effectively changed from voting shares to shares voted by proxy."

Sophy narrowed her eyes. "Exactly what does that mean?"

"It means"—Brumidge drew breath and shot another glance at Martin—"that instead of controlling the company as, I surmise, you currently do, making whatever decisions you deem fit, you would lose that ability, and someone else—per this document, the other shareholders—would have the legal right to make those decisions on your behalf." He held up a hand. "To be clear, you would still be a part owner in the sense that you would benefit to the usual degree from any distribution of profit made by the company. In other words, you would still receive seventy percent of all payments from the company to the shareholders. If the company was sold, you would receive seventy percent of the sale price. Essentially, had you signed, you would have retained your stake in the company, but would have given up the rights to control the company's decisions. Via this document, those rights would have passed to the other shareholders."

His features like stone, Martin said, "I didn't see any name given for the proposed proxy holder."

"Indeed. Instead of a specific holder, the voting rights are to be equally distributed among the remaining shareholders." Brumidge looked at Sophy. "That's unusual, but not unheard of."

Sophy drew in a huge breath, then in a tight voice said, "So had I signed that document, the right to make any and all decisions regarding Carmichael Steelworks would have passed to my cousins."

Brumidge nodded. "Exactly."

Martin escorted a rather pale and tight-lipped Sophy and her gruffly worried grandmother back to the Bracknell town house. They returned via the mews and entered the kitchen to find Higginbotham waiting.

"Mrs. Canterbury is in the drawing room, ma'am. Hector escorted her here and is waiting with her."

Lady Bracknell nodded. "Thank you, Higginbotham. And Queerly?"

The cook-housekeeper looked up from the table where she was chopping vegetables. "Yes, ma'am?"

"Gird your loins, woman. I suspect we're going to have an impromptu dinner party."

Queerly perked up and eagerly asked, "How many diners, ma'am?"

Lady Bracknell looked at Sophy and arched her brows.

Sophy rapidly calculated. "In addition to her ladyship, I believe there'll be five others."

Queerly was already wiping her hands and hurrying to her pantry. "Excellent! You won't be disappointed, my lady."

"I know, Queerly. I never am." Lady Bracknell led Martin and Sophy into the front hall and thence to the drawing room, an elegantly furnished room at the front of the house.

Hector was standing just inside the door. He looked hugely relieved when Sophy walked in, and he nodded gratefully to Martin.

Sophy's aunt sprang up from an armchair by the hearth. "Sophy! Thank God you're all right. What on earth happened?" Julia swept up to Sophy and embraced her.

Sophy patted her aunt's shoulder and rather unconvincingly tried to reassure Julia that she was well.

Julia stepped back and peered at Sophy's face. "Silly girl," she gently chided. "I can see you're upset."

"Yes, well." With a distracted wave, Sophy urged her aunt back to the armchair, then sat on the long sofa. "Strange to say, that's not due to being kidnapped but rather the reason why."

Lady Bracknell huffed as she sank into another armchair by the fireplace. "A bit of a facer, what we've just learned. I'm not sure I fully comprehend the implications."

"Nor I," Sophy admitted.

The clatter of carriage wheels on the street outside drew Martin to the as-yet-uncurtained window. He looked out, then reported, "It's Oliver and Charlie." Being careful not to be seen, he drew the curtains over the windows, then turned to the ladies and directed a half smile Sophy's way. "At least they've brought my curricle and horses back."

A brisk tattoo on the front door was followed by a muted exchange with Higginbotham, then the door opened, and Oliver and Charlie strode in. Both halted just inside the room and looked from Martin to Sophy, and the tension that had ridden them visibly eased.

"You're all right," Oliver stated.

Charlie added a heartfelt, "Thank God." He walked to a chair and dropped into it. "We came back from our ride to find the Elliots and Old Joe and Reggie quartering the garden. We helped, but found no sign of you. We had no idea where you'd disappeared to. We were organizing a search when the messenger arrived."

"We drove straight back." Oliver grinned at Martin. "I like your horses."

Martin arched a brow. "So do I." He waved Oliver to another chair and moved to sit beside Sophy. "Now we're all here"—he caught Sophy's eye—"I suggest we start at the beginning. We were strolling in the shrubbery when I was hit rather viciously over the head and lost consciousness."

Sophy picked up the tale, explaining how the two thugs had taken her and Martin to a hut on the moors, where they were visited by the thugs' leader and she was given a document to sign in return for being set free.

Oliver frowned. "So you were essentially being held hostage in order to get your signature on a document?"

When Martin and Sophy nodded, Oliver asked, "What was the document?"

Martin caught Sophy's eye. "We'll come to that in a moment."

Sophy nodded and continued, recounting how the leader had confessed to being behind the accidents at the steelworks. "All on the orders of some man who'd hired him—him and his men."

Charlie was frowning as he followed the tale. "Was the document something the leader wanted you to sign for his own benefit, or was that also a part of what he'd been hired to do?"

"The latter." Sophy glanced at Martin.

He added, "The document originated with the man who hired the thugs we met."

Charlie and Oliver both nodded, and Sophy went on, "I stated I couldn't possibly sign such a document given I couldn't understand what it said."

"I was still feigning unconsciousness at that point," Martin explained, "and Sophy persuaded the leader to give us an hour for me to recover and read the document and explain it to her."

"Apparently," Sophy said, "he—the leader—had to return to town, so he was willing to give us that time."

"Once he left..." Martin outlined the events that had led to them arriving at Lady Bracknell's house. "After explaining matters to her ladyship, we sent word to you." He glanced around the circle.

Lady Bracknell stirred. "The document Sophy was pressured to sign was a legal one and all but incomprehensible. We needed a solicitor to decipher it, and luckily, we had just enough time to consult Martin's man in town."

Her ladyship looked at Martin, and he filled in, "The document is one that would have transferred the voting rights of Sophy's shares in Carmichael Steelworks to someone else." With Charlie there, he didn't specify to whom the voting rights would have gone. Martin wasn't sure how best to broach the question of Charlie possibly being involved in the campaign against Sophy.

At that moment, he didn't know how he—or she or Lady Bracknell—felt about Charlie.

Oliver was frowning. "The thugs' leader—the one who brought the document to you. Do you have any idea who he is?"

Sophy and Martin shook their heads.

Martin added, "I heard no names."

"No," Sophy agreed. "But by their accents, all three—the two who seized us and the leader—are locals. Of that, I'm sure."

Charlie leaned forward. He, too, was frowning. "The leader—what did he look like?"

Sophy rattled off a description of the man.

Martin saw a look of horrified comprehension dawn on Charlie's face, and when Sophy mentioned the strawberry birthmark, Charlie softly swore.

"It's not a birthmark," he said. "It's a scar from when he was a child and set a cat on fire."

Seeing the others all staring at him, Charlie said, "That's Vince Murchison."

Martin straightened. "The man who holds your IOUs and tried to force you to rob the steelworks?"

Grim-faced, Charlie nodded. "The same."

"Well," Sophy said, her tone hardening. "Now we know who was behind all the accidents at the steelworks!"

"We know who carried them out," Oliver clarified. "But the person actually behind the accidents—and that document—is whoever hired Vince Murchison and his thugs."

"So it seems." Lady Bracknell nodded, along with everyone else.

Frowning anew, Sophy looked at Charlie. "Earlier, when you were telling us about your IOUs and what this Vince Murchison told you to do at the steelworks, you said he wanted you to sign some document as well."

Charlie blinked, then nodded. "That's right. I'd forgotten about that."

"Do you have the document with you?" Martin asked.

Charlie was already hunting through his pockets. "Yes!" He pulled out a wad of folded paper from an inner pocket. "Here it is."

Martin held out his hand, and Charlie handed the document to him. Martin unfolded it, swiftly scanned it, then passed it to Sophy. To the others, he said, "It's the same document, just with Charlie's name instead of Sophy's."

"So," Charlie said, clearly wrestling with the implications, "if I'd signed, I would have given up my voting rights in Carmichael Steelworks, just like Sophy?"

Martin nodded. Sophy handed the document to Lady Bracknell, and Oliver rose and went to read over her shoulder. Her ladyship humphed. "It's just the same." She flipped to the end of the document. "And just like the document Sophy was given, this doesn't stipulate a specific person to whom the voting rights will transfer, just that they will be equally divided between the other shareholders."

Martin looked at Sophy, then at Charlie. "To be perfectly clear, aside from the two of you, who are the other shareholders in Carmichael Steelworks?"

Sophy looked at Charlie, then in unison they said, "Edward."

"There is absolutely no one else?" Martin pressed.

Charlie and Sophy, both thin-lipped, shook their heads.

"Just Edward," Sophy confirmed. "There is no one else."

Martin looked from one to the other, then at the dawning comprehension in Julia's, Hector's, and Lady Bracknell's faces.

Oliver simply looked grim.

"So"—leaning his forearms on his thighs, Martin clasped his hands between his knees—"if Sophy had signed the document put before her, and Charlie had signed the document given to him, control of the steelworks would have passed to Edward."

Everyone was silent as that sank in, then Sophy met his gaze. "Not just control, but complete and absolute control. Whatever Edward decided, there would be no gainsaying him."

Martin looked around at the sober, serious, quite somber faces. "It appears," he concluded, "that first to last, this entire series of incidents has been directed at, on the one hand, damaging the steelworks and, on the other, placing complete control of the business into Edward's hands."

The others all looked at him. No one disagreed.

They were still grappling with that revelation when Higginbotham arrived and announced that dinner was awaiting their pleasure, and they adjourned to the dining room.

Martin noticed that Hector, who had listened silently to the proceedings, slipped away to the kitchens, no doubt to take his meal with the other staff.

The oval table had been set for six, and Lady Bracknell directed them to various seats, with Julia at the foot of the table while her ladyship claimed the carver at its head.

Martin held Sophy's chair for her, then sat beside her. Oliver settled opposite, with Charlie beside him, across the table from Sophy.

Silence—or rather, their churning thoughts—still held them.

The soup was served, and her ladyship, anticipating the likely discussion to come, waved Higginbotham and the footmen away.

As those at the table picked up their soup spoons, Charlie grumbled, "I thought that blasted document had something to do with my debts." He caught Martin's eye. "Other than affect my voting rights, is there anything else that document does?"

Martin savored his first mouthful of oyster soup and shook his head. Briefly, he outlined what Brumidge had told them about the customary use of the instrument. "It's limited to changing the voting rights of shares and nothing else."

"Changing the voting rights is more than enough." Sophy looked around the table. "So, is Edward behind all of this? Is he Vince Murchison's 'gaffer'? Is Edward the one who hired Vince and his thugs to damage the steelworks?"

No one leapt to answer her.

Oliver had been frowning in thought. "I'm no legal expert, but once those documents were executed, given there's no theft as such involved, I imagine getting them rescinded and the outcome reversed wouldn't be easy or even straightforward."

"Given how the courts work," Martin pointed out, "it might take years."

"Years during which Edward would have unchallenged and unchallengeable control of the business." Sophy's expression grew dark. "And I can readily imagine that, as I'm a female and Charlie is widely viewed as a reckless profligate, Edward would be in an excellent position, socially, morally, and legally, to dismiss any formal appeal to have the documents overturned."

After a moment, she glanced at Charlie. "Thank God we didn't sign, so it won't come to that."

Oliver caught Martin's eye. "A lot can be done with a business in two months, let alone a year."

Martin nodded. "Irreversible changes."

Julia set down her soup spoon, dabbed her napkin to her lips, then in a surprisingly steadfast voice, stated, "I simply cannot see Edward having a role in any of this." She looked around the table, her expression adamant. "He's stuffy and starchy and difficult to like, but that stuffiness and starchiness are because he holds himself—and everyone else—to the highest possible standards of behavior. He's rigid and unbending and prides himself on being what we term 'correct.'" She shook her head. "I honestly can't see him being this"—she gestured—"devious."

The rest of the company regarded her, then Lady Bracknell huffed. "I have to say I'm having the same problem casting Edward as the villain. He's such a priggishly *righteous* soul. To be so underhanded…" She, too, shook her head. "I really don't think he has it in him."

Across the table, Martin exchanged a look with Oliver. They both knew of instances of righteous façades concealing much darker natures.

Beside Martin, Sophy sighed. "I'm having much the same problem. Despite Edward being the only person to benefit from the execution of those documents, I'm having great difficulty seeing him planning all this, much less hiring the likes of Vince Murchison."

Charlie slumped back in his chair. "I can't even imagine Edward knowing who Murchison is, much less making contact with him."

Sophy tipped her head Charlie's way. "And even more to the point, I cannot understand why, apparently entirely out of the blue, Edward would have developed such a compelling desire to run the steelworks." She met Charlie's eyes, then glanced at Martin. "He has never shown the slightest interest, not even when my father encouraged him to claim a position in the business—any position he wished."

Lady Bracknell huffed. "I remember that. I was present at that meeting, and from the way Edward reacted, you would have thought Edmund had offered him a position as the lowliest of workers rather than one at Edmund's right hand!"

Julia was nodding in emphatic agreement.

They fell silent as Higginbotham and the footmen reappeared and cleared the soup plates and brought forth the dishes of the main course. All was served as her ladyship directed, then she waved the staff from the room again, and they addressed their plates.

After they'd been eating for several minutes, Martin glanced at Oliver, then spoke to the table at large. "If we accept your collective insights regarding Edward as accurate and, from that, postulate that he knows nothing about the activities of Murchison and his thugs, that leaves us facing the question of whether Edward knows about the documents.

Those documents which, if signed, would give him sole control of the steelworks."

When the others all frowned as if unsure where that got them, Martin went on, "For argument's sake, let's say that Edward knows nothing about the documents. If so, then it appears he's being set up to be used as someone else's puppet." He looked up and down the table. "From what you know of Edward, is that possible? And if so, who might be the one planning to pull his strings?"

Charlie's face cleared. "Ah—I see." He set down his cutlery and reached for his wine glass. "I have to say, that sounds much more likely. Edward thinks he's thoroughly up to snuff, but in reality, he's led a very sheltered life and, therefore, is quite naive, especially when it comes to other people."

From their expressions, Lady Bracknell, Sophy, and even Julia agreed.

"But," Charlie continued, "if Edward is being used as someone else's pawn—or should that be someone else's unwitting stalking horse? Regardless, the person looking to pull his strings won't be Murchison or anyone like him, for precisely the same reason that Edward would never have approached Murchison in the first place."

Julia put in, "Edward would consider all such people far beneath his notice."

"Exactly." Cradling his wine glass, Charlie warmed to his theme. "Edward is an arrogant snob who would never sully himself—or his belief in his own superiority—by consorting with those he deems the underclass. I grant you the older Murchison, Walter, is rather more presentable than Vince, but even Walter is a rough sort with only the thinnest veneer of respectability. Neither brother—or any of their peers—is the sort Edward would ever lower himself to deal with."

It was obvious that Sophy, Lady Bracknell, and Julia shared Charlie's assessment of Edward.

Her ladyship stated, "To use an old-fashioned but apt description, Edward's a high stickler."

They all ate and ruminated on Edward's character and on where incorporating that into the picture they were forming led them.

Eventually, Martin glanced around the faces. "I've been trying to think of who might be angling to use Edward as his stalking horse." He met Oliver's eyes. "I keep coming back to the mystery man Edward was seen with in the Iron and Steel Club." He tipped his head at Charlie. "And also seen by Charlie in Edward's home. That man isn't a local, and those who saw him with Edward were surprised because Edward rarely socializes, yet he seemed very friendly with this man."

Oliver slowly nodded. "And if I recall the timing correctly, the mystery man first appeared in town—or at least at the club—a little before the accidents started." Oliver paused, then added, "But if it's him, what's his motive?"

Martin grimaced. "I can't see any way to tell, not without knowing more about him. But if he hails from London and he's the one who hired Murchison"—he looked at Charlie—"that would explain how Murchison got hold of your IOUs. If this man is the sort to hire Murchison, then presumably he has contacts at the same level in London."

Sophy was frowning. "If the mystery man brought Charlie's IOUs from London, that suggests he came to town with the intention of getting those documents signed and also making trouble—the accidents and other problems we've been having—at the steelworks."

"Exactly." Martin nodded. "Those IOUs suggest a carefully planned and executed campaign, not any idle, incidental game."

"But"—Sophy spread her hands and looked at him in utter puzzlement—"*why*?" She glanced around the table. "What possible reason would a man like that have for putting the reins of the steelworks into Edward's hands?"

"That, indeed, is the central question." Martin's features hardened. "We need to learn more about this mystery man."

Oliver nodded. "Who he is, where he hails from, and why he's in town."

Charlie's eyes had narrowed. "If we could learn where he's staying, that would be a start." He looked at Martin. "Perhaps Hector and your men could ask around quietly. He sounds like the sort to be staying at one of the hotels."

Martin inclined his head. "True. However, the most direct way to learn what we need to know is, of course, to ask Edward." He glanced at the others. "Unless, as much as none of you wish to think it, Edward isn't entirely innocent."

When Julia opened her mouth to protest, Martin held up a placating hand. "I'm not suggesting that Edward is a party to the accidents or abduction, but even knowing nothing about those, it's possible he's aware of some of the mystery man's plan and is going along for his own reasons." He looked from one to the other. "How much do any of you really know about Edward? His financial position? His ideas for his future? His aspirations?"

No one answered.

After several moments during which they finished their main courses, Sophy set down her cutlery, grimaced, and said, "Whatever this scheme's ultimate motive is, until we know Edward's part in it—whether he's actively involved, whether he's been persuaded to countenance it without actually knowing what's been going on, or whether he's entirely innocent and not involved at all—until we're sure which of those alternatives is true, we shouldn't risk asking him."

Relieved, Martin said, "If we do ask him and he is involved, it's possible all we'll achieve is to alert our mystery man to our interest in him and his doings, and who knows what he might do then?" He met the others' eyes. "We don't know enough about him to chance it."

"So," her ladyship asked, "what else can we do? What should we do next?"

Before anyone could formulate an answer, Higginbotham and the footmen reappeared. Those seated waited while the plates and dishes were cleared and a honey trifle and a syllabub were set before them.

Lady Bracknell waved the staff away. "We'll manage, Higginbotham. Thank you."

Higginbotham bowed and, with the rest of the staff, retreated.

They passed the trifle and syllabub around and served themselves, then settled to consume the sweets.

Sophy pushed a lump of trifle around her dish. "The other person who must presumably know the mystery man's name is Vince Murchison." She glanced at Martin. "We—you and I—are witnesses and victims of him and his men. I saw all three of them. They kidnapped me from my own garden and subsequently made demands that would have effectively taken control of my business from me." She looked up the table at her grandmother. "Surely the police could arrest them for that, then we could wring the mystery man's name from Murchison."

Oliver arched his brows. "Good thinking. Given the sort of man Murchison seems to be, if there's a chance of saving his skin, no doubt he'll oblige with the man's name."

Charlie agreed with that assessment.

Everyone thought an approach to the police was an excellent way to proceed, and an energetic discussion ensued.

What Sophy hadn't anticipated was the universal resistance to her involvement.

"That I was kidnapped," Martin said, "will be more than enough to galvanize the constabulary into action."

She stared at him. "But you were unconscious. You can't identify any of the three thugs."

He shook his head. "I was awake and watching for most of the time Vince Murchison was talking to you, and I saw the other two when I knocked them out before we escaped."

She couldn't argue that.

"Indeed," Martin went on, "that one of his men had coshed me unconscious won't help Murchison's cause." He looked around the faces. "First thing tomorrow, I'll go to the police station and lay a complaint. Once they haul Murchison in, we'll see if he can solve the mystery of our unknown man's identity."

"I'll go with you." Sophy's grandmother's gaze had been resting on Sophy. Now, the old lady glanced at Martin. "I know the police commissioner well and will happily inform the local inspector of that."

Martin inclined his head in ready acceptance. "That certainly won't harm our chances." He glanced at Sophy. "And your presence might help ensure Sophy's name isn't mentioned, at least not officially." He paused, then added, "One would hope Vince Murchison is clever enough not to volunteer that he and his men targeted and seized the granddaughter of a local aristocrat, but if they do let that information fall, then having you along, Lady Bracknell, would be wise."

"Indeed," Julia fervently agreed.

Everyone but Sophy was unreservedly encouraging.

Oliver observed, "It's something concrete we can do—a step forward we can take."

On noting that everyone had finished with their desserts, her grandmother rose, bringing the rest of the table to their feet. "Gentlemen, will you remain here for brandy and port or accompany us ladies back to the drawing room?"

After glancing at each other, the men denied any wish for spirits, and as a group, they repaired to the drawing room. There, they resumed their seats, and the talk turned to what might occur at the police station the following morning.

"One thing you can bank on," Charlie said, "is that the local constabulary will jump at any chance to haul in a Murchison, even if it's just Vince rather than Walter."

"Walter's the older one and runs the outfit?" Oliver clarified.

Charlie nodded. "That's the way it's always worked in Sheffield. As far as I know, when it comes to thugs for hire, the Murchisons are the only group in town." Charlie met Martin's eyes. "That's why the police are so keen to get their hands on something—anything—solid enough to remove the Murchisons from the local scene."

Martin and Oliver asked several more questions about the Murchisons, then the door opened, and Higginbotham wheeled in the tea trolley.

Hector slipped into the room in Higginbotham's wake. He waited, standing beside the door, while Higginbotham helped hand around the cups of tea Sophy's grandmother poured. That done, Hector came forward.

Sophy—and everyone else—looked at him expectantly.

"Ladies. Gents." Hector half bowed. "I've just had word from Portobello Street that the house is being watched by what Tom, the young footman, describes as 'shifty characters lurking in the grounds of the church.'"

Julia looked disturbed, but before anyone could comment, Hector transferred his gaze to Martin and went on, "And Mr. Cynster's man, Jiggs, is downstairs. He says the Kings Head is under surveillance as well, but he sneaked out and is confident he wasn't seen and tracked here."

"Well, well." Oliver looked at Martin. "Whoever is behind this, they really are serious. Now they want not only Sophy but you as well."

"So it seems." Martin sounded unperturbed. He glanced at Sophy. "I think we can safely assume they'll be keeping a close watch on the steelworks as well." He looked at Charlie. "And no doubt, they'll be looking for you, too."

Charlie frowned. "They might not have seen me at the manor. I'm sure they didn't follow me out there."

Martin tipped his head in agreement. "They must have been following Sophy all along. It was she they were intent on kidnapping. You, they thought they already had on a hook, courtesy of your IOUs."

"Well, that settles it," Lady Bracknell declared. "You"—she looked at Sophy, then transferred her gaze to Martin—"and you must remain here rather than risk being found by these dreadful people. You can remain with me until this matter is resolved. Anywhere else is too dangerous."

Anxiety plain in her face, Julia looked at Sophy. "I daresay this house is more secure…"

"Indeed, it is." Lady Bracknell nodded emphatically. "I have more staff, and I will put them on alert—well, they already are, of course." She looked from Sophy to Martin. "And as I don't spend that much time in Sheffield these days, there's really no reason these thugs would even know about this house, much less come looking for you here."

Martin had to admit that was likely, and if him staying there would ensure that Sophy did, too, thus remaining within his protective reach… He met Lady Bracknell's eyes. "Thank you, ma'am. I agree that Sophy and me staying here is likely the wisest choice." He uncrossed his legs and rose. "I'll have a word with Jiggs and have him fetch some of my things from the hotel."

Higginbotham cleared his throat. "It might be best, sir, if one of our footmen returned with Mr. Jiggs and brought your bag here, rather than unnecessarily risk one of your men being seen heading this way."

"Good thinking, Higginbotham!" Lady Bracknell waved the butler off. "Go and see to it, please." She smiled at Martin. "The Kings Head is only a block or so away. Your things will be here in no time."

Higginbotham bowed. "I'll see that your bag is taken up to your room, sir."

Martin nodded to Higginbotham, then half bowed to her ladyship. "Thank you, ma'am." He resumed his seat on the sofa, beside Sophy, and looked at Charlie. "Speaking of the Kings Head being only a block away, heading for Sycamore Street might not be a wise move for you. Do you have anywhere safe you can stay?"

Various options were canvassed, and Charlie gratefully accepted an offer from Oliver to put him up in the second bedroom of the suite Oliver had taken at the King James Hotel in Campo Lane. "It's in the opposite direction to the Kings Head," Oliver pointed out, "so we should be safe enough."

Sophy, meanwhile, had leaned across to speak with Julia; Martin caught enough of the exchange to realize Sophy was reassuring her aunt that, as she routinely kept clothes and accoutrements at her grandmother's house, she needed nothing sent from Portobello Street. "Not for a few days' stay."

Julia accepted that with a still-anxious murmur, but made no further comment.

Shortly afterward, with the teacups emptied and with their safety arranged to the best of their ability, the company rose and drifted into the front hall.

Julia left first, with Hector handing her into her carriage, then swinging up to ride beside the coachman, then Charlie and Oliver ambled off together, just two gentlemen returning from having dinner somewhere.

After Higginbotham closed the door, Lady Bracknell turned to Martin and Sophy and waved up the stairs. "Come along, you two. We're going to have a busy day tomorrow, what with enlisting the aid of the police and interviewing thugs and whatever comes after that."

CHAPTER 12

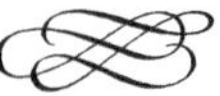

Sophy fell in beside her grandmother as she ascended the stairs, and Martin dutifully climbed in their wake.

"I hope we learn our mystery man's name." Sophy stepped into the gallery. "I'm getting very tired of his games and would like nothing better than to put a permanent spoke in his wheel."

The vengefulness in her voice made Martin very glad she would not be accompanying him to the police station.

He followed the ladies into the gallery. Higginbotham had told him the room he'd briefly used earlier had been prepared for his continued use. That room lay to the right, while Sophy and her indomitable grandmother were heading to the left.

Martin paused and called, "Goodnight, ladies. Pleasant dreams."

Lady Bracknell glanced over her shoulder. "Goodnight, Martin." Facing forward, she airily waved and continued walking. "We can meet over the breakfast table and plan our campaign."

Martin smiled at her retreating back.

Sophy had paused to look back at him. She saw his smile and, in return, smiled conspiratorially. Then she dipped her head and followed her grandmother. "Goodnight."

Martin watched her walk away. "Goodnight," he echoed, then turned and walked in the opposite direction.

The room he'd been assigned lay at the end of the corridor, a handsome apartment with a large and doubtless comfortable bed. He walked in to find that twin lamps, perched on side tables to either side of the door, had been lit, casting a warm glow across the room. A small fire blazed cheerily in the hearth, before which two well-padded armchairs were angled.

His bag was neatly stored beside the tallboy to one side of the fireplace, and his comb and brushes had been laid out on the tallboy's top.

He closed the door, hesitated, then turned down both lamps, leaving the room lit only by the flickering firelight, and crossed to the narrow window set in the wall on the far side of the bed.

He pushed aside the heavy curtain just enough to look out. As he'd expected, the window afforded him a good view of the street in front of the house. Looking to the west, he could see the dark bulk of St. James's Church at the end of the street. Slowly, he scanned the pavements, working eastward from the church and continuing as far as the window allowed.

Not so much as a cat slinked through the shadows.

Good.

He watched for a few minutes, but there was no sign of any watchers. That meant that no one would have seen Charlie with Oliver, either. Martin let the curtain fall and turned back to the room.

Walking past the bed, he shrugged out of his coat and tossed the garment over the back of one of the chairs before the fire. He checked his bag, but the supplies Roland had packed—enough for several days—had been transferred and arranged in the tallboy's drawers.

Martin turned away, taking mental stock.

He halted and frowned.

He'd expected to feel if not relaxed then at least more settled. They'd learned quite a bit about what was going on and had defined a clear path toward identifying who was responsible. They had actions they could take, and he knew what their next steps would be. While the outcome remained undecided, the possibility of learning who was behind Sophy's problems was definite and real.

And yet he felt…unsettled. Restless.

He set his hands on his hips, hung his head, and thought over the events of the day. The drama, the action…

The conversation the thugs had interrupted in the shrubbery.

He pulled up those moments in his mind and replayed the exchange.

Can you see the vision?

He'd asked her that, and she'd been about to reply, and her answer…

Hardly surprising I'm feeling unsatisfied.

And now, of course, he felt even more restless and impatient and *wanting.*

The sound of the door opening had him raising his head and swinging around, only to see, as if his thoughts had summoned her, Sophy slip inside.

She quietly shut the door and looked at the bed. She stared at it for several seconds, then scanned the dimly lit room. When her gaze reached him, she smiled—even in the poor light he saw her features transform—then she calmly walked toward him.

He tightened his grip on his libido to the mental equivalent of white-knuckled.

As Sophy neared, she studied his expression. Was he still in pain? She could read very little from his face. "How's your head?" To her mind, that was the most pertinent question.

He frowned and raised a hand to the back of his head, then his brows rose in surprise. "It's not that bad. It's no longer throbbing and only hurts if I press."

She halted before him, reached up, and followed his fingers to the lump, then gently nudged his hand away and explored for herself. Her eyes on his, she murmured, "It's not as large as it was."

From close quarters, he searched her face. "That's a relief."

She let her lips curve. "Clearly, you have a hard head."

His eyes met and locked with hers. She felt his hands close, gently, about her waist, holding her where she was. Close. Almost against him. The front of his coat brushed tantalizingly over the taut fabric of her bodice.

"I'm fairly certain," he murmured, his voice deep and low, "that you didn't come here to investigate the size of my lump."

Fearlessly, she held his gaze. "I'm here because I'm not about to allow whoever's behind this—our mystery man—to dictate my life. Mine or yours." She paused, studying his eyes. All she saw in the caramel depths was stalwart strength, potent, unwavering, yet controlled. Held reined. Waiting.

She tipped her head quizzically. "Do you remember what we were speaking about in the shrubbery before Murchison's thugs so rudely interrupted us?"

"Vividly."

Delicious tension rose inside her, and she locked her eyes with his. "I can see the vision you conjured, the landscape of our future as it could be. And I want it—want that—just as much as you do."

His eyes searched hers, then his lips lightly curved, and his voice lowered almost to a purr. "I very much doubt that. You cannot possibly want that shining future, crave and yearn for it, as much as I do."

She couldn't stop her lips from curving at the blatant challenge. Couldn't stop herself from responding to the lure. "Trust me, I can. Indeed, I do." Deliberately, she closed the distance between them. "Let me show you how much."

Sliding her hands to his nape, she stretched up against him, then drew his head down, set her lips to his, and with flagrant wanton intention, plunged, heart and soul, into the kiss.

Into the waiting flames. Flames of passion, desire, and hunger that roared and greedily welcomed her into a fiery embrace.

His arms surrounded her and tightened, holding her, then crushing her to him.

She gloried in the spike of greedy need that surged through her and him, spurred by the provocative contact. Her nerves sparked, and her senses expanded as heat swirled and built, beckoning, luring, tempting them on. *This* was what she wanted and, after the drama, the demands, and the tensions of the day, simply had to have, and the same desire burned in him.

That avid mutual hunger was evident in the way their lips ravenously melded, in the way their tongues tangled in successive heated duels. In the desperate craving that surged through them and had their hands gripping, seizing, holding, clinging as their world and their senses spun.

Out of control.

Both of them were, and neither cared.

Since that disrupted moment in the shrubbery, they'd been forced to set aside these needs, yet while dealing with the demands the situation had forced upon them, beneath their outwardly collected façades, *this*—this hunger, these needs—had been simmering, swelling, and building, constantly abraded by all the necessary social touches, leaping at the nearness, the physical closeness dictated by their responses to the ongoing, evolving mystery.

Now, they'd left the mystery and all its demands outside the door. They'd dropped their polite masks and set passion free to surge as it would, unleashed by her decision. By her declaration.

In giddy delight, they let hunger consume them, let desire rage and sweep them away.

She'd never imagined kisses could be so ravenous, so rapacious. He drew back to sup at her lips, only to dive back into the exchange, and she welcomed him with equal passion, with a need every bit as desperate as their tongues caressed and their senses whirled.

His hands, splayed, swept over her back, down over the swell of her hips, urging her impossibly closer. She felt the heated bulge of his erection press, rigid, hard, and hot, against the soft swell of her belly, and a surge of giddy wanting nearly sent her to her knees.

He must have sensed her reaction, for he bent and swept her into his arms. She refused to release him from the heated kiss, but that didn't stop him from carrying her across the room.

And then they were rolling on the bed.

Her breath hitched, then left her entirely as his weight settled over her and his hands—those wicked hands—closed over her breasts. Then a wave of heat, of flame and desire, rolled over her, through her, and she let go and surrendered to passion's tide.

Martin recognized that moment; he felt it in his bones. She and what they'd conjured together, what their combined desires and passions had evoked and unleashed, had blindsided him and, given his experience, well-nigh unbelievably reduced him to reacting like a lovemaking amateur, entirely driven by uncontrollable desires, yet instinct nevertheless remained, and he saw, seized, and clung.

Control as he usually wielded it—absolute and definite—might be beyond him, but it was still in his power to channel, guide, and steer. In doing so, he had only one aim—to shower her with the breadth, the depth, and every iota of the reality of his feelings for her.

Feelings he couldn't explain, even to himself, but that here, in this arena, were, to him, abundantly plain.

She was his all, and it behooved him to make that ineradicably clear.

That was his goal, his agenda, and he devoted himself to achieving it using every means at his disposal.

His hands roved her still fully clothed body, hunger and need thrumming in every touch, in every subtle pressure. She hummed in her throat and, through the kiss and with the greedy insistence of her small hands, urged him on.

Soon, she grew desperate to rid them of the layers that kept their bodies apart, and he was only too ready to assist.

Long practice guided him in efficiently stripping her, but when he would have paused to admire and glory, she fell on him with her own greedy demands.

Her touch, her determination, her drive that clearly matched his own impelled him, temporarily, to share the reins—such reins as they were.

Only to realize, minutes later, that given her inexperience, that wasn't actually the wisest choice.

Too soon, they were locked in a naked tussle, with him wanting to slow their proceedings enough to lavish all possible pleasure on her, and her pressing to race ahead in a manner that would reach the end but miss all the subtler delights along the way.

It was an argument without words, a battle only his years of experience and greater strength and weight allowed him to win.

She slumped back on the pillows and huffed, then through bright aqua eyes peeking from beneath the fringe of her lashes, boldly studied him.

Crouched over her, he grinned his most wicked grin. "Not just ten minutes, remember?"

Her eyes widened slightly, then he bent his head and pressed a hot open-mouthed kiss to her belly, and her lids fell. A second later, her hips lifted and twisted between his restraining hands, and she moaned.

The sound was pure ambrosia to his rapacious soul. Unrelentingly greedy, he set about eliciting further evocative avowals of her delight.

Deliberately and increasingly sure of his path, he showered her with passion. He took his time exploring her body, feeding and teasing her senses and his and expanding her knowledge of earthly pleasure. Attuned to her at a level he never had been with any woman before, he was aware of the reverence investing his caresses, the worshipful hunger imbuing every touch, and let the feelings that fed those emotions flow and spread through him and on, into her.

For the first time in his life, he consciously used the act of making love to communicate, to impress on her what drove his passion, his desires, his needs.

Heated and awash with hunger though he was, he was yet aware enough to see and recognize all those changes, those revelations, for what they were. To comprehend from whence they sprang and acknowledge what that meant.

There was only one real difference between her and all the rest—all who, for him, had come before. She was the lady he wanted and needed by his side for the rest of his days.

He wanted her to be his wife, and that changed everything.

And when, ultimately surrendering to her desperate urgings, he rose over her and, on one long thrust, entered her, that was different, too. More charged, more meaningful, and so much more elementally powerful that it rocked him to his core.

Eyes closed, desperately holding against the impulse to plunder, he dragged in a huge breath, then forced up his lids enough to look at her.

She'd gasped in pain—unavoidable given she'd been a virgin—and her nails had sunk into his forearms, but even as he took in the frown tangling her brows, the tense line eased, then smoothed away. She drew in a deep breath, too, then her grip on his forearms loosened, and she shifted, experimentally lifted.

The instinctive invitation snapped the remnants of his reins, yet as he drew back and thrust deep again, she was with him, eagerly rising to the beat he set, joining him in the age-old dance of passion and desire and heated wanting.

What followed was a journey through a landscape he'd thought he'd known, but hadn't. This sensual wonderland was new, novel, the sensations here more intense, more powerful and potent. The primal compulsion built swiftly, inexorably, until it caught them and swept them on. Unrelenting and unstoppable, that compulsion transformed to an irresistible tide that drove them in a plundering, racing ride over ever-escalating peaks of sensation until, inevitably, tense and tight, they reached passion's pinnacle, and with a last desperate thrust, he sent them soaring.

Together, they clung as pleasure and delight battered them, and desire and passion collided and exploded into ecstasy, nova-bright, brilliant, and overwhelming, and the tumultuous power swelled and shattered them.

Pleasure, sweeter and more intense than he'd ever known, flooded his veins and filled his heart.

That heart thumped heavily against hers as completion swept through him, and he slumped upon her.

Oblivion beckoned, and he felt her arms slide around him, felt her hold him close.

Revelation, comprehension, and promise—all had been manifest in the engagement.

All had been there to be seized and claimed, and together, they had. Unreservedly, with characteristic, clear-eyed determination.

This was where they'd both wanted to be, the step they'd both been waiting, poised, to take.

His lips lightly curving, eyes closed, he let consciousness slip through his fingers and surrendered.

To her and to what had grown between them.

Some unknown time later, he stirred, and despite the tightening of her arms urging him to remain where he was, he lifted from her and, ignoring her incoherent grumbling, settled on his side beside her.

She wriggled onto her side, facing him, but kept her eyes closed, even though the tension in her sleek muscles assured him she was awake.

In the distant glow of the dying fire, he studied her face and saw her lashes flicker. He raised a hand and brushed back a heavy lock of her glorious golden hair, then leaned in and brushed a gentle kiss to her lips.

"Just to be clear," he whispered, "when all this is over, the situation resolved, and we've sorted out Edward and our mystery man and put an end to all threats to Carmichael Steelworks, you and I are going to get married."

One lid lifted a fraction, and she studied his face, then her lips curved in a frankly lascivious smile. With her eyes once again closed, she all but purred, "Indeed we are. You've convinced me of the benefits. That vision of a working partnership you described? We—you and I—are going to make it a reality."

He smiled and kissed her again. "We're going to make it *our* reality."

That was all he needed to hear. All he needed to know.

Smiling to himself, he relaxed into the mattress and felt the last scintilla of tension drain away as sweet satiation—satiation on every level—flowed through him.

He was looking forward to the dawn, to the day and what it would bring. To learning the identity of the mystery man and eradicating all threats to Sophy and the steelworks. All threats to his future.

Glorying in the feel of her soft warmth pressed against him, he wondered how soon they could tie the knot.

The next morning, somewhat later than usual, Sophy hurried down the stairs and turned in to the corridor to the breakfast parlor.

Situated in a rear corner of the house, the parlor overlooked a small garden and, that morning, was bright with sunbeams and warmth. She breezed through the open doorway with a cheery "Good morning," unsurprised to find both Martin and her grandmother already at the table.

"Good morning, my dear." Her grandmother raised her gaze to her face, blinked, then stared.

Sophy made a valiant effort to dim her smile, but doubted she was all that successful. When, not that long ago, she'd returned to her room, she'd glanced in the mirror and been surprised to discover that she had, somehow or other, acquired a definite glow.

No one had ever mentioned that as an outcome of indulging in love-making, but given the time and her need to appear at the breakfast table, there'd been little she'd been able to do to disguise the effect.

Tempted by the aromas, she crossed to the sideboard and realized she was unusually hungry. She collected a small serving from beneath several of the domed dishes, then turned to the table and claimed her usual place on her grandmother's left.

She beamed her thanks at Higginbotham as he filled her teacup, then endeavoring to ignore the way her grandmother was looking back and forth between her and Martin, seated opposite her and looking as unruf-flably handsome as ever, she met Martin's eyes.

After a second, he lightly arched his brows, and she recalled their plan. She glanced at Higginbotham and requested a pot of hot chocolate. Once the butler had left the room, she turned to her grandmother. "Grand-mama, Martin has offered for my hand, and I've accepted."

Her grandmother's eyes met hers and widened in immediate and transparent comprehension, then the old lady swung a sharp, shrewd, and rather narrow-eyed look Martin's way.

He met that incisive gaze without flinching, then directed an indulgent smile at Sophy. "Your granddaughter has made me a very happy man."

Her grandmother snorted, then raised her napkin, patted her lips, and somewhat grudgingly admitted, "I can't say I didn't wish for such an outcome, so"—she smiled at Martin, then nodded to Sophy—"you are both to be commended for having such excellent sense."

Higginbotham hurried in with the hot chocolate, and at his mistress's direction, poured cups for both Sophy and herself.

Then her grandmother raised her cup and, with a wicked gleam in her eye, said, "Let's drink to your engagement and, of course, to the wedding that will follow."

Higginbotham audibly gasped, and a look of hope and expectation bloomed on his face.

Smiling widely, Martin raised his coffee cup and, with a "hear, hear," complied with her ladyship's directive, as did Sophy with her hot chocolate.

But the instant they'd all drunk and her grandmother lowered her cup, Sophy leapt in to say, "However, until we resolve the mysteries presently besetting us, Martin and I would greatly prefer to keep the news within the family."

"Purely until we've seen off these threats." Martin met Lady Bracknell's eyes. "Aside from discussions of engagement balls and weddings being an unnecessary distraction at the moment, we would rather not advertise the nature of our connection to whoever is responsible for the attacks."

From the corner of his eye, Martin saw Higginbotham all but visibly rein in his excitement. Confident that the message of the need for temporary secrecy had been heard and understood, Martin concentrated on convincing her ladyship. "Further to that, I would greatly prefer Sophy especially"—he flicked an understanding glance her way—"not to feel distracted while deciding the details of announcing and celebrating our news."

As he'd hoped, that consideration weighed with her ladyship, too.

"Indeed." Lady Bracknell turned her gaze on Sophy. "Very wise." She nodded to Sophy. "One needs to be able to give one's complete attention to the details when announcing news such as this. One only does so once, after all, and it doesn't pay to muff it."

Sophy met Martin's gaze, then took another mouthful of chocolate and didn't argue.

"With a view to eliminating the obstacles to announcing our happy news," Martin continued, "perhaps we should discuss exactly how to approach the police. Specifically, how much we need to tell them."

Lady Bracknell blinked back to the here and now and nodded decisively. "You're right. We need to decide how best to keep Sophy's involvement in what went on quiet, or at least as quiet as possible." Her ladyship's gaze hardened. "Quiet enough that it won't ever become widely known."

Martin and Sophy agreed unreservedly, and they knuckled down to work out how to achieve that outcome.

It was midmorning when, with Lady Bracknell on his arm, Martin walked into the main police station in Sheffield.

The tiled foyer was a noisy place, with various miscreants seated on benches against the walls and constables striding in and out through the heavy wood-and-glass doors.

After a quick glance around, Martin led her ladyship straight ahead, directly to a raised counter set against the foyer's rear wall.

The sergeant on duty behind the desk glanced idly at them as they approached. His gaze passed over them, and he blinked and quickly straightened. "Ma'am." He nodded respectfully to Lady Bracknell, then transferred his gaze to Martin. "Sir. How can we help you?"

As they'd agreed, Martin replied, "I have information regarding a kidnapping in the area."

In a firm voice, Lady Bracknell added, "My good friend Sir Hubert Swale, who, I believe, is your chief commissioner, always told me that should I ever have need to call on the police force, to ask to see the relevant inspector." She widened her eyes at the sergeant. "Who is that, pray tell? For the case of the kidnapping of a member of an aristocratic family?"

The sergeant's eyes had widened; they widened even more at the mention of the aristocracy.

The speed with which things happened next made Martin glad he'd gone along with her ladyship's wish to use her influence. Within minutes, she and he were escorted upstairs and along a narrow corridor to the rather small office of Inspector Curtin, who, they were assured, was the right man to investigate their case.

Curtin proved to be a neat, rather dapper individual. As they entered, he rose from his chair behind a desk playing host to two towering piles of brown cardboard files, stacked at either end of the blotter. The inspector greeted Lady Bracknell with appropriate deference, but no fawning, then nodded respectfully to Martin. "Sir."

Martin read the question in Curtin's eyes. "My name is Martin Cynster. I've been in Sheffield for the past several weeks, looking into investing in Carmichael Steelworks."

Curtin blinked, then inclined his head. "I see." He waved them to the pair of armchairs that had been hurriedly ferried into his office. Once they sat, Curtin resumed his seat, folded his hands on his unencumbered blotter, and leaned forward, reminding Martin of a hound in expectation of catching a scent. “The sergeant mentioned a kidnapping.” With poorly concealed eagerness, Curtin looked from Martin to Lady Bracknell and back again. “Who has been kidnapped?”

“Was kidnapped,” Martin corrected. “And it was me.”

Curtin’s eyes flew wide, suggesting he had, indeed, recognized the Cynster name.

“I managed to escape,” Martin continued, “and as I’ve now learned the identity of those responsible, I wish to lay charges.”

“Indeed.” Without taking his eyes from Martin, Curtin retrieved a small notebook and pencil from a drawer. “Where and when did this kidnapping take place?”

“Yesterday, midmorning. I was visiting Mistymoor Manor, which is owned by my fiancée, and she and I were strolling in the shrubbery when I was coshed unconscious, and we were seized and removed to an old shepherd’s hut on the moors.”

“Good Lord.” Curtin looked down at his notebook and started scribbling.

Martin saw Curtin fleetingly raise his gaze to Lady Bracknell. No doubt the man was putting two and two together regarding the identity of Martin’s fiancée. They’d accepted that as unavoidable, but there was more than one way to achieve their desired goal.

Curtin looked at Martin. “Who was it who coshed and seized you? Did you see them?”

“Not at that time, but my fiancée did, and I did later, when we escaped. There were two of them, lower-level thugs for hire, it seems.” He rattled off the descriptions he and Sophy had agreed were accurate for the pair. “Once they had us secured in the hut, we were visited by the man they work for, who presented a document he demanded my fiancée sign. We’ve subsequently identified that third, more senior man as one Vincent Murchison.”

Curtin’s expression brightened. “Vince?” Then the implication of what Martin was going to bring about dawned, and Curtin smiled in wolfish anticipation. “You interest me greatly, sir. We would be exceedingly glad to be able to convict Vince Murchison on a charge of kidnapping and get him out of our hair.”

“Excellent.” Martin leaned back. “However, our interest—mine, my fiancée’s, and by extension, Lady Bracknell’s—is in identifying the man who hired Murchison. You see, while he was discussing the terms of our incarceration, Murchison let slip that he and his thugs were also responsible for a series of accidents that, of late, has plagued Carmichael Steelworks. Several of those accidents came close to being lethal. In addition, as part of their campaign, Murchison and his men were responsible for arranging for a dray from the Atlas Works to dump its load of pig iron on one of Sheffield's busiest streets. That accident, too, could have had very serious consequences."

"Great heavens!" Curtin scribbled busily. "With your descriptions of the kidnappers and knowing that their gaffer is Murchison, it's easy to identify the pair as his favorite bully-boys."

When Curtin glanced up, Martin caught and held his gaze. "While we now know Murchison and his men were responsible for all the aforementioned crimes, they are merely the hired help. The ultimate villain behind all these actions—the accidents, the kidnapping, and also a separate but connected attempt at blackmail—is the man who hired Murchison."

Slowly, Curtin nodded. "Do you have any clue as to the identity of this man?"

"He's been seen around town," Martin replied, "but no one we've yet spoken to has been able to give us his name." All of which was true; they didn't want to beard Edward, not until they knew who the mystery man was and could judge how involved Edward might be in his scheme.

Curtin narrowed his eyes. "The obvious way to learn who hired Murchison is to get Vince to tell us."

Martin inclined his head. "Indeed. And given the seriousness of the attacks on the steelworks, recently extending to the Atlas Works as well, we're sure you understand how vital it is to identify that man and, ultimately, put an end to his game."

"Of course," Curtin agreed. "This is Sheffield. We take protecting our industries very seriously."

Lady Bracknell nodded. "Just so. Now, Inspector, I am here to ensure that the name of Mr. Cynster's fiancée remains unconnected to all police proceedings. It's my considered opinion, and that of the lady in question and her family and of Mr. Cynster and his family, that as Mr. Cynster was kidnapped and is willing to bring charges, identifying the lady in question is neither here nor there. It would advance your and the police's cause not one whit and would only generate a degree of sensationalism that I'm sure the mayor and aldermen of the town would much rather avoid."

Curtin dipped his head. "Indeed, your ladyship. On that point, I am in complete agreement with you and Mr. Cynster." He looked at Martin. "If you're willing to lay charges against Murchison, we'll be only too happy to haul him in, and during our interrogation, we'll do our best to induce him to name the man who hired him." The inspector huffed. "Truth to tell, I doubt that will be difficult. Given the right incentive, curs like Murchison are invariably only too ready to turn and bite the hand that's fed them."

Martin smiled; it seemed the inspector was on their side.

"Now, if you will both remain here"—Curtin pushed to his feet—"I'll send some of my men to haul Vince Murchison and his two favorites in, and we'll see what we can wring from them."

Lady Bracknell inclined her head regally.

Martin met Curtin's eyes. "I would like to be present during the interviews. Aside from anything else, I suspect seeing me will cause all three men no small degree of consternation, which you might find useful."

Curtin grinned at the prospect. "I've no objection to you joining me."

"Also," Martin continued, "I've a friend who's been assisting us in dealing with the accidents and trying to learn our mystery man's name. I'd like to invite him—Mr. Oliver Coulter—to join us when we speak with Murchison and his thugs. In such situations, I've generally found that having an extra pair of observant eyes and another shrewd brain is an advantage. Oliver knows the facts of this case as well as I do. He might see something you and I miss."

Curtin hesitated for only a second, then dipped his head in agreement. "Where is Mr. Coulter at present? Can he be easily summoned here?"

Oliver and Charlie had arrived at Lady Bracknell's house just as she and Martin had been about to set off. The pair had volunteered to wait there with Sophy.

Martin gave Curtin the St. James' Street address.

The inspector nodded. "I'll send a constable to fetch the gentleman. Now, if you'll excuse me"—his eyes lit with anticipation—"I'll arrange for Murchison and his boys to be brought in."

Curtin went.

Lady Bracknell arched her brows at Martin. "That went better than I'd hoped."

"Indeed." He glanced at the doorway through which Curtin had gone. "Now, we wait and see."

CHAPTER 13

By the time Curtin returned with the news that Vince Murchison and his two bully-boys were in interview rooms in the basement, Oliver—thrilled to have the chance to sit in on the interrogations—had arrived and joined Martin and Lady Bracknell.

Curtin had had the presence of mind to order a tea tray for her ladyship, and when Martin and Oliver rose, ready to sally forth with the inspector, she waved them on. "Go, go! I'll be perfectly comfortable here."

With Oliver beside him, Martin followed Curtin out of the room, along the corridor, and down several flights of stairs.

"Might I suggest," Martin said, descending in Curtin's wake, "that we start with Murchison's men and see what we can get from them before we confront the man himself?"

"Agreed." Curtin stepped off the last stair and halted.

Martin and Oliver joined him and found themselves at the end of a long corridor with doors on both sides. Two policemen stood with their backs to the wall between the nearer three doors on the left.

Curtin had brought three files with him, each at least half an inch thick. He glanced at them briefly and shuffled them, then looked at Martin and Oliver. "They're in the nearest rooms. Why don't we start with the youngest?" Curtin consulted the uppermost file. "Eddie McBain. He's nervy and will be the easiest to rattle. He's in the first room. Our second thug is John Little, locally known as Little John. He's older and wiser—we might not get much from him." Curtin shut the files. "Murchison's in the third room along."

The inspector's lips lifted in a feral smile. "Ready?"

Martin nodded toward the relevant doors. "Lead on."

Curtin marched to the first door, opened it, and walked through. Martin was about to follow, but just before the doorway, a thought struck, and he halted, then waved at Oliver to precede him. When Oliver quirked a brow his way, Martin whispered, "He'll recognize me and, with any luck, will give himself away."

Oliver's "Ah" of understanding was soundless, and he strolled on, into the room.

Martin waited two heartbeats, then silently followed. He paused in the doorway and looked at the thug perched on a stool on the other side of a bare wooden table. Sophy had labeled him wiry, and he was certainly that. His shackled hands were clasped on the table, his fingers nervously gripping, shifting, and gripping again. No doubt his feet were shackled as well; they shuffled and clinked as he shifted on the stool.

Eddie McBain was thoroughly unnerved, his gaze darting between Curtin, who had claimed the middle chair of the three arrayed on the nearer side of the desk and set his files on the table before him, and Oliver, who was subsiding into the chair on Curtin's left.

"Now then, Eddie," Curtin commenced. "I'm Inspector Curtin, and these gentlemen are assisting me in this matter."

Martin saw the moment Eddie registered that there was an empty chair and a gentleman yet to arrive. Eddie's gaze streaked to the doorway, and he saw Martin, who took that as his cue to slowly walk in and, equally slowly and deliberately, shut the door, all the while keeping his gaze on Eddie's face.

Eddie blanched. His eyes huge, he froze.

For a moment, Martin wondered if the man would faint.

Curtin had been watching Eddie closely and, almost as if they'd rehearsed the moment, acidly remarked, "Indeed. I believe you and Mr. Cynster are already acquainted, Eddie."

Eddie swallowed, then a hint of color returned to his pasty cheeks and, as Martin drew back the chair on Curtin's right and elegantly sat, Eddie raised his shackled hands and pointed at Martin. "Here! He knocked me out, he did."

"Really?" Curtin sounded interested and potentially sympathetic. "When was that?"

"When we was up on the moors at that shepherd's hut…" Eddie trailed off as his brain caught up with his tongue, and he looked at Curtin as if only then realizing the man was a fox and he was a rabbit.

Curtin's smile was all edges, but he nodded encouragingly. "The hut on the moors in which you and your friend had incarcerated Mr. Cynster after coshing him unconscious and kidnapping him from the gardens of Mistymoor Manor. Indeed. So what can you tell us about that, Eddie? Why were you there?"

"I…" Eddie was thoroughly rattled. He continued to stare at Curtin. When the inspector waited with apparently limitless patience, Eddie licked his lips and said, "Well, it were my job, see?"

"In what way?" Curtin inquired. "Who hired you?"

"The gaffer, o'course." When Curtin again waited, Eddie burst out, "Vince. You know I work for Vince Murchison."

"We knew that, yes, but you might have taken a job with someone else." Curtin jotted a note. "We just need to be sure of our facts, and now, we are."

Martin sat back and admired the inspector's style. The man was demonstrably good at this. There was little doubt he'd earned his rank. With Oliver and, even more distractingly, Martin flanking him, Curtin likely appeared to Eddie as the lesser of three largely unknown evils.

Eddie was eying Martin with increasing wariness. "And for the record, like, it wasn't me who coshed the gentleman. I just helped… manage things."

"Hmm." Curtin continued to write in Eddie's file. "And got knocked out for your pains and, later, no doubt hauled over the coals by Vince, and now arrested." Curtin paused in his scribbling and looked squarely at Eddie. "How do you feel about that, Eddie?"

Curtin had pegged Eddie's intelligence correctly. His gaze on the table, Eddie frowned in thought, then offered, "Not good." He slumped on the stool and, voice lower, grumbled, "I wish Vince had never taken the job."

Curtin nodded. "That would, indeed, have been the wiser course. Who did Vince take this job from?"

Looking glum and dismal, Eddie shook his head. "Don't know. Never saw the geezer."

"Were the accidents at the steelworks part of the same job?" Oliver asked.

Without looking up, Eddie nodded. "Aye. We was to find things to make go wrong—things that would create problems and"—his voice lowered to a whisper, and he hunched on the stool—"possibly even hurt some of the workers."

Curtin's tone turned cool and disapproving. "In this town, attacking a steelworks and steelworkers is regarded as a very serious crime, Eddie."

Gloomily, Eddie nodded. "I know. Didn't sit right with me at the time but…" He shrugged. "Job's a job, you know?"

"Did Vince ever help stage the accidents?" Martin asked.

"Nah, not him. Just me and…me mate. Both of us've crewed at one or other of the works before, so we knew what to do. Vince just told us to make it look good, like what happened might have been an accident."

Curtin had been diligently writing. Now he put in a last period, looked at Martin, then glanced at Oliver. "Any further questions for Eddie here?"

Martin shook his head, and Oliver murmured, "I can't think of anything worthwhile."

"Right." Curtin closed his file and looked at Eddie. "I'm going to send you to the cells. What exactly you'll be charged with"—he slid a glance at Martin—"I can't yet say, but you'll hear soon enough."

Eddie made a defeated sound and slumped even lower.

Martin pushed back his chair, rose, and followed Curtin from the room.

The three of them gathered in the corridor. Curtin sent one of the constables to escort Eddie to a cell, then turned to Martin and Oliver and, rather eagerly, met their eyes. "Let's do that again—enter in that way. We're going to need all the edge we can muster with Little."

They duly entered the second of the interview rooms as they had the first. When Martin paused in the doorway, he instantly agreed with Curtin's assessment.

Previously, Martin had seen Little only from above, then after he'd rendered the man unconscious. Aside from being nearly twice Eddie's width, John Little was a much harder, more experienced bruiser, altogether a different prospect. A heavyweight accustomed to using his fists, he had a degree of intelligence, too, and his expression remained impassive as he watched Curtin and Oliver. Although perched on a stool, hands and legs shackled as Eddie's had been, Little was sitting bolt upright, apparently relaxed yet alert, tense, and ready to defend himself. He stared unyieldingly at Curtin as the inspector and Oliver settled in their chairs, and Curtin introduced himself and his assisting gentlemen.

As Eddie had, Little realized one man was missing, and his gaze shot to the doorway.

He had better control over his reactions than Eddie, but expecting that, Martin smiled tauntingly, and Little couldn't stop his snarl. He half rose, but then saw Curtin watching, waiting expectantly, and forced himself to sink back to the stool.

Deliberately projecting an insufferable degree of arrogant assurance, Martin sauntered forward to claim the final chair.

As entirely unperturbed, he sat and elegantly crossed his legs, Little, unable to help himself, spat, "You!"

Faintly smiling, Martin met Little's narrowed eyes.

Little studied him. There was a hint of grudging respect in Little's gaze as he growled, "You was supposed to be a namby-pamby gentleman from London. Not the sort to leap off a roof onto a man and hit him in the head like a pile driver."

Martin arched a brow. "Your—and your master's—mistake."

"Aye, this caper was a mistake, all right." Little transferred his gaze to Curtin. "So get on with it already. The sooner you ask your questions, the sooner I can get my nap."

Curtin smiled, oozing calm confidence. "We already know that you were the one who coshed Mr. Cynster and that you are partly responsible for the accidents that have recently plagued Carmichael Steelworks. We have reliable and solid identification and testimony on both counts." Curtin waited while that sank in.

Little hunched over his clasped hands, and his frown, now directed at the table, deepened.

"We know," Curtin continued, his tone almost gentle, "that in doing those things, you were, as usual, working for Vince Murchison."

Little looked up and scowled. "Who told you that?"

"Come now, Johnny. Half of Sheffield knows that."

Little grumbled and looked at his hands, now curled into fists.

After a moment, Curtin continued, his tone more definite, "We also know that Vince—again, as usual—was working for someone else. He and, therefore, you were following someone else's orders."

Little didn't deny that. From beneath his lowered brows, he looked at Curtin, clearly unsure where the inspector was leading him.

Smoothly, Martin said, "We're really not that interested in you, your friend, or even Murchison, John. We're much more interested in learning the identity of the man who hired Vince and, through him, you."

Curtin nodded and, when Little looked back at him, said, "So what can you tell us about that man, Johnny?"

Little glanced again at Martin, then shot a look at Oliver before returning his gaze to Curtin. "I'm for this, aren't I?"

Slowly, Curtin nodded. "'Fraid so. You've stirred up a hornet's nest this time, and you aren't going to escape being stung."

Little pulled a face, then with a hint of shrewdness in his eyes, looked at Martin. "If I tell what I know…?" He grimaced. "It isn't much, but… what then?"

"Then," Curtin said, "if Mr. Cynster is so inclined, we can arrange for your sentence to be transportation rather than the noose. Those accidents were bad enough, especially in this town, but the kidnapping?" Curtin shook his head. "There's no escaping paying a price for that."

Little grimaced again, stared at the table for several moments, then nodded to himself and looked at Martin. "I'll tell what I know, but it doesn't amount to much."

"So you said." Martin met Little's gaze levelly. "And as I said, I'm more interested in that man than I am in you, so any piece of information, no matter how small, might be valuable."

"Well, then. I only saw him the once, the first time Vince met him. It was me and Vince and him and his guard. His guard was like me. He'd spent time in the ring, but he wasn't the chatty sort." Little paused as if remembering. "Real cold one, that, and his master mighta been worse. Didn't get much from either man to judge, if you know what I mean. No little smiles, nothing in their faces to show what they were thinking. No tells."

Little looked at Martin. "Anyhow, him in charge was oldish—fifty-something. His face was…craggy. Hard and…well, like cut from a rock. His eyes made you shiver. They were palest-green chips of frozen ice. He had silver-gray hair, pomaded and all, and was very well turned out. His gloves were kid, his top hat real silk, and his overcoat was the best I've seen in an age. Softest wool, it looked, and perfectly cut. London without a doubt.

"The thing is, though"—Little looked at Oliver, studying him for several seconds, then returned his gaze to Martin—"the man looked like a toff. He spoke like a toff, quiet-like and clear in his speech. Never raised his voice. But it was all an act, see. You just knew it was. He wasn't like you two—you're real toffs. You carry that like a cloak that never ever slips. It can't slip because it's who you really are. He, though...I pegged him as a vicious streetfighter-type posing as a toff."

Little paused, clearly thinking back to that meeting, then shook his head regretfully. "After the man explained what he wanted done and, silly beggar, Vince agreed and the pair left, I told Vince—begged him—to go after the geezer and return his down payment." Little heaved a huge sigh. "But Vince wouldn't, would he? And look where it's got us."

After a moment of contemplating that, Little looked at Martin. "That's all I've got. Enough?"

Martin studied the man, then nodded. "How's your head?"

Little huffed. "Probably about the same as yours."

"I figure that makes us even, then." Martin pushed back his chair. "Depending on what we get from Vince, I might see my way to dropping the kidnapping charges." That would greatly reduce the possible threat to Sophy's reputation. "The charges relating to the accidents will, however, remain."

Little considered that, then dipped his head. "Fair enough."

"One last thing," Curtin said. "Do you know where this toff-who-isn't-a-toff is putting up?"

Little shook his head. "Nah, sorry. Vince caught up to him on the street, and they met at Vince's place, not the other way about."

Curtin shut Little's file. "Never mind. With that description, we should be able to hunt him down." He rose and nodded to Little. "I'll have you taken to a cell. You'll learn what charges you'll face later."

With Oliver trailing him, Curtin followed Martin from the room.

Martin halted in the corridor. While Curtin gave orders for Little to be transferred to a cell, Martin said to Oliver, who had halted beside him, "That was the best description we've yet got of our man. And if Little is correct—and it's likely he is—and our mystery man is not actually the gentleman he pretends to be, that would explain why no one in Sheffield seems to know who he is."

Oliver nodded. "He wouldn't move in the circles in which we've been making our inquiries."

Curtin joined them in time to hear that. "Given Sheffield is not his home turf, it's likely he's lying low, although other than the Murchisons, there's no underworld figure of any note he'd need to be wary of." Curtin frowned. "But as he's dealing with the Murchisons, I can't see why he'd be hiding from them."

Martin shrugged. "He could simply be one of those villains who prefers to operate from the shadows."

Curtin tipped his head. "True." He juggled his files, then looked at the next closed door. "Shall we?"

"Same entrance?" Oliver asked as they approached the door. He glanced at Martin. "Did Vince see you when you were laid out?"

Martin nodded. "He did, indeed, and I saw him as well."

"Excellent." Curtin reached for the bolt that secured the door. "Let's see what we can drag from young Vince."

Curtin went in. Oliver grinned at Martin and followed.

Martin waited until he heard Curtin introducing himself and his "gentlemen assisting," then stepped into the open doorway.

Vince saw him immediately. He froze for a second, and his arrogantly cocky expression faded. A certain wariness seeped into his features as Martin closed the door, walked forward, and with a flat and unfriendly gaze directed at Vince, claimed the chair on Curtin's right.

"Now, then." Curtin gestured at Martin. "I'm sure you recognize this gentleman."

Vince fixed his gaze on Curtin's face. "Never saw him before in my life."

Curtin huffed a laugh. "Come now, Vince."

"No. I mean it." Vince shifted his gaze to Martin and narrowed his eyes. "And he can't tell you any different."

Martin quirked a brow and, with languid superiority, retorted, "Can't I?"

"No, you can't!" Vince leaned across the table. "You were unconscious the whole t—" He broke off.

"Too late." Martin smiled. "If it's any consolation, I was, in fact, conscious. I just didn't want you to know that."

"Consequently," Curtin rolled on, "you will be charged with ordering the abduction of Mr. Cynster here, a member of a major aristocratic family." Curtin looked up and met Vince's widening-in-horror eyes and nodded. "Ducal dynasty, as a matter of fact."

"I didn't know that! I was told he was just some London gentleman who was sweet on Miss Carmichael, and if we happened to grab him as well as her—" With a visible effort, Vince swallowed the rest of his panicked words. He hauled in a deep breath, then sat back and folded his arms across his chest. "I'm not saying anything more."

He pressed his lips tight as if to ensure that.

Unperturbed, Curtin smiled. "That's all right. We don't need anything more from you, at least not in terms of defining the charges to be laid at your door. Where was I? Ah, yes. You will be charged with abducting Mr. Cynster, and as he is here, ready to bear witness, our case is cut and dried."

Vince's unlovely features worked, then he blurted, "You won't charge me." He glanced at Martin, and Vince's expression turned sly. "You won't want it known there was a lady involved, and if I have to cop to grabbing you, I'll tell the judge and all in the courtroom about her, too. Lovely piece, she was. Pity to besmirch her reputation an' all, but if you're set on trying me…" Vince shrugged. "Well, all I can say is it won't be my fault if she gets ruined in the process."

Martin leaned his arms on the table and lowered his head so his eyes were level with Vince's. "If you wish to see the inside of any courtroom," he said, his voice low, quiet, his tone utterly deadly, "I suggest you forget you ever laid eyes on my fiancée."

Trapped by Martin's gaze, unable to look away, Vince blinked, several times.

Martin sat back and smoothly went on, "However, what whoever it was who put that idea into your head failed to mention is that as my fiancée was with *me* the entire time—and your own men will testify to that—there is no scandal to be avoided. All you mentioning her will achieve is to guarantee you a trip to the gallows for abducting a high-born lady."

Vince swallowed. Even when Martin glanced at Curtin, Vince couldn't seem to shift his gaze, transfixed by the lethal menace Martin had exuded.

Curtin met Martin's eyes and, after successfully fighting back a grin, turned his head to gaze levelly at Vince. "As it happens, Vince, we're very much interested in identifying and having a little chat with the man who gave you your orders, both with regard to the accidents at Carmichael Steelworks and also the kidnapping of those you and your men so unwisely seized." Curtin glanced at the file open before him. "And I believe there's a matter of IOUs being used as blackmail to induce a well-born member of Sheffield society to commit a criminal deed, although I believe we've enough to be going on with in terms of charges. So"—with Martin having leaned back, Curtin had succeeded in reclaiming Vince's attention—"let's get down to the nuts and bolts, shall we? I'm in a position to lighten your charges if you can give us solid information about the man who hired you."

Oliver added, "We already have a detailed description. We wish to learn the man's name and where he can be found."

His gaze on Vince, Curtin nodded. "You must know both."

Vince stared, blinked, and stared some more as his expression grew bleaker and bleaker.

Puzzled, Curtin arched a brow. "Come now, Vince. That's not such a great thing to ask."

When, plainly torn, Vince still hesitated, Martin said, "By giving you the orders he did, this man has used you and your men in a very dangerous game. Dangerous to you and your men as much as to anyone else. It was a hugely risky campaign, but as it was you and your men who would get caught, the man who hired you had little to lose—unless you tell us his name. That will take the weight of the charges off you and your men and lay that weight where it correctly belongs—on him."

"So," Curtin gently prompted, "who was it, Vince?"

Oliver added, "All you need to do is tell us his name."

Vince opened his mouth, then forced it shut again. He looked at the three of them, then shook his head. "You don't understand. I would if I could, but I daren't."

Curtin sighed and settled to reassure Vince that there was no reason to fear any repercussions if he told them the man's name. "We'll have him in the cells quick as a wink. You just need to tell us who he is."

Vince laughed hollowly. "See?" He appealed to Martin and Oliver. "That's it—the thing you don't understand about this geezer. He's well known, he is, even to the likes of us up here, and the stories about what happens to anyone who goes against him…" Vince shuddered, and there was no question that he was genuinely terrified.

After a second, his expression hardened. "I can't say my piece against him if I'm dead—dead in some horrible way—and there's no use you telling me that you and the boys here"—with his shackled hands, Vince gestured around them—"will keep me safe. Not from the likes of him. The law's never been able to catch him for anything, not even in London and with Bow Street on the case."

Vince paused to draw breath, then slowly, stubbornly, shook his head. "No. I can't do it. I can't tell you who he is."

From that position, he wouldn't be swayed.

Eventually, Curtin sat back, studied Vince, then sighed in resignation.

"In that case, I'll have to invite your brother in and see what he has to say."

The suggestion galvanized Vince. "No, no!" Then he swallowed and lowered his panicked voice. "This wasn't a job I did for Walter. He doesn't know anything about me taking it."

Curtin stared at Vince, then said, "Pull the other one, Vince. There's no way a villainous cove from London came up to Sheffield looking to hire muscle and came straight to you. The only person our villain would have known to ask for is Walter."

Vince deflated and hung his head. "He did, all right? He came up and talked to Walter, and Walter decided the job wasn't for us. Going soft, Walter is. I mean, at that point, all the man was asking for was a little help setting up a few accidents at the works. Nothing me and the boys couldn't handle, but Walter said to leave it. He wasn't interested, so…I decided to strike out on my own. I followed the man, and he came back to my office and heard me out and gave me the job." His head hanging even lower, Vince mumbled, "I should've listened to Walter."

Puzzled, Curtin asked, "What did Walter say? What reason did he give for turning down the job?"

Vince gave a half-hearted shrug. "He told the geezer that he was shorthanded at the moment and couldn't accommodate him with anyone suitable, meaning men up to the task. All polite and respectful-like. The geezer didn't like being turned down—anyone could see that—but he accepted it and left. Once he had, I asked Walter what he was up to, and he said he wasn't comfortable dealing with villains of that sort. Too risky, he said." Vince grimaced. "I should've listened to him."

Unable to do anything other than agree, Martin rose, as did Curtin and Oliver, and the three of them left the room. Once in the corridor, Curtin waved them toward the stairs, leaving the two constables to escort Vince to the cell they had waiting for him.

Halting at the foot of the stairs, Curtin turned to Martin. "I have to say, I don't like this. For Vince to refuse to save his own hide out of fear of this man is worrying enough, but for Walter to refuse to deal with the man at all is another thing altogether."

Oliver slid his hands into his pockets. "I take it Murchison Senior is the sort whose opinion of a villain is likely to be sound."

Curtin nodded. "Walter's been the king of the Sheffield underworld for decades."

"So," Martin said, "an experienced villain."

"Indeed." Grimly, Curtin shook his head. "Whoever this man is, he's not the sort we want around here."

Martin exchanged a glance with Oliver, then ventured, "The most important fact we need to learn is the name of this not-a-gentleman villain. It seems the only clear path left to us is to have a chat with Murchison Senior regarding the man he declined to deal with and hope he'll divulge the name."

"Hmm." Curtin narrowed his eyes in thought. "Perhaps if we dangle the carrot that if Walter cooperates, we'll drop the kidnapping charge against his brother." He angled a questioning glance at Martin.

Martin nodded decisively. "The charges relating to the steelworks' accidents are more than enough to send Vince and his boys off to the colonies. The kidnapping? In the end, it didn't cause any lasting harm so…" He shrugged. "Yes. In return for the name of the man behind the many threats against the steelworks—the reason for which we still don't know—I'll agree to withdraw the kidnapping charge."

"Good." Curtin turned and led the way up the stairs. "Walter and Vince have always been close. Playing on Walter's protectiveness is definitely worth the attempt. Aside from all else, he can't be relishing the notion of having a bigger shark swimming in what, until now, has been his pond."

They reached the ground floor, and Curtin paused to say, "If you'll wait in my office and keep her ladyship company, I'll organize to have a couple of the lads bring Walter in for a quiet chat."

Martin and Oliver agreed and continued up the stairs.

Apparently, the Murchison abode was somewhere close. Martin and Oliver had only just finished describing all that had transpired downstairs to a hugely curious Lady Bracknell when Curtin strode up and paused in the open doorway to his office.

"Sorry," he said with an apologetic smile. "I got waylaid. But we're in luck. Walter was at home, and when my men told him Vince was in the cells, he agreed to come in without fuss."

Curtin stepped back, and Martin and Oliver, after making half bows to her ladyship and being impatiently waved off, joined him in the corridor.

As they strode once more for the stairs, Curtin volunteered, "The men who fetched Walter told me he seemed puzzled. He asked them what Vince had been taken up for, not that they told him, of course."

"That fits with Vince's story that Walter didn't know about Vince taking the job," Oliver said.

"Hmm. I'm just not sure how Walter not knowing is going to play out," Curtin replied.

They reached the bottom of the stairs, and Martin saw a pair of constables standing with their backs to the corridor wall to either side of the first door along. He slowed and glanced at Curtin. "Walter has no idea who Oliver and I are. In this case, it might be worthwhile for you to introduce us by name."

Curtin thought, then nodded. "That can't hurt." He tipped his head, his gaze on Martin's face. "How much should we tell him about his brother's doings?"

Martin rapidly considered, then replied, "Tell him the whole story. He doesn't sound like the sort who would be silly enough to spread the tale."

"You've got that right." Curtin continued along the corridor. "In terms of intelligence, Walter is a very far cry from Vince."

With a nod to the constables, Curtin opened the door and went in. Oliver followed, and this time, Martin was at his heels.

Walter, it transpired, was also a far cry from Vince in appearance. At least a decade older, in build, Walter was a larger but softer version of Vince, but beyond that and a vague similarity in their features, they seemed very different men. Instead of Vince's clerk-like attire, Walter's well-trimmed hair, good-quality suit, and neat shirt, waistcoat, and collar gave him the air of a respectable merchant, one careful of his pennies but nevertheless accustomed to the better things in life.

Indeed, Walter had the look of a man who had lived a full and varied life, and the experience of those years was etched in his features, presently set in an unreadable expression. His hard brown eyes held a distinct glint of shrewd intelligence, and while his round, rather heavy-jowled face should have been unprepossessing, somehow, it wasn't.

While not in any way striking, Walter Murchison was the sort of man one noticed.

They sat in the three chairs facing Walter, who appeared quite comfortable on the stool opposite.

Walter nodded to Curtin. "Inspector."

Curtin started to nod back, then stopped and, frowning slightly, waved rather curtly at Martin and Oliver. "Mr. Cynster and Mr. Coulter are assisting me in this investigation, the one involving your brother."

Walter recognized both surnames, but beyond a quick blink, showed little other reaction. Politely, he inclined his head to Martin and Oliver, then refocused on Curtin. "I see. And what is it you believe my brother's been up to now?"

Between them, briefly yet comprehensively, they described Vince's recent activities.

As the magnitude of what his younger brother had done became clear, despite Walter's really rather good poker face, Martin saw chagrin, then anger close to fury and, finally, stoic resignation flow behind Walter's agate-like eyes.

Curtin concluded with the charges likely to be laid against Vince and his men.

When, that done, Curtin glanced at Martin, Martin nodded encouragingly, leaving it to Curtin to dangle their carrot; he knew Walter better than Martin did. Sitting back, Martin watched Walter with a sinking heart; he had a feeling their approach wasn't going to work.

Curtin made a good case, playing on what had plainly been Walter's long-standing habit of protecting his younger sibling.

And Walter definitely considered giving them the name they sought.

However, in the end, Walter shook his head. He met first Martin's, then Curtin's eyes. "Understand this"—decision rang clear and firm in Walter's tone—"if I could save Vince without putting others—others even closer to me—at risk, I would. But in this, Vince has made his own bed, against my stated wishes what's more, and given the circumstances, there's nothing I can do for him."

Walter paused, then continued, "It might interest you to know, Inspector, that I've recently decided to…shall we say 'reinvent myself.' As a shopkeeper of sorts, an agent for various importers and exporters. There's money and plenty of it to be made in that endeavor in this town, and I've decided that's to be my new life. My recent meeting with the man in question has only hardened my resolve to no longer play any part in those…circles. To take any hand in that sort of enterprise."

Walter tipped up his chin. "I promised the missus and the bairns I'd make a clean break, and I have." He paused, then in a regretful but firm tone, went on, "Not even for Vince would I put my family at risk." He met Martin's gaze with unflinching candor. "And believe you me, telling you the name you're after would definitely put not just my skin at risk but theirs, too, and I can't—won't—do that."

Martin couldn't argue. Every instinct he possessed was telling him that Walter Murchison was speaking the literal truth.

Walter held his gaze a second longer, then looked at Curtin. "I'm actually sorry I can't oblige, because I truly would like the man we're speaking of to be gone. Anywhere—I really don't care where—but I truly would rather he wasn't looking to move into Sheffield."

Walter arched a brow at Curtin. "Now, if there's nothing else, Inspector, I should be getting on."

Curtin studied Walter, then shook his head. "No. Nothing else." They all rose, and Curtin nodded to Walter. "Thank you for coming in."

Walter blinked, then sighed. "Can't say it was a pleasure, but…" He paused, then said, "If Vince asks if you've spoken with me, tell him I said that he knowingly did this against my wishes and behind my back, and I'm not having him pull me into the briars this time."

Curtin nodded. "If he asks, I'll tell him."

They stood back and allowed Walter to leave first. A surprised constable looked into the room, and Curtin waved him off. "He's free to go. See him out."

The constable looked faintly shocked, but hurried off in Walter's wake. They listened to Walter's heavy footsteps stumping up the stairs, and Curtin whistled through his teeth. "If I didn't like the sound of this man before, I'm truly apprehensive about him now."

Oliver exchanged a weighty look with Martin. "Walter's reaction to our mystery man does not bode well."

"No, indeed." Martin frowned. "So where does what we've gleaned from our local villains leave us? Have we got any farther forward?"

Curtin thought, then huffed. "Well, speaking for the Sheffield Constabulary, I rather think it's been a very good morning. Apparently, we have both Murchisons off the streets. Vince is going far away for a very long time, and Walter is retiring." Curtin brightened. "The police commissioner will turn cartwheels when he hears."

Oliver looked surprised. "Were they really that bad?"

Curtin snorted. "In Walter's heyday, they were a scourge." He paused, then added, "But as we've just seen, that was all down to Walter. When he was giving the orders, they were a formidable crew. Vince, though..."

"Isn't up to it." Martin shoved his hands into his pockets and looked at Oliver. "As far as I can see, despite a solid morning's work, we've still got the same two major questions before us. Who is the mystery man behind the accidents and the attempts to place control of Carmichael Steelworks into Edward Carmichael's hands?"

Oliver nodded. "And our second question is why."

Martin looked at Curtin.

The inspector shook his head. "I'm truly sorry we've got nowhere today, but I'm now as concerned as you are about what this man means to do and why he's chosen Sheffield for his scheme." Curtin met Martin's gaze. "If you have any further ideas on how to learn the answers to those questions, I'll be happy to do whatever's in my power to help."

"Perhaps," Martin said, "given the description Little gave us, you could have your men ask around—quietly—to see if they can find where our mystery man is staying. He must be somewhere in town or close to it, but"—he caught Curtin's eyes—"we don't want to alert him to our interest. Not yet."

Curtin agreed. "I'll put out an order to all the constables on the beat."

"Thank you. If you learn anything, I'll be at Lady Bracknell's house in St. James' Street." Martin looked at Oliver. "We'd better go and fetch her ladyship and return there."

Oliver nodded. "Before someone waiting there loses patience and comes looking for us here."

CHAPTER 14

Sophy was pacing back and forth before the windows in her grandmother's drawing room, keeping an eye on the street, when sounds in the front hall informed her that the delegation that had gone to the police station had returned via the mews.

She whirled to face the drawing room door, expectation leaping in her breast.

From where he was lounging in the armchair opposite Julia, seated on the sofa, Charlie looked up, equally hopeful and eager. He'd arrived with Oliver just after Martin and Sophy's grandmother had departed. When Oliver had been summoned to the police station, Charlie had remained to keep Sophy and Julia—who had arrived shortly after the two men—company. All three of them stared at the door as it opened, and Lady Bracknell swept in.

Sophy took in her grandmother's set and anxious expression, and her heart plummeted.

Martin and Oliver followed her grandmother into the room, and Higginbotham quietly shut the door.

Sophy locked her gaze on Martin's face. "What happened?"

"Well"—her grandmother sank onto the sofa beside Julia—"speaking for myself, I drank a quantity of tea and otherwise waited." Her grandmother looked pointedly at Martin and Oliver.

Martin waved Sophy to the other sofa. "Come, sit, and we'll tell you what little we learned."

Charlie had been studying Oliver's and Martin's faces. "From your expressions, I take it that little wasn't good."

"No." Oliver slumped into the other armchair. "It wasn't, however, the sort of information it would be wise to ignore."

"Indeed." Martin sat beside Sophy. He frowned and murmured, "Where to start?"

"The beginning is usually the best place," her grandmother tartly informed him. To the others, she said, "We spoke to an Inspector Curtin, who proved most helpful. He listened to Martin's tale and immediately set about bringing the thugs in for questioning."

"From our descriptions, Curtin recognized the men who carried out the kidnapping," Martin said. "While Curtin was arranging for Vince Murchison and those men to be brought in, we sent for Oliver."

"I arrived just in time to sit in on the first interview," Oliver said.

"That was with the younger man, Eddie McBain," Martin continued. "He gave himself away by recognizing me, then admitted to kidnapping us under orders from Vince Murchison. Eddie let fall that he and the older thug, John Little, rigged the accidents at the steelworks as well, and that was also under orders from Vince, who in turn had taken his orders from some man Eddie had never met. To Eddie, it was simply a job, as indeed was the case for Little as well. However, Little had been present when Vince met with the man who hired them."

His chin sunk on his chest, Oliver said, "Unfortunately, Little never heard the man's name. He did, however, give us a fairly detailed description." Oliver glanced at Charlie. "Enough to feel certain that Vince's 'gaffer' was the man seen with Edward in the Iron and Steel Club and also by you with Edward at his home."

Frowning, Charlie shook his head. "This gets more and more confusing. What is Edward doing with such a man?"

No one had any answer to offer.

Sophy turned to Martin. "What about Murchison? Did you learn anything from him?"

Martin grimaced. "Not what we wanted to learn. Despite considerable pressure being brought to bear, Vince was too afraid of the man, of his ability to retaliate, to give us the man's name."

Julia looked increasingly concerned. "That doesn't sound at all heartening."

"No, indeed," Martin grimly agreed. "And there was worse to come. Vince's older brother, Walter, had been the mystery man's first choice as his hireling, but Walter declined. Vince admitted that, and in desperation, Curtin brought Walter in. Compared to Vince, Walter is considerably older and infinitely wiser, and despite being a seasoned villain himself, he had no wish whatsoever to be drawn into our mystery man's scheme. Unbeknown to Walter, Vince had gone after the man and offered his services and was hired to do the job." Martin glanced around the faces. "Unfortunately, like Vince, Walter was unwilling to risk the mystery man's wrath by telling us his name."

Oliver grunted. "Not even to save his brother."

Sophy's grandmother leaned back against the sofa cushions and stared at Martin, then at Oliver. "So you're saying that seasoned villains are too frightened of this mystery man to even utter his name?"

Martin nodded. "That's the situation in a nutshell. Curtin will alert his constables and we'll see if, armed with the man's description, they can learn where he's staying, but other than that, we're no closer to identifying him than we were yesterday."

Sophy muttered, "Or the day before that."

The door opened, and Higginbotham entered. "Luncheon, my lady?"

Sophy's grandmother glanced at the clock, then nodded decisively. "An excellent notion, Higginbotham." She pushed to her feet, bringing everyone else to theirs. "We need distraction, and partaking of luncheon will fit the bill nicely."

They filed out in the old lady's wake and were soon seated around the dining table, serving themselves from the platters Higginbotham and the footmen had set out.

While she ate, Sophy monitored the atmosphere around the table; all of them were now sufficiently relaxed with each other to allow their emotions to show. They were cast down, disappointed, even disheartened; all those feelings were there, on display as they commenced the meal, and weighing on them all was the implication of how dangerous their mysterious adversary was.

But gradually, they came about.

The conversation, what there was of it, remained desultory, and all remarks made had to do with their search for the unknown man's name, yet bit by bit, determination rose and strengthened, and focus returned.

Eventually, Martin looked across the table at Oliver. "Correct me if I'm wrong, but at present, the only route open to us to learn the mystery man's name is to ask Edward."

Oliver met Martin's eyes and nodded. "That's the way I see it, too."

As Martin and Oliver had intended, their comments sparked a discussion—a revisiting—of everyone else's view of Edward and his likely involvement with the mystery man and his scheme to place Edward in charge of the steelworks.

Julia trenchantly declared, "Edward won't be involved. He'll know nothing about it, mark my words."

Sophy caught Charlie's eyes, then grimaced. "I'm still of that mind myself." She arched her brows at Charlie. "You?"

Charlie shook his head. "I'm not in Edward's pocket, and I admit I haven't been around much in recent years, but I really can't see him being a party to this." Charlie looked at Martin. "An unwitting stalking horse, as you suggested, absolutely yes. I can easily imagine a clever manipulator—and the chances are our mystery man can wear just such a hat when it suits him—could easily lead Edward to…" Charlie paused, then tipped his head. "Well, I could imagine our mystery man beguiling Edward to the trough, but I still don't think anyone could make him drink—not if drinking wasn't the right thing to do."

Sophy nodded decisively. "I concur. Edward won't be knowingly involved in anything underhanded, much less criminal."

Her grandmother slowly nodded. "The 'knowingly' is key."

Martin and Oliver exchanged a look, then Martin said, "If we accept your reading of Edward's character as correct, then the most straightforward way to learn the mystery man's name is to approach Edward directly, explain the situation, and ask him who the man is." Martin looked around the table. "Is that what you would recommend?"

After several minutes of further discussion, all agreed.

Sophy looked around the faces one last time, then nodded. "So we'll go around to Sycamore Street and talk to Edward. At this hour, he's likely to be at home."

"Indeed." Her grandmother set aside her napkin. "No time like the present, especially as we know so little of what this villainous man intends."

"Not only that." Looking rather grim, Charlie eased back his chair. "It's just occurred to me that the police have hauled in the Murchisons, but given no one's come knocking on the mystery man's door, if he's been keeping an eye on those people in whom he has an interest, he's likely confident that neither Murchison has passed on his name. He'll feel comfortable knowing that both Murchisons appreciate the depths of his villainy and won't cross him." Charlie looked across the table at Martin. "But Edward…"

His expression grim, Martin continued, "Most likely knows nothing of the man's reputation and wouldn't be swayed even if he did."

Charlie went on, "Edward is a weak link in the man's scheme. If the villain feels threatened…"

Eyes widening, Sophy looked from Charlie to Martin. "Good Lord! Do you mean that Edward might be in danger because he can tell us the man's name?"

"Us and the police." Oliver tossed down his napkin and pushed back his chair.

A sense of urgency gripped them all.

Martin rose, and Sophy sprang to her feet.

Her grandmother and Julia, both with determined expressions on their faces, were also rising.

Stumping forward, her grandmother waved toward the door. "Let's go. Into the mews. If we take my traveling carriage, we can all fit, and if anyone's watching either house, they won't see us."

While everyone donned their coats and hats, Sophy's grandmother ordered the carriage readied. When Higginbotham informed them that the conveyance was waiting in the mews, they filed out of the house by the rear door and climbed into the large closed traveling coach.

Sophy snaffled a seat by one window. Her grandmother sat beside her, with Julia on her other side. Martin sat on the rear-facing seat opposite Sophy, with Oliver next to him and Charlie beyond.

Remaining shrouded in the gloom within the vehicle, Sophy scanned the pavements as the carriage rolled sedately through the center of the town, eventually crossing Norfolk Street to reach Surry Street and, finally, Sycamore Street.

Immediately before the corner of Sycamore Street, the carriage drew in to the curb.

Charlie opened the far door and stepped down to the street. He looked back and said, "Keep your eye on the drawing room window. If he's there and the coast is clear, I'll close the curtains."

"We'll be watching," Martin replied.

Charlie shut the door and vanished.

The carriage remained stationary for what seemed an age, but according to Martin's watch, which he consulted at Sophy's request, the period was only their agreed five minutes long. At Martin's nod, Oliver rose and tapped on the flap in the roof, then sat again, and the carriage jerked and rolled on, around the corner.

After some discussion, they'd agreed that they had to assume that the mystery man might be maintaining a watch on Edward's house, so Charlie had volunteered to go in via the mews and the kitchen door. If Edward was at home and alone, Charlie would signal via the drawing room window that faced the street.

They'd explained as much to her grandmother's coachman, and he'd suggested pulling up opposite the house next door. That should, he'd said, give them a decent view of the drawing room window of Edward's house, and when the carriage rocked to a halt, Sophy peered out, and sure enough, she could see the window clearly.

Martin followed her gaze. "It shouldn't take Charlie much longer."

A minute later, she spotted movement in the dimness on the other side of the glass. She sat up. "He's there." She waited, then the curtain was slowly drawn across the glass. "And there's the signal."

Oliver duly rose and tapped the flap in the roof. A second later, the carriage rolled slowly forward and on. The coachman drove around the corner, then down the narrow mews behind the row of well-to-do town houses.

The carriage slowed, then halted, and Charlie hauled open the door to reveal the back gate of Edward's house.

Charlie handed down Julia, then Sophy's grandmother. Oliver and Martin followed. Sophy was the last one out, gripping Martin's hand tightly as he steadied her down the carriage steps.

They hurried to catch up with the others, who were treading the path to the kitchen door. Charlie led them inside, along a short corridor, and into a decent-sized kitchen.

A cook and a maid looked up in surprise.

The cook quickly wiped her hands and hurried forward, bobbing in obeisance. "Your ladyship. Mrs. Canterbury. Miss Carmichael." The buxom woman shot a glance at an inner door that opened to reveal Edward's butler, Calwell, rapidly shrugging on his coat.

He saw them gathered in the kitchen and looked shocked. "Your ladyship! Master Charlie."

Sophy's grandmother waved placatingly. "Yes, yes, Calwell. All most irregular, I know, but we're here to see your master, who we understand is in. Don't worry. We'll see ourselves through."

But Calwell would have none of that. He hurried to escort them along another corridor and held open the green baize-covered door at its end. As they filed past into the front hall, Calwell ventured, "I'll just announce you—"

"No need, Calwell," Charlie said. "M'brother's in the library, and I rather think we'll join him there." More softly, he added, "Where we'll be out of sight of any interested eyes."

"But…" Calwell looked scandalized. "At least…" He appealed to Sophy's grandmother. "Tea, my lady?"

"Perhaps later, Calwell. We'll ring." With that, her grandmother grasped Charlie's arm and swept on down the corridor toward the library.

Julia, Sophy, Oliver, and Martin followed in her wake, leaving Calwell dithering in the front hall.

On reaching the library, Charlie set the door swinging wide and ushered Sophy's grandmother through. As the rest of them followed, with Charlie lingering to shut the door behind them, Edward, who was sitting in a wing chair by the fireplace and reading a book, without dragging his eyes from the page, murmured, "Hmm? What is it, Calwell?"

"Edward!" Her grandmother rapped her cane on the floor; the resulting sound ricocheted about the room.

Edward jerked and looked around, then shot to his feet. "Lady Bracknell! Cousin Julia." His gaze wandered farther. "Sophy?" Confusion writ large in his face, Edward glanced at Martin and Oliver, then looked again and blinked, presumably recognizing them from their previous meeting at his club. Slowly, Edward returned his gaze to Sophy, his expression reflecting surprise and deepening confusion. "What's this about?"

Determinedly, she walked forward, making for one of the two leather-covered sofas. "We have a matter we wish to discuss with you, Edward. And yes, all of us need to be here."

"Indeed." Her grandmother followed and sank onto the second sofa.

"Yes, of course." Obviously entirely at sea, Edward looked from one to the other and weakly waved to the available chairs. "Always pleased to talk about…well, whatever you wish."

He watched Martin and Oliver come forward and nodded rather warily. "Cynster. Coulter."

Nodding back, Martin smiled reassuringly. "Carmichael. We meet again."

As they all chose seats—Julia beside Sophy's grandmother, Martin beside Sophy, and Charlie and Oliver in armchairs—Edward dithered, then nudged the chair he'd been occupying around to face them and slowly, uncertainly, sank into it again.

Sophy leveled her gaze on Edward. "We've had several rather disturbing incidents occur over recent weeks." The others had agreed that she should be the one to commence the litany of all that had occurred. "At first, it was..." Matter-of-factly, she listed the accidents at the steelworks before moving on to Charlie's unexpected involvement, then quickly—before Edward could distract himself by commenting on his younger brother's profligacy—she continued with a step-by-step account of her and Martin's kidnapping, subsequent escape, and retreat to her grandmother's house.

As per their plan, she deliberately omitted their visit to Brumidge's chambers and what they'd learned there, merely mentioning in passing the documents she and Charlie had been pressed to sign.

"After discussing our options at length," she concluded, "we decided to involve the police."

"The police?" Edward looked scandalized. He glanced at Martin and Oliver, then at Sophy's grandmother and Julia. "I say, is that wise? I mean…one doesn't want it bruited about that one might have reason to involve the constabulary."

"In this case," Martin stated, and his tone did not invite argument, "it was our most direct option through which to learn the mystery man's name." He briefly described the police's assistance and who they had interviewed, ending with, "We came away with the clear understanding that the man behind the accidents at the steelworks, the attempt to involve Charlie in those crimes, Sophy's and my kidnapping, and ultimately and most importantly, the efforts to get Charlie and Sophy to sign those documents is a villain so feared by the senior local underworld figures that they will not utter his name, even when the alternative is the hangman's noose."

Edward frowned. "He sounds a most unsavory character."

Martin dipped his head in agreement. "The other piece of information we gleaned from those interviews was a reasonably sound description of the man involved." He caught and held Edward's gaze. "To whit, the man looks to be in his fifties and has a hard-featured, craggy, rough-hewn face and cold, pale-green eyes. He speaks and dresses well, indeed, as a gentleman. He has silver-gray hair, well-tended and pomaded."

Edward's frown started to fade.

Martin continued, "The one identifying feature that was universally noted by everyone who saw him was the style and quality of his black overcoat."

Edward's expression leached to blankness. He stared unseeing at Martin, then swallowed, refocused, and weakly repeated, "Black overcoat?"

Martin nodded. "Just like that worn by the man seen talking in friendly fashion with you in the Iron and Steel Club. The same man Charlie saw being entertained by you here, in this very room."

Edward stared, patently stunned and not wanting to believe. "No." He shook his head. "It can't be he."

Martin studied Edward for a second, then calmly stated, "One other fact you need to know is that those documents that, under this man's orders, Charlie and Sophy were pressured to sign, if signed, would have transferred the voting rights of Charlie's and Sophy's shares in Carmichael Steelworks to the remaining shareholder. We've had a solicitor check over those documents, and if Sophy and Charlie had signed, you, Edward, would have gained effective, complete, and unchallengeable control of Carmichael Steelworks."

"What?" His expression a roiling mix of astonishment, confusion, and disbelief, Edward shook his head. "That makes no sense." He looked at Sophy. "You know I've never had any interest in managing the steelworks."

She nodded. "Yes, I know." She gestured at the others. "We all know that. That's why we're here, trying to figure out what's going on."

Martin continued, "Even if Sophy and Charlie challenged the documents and tried to have them reversed, it would likely take years of going through the courts, and even then, who knows what would have happened?"

Edward continued to shake his head, but now in the manner of someone appalled. "I don't understand. Why would anyone—this man as you say—do such a thing?"

"That," Oliver said, "is what we need to work out, and as it's you he's seeking to involve in his scheme, we're here to learn what you know of it and him."

Edward stared at Oliver, then sought refuge in prim starchiness. "Mr. Coulter." Edward glanced at Martin. "And Mr. Cynster. I know you're both interested in investing in this town, but I confess I fail to understand why you are here, embroiled in what seems to be private family business."

Lady Bracknell made a rude sound, dismissively waving aside the objection, while Julia bent a sternly reproving look on Edward, which only left him even more confused.

Martin calmly informed Edward, "I'm here because Sophy has agreed to marry me, so I'm present in the role of her fiancé."

Sophy's aunt gave a joyful squeak and, beaming, leaned across to grip Sophy's hand.

Leaving Sophy to deal with her aunt, Martin glanced at Oliver and saw his pleased—and rather knowing—smile, alongside Charlie's delighted surprise. "As for Coulter," Martin continued, determined to keep the discussion on track, "he's a friend who has been helping us unravel the facts of this case."

He returned his gaze to Edward. "All that we've discovered has led us here, to you, Edward. We need to know what our mystery man wants with you, and most importantly, we need you to tell us who he is and what you know of his goals."

Edward stared at Martin for several long moments, then rather pompously stated, "I cannot believe you have any of this right. You've confused your mystery man with the gentleman with whom I'm acquainted, that's all."

Martin was beginning to have greater sympathy for Charlie. "Is that so? Then perhaps you could tell us who else fits the description we have and has an interest in underhandedly ensuring control of the steelworks passes to you."

Edward frowned. "I told you. I have no notion of what that's about."

Lady Bracknell snorted. "Give over, Edward. Who the devil is the man you were seen talking to, and what the devil was he talking to you about?" She stared belligerently at Edward, then spread her hands. "If all is as above board as you insist, what have you to fear?"

Her ladyship's jibe touched Edward on the raw. He colored, then lips primmed, turned back to Martin and Sophy. "If you must know, the gentleman I've been speaking with is a wealthy landowner who has many properties all around the country."

"And his name?" Martin asked.

"Blackwell." Edward tipped up his chin and, in a superior manner, stated, "His name is Mr. Cornelius Blackwell."

"Blackwell?" The exclamation burst from Martin's, Oliver's, and Sophy's throats.

It was clearly their turn to be shocked. All three stared at Edward, appalled and utterly aghast.

Their horrified reaction wasn't what Edward had expected. He frowned at them. "Yes."

Charlie's mouth had fallen agape. He snapped it shut, stared at his brother, then softly cursed and asked, "Good Lord, Edward! Don't you know who Cornelius Blackwell is?"

Uncertain, Edward repeated, "He's a landowner. He said he owns properties around London, Birmingham, Manchester, and Nottingham."

"*Slum* properties, Edward. My God!" Charlie shook his head in disgust. "Of all people, I would never have picked you to be happily consorting with the likes of Blackwell."

"Even I know who Cornelius Blackwell is." Sophy crossed her arms and frowned at Edward.

"Well!" her ladyship said. "Neither Julia nor I have the slightest clue, so please, someone, explain."

His tone unusually steely, his gaze condemnatory, Oliver obliged. "Cornelius Blackwell is, technically, a landowner. He owns the largest estates of slum housing in London and in those other cities you mentioned."

Martin elaborated, "Blackwell is known for building what he terms 'houses for workers.' His buildings look good enough when new, but the work is cut-price and shoddy, and the houses—usually row houses cheek by jowl—quickly deteriorate into effective slums, but by then, he's lured workers with families into rental contracts. Most if not all do not understand the detailed clauses in those contracts, but the terms of those leases effectively make them and their families into more or less indentured slaves for the rest of their lives."

"It's the worst sort of usury," Charlie declared.

Edward stared at his brother. "There must be some mistake." But from his tone, even he no longer believed that.

Martin glanced at Oliver. "I assume Blackwell's usual goals explain his interest in making Edward the controlling shareholder of Carmichael Steelworks."

Edward frowned. "What do you mean?"

Martin studied Edward for a moment, then explained, "I suspect Blackwell's move to make you the controlling shareholder is because he believes he can influence you, either to go into business with him or to sell him the steelworks. Either would satisfy him, I expect."

"But…" Edward returned to shaking his head. He looked at Sophy. "I have no interest in running the steelworks. You know I've never harbored the slightest desire to take over the reins."

Sophy nodded. "I know that, but does Blackwell know that?" She, too, studied Edward. "Did Blackwell talk to you about the steelworks? Perhaps ask what you thought of the current management?"

Edward looked decidedly uncomfortable. When Sophy arched her brows and waited—and everyone else also looked at him questioningly—he cleared his throat and managed to get out, "I might have…said something. He might have…misinterpreted and got the wrong idea…"

Resigned, Sophy sighed and filled in, "You took the opportunity of a new listener to fill his ears with how you disapproved of me—a female—running the company. Blackwell took that as meaning you felt you could do a better job, were you in a position to take over."

"But I've never wanted to take over!" Edward looked faintly ill.

Sophy tipped her head, acknowledging that. "But that's not what Blackwell heard. And by way of undermining my standing as current manager of the steelworks, thus paving the way for your takeover, he set about arranging for our string of accidents."

"He would have thought," Martin said, "that if he were to arrange for you, Edward, to assume control of the company—all neatly legal—you would be grateful."

Oliver was nodding. "Grateful enough to hear him out when he made his pitch to buy the steelworks." He glanced at Martin. "Given it's a profitable enterprise, Blackwell might even have allowed the steelworks to continue operation for a few years while he got all his arrangements in place."

"But eventually"—Charlie looked grim as he took up the baton of explaining all to Edward and her ladyship and Julia—"Blackwell would have shut the steelworks and converted the site into his 'houses for workers.' I've seen them in London, in the East End. They're…soul-destroying places. The people live a hand-to-mouth existence while they pay increasingly onerous rents to Blackwell."

"He entices families in with low rents to begin with," Martin said, "then steadily increases the payments until they reach the upper limit of what the family can afford. The families can leave after ten years, but if they do, they leave absolutely penniless and with little prospect of finding other accommodation close to where they work, so many stay simply to have a roof—however leaky—over their heads. But by then, most of the family's income will be paid every week to Blackwell."

Lady Bracknell looked stunned. "And that's what he planned to do with the Carmichael Steelworks' site?"

"Most likely," Oliver replied.

To his credit, Edward appeared genuinely horrified. "But...while I can understand Blackwell thinking that I would welcome the chance to take over the steelworks, why would he think I would sell the place to him to be used in such an...an *unconscionable* way?" Edward stiffened and looked around the circle of faces. "No one who knows me would ever imagine I would countenance the steelworks being replaced by a slum."

Martin hesitated, then voiced a thought that, during their time with Edward, had been solidifying in his mind. "I think the documents were a part of that."

Sophy and Charlie glanced at him. "How so?" Sophy asked.

"I *think*"—Martin emphasized the word to underscore he was hypothesizing—"that Blackwell was counting on you, Edward, leaping at the chance to usurp Sophy and take over the steelworks." Martin held up a hand to still Edward's repeated protest. "I accept that you didn't mean anything of the sort, that Blackwell overextrapolated from your probably unwise rant. However, from Blackwell's point of view, I suspect he believed that, when he presented you with those signed documents that effectively handed you control of the steelworks, you would have leapt to take advantage without properly considering how those documents came to be signed."

"Ah." Oliver nodded. "I see. And that sounds just like Blackwell."

While Charlie's and Sophy's expressions showed they also understood Martin's reasoning, Edward, Lady Bracknell, and Julia remained transparently at sea.

Before her ladyship could demand further elucidation, Martin continued, "As Oliver said, Blackwell is the sort to be patient. He doesn't need to rush and is willing to play a very long game. Most likely, he would have left you running the steelworks for a few years, then turned up with his offer to buy the site. He would have worked on you to accept it, take his money, hand over the keys, and go away. He might even have dabbled in a little sabotage to make selling more attractive to you. Regardless, at some point, he would have pressured you to sell to him. And if you tried to refuse...well, he would already hold in his hands all the necessary facts to blackmail you over the documents you'd needed and relied on to take control of the company."

Edward remained confused. "But I know nothing about those documents! Nothing!"

"But, Edward," Charlie said, "who else would have even thought to have such documents drafted? The only person who stands to gain from having them executed is you."

Arms still crossed, Sophy nodded. "And doubtless the legal firm who did, in fact, draft the documents will be happy to come forward and swear it was you who instructed them to prepare them."

Martin leaned back and, when a thoroughly shocked Edward looked at him, shook his head. "I seriously doubt anyone would believe it wasn't you who had those documents prepared, then hired thugs to force Sophy and Charlie to sign."

Edward paled. In a smaller voice, he said, "But it wasn't me!"

Martin tipped his head. "But Blackwell would have made a cast-iron case that it was."

Lady Bracknell had finally seen the whole picture. "You would have been ruined, Edward, and forced to sell—to Blackwell."

"You really have to admire the man's ability to manipulate others," Oliver said. "No matter which way the situation played out, if you'd ever assumed control of the business, which you could only have done by using those documents, you would eventually have sold to Blackwell, and that's really all he cares about—getting his hands on that site."

Martin concluded, "Blackwell thought he'd found a way to buy a prime site in Sheffield, possibly for a fraction of what it's worth, by exploiting what he mistakenly perceived as your weakness, Edward—namely that you wanted nothing more than to usurp Sophy's position at Carmichael Steelworks."

Martin's summation set Edward bristling.

"This… This…" he spluttered. "My God—this is *appalling*!" His color rose. "I understand what you're saying now, and dash it, Blackwell's played me for a fool! How dare he take it upon himself to act, as it were, in my name?"

His features darkening, Edward abruptly stood. "I'm going to go around right this minute and confront the blighter and tell him what's what!"

Startled, Martin took in Edward's set face, the fury that edged his lips with white, and evenly said, "That might not be the wisest course." When

Edward looked his way, Martin caught his eye. "When you take on a villain of the caliber of Blackwell, it's best to take stock first." He arched a brow at Edward. "What are you going to do about his guards?"

Edward blinked. "He has guards?"

"At least one, and I suspect there'll be more. If you go around breathing fire and brimstone and demanding to see Blackwell, they're likely to get in your way."

Slowly, Edward sank back into his chair. "What, then, should we do?"

Faintly frowning, Martin glanced at Oliver. "That, indeed, is the question."

For a moment, silence reigned, then Lady Bracknell said, "Well, I suggest we talk to Inspector Curtin and see what he and the police commissioner have to say."

Given Edward's disinclination to have anything to do with the constabulary, unsurprisingly, that proposal sparked a vigorous debate.

Martin sat and listened while silently evaluating his own inclinations.

In times past, members of his family would have reacted exactly as Edward wished to. They would have roared around and driven Blackwell off, using whatever means fell to their hands, which, in those days, would likely have included physical retaliation.

In truth, Blackwell was the sort of villain that Martin's father, uncle, and their cousins—indeed, all that generation of the upper aristocracy—wouldn't have hesitated to remove permanently. And everyone involved, including the authorities, would have nodded and deemed that an appropriate and acceptable outcome.

Viewed from the widest perspective, namely that of the ultimate good for all of society, such an outcome might still be considered by many as righteous, yet Martin had a strong suspicion that, in this day and age, the authorities would be very uncomfortable, even antagonistic, should he dispose of Blackwell in such high-handed fashion.

Times had changed.

So had villains.

How one dealt with them had to change as well.

Men like Blackwell grew to be feared by their peers and victims alike precisely because they'd learned to live within the modern system and had discovered how to make it work for them.

These days, dealing with the likes of Cornelius Blackwell required a very different approach.

Although Martin wasn't of his father's generation, he still felt the same overwhelming need to exact retribution from the man who had dared to strike against the woman Martin viewed as his. His to care for, his to protect. Those impulses were ingrained in him; they compelled in a way he could neither deny nor ignore. He had to—had to—retaliate against Blackwell, but the paramount objective that drove him was to eliminate the threat Blackwell posed to Sophy, Carmichael Steelworks, and indeed, Sheffield as a whole.

The town was going to become Martin's permanent home. Obviously, his defense of it was slated to begin immediately.

Luckily, when it came to the way the world now worked, courtesy of his years in America and his subsequent campaign to establish himself in England, he had experience beyond his years to call on. He'd learned how to operate within the current structures, and his personal wealth testified to how successful he'd been in that.

With those considerations circling in his brain, he sat beside Sophy, his arm across the back of the sofa, and coldly and carefully considered their options. In confronting a man like Blackwell, their approach needed to be not hotblooded but coldblooded, with every move calculated and executed with power and precision.

The argument over appealing to the police had grown heated.

With a plan slowly forming in his mind, Martin stirred and, cutting across a pointed exchange between Charlie and Edward, evenly stated, "One thing I've learned over my past twenty years of business dealings is that there is never any point in wishing matters were other than they are."

As Martin had hoped, the somewhat tangential observation drew everyone's attention. Charlie and Edward broke off their fraught argument, while Oliver, Lady Bracknell, and Julia looked at Martin hopefully.

Sophy swiveled to face him. "You've been very quiet. Thinking?"

Soberly, he nodded. "And after considering all the information we currently have, I believe that the only way to successfully deal with a threat of the kind posed by Cornelius Blackwell is, first, to identify exactly what our ultimate goal is and, subsequently, to work toward that single-mindedly while simultaneously searching out and exploiting Blackwell's weaknesses."

Oliver nodded. "That sounds like the sort of plan we need."

Charlie frowned. "What sort of weaknesses would a man like Blackwell have?"

"We'll get to those," Martin said. "But first, let's define exactly what we want to achieve in dealing with him."

"We're not selling him Carmichael Steelworks," Sophy promptly replied, and both her cousins looked equally obdurate.

Martin dipped his head in acknowledgment. "That's understood, but simply taking that stand—essentially refusing Blackwell's offer and telling him to go away—is going to be seen by him as a challenge. He'll react by doing everything in his power to make you bend and sell, and he won't give up. By openly defying him, you'll have made yourself a threat to his rule, one that he will absolutely have to crush. He can't afford not to, can't afford to let you get away with it. His reputation would be badly dented. So what will you do when he retaliates?"

Sophy—and Lady Bracknell, Julia, Edward, and Charlie—looked taken aback, but as his words impinged, their expressions clouded, and they frowned.

Martin lifted his arm from the sofa's back and looked around the circle of faces. "We need to go further. We need to eliminate the threat that Blackwell—through his designs on the steelworks—poses to Sophy, the Carmichael family, the steelworks and all who work there, and ultimately, to Sheffield itself."

No newcomer to such strategic thinking, Oliver nodded. "So how are we to eliminate that threat"—he grinned understandingly at Martin, transparently sharing his inherited proclivities—"other than in the time-honored way?"

Martin dipped his head. "Indeed. In this instance, strength—physical, legal, or even political—won't help us, because Blackwell knows how to either wield his own or circumvent such attacks." He glanced around the frowning faces. "In the areas in which he's established, his influence is extensive. His slum holdings become a hotbed of crime—unsurprising given how pressed those who live there are to make the money to pay his rents—and rumor has it that Blackwell himself gains through those criminal gangs, although that's never been proved."

"Not for want of trying," Oliver observed.

Martin nodded. "In our case, of greater concern are the reports that Blackwell is very good at finding levers to pull to influence officials at all levels of local government. His typical modus operandi is to have several key officials in his pocket, certainly once he becomes a recognized landowner." Martin glanced at Lady Bracknell, who was looking increasingly concerned. "It's unlikely he'll have set down roots in Sheffield as yet. Or so we can hope."

Rather pale, Edward stated, "He's definitely not the sort of 'investor' we need in our town."

Frowning, Julia tentatively offered, "Can we somehow make him no longer want the steelworks?"

Lady Bracknell huffed. "Preferably make him rethink 'investing' in Sheffield at all."

Martin nodded at both ladies. "That, I think, is the right approach, but we need him to make that decision himself. To Blackwell, this is like a chess game. In order to checkmate him and have him accept defeat and go away, we need to be cleverer than he is in moving the pieces on the board."

"You mean," Sophy said, "that we have to...manipulate things so that he decides it's no longer worth his while to pursue purchasing the steelworks?" When Martin and Oliver nodded encouragingly, she focused on Martin. "Do you mean setting up as a workers' landlord ourselves? Thus removing his advantage by acting before he does and satisfying the need he would otherwise prey on?"

Martin blinked. "I hadn't thought of that, but removing the need that allows predators like Blackwell to establish themselves in a community is a thought for later on."

"First," Oliver said, "we need to find a way to persuade Blackwell that buying into Sheffield isn't, after all, for him."

"And much as it might go against our grain, we need to set things up so that he can retreat without losing face." Martin glanced at the others. "With a man like Blackwell, that's important. We don't want to push him into any corner. If we do, he'll dig in, grow more stubborn and aggressive, and fight even harder and with even less conscience. If at all possible, we need to avoid that."

"Persuading Blackwell to leave Sheffield." Edward looked at Lady Bracknell. "Given all we've learned of what he's done, surely your friend the police commissioner and that inspector can drum up a case against him." Edward primmed his lips, then stiffly offered, "In the circumstances, I would be willing to give evidence to identify him."

Lady Bracknell looked at Martin. "I would be happy to return to the police station and see what's possible. I'm sure I speak for all of Sheffield in saying we don't want the likes of Blackwell here, not in any way, shape, or form."

Martin inclined his head. "Be that as it may, no matter that we can all see that Blackwell's our villain, without testimony from the Murchisons, which we won't get, there's no demonstrable link between Blackwell and the accidents, blackmail, or kidnapping. Nothing that would stand up in court. Without the Murchisons' evidence, there's nothing the police can—or indeed, should—do, no matter what we'd prefer. We need to remember what I said before, about men like Blackwell knowing how the authorities work. Direct confrontation, direct opposition, won't get us were we want to go."

Her ladyship huffed. "What you're saying is that we'll get no joy from any of the authorities."

"Not in terms of restraining Blackwell," Oliver replied. "They have no grounds to act against him. He's far too canny for that."

After glancing around at the dejected expressions, Martin said, "Sometimes, in order to counteract men like Blackwell, one needs to be as devious—or rather, more devious—than they."

Charlie brightened. "Is this where Blackwell's weaknesses come in?"

"So to speak," Martin replied.

Charlie's frown returned. "Then I ask again, what weaknesses does Blackwell have?"

Martin leaned back and glanced at Sophy, then at Oliver. "As to that, I think that overcoat of his is a very big clue."

"Oh?" Oliver tipped his head, considering that.

"I have an inkling of a plan." Martin proceeded to describe what he thought might, just might, succeed in persuading Cornelius Blackwell that setting up in Sheffield wouldn't be worth his time.

As he spoke, understanding dawned on the others' faces.

When he reached the end of his current thinking, he looked around again. "Obviously, we'll need to organize and arrange everything down to the very last detail, but…what do you think?"

Enthusiastic suggestions rained down upon him, and together, united in clear and common cause, the company knuckled down to work on their plan to rid Sheffield of Cornelius Blackwell.

CHAPTER 15

Consequent on Oliver being struck by sudden and quite brilliant inspiration as to where they might find some actual hard evidence as to Blackwell's plans, Oliver, Martin, and Lady Bracknell made a covert dash to the Town Hall.

They took Edward's town carriage, leaving Lady Bracknell's traveling coach for the others to use in their equally surreptitious retreat to the house in St. James' Street. Everyone had agreed that her ladyship's house was the best appointed to be their headquarters as they worked to get everything into place for the face-to-face meeting with Cornelius Blackwell that formed the centerpiece of their strategy.

On arriving at the Town Hall, Lady Bracknell swept up to the counter and blithely exerted her influence as a resident of note, and in short order, she, Martin, and Oliver were conducted to a basement room by an obsequious but helpful clerk.

"The property records are in this section." The slender man pointed to a row of metal cabinets lining one wall. He glanced at Martin and Oliver. "What type of property is it, and how far back do you need to search?"

Martin and Oliver exchanged a look, then Oliver replied, "Vacant land or derelict buildings within the town boundaries."

Martin added, "Most likely to the west."

"Last five years?" Oliver cocked a brow at Martin. "He is said to be a long-term planner."

Martin nodded. "Five years should do it."

The clerk huffed, then directed an unctuous smile at her ladyship. "I should be able to help with that. There aren't that many vacant blocks left within the town boundaries, even to the west."

Martin hesitated, then said, "The area we're particularly interested in is bounded by Broad Lane to the north and West Street to the south."

"Ah." The clerk advanced on the cabinets. "That's nicely specific. It shouldn't take long to retrieve the relevant files." He hauled open a cabinet drawer, then paused to ask, "Forward from five years back or from the present going back five years?"

"The latter," Oliver said. "That's likely to be faster."

"Also easier," the clerk mumbled, diving into the drawer. Straightening, he hauled out an armful of files. "You'll need to look through these and see if any fit your bill."

Oliver took the first stack, set the pile on the long table that ran down the room, and started opening and reading the contents of the files.

Martin took the second armful, and Lady Bracknell accepted the third.

The clerk hovered. "I could help if you told me what you're searching for."

Without looking up, Oliver replied, "We can't actually specify well enough, but we'll know when we see it."

They were each on their second stack of files, and the clerk was growing bored, when Martin looked up from the file he'd opened. "This is it." He looked again at the diagram of the parcel of land involved. "Or at least a part of it."

Oliver and Lady Bracknell crowded around to see.

Eyes narrowing, Lady Bracknell said, "That land is two blocks away from the steelworks."

Martin nodded. "Directly west, but there's another parcel of land between." He looked at the clerk and showed him the map of the site. "Is there any way we can narrow our search to the blocks surrounding this one?"

"Oh yes." The clerk's eyes gleamed. "If you'll just show me the number on the front of that file?"

Martin obliged, and the clerk thought, then rattled off a series of other numbers. "Those are the identifiers for the surrounding blocks. The files should be somewhere among those we have stacked on the table."

With renewed purpose, they sorted through the files and found several adjoining properties that had been purchased over the past four years.

Like the block Martin had found, all had been bought by a CB Enterprises whose address was that of a solicitor's chambers in London.

At Martin's suggestion, they extended their search to adjoining properties of the adjoining properties and turned up even more purchases by CB Enterprises.

When the clerk finally decreed that they'd exhausted the possibilities, he helpfully arranged the diagrams of the blocks owned by CB Enterprises boundary to boundary on a clear section of the table, and the four of them stood looking down at the result.

"Good Lord," Oliver breathed. "No wonder he wants the steelworks so badly."

Martin nodded. "He left it until last because he knew it would be the most difficult to acquire."

"Perhaps he hoped the business might weaken over the years," Oliver offered.

The clerk stared at the diagrams. "I can't believe that one entity has acquired such a swath of land without anyone noticing!" His expression firmed, and he glanced upward. "The higher-ups will want to know about this and no mistake." He looked back at the files, then tipped his head. "But I suppose, with the purchases spread over four years, there's really no reason anyone would have known."

Her lips setting in ominous fashion, Lady Bracknell shook her head. "If this...development ever comes to pass, the town—certainly that area—will be ruined."

"From the east side of Bailey Lane, west"—Martin drifted a hand over the files—"all the way to the block facing the church, covering all the land between Broad Lane and Portobello Street."

"It would be one massive enclave." Oliver stared at the evidence of the extent of Cornelius Blackwell's scheme.

Martin pulled out a notebook. Hunting for his pencil, he nodded at Oliver. "Read out the address of each site and the price he paid. That's something we'll need to know."

Oliver frowned, but reached for the first file. "Why?"

"Because," Martin said, checking his pencil's point, "as I said earlier, we'll need to be prepared to offer our fine gentleman a way out. Meaning a way to quit Sheffield without a massive financial loss."

"Ah. I see." Oliver opened the first file just as a bell rang stridently throughout the building.

The clerk looked upward. "Five minutes. That's all we have before they lock the front doors."

Oliver and Martin exchanged a look—if anyone tried to lock them in, they'd simply find a way out—then Oliver rattled off the first address and the sum that had been paid for that block.

Lady Bracknell picked up a file. "If we all help, this will go more quickly, and we can leave without having to run up those stairs."

Martin wrestled his lips straight at the thought of her ladyship running anywhere, much less up any stairs, and continued swiftly jotting down the information the other three flung at him.

They reached the building's front doors just as the porter was about to swing them shut.

Energized, they returned to St. James' Street and walked into her ladyship's dining room, where the dining table, extended to its full size, had been commandeered and now formed the center of a hive of activity. Julia and Sophy sat facing each other at one end, rapidly writing notes. As they finished each letter, they handed it to either Edward or Charlie, who, seated farther along the table, dutifully blotted and folded the sheets, then inscribed the outside of each with the correct direction before handing the letter to Higginbotham.

The butler, in turn, was sorting the missives into small piles, which he dispatched with a footman for delivery every time one of the footmen returned to the house and presented himself for duty.

Higginbotham looked up as Martin, Oliver, and her ladyship entered. "My lady, you're back." The butler nodded to Oliver and Martin, then added, "Mr. Cynster, thank you for sending your men to help. At present, all three are out delivering notes."

"I'm sure they're pleased to have something to do." Martin smiled. "And the exercise will give them a chance to hone their knowledge of Sheffield's streets."

He saw Sophy glance up at him, then she smiled and went back to her writing.

"Well?" Charlie dropped the letter he'd just finished addressing on Higginbotham's salver and looked expectantly at Martin, Oliver, and Lady Bracknell. "Did you find anything?"

All three of them smiled.

"Indeed, we did." Martin pulled out his notebook as Oliver sat beside Edward. Oliver drew Edward's copy of the list of those to be informed of the upcoming meeting closer and perused it. Lady Bracknell walked around the table to claim the chair beside Sophy. Her ladyship checked Sophy's copy of the list and Julia's as well, then picked up a spare pen, drew a sheet of paper close, and started to write. There were a lot of letters they needed to send out in a very short space of time.

"Oliver's notion paid off." Martin drew out a chair at the table, sat, and thumbed through his notebook to the correct page. While the others worked, he read out the list of properties CB Enterprises had acquired over the past four years.

When he reached the end and looked up, he found Sophy, Edward, and Charlie staring at him.

"Good Lord!" Sophy looked stunned. "That's...a massive tract of land."

Edward looked faintly ill. "From the edge of the church's property all the way to Bailey Lane." He shook his head. "And all of it slated to become one giant slum?"

Charlie looked grim. "If Blackwell adheres to his usual methods, it won't look like a slum to begin with."

Martin nodded and reached for a spare sheet of paper. "Within two years, it would start to look shabby and go downhill from there."

After various dark mutterings, the others returned to their allotted tasks. Meanwhile, Martin made a list of the properties and the amount Blackwell had paid for each. He added up the total and regarded it with an inward grimace. More than he liked, but nowhere near more than he could afford.

At the head of the table, pens were downed, and after a quick check of the various lists, Julia and Sophy sighed, stretched their arms, and relaxed.

A minute later, Edward and Charlie finished addressing the last of the notes and tossed them on the salver for Higginbotham, who immediately retrieved them and handed the final batch of letters to a waiting footman, who promptly vanished into the hall on his quest to deliver them.

"Done!" Charlie flung down his pen and stretched his arms above his head.

"Well, my dears." Lady Bracknell pushed herself out of her chair. "We've all labored long and hard and hopefully successfully, and now we have just enough time for a sherry before dinner. Might I suggest we repair to the drawing room and let Higginbotham clear and set this table?"

They duly adjourned to the drawing room and, once the sherry was dispensed, were soon engrossed in a discussion regarding their next decision, namely, which of the available premises to use for the critical meeting with Blackwell.

"It can't be held at any of our houses," Julia stated with finality.

"Absolutely not," Sophy agreed. "It has to have the right ambiance, and a drawing room simply won't do the trick."

"I daresay," her ladyship said, "that if we asked, the lord mayor would allow us to use one of the Town Hall's meeting rooms."

Edward frowned. "Given the manner in which you want to approach Blackwell, don't you think the Town Hall might be a little too…well, formal and distant?"

Oliver huffed. "If we use the Town Hall, I would be more worried that Blackwell will be put on guard over the possibility of just the sort of ambush we are, in fact, endeavoring to engineer."

"I agree." Martin caught Sophy's eye. "You have a boardroom at the steelworks, don't you? What about using that?"

Sophy tipped her head, clearly envisioning it, then slowly nodded. "That might work very well. There's an anteroom to one side, and we could rearrange the boardroom table so that it functions more like a desk…" She met Martin's eyes. "And Blackwell would assume we were asking him there to discuss a potential sale, so he would come with his thoughts fixed in that direction."

Martin nodded. "And that would definitely be to our advantage."

Sophy sipped her sherry, then lowered the glass and observed, "You, Oliver, and Grandmama finding the evidence to back up our conjecture about what Blackwell is up to was a stroke of luck. Once they hear of that, everyone else will be as determined as we are to see Blackwell routed."

"And to ensure he never comes back." Martin drained his glass, then Higginbotham arrived to announce that dinner was ready to be served, and the company rose and trooped back to the dining room.

All evidence of their earlier activities had been cleared away. They sat, and Higginbotham and the footmen served the various dishes. Conversation was muted and rather perfunctory as they all went over in their minds what they wanted to accomplish and what they hoped would happen the next day.

As they settled to consume the main course, her gaze on her plate, Sophy grumbled, "I wish we hadn't decided to wait until the afternoon. That seems such a waste of time." She was itching to execute their plan and rid herself, her family, her steelworks, and her town of Blackwell.

She sensed rather than saw the amused understanding in Martin's gaze as it touched her face, but his tone was the epitome of calm reason when he replied, "We need to assemble as much support as we can muster to give ourselves the best possible chance of triumphing over Blackwell and deflecting his ambitions, and for that, the afternoon is the safer option."

She huffed. "Logically, I know that, but I do so want this over and done with."

From the corner of her eye, she saw Martin shrug slightly.

"That's understandable, but the afternoon it is." He glanced around the table. "The larger concern is how many of those we've contacted will agree to play their part."

The comment sparked a fresh discussion—about likely numbers and the accommodations required—that lasted until the desserts were set before them and Higginbotham and the footmen departed, bearing away the plates and emptied platters.

It was Edward who, poking at a serving of gooseberry fool, voiced a question that Sophy suspected was rolling around in all their minds. "Do you truly think"—Edward glanced at Martin, then Oliver—"that denied the Carmichael Steelworks site, Blackwell will discard all his plans and withdraw from Sheffield? Won't he simply look about for some other site?"

When everyone looked at Martin, he set down his spoon and, plainly organizing his thoughts, took a sip of wine, then he set down the glass and replied, "There are two factors that, we hope, will work in our favor and push Blackwell into deciding that retreat from Sheffield is his best option. The first is that the steelworks' site is geographically central to his scheme. Without it, his holdings are fractured and, for his purposes, much less useful, no matter whether he seeks another site or not."

Oliver was nodding. "Blackwell's had his eye on the steelworks for years, ever since he first started assembling his Sheffield property portfolio. What's held him back from approaching the family until now—until the steelworks has become a critical acquisition for his project—is, I suspect, that Sophy and her father before her have been steadily growing the business. This is pure conjecture on my part, but I'd be willing to wager that around four years ago, before Blackwell started acquiring the surrounding sites, he would have approached your father about buying the steelworks. For some reason, he formed the opinion that Carmichael Steelworks would go into a decline, and eventually, he would be able to pick up the land, very likely for a song."

"Four years ago?" Sophy frowned. "At that time, there was an issue about buying the new Bessemer converters. We had to do it, or we wouldn't have been able to continue, at least not for long. The business didn't have the cash to fund the expense, and the banks weren't keen because the technology was new and, to their minds, unproven, and they couldn't understand why it would make such a difference to our bottom line."

"So the purchase of the converters was stalled?" Martin asked.

She nodded. "For a few weeks. In the end, Papa put in the money himself, and once we bought the converters and installed them, our profits soared." She shrugged. "Just as we'd predicted."

"There you are, then." Oliver grinned. "Blackwell's not a steel man. He had a similar expectation as the banks. He assumed you wouldn't be able to buy the converters and, even if you did, that you'd end in debt. He convinced himself that, one way or another, he would, at some point in the future, be able to buy Carmichael Steelworks."

"Either as a failed or failing business. He thought that was a sure bet." Martin met Sophy's eyes and smiled. "Only it wasn't."

"And now," Oliver continued, "he's caught. He has to get his hands on the steelworks' site or his grand plan of creating a workers' estate will literally fall to pieces."

"And he's not going to be able to buy Carmichael Steelworks." Sophy stated that with absolute determination. "We'll convince him of that at our meeting, well enough to put the matter beyond question, even for him."

They all took a moment to envision that, then Edward looked at Martin. "You said two factors. What's the other?"

"That," Martin admitted, "is based on my estimation of what's really important to Blackwell. His true, underlying, most personal aim. If my reading of that is correct, then having the support of the others we've called on will be crucial. I'm hoping that by acting in concert, we'll be able to push him over the invisible line into a not-exactly-willing-but-unresisting retreat."

Lady Bracknell tossed her napkin on the table and pushed back her chair. "Let's adjourn to the drawing room and take final stock there."

In a loose group, they trailed her and Julia to the drawing room and resumed their now-accustomed seats.

"I've instructed Higginbotham to bring in the tea trolley as soon as he's free to do so." Lady Bracknell looked around the assembled company. "Tomorrow is going to be a long day."

They fell to discussing the roles each of them would play throughout the following day, then moved on to speculating how matters might pan out. Eventually, Higginbotham wheeled in the tea trolley, and they gratefully accepted and drained their cups, then Julia, Edward, Oliver, and Charlie rose to leave.

With Sophy and her ladyship, Martin walked out to the front hall to farewell the others. Everyone had agreed that he and Sophy should remain in St. James' Street for the moment, and Roland was hovering in the shadows at the rear of the hall, waiting for any instructions Martin cared to give.

He saw the others off first. All four assured Lady Bracknell, Sophy, and him that they would return in good time to help with the final arrangements for the first stage in their plan, namely the luncheon her ladyship would host tomorrow.

Lady Bracknell welcomed all offers of help. "For we won't know until an hour or so before exactly how many will be attending." She glanced at Higginbotham. "Quite like old times, Higginbotham, playing host to so many at once."

"Indeed, ma'am." Higginbotham bowed. "The staff are looking forward to the challenge."

Martin grinned, as did Sophy, then Higginbotham swung open the door, and the others stepped out.

Hector went first, accompanying Julia and assisting her into the waiting carriage. Edward insisted on taking Charlie and Oliver up in his town carriage and delivering the pair to Oliver's hotel before heading south to Sycamore Street.

The instant the front door shut, Lady Bracknell heaved a huge sigh and swung toward the stairs. "Come along, Sophy, my dear. I need my beauty sleep if I'm to act as hostess for our luncheon tomorrow."

Sophy cast a questioning look Martin's way. He pointed at Roland, waiting in the shadows, then nodded.

With a secretive, expectant smile on her lips, Sophy looped her arm with her grandmother's, and together, the ladies ascended the stairs.

Martin watched them go, then Roland came forward.

After conveying his orders for Roland, Figgs, and especially Tunstall for the following day, Martin dismissed Roland to return to the Kings Head and, finally, headed up the stairs.

His hostess was long gone, but Sophy was waiting in the gallery. She turned to him as he neared, and a tempting smile curved her lips. "I've sent my maid to bed."

He arched a brow. "Have you?"

"I have, indeed." She linked her arm with his and paced on beside him. "I'm all yours."

He fought to hide the surge of possessiveness that declaration provoked. Noting that she was propelling him—rather determinedly—toward his room, he asked, "What are your plans?"

He'd thought to distract her or at least slow her down, but she had an answer ready. "Grandmama is right. We've done all we can, and now we need to set everything down, trust in our preparations, and stop thinking and fretting long enough to get some sleep."

"Is that so?"

She nodded and, from the corner of her eye, caught his amused gaze. "And I've realized that we'll both accomplish that much more readily if I join you in your bed."

He had to laugh. "I see."

"Indeed." With provocative assurance, she tipped up her chin. "I rather think my conclusion is incontestable."

"I'm not arguing." They'd arrived at his room, and he reached for the doorknob and set the door swinging wide.

She swept into the room, halted, and turned. She allowed him just long enough to cross the threshold and shut the door before launching herself into his arms.

Laughing, he caught her and met her hungry lips with his. Equally hungry, equally greedy for the succor they both could take and give.

With her locked within one arm, her svelte body stretching upward against his, her soft curves pressing into his harder frame in blatant and potent temptation, he knew she had it right. Together, they had precisely the right prescription to stop each other from thinking, to suspend each other's thoughts.

And tonight, they needed that mental surcease.

He raised a hand, cradled her jaw, and held her captive as he plunged them both deeper into the passionate exchange.

At her command, with ready acquiescence, he put aside all thought and let instinct guide him.

If she was all his, he was all hers, and at that moment, nothing else mattered.

Later, with her body, mind, and senses awash in the glow of aftermath, Sophy lay curled against Martin's side and listened to their slowing hearts, listened as their breathing gradually returned to normal.

Several minutes later, she breathed in, then out. Then whispered, "I was wrong. I'm still thinking."

He huffed wryly. "So am I." After a moment, he went on, "But from where I lie…"

When he said nothing else, she prompted, "What can you see?"

He exhaled, his chest falling, his big body growing more relaxed. "I've been weighing up the chances of Blackwell feeling compelled to retaliate against us—against you or me personally or against the steelworks."

"And?"

"And I can't see him wasting the time and effort on what should, by then, feature to him as a lost cause." He paused, then added, "If years from now, a chance arises to harm us business-wise, I would fully expect him to seize it, assuming the action posed no threat to his own endeavors. But if our plans play out as we hope, then tomorrow or the day after? No. Despite his reputation, if I've read him correctly, I can't see him acting spitefully and maliciously purely in order to be spiteful and malicious—to pay us back with no real benefit, reputational or otherwise, to him."

He sighed, then angled his head to look down and meet her eyes. "So much of our plan hinges on me having read him aright. I pray I've interpreted the signs correctly—that although Blackwell is, indeed, a villain through and through and has clawed his way up in truly villainous fashion, he's stepped away from being 'just a villain' and has ambitions to be more."

"That's what you meant about his coat."

He nodded. "It's part of his costume in transforming himself into the businessman he wants to be and, even more importantly, that he wants others to see him as." After a moment, he added, "Blackwell wants to move into the world you and I inhabit. He's inching into the fringes, but he only has a toehold as yet. In essence, I'm wagering everything on him not wanting to surrender his hard-won gains for any petty retaliation. If his determination to better himself has got him this far, I'm hoping that commitment to his own cause will compel him to rein in any impulse to lash out, now or in the future."

"Regardless"—she shifted against him, getting more comfortable—"we need to do as we've planned. We need to stop him in his tracks and convince him to pull back from Sheffield. It's the only way forward for us and, indeed, the entire town."

He glanced at her again; she felt his gaze rove her face. "That's the true nature of the threat Blackwell poses. If his plans go ahead, they will ruin the bright future you and I can see not just for us but for everyone who lives here."

"And that's why we"—she patted his warm chest—"are going to be even wilier than he, and with the help of all those who answer our call, we'll see him comprehensively routed."

She tipped back her head and met his eyes, letting her determination and assurance shine.

Martin drank both in and felt her conviction resonate inside him.

He still wasn't one hundred percent certain their plan would succeed, but with her by his side, so fierce and resolute, they were as best placed as they could be to pull off the tricky, rather delicate stratagem.

They just had to manage it without any missteps.

Like walking a tightrope.

He looked into her face for a moment more, then raised his head and dropped a kiss on her nose. "Sleep," he whispered.

He let his head fall back on the pillow, closed his eyes, and felt her curl and settle against him.

Satiation spread through him, golden and deep, and he felt his lips curve in a silly smile.

The last of the day's tension flowed away, and sleep came rolling in.

CHAPTER 16

Seated at the middle of one of the long sides of the boardroom table at Carmichael Steelworks, Sophy fought to calm her nerves. On her left, Edward fidgeted nervously, while Charlie, in the chair to her right, stared tensely across the table at the closed door that led to the outer office.

She glanced over her right shoulder. Martin was lounging against the paneled wall and was effortlessly projecting the image of a relaxed and untroubled aristocratic gentleman. She assumed it was a façade and he was nowhere near as unconcerned as he appeared, but there was no way she could tell.

He was stationed in that position, two steps from her and the table, supposedly to underscore that he held no shares in the company and was therefore not involved in the matter at hand, but in reality, he was there to partially conceal and draw the eye from the door to the adjoining anteroom, which was fractionally ajar.

Perfectly groomed and dressed in a suit of restrained elegance, he was admirably suited to the task of capturing and fixing any gaze that wandered in that direction.

A light tap on the door to the office sent her nerves leaping and transfixed her attention on the wooden panel. This was the moment they'd all worked frantically hard to prepare for. She drew in a breath and surreptitiously held it. "This will be him," she murmured to Edward and Charlie.

They were as ready as they would ever be. Clasping her hands on the pristine blotter before her, she raised her chin and commandingly called, "Come in."

Harvey opened the door and ushered in Mr. Cornelius Blackwell.

She stared at the man who had caused so much consternation in her life. Hers and many others' as well.

That morning, she and Martin had barely made it to the breakfast parlor before a deluge of replies to their letters of the previous evening had started pouring in. It was soon apparent that enough of the right people were ready to back their scheme; judging by the replies, Blackwell's name alone had been enough to ensure that. With the required support guaranteed, she'd written a polite letter to Blackwell, merely stating that his interest in Carmichael Steelworks had come to her attention and suggesting a meeting with her and the other shareholders in the boardroom at the works.

She'd stipulated three o'clock that afternoon as an appropriate hour and had dispatched the missive by footman to the hotel in Castle Street that Blackwell had told Edward he was patronizing; subsequently, Martin's men had confirmed that Blackwell was, indeed, in residence. She'd instructed the footman to wait for a reply.

Unsurprisingly, Blackwell had responded with alacrity, returning a simply worded acceptance with the footman.

Thereafter, she hadn't had a minute to call her own, what with helping to manage the luncheon her grandmother had hosted, during which they'd described to the assembled guests just what had been occurring at Carmichael Steelworks and what they'd subsequently learned of Blackwell's intentions. Once the exclamations and protestations had died down, Martin had explained their plan to derail Blackwell's scheme, at least with regard to Sheffield.

While in general concise and succinct, Martin had taken the time to elucidate his reasoning. Sophy had noted how the atmosphere in the room shifted and clarified as more and more of those present understood his tack, agreed with his thinking, and came around to wholeheartedly supporting their plan.

Their plan to convince Cornelius Blackwell to give up his vision of building slum housing over a large area of Sheffield.

She watched as Blackwell approached the table. He was tall, wide-shouldered, and lean, with a slight stoop, and was wearing the black overcoat that had so defined him. His gaze swept the room, taking in Edward, herself, and Charlie. That cool, assessing gaze lingered for a moment on Martin before Blackwell returned his attention to her.

Unhurriedly, she rose, and Edward and Charlie came to their feet, flanking her. With an entirely mild expression on her face, she nodded in greeting. "Mr. Blackwell. I'm Miss Carmichael."

With surprising grace, Blackwell returned the gesture. "Miss Carmichael." His voice was rough and deep, almost grating in quality.

Sophy waved at Edward. "I believe you're acquainted with my cousin, Edward. And this"—she indicated Charlie—"is Edward's brother, Charles Carmichael."

She waited while the men exchanged nods and single-word greetings, rather clipped on her cousins' parts, then she half turned and smiled warmly in Martin's direction. "And this is Mr. Martin Cynster, my fiancé."

Returning her gaze to Blackwell, she caught a fleeting flicker pass through his eyes—possibly recognition of the Cynster name or, alternatively, speculation over her engagement and what that might mean for her continuing in her role at the steelworks.

"Mr. Blackwell."

At the edge of her vision, she saw Martin nod in languidly distant fashion; he was to play the part of disinterested spectator, at least to begin with.

Blackwell inclined his head in response, the movement rather more wary than with her cousins. "Mr. Cynster."

Adhering to her businesslike manner, she gestured to the single chair on the other side of the table, set directly opposite her own. "Please, Mr. Blackwell, take a seat."

She sat as Blackwell moved forward.

He drew back the chair and gathered his black coat before sitting. He'd removed his gloves, and his hands were large, the fingers long, their backs scarred. Examining his coat, Sophy could understand why people remembered it; from the way the fabric hung and moved about his body, it was plainly luxurious, soft and thick, densely black, and the garment was superbly cut to suit Blackwell's tall, broad-shouldered frame.

That the coat had come from one of London's foremost tailors was beyond doubt. She agreed with Martin's assessment; Blackwell wore it as a badge, as a visible assertion of who he believed he was.

Or rather, who he wanted others to believe him to be.

She seized the moment to swiftly study him. His face did, indeed, appear hewn from rock, the planes hard and sharp-edged. His eyes were a pale, washed-out sea green, deeply set beneath the overhang of his wide brow, and his lips were thin and pale, showing little contrast against his pale skin.

His was a face that was difficult to read; there was little movement in the hard lines, little evidence of emotion to give a watcher any clue as to his thoughts.

The only sign she detected lay in the pale, cold eyes that rested, with just a hint of expectation, on her.

That was good; expectation she could work with.

She bestowed a polite, business-appropriate smile. "Mr. Blackwell, I've asked you here today to"—artfully, she glanced at Edward, then returned her gaze to Blackwell—"allow us an opportunity to discuss our views on the future of Carmichael Steelworks."

Although nothing changed in Blackwell's face, she immediately sensed a heightened alertness emanating from him; it seemed he was eager to engage. Smoothly, she went on, "I understand from Edward that you've shown some interest in our business and wondered at the direction of your thoughts. I invited you here today hoping you would share those with us."

He regarded her steadily for several seconds, then replied, "I do have some ideas regarding the business, by way of making the most of what's here. However, Miss Carmichael, any involvement of mine would be contingent on acquiring, at the very least, a controlling position in the company."

That was her cue to dart a look Martin's way, hopefully fostering the notion that, once they were wed, she would be stepping back from her current role regardless. That was what Blackwell would expect of any lady marrying into a family of the social standing of the Cynsters. "Well," she said, her tone uncertain. She returned her gaze to Blackwell. "One can make no promises, of course, but that we are here, myself and my cousins, ready to listen to your proposal, should, I believe, speak to our willingness to entertain your ideas." She gestured. "Obviously, what you choose to reveal will be crucial in determining our best way forward."

Blackwell regarded her steadily. His unnervingly immobile features gave nothing away, yet she strongly suspected he was debating how much she knew of him and his affairs and weighing up how candid he should be, how much of the reality of his plans for the steelworks he should lay bare.

Behind Sophy, Martin shifted, drawing Blackwell's gaze. In the tone of one with limited patience yet also trying to be helpful, he drawled, "Perhaps, Blackwell, you might start by explaining your interest in steelmaking."

When Blackwell blinked and didn't respond, Martin rephrased, "For instance, what are your intentions regarding any alterations to the steelworks' operation?"

"Yes, indeed." When Blackwell looked her way, Sophy clasped her hands on the blotter again and, leaning slightly forward, looked encouraging, as if willing Blackwell to expound on his thoughts.

As they'd rehearsed, Edward huffed and, frowning slightly, waved dismissively. "I'm really not sure we need to interrogate Mr. Blackwell on that issue, do we, cousin?"

Sophy frowned and turned to look at Edward, but before she could speak, Charlie cut in.

"What Edward means," Charlie explained, "is that neither he nor I will have any interest in what happens at the steelworks after we've sold our share and"—he met Sophy's eyes as she turned to him—"regardless of whether you choose to retain an interest or not, the reality is that you won't have time to be as active in the business as you've been to date." Charlie flicked his eyes Martin's way. "You'll have other demands on your time."

Martin watched Cornelius Blackwell drink in the subtle and not-so-subtle messages Sophy, Edward, and Charlie were feeding him.

Sophy's expression turned mulish as she stared at Charlie.

He raised his hands defensively. "I'm just pointing out that, once Mr. Blackwell takes control of the company, your interest in what happens at the steelworks will, naturally, fall away."

"It won't really be any concern of yours, Sophy," Edward stated in a blatantly superior tone. "Not when you no longer have the controlling stake."

Judging from the gleam in Blackwell's eyes, the three had said enough to convince him that they were, indeed, inclined to sell. Rather than risk them overstepping, Martin decided it was time to move on to the next act in their pantomime. Holding to his lounging pose, he evenly said, "I understand, Blackwell, that you own the block across the street.

Indeed, that you own all of the land from the steelworks' western boundary to the park around St. George's Church, and you also hold the title to the row of houses to the east, along the eastern side of Bailey Lane."

Blackwell's expression set like stone, and he grew preternaturally still.

As if unaware of those subtle changes, Martin rolled on, "Consequently, your purchase of the steelworks will consolidate those holdings into one sizeable area." Utterly innocently, he tipped his head and asked, "What do you plan to do with all that land?"

Silence ensued, but Sophy broke it, leaning forward eagerly and asking, "Do you intend to expand? Or…?"

Blackwell's sharp and penetrating gaze shifted to rest on Sophy's face.

Everyone listening—the four at the table and the small army in the anteroom at their backs—held their breaths.

Whatever Blackwell saw in Sophy's expression, it wasn't his doom. His features eased. His gaze still on her face, he rather grudgingly admitted, "I'm hoping to—intending to—build housing for steelworkers on the site."

Sophy's face lit. "Oh, what an excellent idea! I take it you have experience in such projects?"

When Blackwell inclined his head, she rolled on. "Wonderful! Well, that will make it easier to attract and hold workers." She rattled on for a full minute, enumerating the benefits to steelworkers in living close to the works themselves, then all but glowing with approval, she smiled at Blackwell and inquired, "Who will you be bringing in to manage the steelworks? Do you have someone in mind? Or will you look to our current foreman to step into the role?"

Blackwell's lashes flickered for a second, then he once again met Sophy's gaze. "I have to admit that, as yet, I haven't planned quite that far ahead."

"Oh." Sophy looked faintly puzzled. "I see." She blinked, then ventured, "I just thought…"

She glanced at Martin as if seeking his opinion.

He obliged by asking Blackwell, "What are your projections for profits from the steelworks? How do you intend to grow the business…" He narrowed his eyes on Blackwell. "But I forget. You haven't yet examined the books, have you?"

One of Blackwell's hands twitched as if he'd started to close it into a fist, realized, and halted the telltale action.

Martin sensed the man was starting to feel unsure, uncertain of his footing.

Sophy looked delightfully confused. "That's true. So how—"

Edward leapt in to say, "Oh, I don't think we need to bother Mr. Blackwell about such details, do we?"

Charlie folded his arms, leaned back in his chair, and flicked a faintly irritated glance at Martin. "None of our business, really. Not once we're no longer part owners."

Blackwell seized the opening. "Just so." He fixed his pale gaze on Sophy. "Let me worry about the future. There's plenty of time to work out the details. From all I've heard, Carmichael Steelworks is a nicely profitable business."

Sophy nodded. "Indeed, it is. And of course, being a businessman, you'll ensure it remains so." She returned Blackwell's gaze. "Won't you?"

Blackwell's previous uncertainty had faded; he was confident that he had her—and Edward's and Charlie's—measure. "Once the steelworks passes into my hands, if it continues to be profitable, well and good. But you must understand it will need to hold its own within my portfolio of properties." His features shifted into what, for him, was presumably a reassuring smile. "As long as the rate of return on my invested capital is as high or higher than my other enterprises, then why would I make any dramatic changes?"

Sophy smiled back, but almost immediately, the expression faded, transforming into a puzzled frown. "Your other enterprises… What are they?"

She appeared to be genuinely interested and not at all antagonistic; with such thespian skills, she could, Martin felt, have graced any stage.

Blackwell didn't hesitate to explain, "As I mentioned earlier, my principal interest is in building houses for workers. In my experience, rather than investing directly in manufacturing industries, there's considerably more profit to be had through providing housing for the workers required to run such businesses."

"As you do in London, Birmingham, Nottingham, and Manchester?" Martin pushed away from the wall and prowled to stand by Sophy's shoulder.

Blackwell's eyes tracked him, then Blackwell's expression hardened. He nodded curtly. "Exactly."

Immediately, Blackwell returned his gaze to Sophy, then he looked at Edward and, lastly, at Charlie. "Right, then. That's enough talk of the business. Miss Carmichael, gents. If we're to do any deal, I suggest we start talking numbers."

Sophy held up a finger. "Just so we're clear, Mr. Blackwell. Am I correct in thinking that you have no genuine interest in ensuring that Carmichael Steelworks has a future as a going concern? Specifically, as a steelworks?"

Her tone remained even, giving Blackwell no hint of what answer she wished to hear.

Sophy didn't give him a chance to think. Leaning forward, in a voice devoid of judgment, positive or negative, she said, "It's just that wiping out a business that generates a tidy profit and employs so many workers in order to build housing, which, after construction, doesn't employ anyone and is completely nonproductive, so to speak, doesn't make a great deal of sense to me."

Her delivery left Blackwell having to guess whether she was asking for further enlightenment or criticizing his proposal. He glanced at Edward and Charlie, clearly hoping one or the other would come to his aid, but they remained blank-faced and silent.

Sophy waved dismissively, drawing Blackwell's gaze back to her. "If you can't sway me, then what they say doesn't matter. I hold the controlling interest in Carmichael Steelworks."

She'd made the statements sound like a challenge, and praise be, Blackwell rose to the lure. "In that case," he said, "perhaps the profits that my supposedly 'nonproductive' housing will generate might overcome your resistance."

Sophy sat back and arched a brow. "And those are?"

Eyes narrowing, Blackwell declared, "I would put up six-story buildings across the entire combined site." He leaned forward, and his pale gaze glimmered with avaricious zeal. "At the opening rental rate, that will generate upward of a thousand pounds a month. And as the town expands and more workers stream in and the demand for housing grows, I'll put up the rents." He glanced at Martin. "My projection for the monthly take in five years' time is at least ten thousand pounds."

Sophy blinked. "Good Lord!" The exclamation was weak.

Taking that to mean he'd dazzled her with the monetary possibilities,

Blackwell shifted his gaze to Martin and nodded. "I've heard you're a businessman and a pretty ruthless and successful one, too." He tipped his head toward Sophy. "You should have a word with your fiancée and ensure she sees the light. After all, once the pair of you tie the knot, what's hers becomes yours." He paused, then looked at Sophy and smiled intently. "And then it won't matter what she thinks."

Sophy stiffened.

Before she could explode, Martin spoke, reclaiming Blackwell's attention. "In all honesty, Blackwell, I see no reason to attempt to change Miss Carmichael's mind. Her reservations regarding your housing proposal seem entirely well-founded. Because of course"—he stepped back and, reaching out, drew open the concealed door in the paneling—"there's more to being a part of Sheffield or, indeed, any town than simply owning land or a business, no matter how profitable."

Through the doorway thus revealed, a procession of people filed into the boardroom. Blackwell's eyes flared in shocked surprise. As well-dressed gentlemen and ladies continued to walk in, all leveling censorious looks at him, his features fell slack, his expression blanking.

The town's luminaries, dignitaries, and most prominent businessmen had turned out in force. Thanks to Sophy's grandmother, even the major hostesses were there.

Martin moved down the long table to stand at its end as the tide of influential, important, and distinguished locals continued to flood in. The police commissioner and Inspector Curtin were among the crowd, but kept to the rear. They were there to act as official witnesses and representatives of the law if required. Oliver, a non-local, hung back as well. Among the last to appear was the lord mayor, with his chain of office glinting on his chest.

Keeping unnervingly mum, the company fanned out, filling the room to either side of the long table and lining up behind it, standing along the wall. Given that all who had answered the call were determined to keep their eyes on Blackwell's face, despite the room's size, the assembled throng settled in densely packed ranks with their gazes trained on him.

Blackwell clenched his jaw; although beyond that, his features didn't appreciably alter, Martin sensed he was exceedingly wary.

When the last gentleman through the connecting door closed it and the shuffle of footsteps faded, Blackwell—transparently aware that he was well and truly out of his depth—glanced at Edward. "What's this?" For the first time, there was an edge of nervousness in his tone.

Stone-faced, Edward simply stared back.

No one else volunteered an answer.

Increasingly uncertain, avoiding Sophy—now regarding him as stonily as anyone—Blackwell reluctantly looked at Martin. "Who are all these people?"

Martin glanced at Sophy, passing the question to her.

She inclined her head fractionally to him, then returned her attention to Blackwell. Calm, collected, and assured, she smiled coolly and gestured to the assembled horde. "This, Mr. Blackwell, is the might of Sheffield. These are the people who made this town what it is, and they are devoted to seeing it prosper. All of it, the workers as well as the businesses and the business owners."

She looked invitingly at the lord mayor.

He inclined his head to her, then focused on Blackwell. "Many of those here are aware of your reputation, Mr. Blackwell. We've now heard your proposal for Sheffield, and we wish to inform you that should you press ahead, that proposal is doomed to failure. We will never allow such housing as you propose to be built within the town's boundaries."

The imposing figure of John Brown stood among the front ranks of those assembled. His gaze resting heavily on Blackwell, he rumbled, "I'm John Brown. Many call me the Father of the Sheffield Iron and Steel Trade." He glanced around the circle of his peers and smiled confidently. "With good reason."

Many softly laughed and, with patent good humor, nodded, indicating he spoke for them and encouraging him to continue.

He looked back at Blackwell. "Together with all those gathered here today, I wish to inform you that there's no place in this town for men like you, looking to make your fortune off the backs of our workers. Between us, we own the vast majority—" He paused to glance over the ranks again, noting those present, then amended, "Actually, all the steelworks and associated industries in this town, and we will ensure that none of our workers falls into the trap of taking a lease on such housing as you propose, be it yours or anyone else's."

Several in the crowd murmured affirmations, most along the lines of "The success of our business depends on our workers, and we're not likely to forget that."

Then Tom Vickers stepped forward and met Blackwell's eyes. "Colonel Thomas Vickers of Naylor Vickers." He nodded at John Brown. "And I second everything my colleague said. We're a collegiate group in this town. We want the best for it, for us, our workers, and all who live within its borders. Speaking for myself, although I daresay this applies to others here as well, that isn't due to any altruistic belief but rather one based on cold, hard experience in running a business where success depends on the efforts of many. Put simply, the success of the Naylor Vickers business relies on the health and well-being of our workforce."

"Hear, hear" rumbled through the room.

Tom tipped his head in acknowledgment. "You see? We all know on which side our bread is buttered. Consequently, now we know what you're proposing to do, we, collectively, will ensure you or, indeed, anyone similarly inclined do not succeed. No matter what approach is taken, one of us will learn of it—nothing could be more certain, not in this town—and as a group, we will step in and do whatever's necessary to scuttle such plans."

"If necessary," the lord mayor said, "we'll enact town ordinances to block such developments."

Blackwell was thoroughly stunned. He was transparently having trouble taking in the enormity of the resistance marshaled against him.

Lady Bracknell, who, with the other major hostesses, had come in with the gentlemen, trenchantly stated, "We, none of us, want such tenements in our town, and acting together, we wield more than enough influence—socially, civically, politically, and financially—to ensure such projects never see the light of day." She all but glared at Blackwell. "Yours or anyone else's, sir!"

The round of "Hear, hear!" that followed left Blackwell in no doubt whatsoever that his project in Sheffield was doomed. However, they'd been careful to target their comments not at Blackwell himself but rather at his proposal or any similar project.

For Martin's money, it was Lady Bracknell's proud and haughty denunciation that punched the final nail into the coffin of Blackwell's development. Martin knew that once the senior ladies of a town took a stance on anything, changing their husbands' minds became a lost cause, but he doubted Blackwell had as much experience with the species as he. However, since setting eyes on Blackwell, Martin had grown increasingly certain that the man harbored a vision of, at some point, buying his way into society, and in that respect, her ladyship had just punctured any such dreams, at least if Blackwell attempted to push on with his plans.

If he didn't…

This moment was the critical point when things could go either way. When Blackwell could be tipped into acting in a manner that would satisfy them all or, conversely, in a way that would do no one any good.

If he felt backed into a corner, dug in, and decided to fight like the vicious street fighter rumor had it he'd once been, the town and everyone living there would be in for an uncomfortable few years. Alternatively, even vicious street fighters harbored dreams.

Would Blackwell opt to fight or to follow his dream?

Blackwell's pale gaze, which had been scanning the opposing ranks, returned, slowly, to Sophy.

She smiled confidently yet with a hint of cold steel in her expression. "Just business, Mr. Blackwell. Please understand that this is nothing personal. Our reaction would have been exactly the same toward any such development proposed for this town."

That was Martin's cue. He shifted, drawing Blackwell's attention, then dipped his head in acknowledgment. "As you earlier noted, I'm a businessman. I can appreciate that you've sunk significant capital into purchasing the sites surrounding Carmichael Steelworks. The largely vacant blocks to the west, all the way to the park around the church, and also the row of houses along Bailey Lane to the east. That's quite an investment."

"You could say that," Blackwell growled. He cast a narrow-eyed look at the mayor. "And as far as I know, there's no law defining what a man can do on his own land, not even in this town."

"No specific law, perhaps," Martin conceded, "but there are, I'm sure, many regulations, and as both you and I know, Mr. Blackwell, nothing is certain in life and bureaucracy other than that bureaucracy will get in the way." That surprised a huff of wry laughter from Blackwell, and he returned his attention to Martin.

"And," Martin smoothly continued, "like it or not, one has to take into account the reaction of the populace"—with a tip of his head, he indicated the representatives of the town—"especially those with the power to obstruct and, ultimately, deny." He paused, then went on. "I'm sure you've realized that's the situation you now face, but as, prior to today, you could not have foreseen or anticipated such resistance to your project, I'm willing to make a one-time offer for your current holdings in the town."

A slight widening of Blackwell's eyes was the only sign of his surprise. There was certainly no immediate show of interest, but from

Blackwell's studiously blank expression, Martin suspected he was thinking furiously.

Along with everyone else in the room, Sophy held her breath, watched Blackwell like a hawk, and waited to see if he would accept the way out Martin was offering.

A way out—an olive branch of sorts—endorsed by everyone there; all they had to do—all Martin had to do—was convince Blackwell to take it.

During the luncheon in St. James' Street when they'd explained all to the assembled throng—to the might of Sheffield, as she'd dubbed them—they'd discussed the best way to get Blackwell to quit the town entirely, including selling the land he'd acquired. Martin had explained his reading of Blackwell—all speculation as, at that point, they hadn't yet met the man—but from his knowledge of Blackwell's reputation and the way Blackwell had conducted himself with Edward, Martin had insisted that their best way forward was, as far as possible, to treat Blackwell as a legitimate businessman.

There was no gainsaying that his hold on the properties he'd bought was, indeed, legitimate.

Martin had suggested that the surest way to get Blackwell to give up his holdings—and therefore his ambition of establishing himself in Sheffield—was to offer the man a deal.

A business deal. One that would allow Blackwell to walk away without loss, either financial or in standing.

As Martin had the deep pockets required to fund such an offer on the spot and, as he'd added with a glance at her, he had a vested interest in the outcome, he'd offered to buy the titles to all the Sheffield land Blackwell owned.

The more hotheaded of the group had wanted to simply run Blackwell out of town, but the lord mayor and the police commissioner had pointed out that the days when such actions could be condoned were long gone. Then the more senior members of the group—those who wielded the most business clout—had agreed with Martin's assessment of Blackwell and had backed his plan as the one most likely to secure the outcome they all desired, namely, Blackwell leaving Sheffield permanently.

Eventually, all had accepted that to effectively rid the town of Blackwell, he had to be persuaded that it was in his best interests to leave.

The might of Sheffield had done their part. Now, it was up to Martin.

The silence had stretched for nearly a minute before Blackwell, his entire attention fixed on Martin and his tone distinctly grim, asked, "What's your offer?"

Martin named a price, and Blackwell's lashes flickered. He'd expected some other amount; Sophy felt sure he'd expected less.

But that reaction was fleeting, there and gone, and he snorted. "That's what I paid for the land."

Unperturbed, Martin nodded. "I know. Given there is now no prospect of you using the land for the purpose you intended, rather than try to take advantage of your situation, I decided that a fair price to offer would be exactly what you invested."

Eyes narrowing, Blackwell countered, "I bought some of those blocks four years ago."

Martin inclined his head. "You took a risk purchasing those blocks before you secured the steelworks' site. As it transpired, that wasn't a wise decision, and now the project has run into powerful headwinds."

Blackwell persisted, "Those blocks are worth more than that to me because of the use I intended to put them to."

"But that's not going to come to pass. Because of matters outside your control, your Sheffield project is not going to proceed." Martin lightly shrugged. "Everyone in business suffers reverses from time to time. Isn't it better to acknowledge that and walk away with your initial investment intact rather than risk further erosion of your capital?"

Blackwell huffed, but he was clearly thinking, susceptible to the business logic Martin was propounding.

More quietly, Martin added, "Of course, as I don't intend to use the land in anything like the manner you intended, then the value of that land to me is arguably lower."

Blackwell's gaze locked on Martin's face. After a second of studying Martin's uncommunicative features, Blackwell pursed his lips.

Apparently reading that as some sign, in the same quiet but even tone, Martin went on, "Make no mistake. This is a one-time offer. You can take it or leave it. Either way, it's no skin off my nose, but of course, both you and I know that the instant you walk out of that door"—he nodded at the door to the outer office—"your chance of selling that land to anyone else at the same price will vanish."

Blackwell's expression had blanked again, but there was a watchfulness—a considering weight in his gaze—as he continued to study Martin.

Silence stretched. Sophy was amazed that none of the others ventured to break it, not even by shifting restlessly. Like her, they were hanging on the outcome, and apparently, all were willing to leave the stage to Martin.

Then, his expression hardening, Martin caught and held Blackwell's gaze. "You know news of this will get out. That's guaranteed. If you want to preserve your reputation, it would be easy enough to put it about that you'd been misled as to the availability of the Carmichael Steelworks' site. That business conditions for the steelworks had changed—as, indeed, they have—and that made it impossible for you to acquire the business. Consequently, as the steelworks' site is central and, more, crucial to the commercial viability of your intended project, you deemed it preferable to pull out of Sheffield entirely, and you were lucky enough to find a buyer willing to take your landholdings off your hands, allowing you to walk away without loss."

Although Martin hadn't explicitly stated it, Sophy thought that it couldn't be clearer that he was offering Blackwell a chance to retreat without losing face among his peers.

She watched while Blackwell absorbed the implications.

Eventually, his gaze steady on Martin's face, Blackwell nodded. Once. "All right. For the same price I paid for them, then."

Martin looked across the room at his secretary, Tunstall, who'd been standing in the lord mayor's shadow.

Tunstall rounded the table and handed Martin a sheaf of documents. "The contracts of sale as requested, sir."

Blackwell barked out a laugh, quickly smothered. From beneath the shelf of his brow, he regarded Martin with, it seemed, fresh eyes. "Came prepared, did you?"

Sorting through the documents, Martin merely said, "Let's just say that everyone here wants to see this business settled today. Apropos of that…" He paused to hunt in one pocket, then drew out a folded paper and passed it to Charlie.

Charlie took it and handed it on to Sophy. She received the folded slip, unfolded and straightened it, then turned it around and, leaning forward, held it where Blackwell could read it.

He did and huffed again. "Definitely prepared." He shot a sharp glance at Martin.

One of the others had gone to the door to the outer office and returned with an ink pot and two pens. The ink pot was set on the table beside Blackwell, along with the pens. Still perusing the documents, Martin rounded the table and walked toward Blackwell. "These all seem in order."

With the attitude of one stifling a sigh—one of surrender—Blackwell held out a hand. "Let me look them over."

Martin handed the documents to Blackwell, then picked up one of the pens.

He waited with unrufflable patience while Blackwell examined the documents, then after a quick glance at the bank draft Sophy was still holding, Blackwell grunted, picked up the other pen, dipped it in the inkwell, and signed the documents, one after the other.

As he did, he pushed each along the table to Martin, who duly dipped the pen he held and signed as well.

When the last of the sale agreements was signed, Martin looked at Blackwell, then glanced at Sophy and nodded.

She offered Blackwell the bank draft.

He reached across the table and took it, then nodded to her. "Miss Carmichael. I can't say it's been any sort of pleasure doing business with you." He looked at Martin. "With the pair of you." Blackwell tucked the bank draft into his coat pocket, then rose. "This has, however, been… How do they put it? An experience to learn from."

He nodded to Martin with a degree of respect he'd shown to no one else.

Then for the second time since he'd walked in, Blackwell allowed his lips to fractionally curve. He glanced around at the assembled denizens of Sheffield and patted the pocket containing the bank draft. "I daresay there are other towns that will prove more salubrious to my health."

With that, he half bowed, then turned toward the office. Steadily and unhurriedly, he walked to the door, opened it, and left.

The door closed behind him, yet everyone waited as they were, unsure.

Two seconds later, the door opened, and a grinning Harvey looked in. "He's gone."

The exhalation of relief that swept the room was intense and audible, more so given how many were there.

"We did it!" Sophy beamed at Martin, and when he grinned at her, she pushed Charlie out of the way and rushed around the table.

Expressions of relief and joy erupted on all sides. Men clapped each other on the back, and many now felt free to voice their worst fears and their delight that all had been resolved so neatly. Congratulations rained down on Martin's head. His hand was wrung, his shoulders thumped, but the best reward of all was Sophy flinging herself into his arms, hauling his face to hers, and kissing him soundly.

"We did it!" She bounced in his arms.

Smiling fit to burst, Martin caught her up and swung her around. He set her on her feet and, beaming himself, looked into her eyes. "We did. He's gone, and thank all the angels, he's far too clever to even think of coming back."

CHAPTER 17

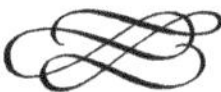

Sophy's grandmother, encouraged and assisted by several of her peers, insisted on hosting a celebratory dinner in St. James' Street that evening.

Most of those who had been present in the Carmichael Steelworks' boardroom attended, happy to eat, drink, and merrily toast their seeing off of a threat the majority had only learned of the previous day. Those more deeply in the know were significantly more relieved.

Martin found himself under siege from both the hostesses, who had learned of what they termed his "conquest of Sophy" and had seized on the likelihood that he would, therefore, continue to grace their circles, and the businessmen, who had realized a newcomer had moved onto their patch and now possessed a significant landholding. All wanted to welcome him and assure him of their interest in his future in Sheffield.

John Brown and Tom Vickers finally managed to extract Martin from the adoring throng.

"So," Vickers asked, coming straight to the point, "what are your intentions regarding Carmichael Steelworks?" He arched a brow, then Sophy came up to take Martin's arm, and Vickers smiled at her. "Sophy, my dear, I was about to ask your intended whether he planned on taking a position in the business."

Smiling as well, Martin slanted a questioning glance at Sophy and received a smug smile and an encouraging nod in reply. He returned his gaze to Vickers. "Not as such. I have several other businesses that claim my time, and in my view, Carmichael Steelworks is already in sound and highly capable hands."

John Brown chuckled. "A wise decision. But I wanted to ask whether you had any plans for the land you've just acquired. I believe most of it is vacant or derelict, and in that area, that leaves the way open for building almost anything."

Martin glanced at Sophy. They hadn't had much time to discuss the possibilities, but buoyed on success, on the return journey from the steelworks, they'd excitedly exchanged a few thoughts. "Nothing's been decided, of course, but"—he looked at Brown and the equally curious Vickers—"one of the ideas Sophy and I are considering is to use part of the site for an adjacent factory—an expansion of sorts—to work on further developing specialist alloys with an initial focus on making steel safes."

Both men were interested in hearing more of that, and the exchange of ideas drew all four deeper into the sort of technical discussion that kept all others at bay.

Eventually, Brown commented, "It seems to me that such a factory will only require a single block." He arched a brow at Martin. "Do you have any ideas for the rest of the land?"

Again, he looked to Sophy, and she nodded, encouraging him to reveal their most-recent notion. Returning his attention to Brown and Vickers, he said, "Sophy and I have only just started discussing this, so as yet, there's little flesh on the bones. However, the crux of our thinking is that Blackwell saw and intended to exploit what, in essence, is a vulnerability of our industries, namely, that we require a sizeable workforce that lives within easy reach of our sites. Given the predominance of such industries in Sheffield, that translates to a vulnerability for the town. Therefore, in order to safely grow our businesses, we need to look into where and how and under what circumstances our workers can be housed."

Brown was nodding. "That was certainly the issue when it came to Blackwell, and I'm the first to admit that, as a group, we haven't applied much thought to the problem."

"The looming problem, as you rightly point out." Vickers frowned. "It's on our horizon, but not here yet, which explains why we haven't yet focused on it. But we should."

"Indeed," Sophy said. "Before it descends on us and causes unnecessary problems."

"Which is why," Martin went on, "Sophy and I intend to look into using some of the land Blackwell amassed to create suitable housing for workers."

Sophy grinned at Brown and Vickers. "Obviously, for *our* workers." She arched her brows at them. "We could make it a challenge to see who provides the better houses, the better conditions to attract and hold the workers we all need."

Vickers laughed. "Our family would be up for that, and our Naylor cousins, too." He met Sophy's, then Martin's eyes. "I know you're right. In the future, we're going to need more workers, and if Sheffield starts now, we'll be able to hold our best workers and attract others of the right caliber using the lure of decent housing."

Brown nodded decisively. "That's definitely something we all should start thinking about." He saw the lord mayor, still wearing his chain, caught the man's eye, and waved him over. "Come and listen to the ideas these two have about workers' housing. Insightful and definitely something you and the aldermen need to support."

The lord mayor promptly professed himself to be very ready to support any notion Martin and Sophy cared to put forward. The group expanded as several others joined them, including two ladies who, speaking from the perspective of their charity work, declared the notion of worker housing to be an excellent idea. Eventually, a tentative plan was made to meet the following week at the Town Hall to continue the discussion with the various officials who oversaw such developments.

Higginbotham, at his supercilious best and enjoying himself hugely, appeared to announce that dinner was served.

Under cover of the melee as Lady Bracknell organized her guests, the lord mayor, who was to lead her ladyship in, followed by Sophy on Martin's arm, smiled at Sophy, then nodded meaningfully to Martin. "You've made your mark in this town, sir. You need have no doubt whatsoever about that. And"—the lord mayor's eyes twinkled as he glanced at Sophy—"I'm very certain that I speak for all the townsfolk in saying how glad we are to learn that you don't plan on leaving."

Martin looked at Sophy and felt contentment rise. "Indeed, sir. I intend to remain in Sheffield for the foreseeable future."

And very likely, for the rest of my life.

Lady Bracknell swept up and claimed the lord mayor's arm, and the procession set off for the dining room.

Still smiling, Martin caught Sophy's gaze.

Happier than she could remember being, Sophy squeezed his arm, then faced forward and glided on.

Although there were no guests of honor as such, she and Martin were indubitably the focus of all attention. Aware of that, her grandmother placed them side by side halfway down the long, extended table. Luckily, the senior ladies were clustered closer to either her grandmother at one end or Julia and Edward at the other, allowing Sophy to glibly and shamelessly redirect all queries as to her and Martin's engagement and their likely wedding date to her older female relatives, on the grounds that, in such matters, they had much more experience on which to draw than she.

Needless to say, speculation was running rife, especially as to how big an occasion their wedding would be. Most there had heard of Martin's family and, from various perspectives, were keen to view the reality.

Inspector Curtin was seated opposite Sophy, and as the soup was served, he confirmed for her and Martin—and all the others who were eagerly listening—that the rift between the Murchison brothers caused by Vince defying Walter and working for Blackwell behind Walter's back had, indeed, spelled the end of the Murchison family's reign as kings of the Sheffield underworld.

"Good riddance, too," the commissioner put in from farther up the table. "I've already dropped a word in the Lord Lieutenant's ear, and he's as thrilled and relieved as I am."

"Apparently," the inspector went on, "Walter truly is turning respectable, and with Vince now gracing our cells and soon to face the Assizes, the rest of their not-so-merry band are at something of a loss. It seems that none of the thugs have the nous to run the businesses—the dens and so on—and one by one, they're shutting down."

The commissioner brandished his spoon at the inspector. "We'll need to be on our guard against any joker thinking to move in, but regardless"—he half bowed to Sophy and Martin—"the reduction of crime in the city is another excellent outcome of your recent adventures."

After that, the conversation moved on to other matters.

Under cover of a discussion about making greater use of canal barges to move iron and steel around the town and surrounding areas, Sophy glanced at Martin's profile, then leaned closer and, her gaze on his face, whispered, "You've certainly carved a place for yourself in Sheffield's heart."

He looked at her, then even more quietly replied, "The only heart that matters to me is yours." Under the table, he caught and gently squeezed her hand. "All I want is to fill the position by your side. Anything else is a bonus."

She smiled softly back. "You have my heart, all of it, not just a part."

His answering smile was the epitome of devilishly sweet. "That's only fair. You have all of mine."

~

Sophy was still smiling when, together with Martin, she stood beside her grandmother in the front hall and waved their happy guests away.

Her aunt Julia was among the last to leave. Julia had insisted on attending the meeting with Blackwell and, like the others there, had been highly impressed by Martin's handling of the situation. Now, standing beside Sophy and watching Martin talking to Oliver, who was heading back to London the next day, Julia murmured to Sophy, "A cool and steady head." Julia smiled and patted Sophy's hand. "He'll do."

Sophy laughed and kissed her aunt's cheek. "I most definitely agree."

She was, however, entertaining visions of making his head much less cool and definitely less steady when they finally got to celebrate their success in private.

Julia gave up waiting and departed, pausing to farewell Martin and Oliver, then allowing Hector to steady her down the steps.

Finally, Martin and Oliver shook hands, and Oliver saluted Sophy and Lady Bracknell, then strode out of the door, down the steps, and into the night.

Sophy joined Martin in the open doorway and gazed at Oliver's retreating figure. "Will we see him again, do you think?"

"I certainly hope so." Martin met her eyes and grinned. "He and I are considering investing in a project in Rotherham. Another use for the iron my foundry there produces."

"Oh?" Sophy arched her brows. "Given I'm hoping to cut an excellent and favorable deal with you for your pig iron, I'm not sure I like the sound of more competition."

Martin laughed and turned her in to the hall, allowing Higginbotham to close the front door. "I've already got plans to expand the foundry, so you needn't fear us not meeting Carmichael's demand."

She tipped up her chin and magnanimously declared, "Well, then, Oliver can have some."

Her grandmother had paused at the bottom of the stairs and looked inquiringly their way.

Still smiling, Sophy was about to step out to join her, but Martin squeezed her hand and held her back. Surprised, she looked at him.

He met her gaze. "Can you spare a few minutes?"

She blinked at him. "Here?"

"In the drawing room." He cast a swift glance at her grandmother, then looked back at her. "There's something—several things, actually—I believe we should discuss."

She was fairly certain he didn't mean pig iron. A flutter of expectation erupted inside her. Intrigued, she inclined her head. "All right."

She looked at her grandmother and saw her already on the stairs.

Her grandmother waved over her shoulder. "I'm for bed. I'll see you both tomorrow. Goodnight, my dears."

"Goodnight," Sophy and Martin chorused.

On the landing, her grandmother glanced back and, with a definite twinkle in her eye, advised, "Don't stay up too late."

With that and a knowing grin, her grandmother swept on, up the second flight.

Sophy turned to Martin and arched her brows.

In response, he stepped back and waved her to the drawing room.

She obliged and preceded him through the door. The staff had been busy, and the room had already been set to rights. The curtains were drawn against the night and—no doubt at Martin's instructions—a small fire burned cheerily in the grate.

One of the smaller sofas had been positioned to catch the warmth thrown out by the flames. Wondering just what Martin wanted to discuss, she drew in her silk skirts and sat.

He sat beside her, angled to face her, and captured one of her hands in his. He searched her eyes, a contented smile warming the caramel depths of his gaze.

She arched her brows again. Some heretofore unknown emotion had risen and blocked her throat.

His lips curved, that lurking smile manifesting. He raised the hand he held to his lips. "I thought"—his eyes locked with hers as he planted a kiss on her knuckles—"that it was time we decided on the parameters of our partnership."

Trapped in his gaze, she tipped her head. "Partnership?"

He nodded. "Our partnership in each and every sphere. To begin with, we should define what we each want business-wise." He looked into her eyes. "How do you want to manage Carmichael Steelworks?"

She stared back as she thought, but the truth was easy to define. "I want to remain working there, in the same way I currently do, as majority owner, overseeing production, managing orders, and doing all the things that fall to me to do."

Somewhat to her relief, he nodded, and a wry smile lit his eyes. "I'm hoping, at some point, to lure you into spending some time helping to establish our new venture across the street and lending your expertise in deciding which alloys will not just be best for our products but will also set them apart."

She laughed and gripped his fingers. "You won't have to ask twice. I would love to contribute to such an enterprise." She sent him an arch look. "In common with all the steel men at our gatherings today, I would be delighted to be associated with bringing a new industry to Sheffield." She grinned. "Indeed, judging by the way their ears pricked when you mentioned your new undertaking, I predict you'll be fighting them off."

He smiled and raised her hand to his lips again. "It's you I want by my side. From the beginning to the end. All the others are incidental."

She sighed and batted her lashes at him. "You say the nicest things, sir."

He laughed and squeezed her fingers. "All right. Between us, we have that much clear." He met her gaze. "You'll remain managing the steelworks and will help me set up the new plating works next door." His lips firmed, and he added, "And yes, I definitely want to bid against Atlas to supply your pig iron. I can guarantee the lowest price and also your input into the smelting conditions."

"Ah." She shifted to face him. "Now, you have my full attention, sir."

His grin turned smug. "I thought that might do it. Mind you, in return, I'll expect excellent deals for procuring Carmichael steel for my knife and wire-and-cable factories, and perhaps, together, we might explore making steel buttons."

She beamed. "That all sounds quite splendid." Entirely sincerely, she went on, "I can barely wait to see it all come into being." She gripped his hand more tightly. "Our life together is going to be filled with inventions and exciting new endeavors."

"Indubitably." Martin had discovered he truly adored making her smile like that, with excitement flashing in her turquoise eyes and her smile radiating happiness. He lowered their hands. "That, I believe, resolves the immediate questions regarding the merging of our business interests. The rest can come with time."

She nodded, and he continued, "That brings us to our more personal decisions." He summoned a serious expression and trained it on her. "Now that we've eradicated the threat to the steelworks, you are going to make an honorable man of me by marrying me, aren't you?"

She struggled to keep her lips straight, but lost the battle and laughed. Then she leaned close and brushed her lips to his. "Yes. I most definitely am." She drew back, and her smile faded, replaced by a faint frown. "About our wedding—"

"We have to have a proper wedding."

She studied him, no doubt wondering at his adamant tone and the determined set of his jaw. She arched a brow. "Can it be just a small one?"

Lips firming, he shook his head. "You don't know my family. You'll understand once you've met them. I'm one of the youngest of my generation, and the wider family will definitely expect a huge wedding with all due pomp and ceremony."

"Really?" She blinked. "You haven't told me all that much about your family."

He sighed. "I suppose this is the point when I should warn you about all the relatives and connections you'll acquire through marrying me." She looked at him encouragingly, and he started working through the long list, commencing with his brother-in-law, the Earl of Alverton, and continuing through the wider Cynster family, touching on the other major ton families to whom they were linked by marriage.

When he reached the end of his recitation, she stared at him. "Good Lord. I had no idea, but it's no longer any wonder that Blackwell reacted as he did when I introduced you. It wasn't just you he knew about sufficiently to be wary but your family as a whole."

He nodded. "There are benefits. Aside from all else, the Cynster connection will make the steelworks and all our enterprises well-nigh impregnable on all fronts—financially, politically, and socially." He paused, then glanced at her. "I should also mention Lord Randolph Cavanaugh, who was something of a mentor of mine, along with Alverton, when I first returned to England and started investing in businesses. I think you would enjoy meeting Cavanaugh's wife, Felicia, and her brother, William John Throgmorton. The pair are inventors and specialize in steam-powered machinery."

"Throgmorton?" Sophy's eyes widened. "I've heard the name. One of the steam winches in the main shed is a Throgmorton design."

Martin smiled at the distracted expression that overlaid her features as, without doubt, she imagined what might be possible were she to meet Felicia and William John.

Then she blinked and looked at him again. "You also haven't told me how you came to make your fortune. Was it family money you invested and grew?"

He considered saying it was, but partnerships were based on trust. "No. It wasn't." Resigned, he captured her gaze and tightened his hold on her hand. "I was once a young, reckless, and very inexperienced man."

He told her all of it—of his ill-advised flight from England, drawn by the lure of the colonies, and his years of hard, dogged, determined work there. "I was little more than a clerk to begin with." He continued, describing how he'd risen through the ranks of the import-export business that had hired him. "Primarily because of my diction and the ability to interact with people of any social rank. I was never intimidated by anyone, you see."

When she smiled as if perceiving some revelation, he asked, "What?"

Her smile deepened. "Your ability to interact with those of any social rank." She tipped her head, studying him. "That was something I noticed about you in the hours after we first met. You knew how to speak with the men in the shed. Very few of our class do."

"Yes, well. Now you know why and where and under what circumstances I learned the knack. I had to in order to survive." He paused, remembering those times. Then he drew breath and told her the rest—of the events that led to him returning to England and reconnecting with his family. Those were memories that, even now, made him inwardly squirm.

But he told her all. She deserved to know.

When he finally reached the present, more or less, and fell silent, she continued to study him as if fascinated with what she saw. Eventually, she smiled. "Your years in America explain how, at the shepherd's hut, you knew what to do to knock out those two thugs." She arched a playful brow at him. "I did wonder, you know."

He grunted and waited, but she simply continued to look at him as if waiting herself… He frowned. "Is that all you have to say about my past? I was no better than one of your workers for years, and yet here I am, claiming your hand."

She blinked, then searched his eyes. He had no idea what she saw there, but her expression softened and, turning fully to him, she raised both hands and framed his face.

She looked into his eyes and softly said, "Your past—all of it, the sum total of it—is what made you the man you are today. The man who saw a situation for what it was and stepped in and protected me, my family, my business, my workers, and the entire town from a cunning and wily enemy who, once he'd got his hooks into us, would have torn our lives to shreds and preyed on us for decades. Only you understood how to rid us of him without bloodshed. If the others had tried, they would have gone in aggressively, seeking to drive him off by force, and he would have dug in his heels, defied and fought us, and regardless of the outcome, the clash would have caused irreparable damage."

Holding his gaze, she evenly stated, "You alone saw the path to victory, and you had the wherewithal—the character, the knowledge, the traits—to convince us all to go along with your plan. That was—" She broke off, clearly remembering the scene in the boardroom, then shook her head in open wonder. "An amazing feat. I've never been a part of anything like that—a collective effort of such power."

She refocused on his eyes and smiled. "The man you are now is the man I need beside me as I—we—steer Carmichael Steelworks into a future bright with possibilities." She searched his eyes once more, then simply said, "You, as you are, are the man with whom I can see a future —a future I want to seize. I've never been visited by this degree of certainty before, not over anything else in my life."

He looked deep into her turquoise eyes and saw that those words were her truth, uttered with unflinching honesty. Finally, some knot, some constriction buried deep inside him, eased, unraveled, and fell away. Lightness—happiness—rushed in and took its place. He smiled, raised a hand and caught one of hers, and pressed a fervent kiss to her fingertips. "Beside you. There's nowhere else on earth I want to be. Now and forever."

Her smile was brilliant, then she leaned closer and, as he bent his head, lifted her lips to his.

They kissed, and between them, passion welled, rose, and surged, eager and wanting.

By the time they broke apart, they were both breathless and hungry.

They searched each other's eyes, saw their desire and need mirrored in the other, and shared a giddy laugh.

She leapt to her feet, seized his hand, and tugged him up. "Come on!

It's clearly past time we headed upstairs to appropriately celebrate our resounding success."

Smiling every bit as broadly, as eagerly expectant as she, he rose and allowed her to tow him to the door.

He'd come to Sheffield seeking to secure the final piece—the final enterprise—to complete his portfolio of steel-based industries.

And while he'd found that, he'd also discovered and secured something infinitely more precious.

His place.

The right place for him to fit, the right place in which he could prosper and grow.

Into the man he knew he had it in him to be, standing alongside her.

EPILOGUE

SATURDAY, JUNE 13, 1863. MISTYMOOR MANOR, STACEY BANK, PEAK DISTRICT.

Just over three weeks later, Martin had his most deeply desired wish fulfilled when he and Sophy were married before the altar in Sheffield Parish Church.

They'd had to move the ceremony to the larger church to accommodate all those who'd wished to attend. In addition to both their families and all the invited guests who had traveled from all over the British Isles, the congregation had included the majority of staff from the Carmichael houses plus most of the workers from the steelworks as well as all those who had been present in the Carmichael Steelworks' boardroom on that memorable day when Cornelius Blackwell had been forced to retreat from the town.

Inevitably, the tale of what had transpired that day had got out and done the rounds of the pubs and the clubs, no doubt embellished through every retelling, until Martin couldn't walk down any street without being greeted and thanked for the town's deliverance.

At first, he'd protested, but in the end, he'd given up and resigned himself to being known far and wide as the Savior of Sheffield. John Brown—the Father of the Sheffield Iron and Steel Trade—had been the first to laugh and warn him that such names, bestowed by popular acclaim, stuck to a man for life.

But for today, Martin mentally set the unexpected title and mantle aside and concentrated on—reveled in—simply being himself. Courtesy of recent events, he finally truly understood who and what Martin Cynster was. He'd discovered he was a man who wanted a loving wife and a family of his own—along with the love that made both possible—just as passionately as his siblings.

As all the rest of the wider Cynster brood.

For years, he'd felt detached, untouched by the same compulsion that had seemed to infect all the others, but it seemed that he—the man inside—had merely been waiting for the right lady to cross his path.

In Sophy, he'd found his mate and the route to his future. A future that was so much *more* than any he'd envisioned before.

After the ceremony, they'd circulated among their guests on the lawns about the church, then all those invited to the wedding breakfast had piled into carriages and followed them—driven by Figgs in an open barouche—to Mistymoor Manor.

The manor would be Martin and Sophy's home and boasted a large ballroom with many glass doors that opened to a flagged terrace. Today, with the sun beaming down outside, the doors had been propped open, and every now and then, a gentle breeze wafted the scents of late blossom and early roses over the chattering and dancing guests.

Martin seized a moment to catch his breath and watch Sophy circle the floor in his cousin Toby's arms; she appeared to be interrogating Toby about what he did these days. Martin wished her joy in getting any meaningful answers. He lifted a glass of wine from a passing footman's tray and stepped free of the mad, giddy throng to the empty space before one open door.

He sipped and studied the crowd. Sophy's family and his were mingling and making the usual connections such families did. Everyone seemed to be thoroughly enjoying themselves. So many of his familial peers—his cousins and second cousins, the children of the fabled group long ago dubbed the Bar Cynster—were married now, he sometimes felt he needed a crib sheet to keep all the names of the spouses straight. And the children! His own nephews and nieces were running amok, weaving through the guests and laughing and calling; he vaguely recalled doing the same at long-ago weddings when he'd been their age.

He smiled to himself at the evidence of the generations rolling on. He'd just taken another sip of the very fine burgundy he and his brothers had unearthed in the manor cellars when his sister, Therese, swanned up and joined him.

She halted beside him and, in her usual fashion, critically surveyed the scene. Then she smiled. "I always thought a June wedding in the Peak

District would be spectacular, and you and Sophy have proved me right." Therese cast him an affectionate look. "I'm not sure you noticed—you didn't seem to be focusing on anything beyond your bride—but the church was packed. To the rafters. You are clearly a much-loved person in this town." She nodded at him approvingly. "You've found your place."

He met her gaze for an instant, then gestured to the crowd. "We all have, haven't we?" His gaze deflected to Sophy and Toby. "All except…"

Therese had followed his gaze. "Indeed. But he, too, will find that Fate chooses her own time and, ultimately, will not be gainsaid." Her gaze wandered farther, seeking out other heads in the melee. "Just think of the surprises in that branch of the family. First Pru, then Nicholas and Meg. None of us foresaw any of those matches, yet once they occurred, you had to wonder at the inevitability of the connection. It seemed so obvious once they found their other halves that those people were the right ones for them."

He grunted softly. He had to agree.

His brothers ambled up, and the talk turned general, the siblings sharing what they and their burgeoning families had been up to and also how their expanding interests were faring.

Inevitably, however, given the reason for the gathering, their thoughts turned to who would be next—a game Christopher, Gregory, and Therese's husband, Devlin, who by then had joined them, had played at every wedding since their own.

"No contest, this time," Devlin pointed out as they all looked to where Toby was now chatting with Sophy and several others. "He's the last one." Devlin glanced at Martin. "He's the same age as you, isn't he?" When Martin nodded, Devlin stated, "In that case, he's running out of time."

Christopher nodded. "It'll be soon. He just hasn't realized it yet."

Gregory tipped his head, considering. "Or is it a case of he knows and is taking devilish good care not to stumble into any of Fate's traps?"

Therese made a dismissive sound. "How many more times do I have to remind you? Fate is female, ergo, she'll snare him in the end."

All four males looked at her, then as one, grunted and didn't argue.

Later, when the guests had dispersed and the sun was dipping toward the peaks to the west, Martin and Sophy stole away to the old walled rose garden. It had become their place, their private retreat; other than them, only Old Joe and his brother, Reggie, ever went there.

The wending path lined by massive old rosebushes led to an alcove in the rear wall that housed a stone bench, warmed by the sun.

They sat, and Sophy sighed contentedly and leaned into Martin's side. He raised his arm and looped it about her, settling her comfortably against him.

At first, they simply sat and let the peace and tranquility of the setting steal over them, soothing away the last remnants of tension instilled over the past hectic hours.

Eventually, Sophy softly said, "We're here. Finally."

Martin understood exactly what she meant. He dipped his head and pressed a kiss to her temple. "We are. And our future lies, bright and beckoning, before us."

They were looking forward to plunging in, hand in hand, hearts committed, and minds as one.

He rested his cheek against the silk of her hair and raised his gaze to stare over the rosebushes at the manor's roof.

To date, he'd lived a full, exciting, distinctly varied, and unexpected life. Now, he was looking forward to all the other excitements he'd never thought would be his to experience—being a husband, experiencing fatherhood, crafting a life within a growing family—with a partner the likes of whom he'd never imagined existed, much less might be by his side.

"You," he murmured. He glanced down at Sophy and, when she turned her face his way, smiled into her turquoise eyes. "You've made my future possible. You've opened the door to a future I never knew might be there."

She smiled beatifically. "You've certainly done the same for me."

"And now…?"

"Now, we go forth and claim that future and make it into what we wish it to be. Hand in hand, heart and soul."

"Together," he stated.

"Forever," she replied. She shifted, stretched up, and kissed him.

And as the sun dipped low, they set out to explore all that Fate had gifted them as they started the journey to ultimately realize all the promise their future might hold.

~

Tuesday, November 17, 1863
Lombard Street, London

Martin stood under the weak glow of the third streetlamp on the southern side of Lombard Street and wondered, yet again, at the choice of meeting place. November in London was inevitably a season of fogs, and tonight was no exception. Thick mist coiled around each streetlamp, shrouding what, during the day, was a busy, bustling city street.

Indeed, even at nearly eight o'clock at night, Lombard Street was far from deserted, but human activity was largely confined to the pools of light spilling from the doors of the three public houses strung along the opposite side of the street.

Martin leaned against the wall of the shop before which the stipulated streetlamp rose. He was in London with Sophy, staying at his house in Arlington Street while they considered several businesses to add to their growing portfolio of steel-based industries, as well as finalizing several long-term orders for Carmichael Steelworks.

All was going well on that front. Indeed, their combined interests seemed ever-expanding, and his steel-plating factory was already under construction.

When he'd first received the message that had brought him to Lombard Street, he'd debated whether or not to show it to Sophy, but in the end, he had. Like him, she'd puzzled over what it might mean, and when he'd decided to meet with Blackwell—too eaten by curiosity not to learn the answer—although she'd been concerned, ultimately, she'd placed her faith in him to know what he was doing.

His hands sunk in his greatcoat pockets, he ran his fingertips along the comforting, cool weight of the pair of derringer pistols he'd brought along as insurance. Figgs, Roland, and Tunstall were hanging back somewhere in the shadows. He hadn't spotted them, which made it unlikely that Blackwell and whoever he brought with him would, either.

All Blackwell's missive had contained was a simple request for a meeting to discuss business matters, along with the time and place.

Despite the hour, Lombard Street, in the center of the City, just a block from the Bank of England, did not feature as a likely haunt for villains. Martin couldn't decide whether Blackwell had chosen a street with which Martin had to be familiar to reassure Martin or to lull him into a false sense of security.

He and his men had taken up their positions early. The bells of nearby St. Paul's started tolling for the hour. Their final *bong* was fading when a large, tall, slightly hunched figure wearing a familiar black overcoat turned onto the street at the western end. Striding along the southern pavement, Cornelius Blackwell approached.

Martin straightened away from the wall and waited.

Blackwell halted a yard away and nodded. "Mr. Cynster. Thank you for meeting with me." Blackwell faintly smiled. "I didn't know if you would."

Martin returned the nod. "Blackwell. I have to confess I'm curious as to what business we might have to discuss."

To Martin's surprise, Blackwell looked faintly embarrassed. "Yes, well." Blackwell turned to view the other side of the street. "I chose this place hoping to avoid any impression that I represented a threat." He gestured up and down the street. "Given the weather, I suggest we go in and find a table. Take your pick."

Martin studied the man for a second, then looked across the street. Two of the three public houses were large and likely crowded; they were certainly noisy. The one to the right was smaller and, while bright and cheery and reasonably patronized, had the look of a family establishment. He nodded that way. "Let's try that one."

Together, he and Blackwell crossed the street. At the door, Martin stood back and waved Blackwell through. The moment gave Martin a chance to glance back along the street. He spotted Figgs sliding from the shadows and Tunstall walking openly that way.

Martin turned to the door and followed Blackwell inside.

They found a table in the far corner of the taproom and settled facing each other over pints of ale.

Blackwell took a sip, then setting the glass down in front of him, with his gaze on the frothy head, said, "I didn't ask you here to talk about your business—any of your businesses, not even that new one in Sheffield." Blackwell raised his pale gaze and met Martin's eyes. "I wanted to ask your advice about mine."

Martin blinked, then he took a slow sip of his ale. Lowering the glass, he said, "You want to ask my advice about slum estates?"

"No." Blackwell's lips compressed, then as if forcing the words out, he said, "I've given that game away."

Martin fought to smother his surprise and didn't entirely succeed. "Really?"

"Yes, really." Somewhat testily, Blackwell glanced around, clearly wanting to make sure no one there overheard. "After our…encounter in Sheffield, I got to thinking. I've money now—lots of it. I told you what level of rents I used to squeeze from the tenants, so you can guess how much I've stashed away. And I spoke with Walter Murchison before I left and heard what he was doing, moving on as it were, and I thought, well, what am I going to do with all my money? Just mindlessly doing the same thing over and over again and still not getting what I want… It doesn't make sense. I see that now."

He met Martin's eyes again, and there was determination in Blackwell's gaze.

"So I came back here and thought about it, and I decided to get out. To stop being a landlord. I got my solicitors in and had them work out what I could do. Long story short, I gave all the tenants their leases, free and clear, for however long they want. No further charges. I told my lads that I was getting out of the business. I thought they'd tell me I was going soft and leave to work for some other gaffer, but they didn't. When I told them what I was doing, giving the leases away…well, turns out the heavy handing hadn't been to their taste for some time. They thought letting go was the right thing to do—a good thing to do. For us all."

Blackwell shook his head as if still perplexed by the vagaries of human nature. "Anyway, so now I have all this money sitting in the bank. More than enough for me to see out my life. But the lads…they've been like sons to me, and they need work. So I need to start up some business that will give them all jobs and make enough money in some legitimate way so that they won't see it as charity."

Martin studied Blackwell as the man took a long pull of his ale. As he lowered the glass again, Martin asked, "So where do I come in?"

Blackwell stared at the glass. "I've spent the last weeks looking into you. When I met you in Sheffield, I knew straightaway you weren't like the others in that room, not even like the others who walked in later." Blackwell raised his gaze and narrowed his eyes on Martin. "There's an edge to you. I thought right away that despite your name, you weren't the average ton gentleman. And you aren't, are you? You've been to America and done all sorts of things there, and you learned how to manage a business, how to grow a business, without relying on your name. Without getting any help at all from your station."

Blackwell looked down and waved. "Those others were entitled. They grew up in the business and had it handed to them, or were first in and so made the rules. You…" He paused, then looked at Martin again. "You know how to establish a business when you have no advantages to use as levers."

Martin inclined his head. "So?"

Blackwell hauled in a huge breath, then in a rush, said, "So I want you to advise me as to what business I might get into."

Martin studied the man and couldn't not ask, "What do you want to get out of this enterprise?"

"Satisfaction." The answer came so quickly it was patently the truth. "And jobs for my lads."

"Leaving the lads aside for the moment, what do you mean by satisfaction?"

Blackwell frowned and thought.

Martin took a sip of his ale and wondered what the hell he was doing, responding to the man's appeal.

Eventually, Blackwell said, "By satisfaction, I mean knowing inside that something you've done is good and worthwhile. That you've created something that is useful and will last and remain a good thing once you've passed."

That, Martin had to admit, wasn't a bad answer. He found himself nodding. "All right. So…" He focused on Blackwell, then asked, "How old are you?"

Blackwell looked at him warily. "Why does that matter?"

"Because of the time it takes for a business to mature. I assume you want to achieve satisfaction before you die."

Blackwell huffed and looked into his glass. "I'm forty-five."

Martin blinked. He'd thought Blackwell in his mid- to late fifties.

Blackwell saw his surprise and gestured to his head. "It's the hair. It went gray when I was thirty. M'father was the same. As for the face, it was always like this, so people never can tell my age."

"That's not necessarily a bad thing." Martin studied Blackwell for a long moment. The man didn't flinch or look away.

Am I really going to do this?

Yes, he was, because Blackwell had gone against his own impulses, bared his soul, and asked for help.

"Swear to me," Martin said, "on your mother's grave, that you are no longer involved in any slum estate or in any similar business that exploits others."

Blackwell held his gaze. A slight frown wormed its way onto his face.

"I still own the land the houses are on, but I don't take any money at all from those who live on it."

Martin nodded. "Fair enough on that count. Anything else?"

Blackwell shook his head and, without prompting, formally swore the oath Martin had asked for.

Martin studied him for a moment more, saw nothing but dogged sincerity in his pale eyes, and nodded. "Very well. This is what you're going to do."

~

~

Dear Reader,

In order to complete the romances of Vane and Patience's branch of the Cynster family tree, we've jumped ahead eleven years to learn of Martin and Sophy's romance.

Throughout the previous volumes—those relating the romances of Martin's siblings, Christopher, Therese, and Gregory—Martin has progressively emerged as a man immersed in the task of amassing a portfolio of industrial businesses. He has remained solely focused on that path, ignoring all distractions, especially those associated with finding a wife. It therefore seemed obvious that, if he were to ever find his one true love, he would discover her in some factory somewhere—or as it happened, on a steelworks floor.

Learning about Sheffield in the 1860s, including the details of the then-existing steelworks and the colorful figures that helped establish the town as a center of steelmaking and also learning about the steelmaking process at that time was a fascinating endeavor. As for the problems facing municipalities with the ever-increasing demand for worker housing, those seemed all too familiar! It always amazes me how some issues reverberate through the centuries.

I hope you enjoyed reading of Martin and Sophy's quest to discover who had Carmichael Steelworks in their sights, and the consequent growing understanding of what, to them, was most important in life.

As is now my habit, buried in the Epilogue is a hint of which Cynster is next in line for their story. However, because we've jumped ahead by eleven years, in this instance, the hint points to marriages that, in this volume, have already occurred. So we're heading back to 1854, to pick up the two matches unforeseen by the family, namely Nicholas's tale, to be released in March 2023, to be followed by the romance of Nicholas's younger sister, Meg, later in 2023, while Toby's tale is yet to be told (but it is coming!).

With my best wishes for unrestrained happy reading!

Stephanie.

For alerts as new books are released, plus information on upcoming books, exclusive sweepstakes and sneak peeks into upcoming novels, sign up for Stephanie's Private Email Newsletter https://stephanielaurens.com/newsletter-signup.php

Or if you don't have time to chat and want a quick email alert, sign up and follow me at BookBub https://www.bookbub.com/authors/stephanie-laurens

The ultimate source for detailed information on all Stephanie's published books, including covers, descriptions, and excerpts, is Stephanie's Website www.stephanielaurens.com

You can also follow Stephanie via her Amazon Author Page at http://tinyurl.com/zc3e9mp

Goodreads members can follow Stephanie via her author page https://www.goodreads.com/author/show/9241.Stephanie_Laurens

You can email Stephanie at stephanie@stephanielaurens.com

Or find her on Facebook
https://www.facebook.com/AuthorStephanieLaurens/

COMING NEXT:

THE BARBARIAN AND MISS FLIBBERTIGIBBET
Cynster Next Generation Novel #12
To be released in March, 2023.

Nicholas Cynster rides up to Aisby Grange in Lincolnshire determined to purchase an elusive stallion for the Cynster Stable, only to encounter a strikingly beautiful and very direct young lady who proves to be the lion guarding the gateway to the horse's owner. But before Nicholas can negotiate access, the horse is stolen. In order to reclaim the beast, Nicholas finds himself joining forces with the lady he recognizes as being known throughout the ton for her flighty, frivolous, indeed outrageous behavior…except she's nothing like that.

Available for e-book pre-order in December, 2022.

RECENTLY RELEASED:

FOES, FRIENDS, AND LOVERS
Cynster Next Generation Novel #11

#1 New York Times *bestselling author Stephanie Laurens returns with a tale of a gentleman seeking the road to fulfillment and a lady with a richly satisfying life but no certain future.*

A gentleman searching for a purpose in life sets out to claim his legacy, only to discover that instead of the country residence he'd expected, he's inherited an eccentric community whose enterprises are overseen by a decidedly determined young lady who is disinclined to hand over the reins.

Gregory Cynster arrives at the property willed to him by his great-aunt with the intention of converting Bellamy Hall into a quiet, comfortable, gentleman's country residence, only to discover the Hall overrun by an eclectic collection of residents engaged in a host of business endeavors under the stewardship of a lady far too young to be managing such reins.

With the other residents of the estate, Caitlin Fergusson has been planning just how to deal with the new owner, but coming face to face with Gregory Cynster throws her and everyone else off their stride. They'd anticipated a bored and disinterested gentleman who, once they'd revealed the income generated by the Hall's community, would be content to leave them undisturbed.

Instead, while Gregory appears the epitome of the London rake they'd expected him to be, they quickly learn he's determined to embrace Bellamy Hall and all its works and claim ownership of the estate.

While the other residents adjust their thinking, the burden of dealing daily with Gregory falls primarily on Caitlin's slender shoulders, yet as he doggedly carves out a place for himself, Caitlin's position as chatelaine-cum-steward seems set to grow redundant. But Caitlin has her own reasons for clinging to the refuge her position at Bellamy Hall represents.

What follows is a dance of revelations, both of others and also of themselves, for Gregory, Caitlin, and the residents of Bellamy Hall. Yet even as they work out what their collective future might hold, a shadowy villain threatens to steal away everything they've created.

A classic historical romance set in an artisanal community on a country estate. A Cynster Next Generation novel. A full-length historical romance of 118,000 words.

RECENTLY RELEASED:

THE MEANING OF LOVE
A spin-off from Lady Osbaldestone's Christmas Chronicles

#1 New York Times *bestselling author Stephanie Laurens explores the strength of a fated love, one that was left in abeyance when the protagonists were too young, but that roars back to life when, as adults, they meet again.*

A lady ready and waiting to be deemed on the shelf has her transition into spinsterhood disrupted when the nobleman she'd once thought she loved returns to London and fate and circumstance conspire to force them to discover what love truly is and what it means to them.

What happens when a love left behind doesn't die?

Melissa North had assumed that after eight years of not setting eyes on each other, her youthful attraction to—or was it infatuation with?—Julian Delamere, once Viscount Dagenham and now Earl of Carsely, would have faded to nothing and gasped its last. Unfortunately, during the intervening years, she's failed to find any suitable suitor who measures up to her mark and is resigned to ending her days an old maid.

Then she sees Julian across a crowded ballroom, and he sees her, and the intensity of their connection shocks her. She seizes the first chance that offers to flee, only to discover she's jumped from the frying pan into the fire.

Within twenty-four hours, she and Julian are the newly engaged toast of the ton.

Julian has never forgotten Melissa. Now, having inherited the earldom, he must marry and is determined to choose his own bride. He'd assumed that by now, Melissa would be married to someone else, but apparently not. Consequently, he's not averse to the path Fate seems to be steering them down.

And, indeed, as they discover, enforced separation has made their hearts grow fonder, and the attraction between them flares even more intensely.

However, it's soon apparent that someone is intent on ensuring their married life is cut short in deadly fashion. Through a whirlwind courtship, a massive ton wedding, and finally, blissful country peace, they fend off increasingly dangerous, potentially lethal threats, until, together, they unravel the conspiracy that's dogged their heels and expose the villain behind it all.

A classic historical romance laced with murderous intrigue. A novel arising from the Lady Osbaldestone's Christmas Chronicles. A full-length historical romance of 127,000 words.

THE SECRETS OF LORD GRAYSON CHILD
Cynster Next Generation-Connected Novel
(following on from The Games Lovers Play)

#1 New York Times *bestselling author Stephanie Laurens returns to the world of the Cynsters' next generation with the tale of an unconventional nobleman and an equally unconventional noblewoman learning to love and trust again.*

A jilted noblewoman forced into a dual existence half in and half out of the ton is unexpectedly confronted by the nobleman who left her behind ten years ago, but before either can catch their breaths, they trip over a murder and into a race to capture a killer.

Lord Grayson Child is horrified to discover that *The London Crier*, a popular gossip rag, is proposing to expose his extraordinary wealth to the ton's matchmakers, not to mention London's shysters and Captain Sharps. He hies to London and corners *The Crier's* proprietor—only to discover the paper's owner is the last person he'd expected to see.

Izzy—Lady Isadora Descartes—is flabbergasted when Gray appears in her printing works' office. He's the very last person she wants to meet while in her role as owner of *The Crier*, but there he is, as large as life, and she has to deal with him without giving herself away! She manages—just—and seizes on the late hour to put him off so she can work out what to do.

But before leaving the printing works, she and he stumble across a murder, and all hell breaks loose.

Izzy can only be grateful for Gray's support as, to free them both of suspicion, they embark on a joint campaign to find the killer.

Yet working side by side opens their eyes to who they each are now—both quite different to the youthful would-be lovers of ten years before. Mutual respect, affection, and appreciation grow, and amid the chaos of hunting a ruthless killer, they find themselves facing the question of whether what they'd deemed wrecked ten years before can be resurrected.

Then the killer's motive proves to be a treasonous plot, and with others, Gray and Izzy race to prevent a catastrophe, a task that ultimately falls to them alone in a situation in which the only way out is through selfless togetherness—only by relying on each other will they survive.

A classic historical romance laced with crime and intrigue. A Cynster Next Generation-connected novel—a full-length historical romance of 115,000 words.

THE GAMES LOVERS PLAY
Cynster Next Generation Novel #9

#1 New York Times *bestselling author Stephanie Laurens returns to the Cynsters' next generation with an evocative tale of two people striving to overcome unusual hurdles in order to claim true love.*

A nobleman wedded to the lady he loves strives to overwrite five years of masterful pretence and open his wife's eyes to the fact that he loves her as much as she loves him.

Lord Devlin Cader, Earl of Alverton, married Therese Cynster five years ago. What he didn't tell her then and has assiduously hidden ever since—for what seemed excellent reasons at the time—is that he loves her every bit as much as she loves him.

For her own misguided reasons, Therese had decided that the adage that Cynsters always marry for love did not necessarily mean said Cynsters were loved in return. She accepted that was usually so, but being universally viewed by gentlemen as too managing, bossy, and opinionated, she believed she would never be loved for herself. Consequently, after falling irrevocably in love with Devlin, when he made it plain he didn't love her yet wanted her to wife, she accepted the half love-match he offered, and once they were wed, set about organizing to make their marriage the very best it could be.

Now, five years later, they are an established couple within the haut ton, have three young children, and Devlin is making a name for himself in business and political circles. There's only one problem. Having attended numerous Cynster weddings and family gatherings and spent time with Therese's increasingly married cousins, who with their spouses all embrace the Cynster ideal of marriage based on mutually acknowledged love, Devlin is no longer content with the half love-match he himself engineered. No fool, he sees and comprehends what the craven act of denying his love is costing both him and Therese and feels compelled to rectify his fault. He wants for them what all Therese's married cousins enjoy—the rich and myriad benefits of marriages based on acknowledged mutual love.

Love, he's discovered, is too powerful a force to deny, leaving him wrestling with the conundrum of finding a way to convincingly reveal to Therese that he loves her without wrecking everything—especially the mutual trust—they've built over the past five years.

A classic historical romance set amid the glittering world of the London haut ton. A Cynster Next Generation novel—a full-length historical romance of 110,000 words.

PREVIOUS CYNSTER NEXT GENERATION RELEASES:

THE INEVITABLE FALL OF CHRISTOPHER CYNSTER
Cynster Next Generation Novel #8

#1 New York Times *bestselling author Stephanie Laurens returns to the Cynsters' next generation with a rollicking tale of smugglers, counterfeit banknotes, and two people falling in love.*

A gentleman hoping to avoid falling in love and a lady who believes love has passed her by are flung together in a race to unravel a plot that threatens to undermine the realm.

Christopher Cynster has finally accepted that to have the life he wants, he needs a wife, but before he can even think of searching for the right lady, he's drawn into an investigation into the distribution of counterfeit banknotes.

London born and bred, Ellen Martingale is battling to preserve the fiction that her much-loved uncle, Christopher's neighbor, still has his wits about him, but Christopher's questions regarding nearby Goffard Hall trigger her suspicions. As her younger brother attends card parties at the Hall, she feels compelled to investigate.

While Ellen appears to be the sort of frippery female Christopher abhors, he quickly learns that, in her case, appearances are deceiving. And through the twists and turns in an investigation that grows ever more serious and urgent, he discovers how easy it is to fall in love, while Ellen learns that love hasn't, after all, passed her by.

But then the villain steps from the shadows, and love's strengths and vulnerabilities are put to the test—just as Christopher has always feared. Will he pass muster? Can they triumph? Or will they lose all they've so recently found?

A historical romance with a dash of intrigue, set in rural Kent. A Cynster Next Generation novel—a full-length historical romance of 124,000 words.

A CONQUEST IMPOSSIBLE TO RESIST
Cynster Next Generation Novel #7

#1 New York Times *bestselling author Stephanie Laurens returns to the Cynsters' next generation to bring you a thrilling tale of love, intrigue, and fabulous horses.*

A notorious rakehell with a stable of rare Thoroughbreds and a lady on a quest to locate such horses must negotiate personal minefields to forge a greatly desired alliance—one someone is prepared to murder to prevent.

Prudence Cynster has turned her back on husband hunting in favor of horse hunting. As the head of the breeding program underpinning the success of the Cynster racing stables, she's on a quest to acquire the necessary horses to refresh the stable's breeding stock.

On his estranged father's death, Deaglan Fitzgerald, now Earl of Glengarah, left London and the hedonistic life of a wealthy, wellborn rake and returned to Glengarah Castle determined to rectify the harm caused by his father's neglect. Driven by guilt that he hadn't been there to protect his people during the Great Famine, Deaglan holds firm against the lure of his father's extensive collection of horses and, leaving the stable to the care of his brother, Felix, devotes himself to returning the estate to prosperity.

Deaglan had fallen out with his father and been exiled from Glengarah over his drive to have the horses pay their way. Knowing Deaglan's wishes and that restoration of the estate is almost complete, Felix writes to the premier Thoroughbred breeding program in the British Isles to test their interest in the Glengarah horses.

On receiving a letter describing exactly the type of horses she's seeking, Pru overrides her family's reluctance and sets out for Ireland's west coast to visit the now-reclusive wicked Earl of Glengarah. Yet her only interest is in his horses, which she cannot wait to see.

When Felix tells Deaglan that a P. H. Cynster is about to arrive to assess the horses with a view to a breeding arrangement, Deaglan can only be grateful. But then P. H. Cynster turns out to be a lady, one utterly unlike any other he's ever met.

Yet they are who they are, and both understand their world. They battle their instincts and attempt to keep their interactions businesslike, but the sparks are incandescent and inevitably ignite a sexual blaze that consumes them both—and opens their eyes.

But before they can find their way to their now-desired goal, first one accident, then another distracts them. Someone, it seems, doesn't want them to strike a deal. Who? Why?

They need to find out before whoever it is resorts to the ultimate sanction.

A historical romance with neo-Gothic overtones, set in the west of Ireland. A Cynster Next Generation novel—a full-length historical romance of 125,000 words.

The first volume of the Devil's Brood Trilogy
THE LADY BY HIS SIDE
Cynster Next Generation Novel #4

A marquess in need of the right bride. An earl's daughter in search of a purpose. A betrayal that ends in murder and balloons into a threat to the realm.

Sebastian Cynster knows time is running out. If he doesn't choose a wife soon, his female relatives will line up to assist him. Yet the current debutantes do not appeal. Where is he to find the right lady to be his marchioness? Then Drake Varisey, eldest son of the Duke of Wolverstone, asks for Sebastian's aid.

Having assumed his father's mantle in protecting queen and country, Drake must go to Ireland in pursuit of a dangerous plot. But he's received an urgent missive from Lord Ennis, an Irish peer—Ennis has heard something Drake needs to know. Ennis insists Drake attends an upcoming house party at Ennis's Kent estate so Ennis can reveal his information face-to-face.

Sebastian has assisted Drake before and, long ago, had a liaison with Lady Ennis. Drake insists Sebastian is just the man to be Drake's surrogate at the house party—the guests will imagine all manner of possibilities and be blind to Sebastian's true purpose.

Unsurprisingly, Sebastian is reluctant, but Drake's need is real. With only more debutantes on his horizon, Sebastian allows himself to be persuaded.

His first task is to inveigle Antonia Rawlings, a lady he has known all her life, to include him as her escort to the house party. Although he's seen little of Antonia in recent years, Sebastian is confident of gaining her support.

Eldest daughter of the Earl of Chillingworth, Antonia has abandoned the search for a husband and plans to use the week of the house party to decide what to do with her life. There has to be some purpose, some role, she can claim for her own.

Consequently, on hearing Sebastian's request and an explanation of what lies behind it, she seizes on the call to action. Suppressing her senses' idiotic reaction to Sebastian's nearness, she agrees to be his partner-in-intrigue.

But while joining the house party proves easy, the gathering is thrown into chaos when Lord Ennis is murdered—just before he was to speak with Sebastian. Worse, Ennis's last words, gasped to Sebastian, are: *Gunpowder. Here.*

Gunpowder? And here, where?

With a killer continuing to stalk the halls, side by side, Sebastian and Antonia search for answers and, all the while, the childhood connection that had always existed between them strengthens and blooms…into something so much more.

First volume in a trilogy. A Cynster Next Generation Novel – a classic historical romance with gothic overtones layered over a continuing intrigue. A full-length novel of 99,000 words.

The second volume of the Devil's Brood Trilogy
AN IRRESISTIBLE ALLIANCE
Cynster Next Generation Novel #5

A duke's second son with no responsibilities and a lady starved of the excitement her soul craves join forces to unravel a deadly, potentially catastrophic threat to the realm - that only continues to grow.

With his older brother's betrothal announced, Lord Michael Cynster is freed from the pressure of familial expectations. However, the allure of his previous hedonistic pursuits has paled. Then he learns of the mission his brother, Sebastian, and Lady Antonia Rawlings have been assisting with and volunteers to assist by hunting down the hoard of gunpowder now secreted somewhere in London.

Michael sets out to trace the carters who transported the gunpowder from Kent to London. His quest leads him to the Hendon Shipping Company, where he discovers his sole source of information is the only daughter of Jack and Kit Hendon, Miss Cleome Hendon, who although a fetchingly attractive lady, firmly holds the reins of the office in her small hands.

Cleo has fought to achieve her position in the company. Initially, managing the office was a challenge, but she now conquers all in just a few hours a week. With her three brothers all adventuring in America, she's been driven to the realization that she craves adventure, too.

When Michael Cynster walks in and asks about carters, Cleo's instincts leap. She wrings from him the full tale of his mission—and offers him a bargain. She will lead him to the carters he seeks if he agrees to include her as an equal partner in the mission.

Horrified, Michael attempts to resist, but ultimately finds himself agreeing—a sequence of events he quickly learns is common around Cleo. Then she delivers on her part of the bargain, and he finds there are benefits to allowing her to continue to investigate beside him—not least being that if she's there, then he knows she's safe.

But the further they go in tracing the gunpowder, the more deaths they uncover. And when they finally locate the barrels, they find themselves tangled in a fight to the death—one that forces them to face what has grown between them, to seize and defend what they both see as their path to the greatest adventure of all. A shared life. A shared future. A shared love.

Second volume in a trilogy. A Cynster Next Generation Novel – a classic historical romance with gothic overtones layered over a continuing intrigue. A full-length novel of 101,000 words.

The third and final volume in the Devil's Brood Trilogy
THE GREATEST CHALLENGE OF THEM ALL
Cynster Next Generation Novel #6

A nobleman devoted to defending queen and country and a noblewoman wild enough to match his every step race to disrupt the plans of a malignant intelligence intent on shaking England to its very foundations.

Lord Drake Varisey, Marquess of Winchelsea, eldest son and heir of the Duke of Wolverstone, must foil a plot that threatens to shake the foundations of the realm, but the very last lady—nay, noblewoman—he needs assisting him is Lady Louisa Cynster, known throughout the ton as Lady Wild.

For the past nine years, Louisa has suspected that Drake might well be the ideal husband for her, even though he's assiduous in avoiding her. But she's now twenty-seven and enough is enough. She believes propinquity will elucidate exactly what it is that lies between them, and what better opportunity to work closely with Drake than his latest mission, with which he patently needs her help?

Unable to deny Louisa's abilities or the value of her assistance and powerless to curb her willfulness, Drake is forced to grit his teeth and acquiesce to her sticking by his side, if only to ensure her safety. But all too soon, his true feelings for her show enough for her, perspicacious as she is, to see through his denials, which she then interprets as a challenge.

Even while they gather information, tease out clues, increasingly desperately search for the missing gunpowder, and doggedly pursue the killer responsible for an ever-escalating tally of dead men, thrown together through the hours, he and she learn to trust and appreciate each other. And fed by constant exposure—and blatantly encouraged by her—their desires and hungers swell and grow…

As the barriers between them crumble, the attraction he has for so long restrained burgeons and balloons, until goaded by her near-death, it erupts, and he seizes her—only to be seized in return.

Linked irrevocably and with their wills melded and merged by passion's fire, with time running out and the evil mastermind's deadline looming, together, they focus their considerable talents and make one last push to learn the critical truths—to find the gunpowder and unmask the villain behind this far-reaching plot.

Only to discover that they have significantly less time than they'd thought, that the villain's target is even more crucially fundamental to the realm than they'd imagined, and it's going to take all that Drake is—as well as all that Louisa as Lady Wild can bring to bear—to defuse the threat, capture the villain, and make all safe and right again.

As they race to the ultimate confrontation, the future of all England rests on their shoulders.

Third volume in a trilogy. A Cynster Next Generation Novel – a classic historical romance with gothic overtones layered over an intrigue. A full-length novel of 129,000 words.

If you haven't yet caught up with the first books in the Cynster Next Generation Novels, then BY WINTER'S LIGHT is a Christmas story that highlights the Cynster children as they stand poised on the cusp of adulthood – essentially an introductory novel to the upcoming generation. That novel is followed by the first pair of Cynster Next Generation romances, those of Lucilla and Marcus Cynster, twins and the eldest children of Lord Richard aka Scandal Cynster and Catriona, Lady of the Vale. Both the twins' stories are set in Scotland. See below for further details.

BY WINTER'S LIGHT
Cynster Next Generation Novel #1

#1 New York Times *bestselling author Stephanie Laurens returns to romantic Scotland to usher in a new generation of Cynsters in an enchanting tale of mistletoe, magic, and love.*

It's December 1837 and the young adults of the Cynster clan have succeeded in having the family Christmas celebration held at snow-bound Casphairn Manor, Richard and Catriona Cynster's home. Led by Sebastian, Marquess of Earith, and by Lucilla, future Lady of the Vale, and her twin brother, Marcus, the upcoming generation has their own plans for the holiday season.

Yet where Cynsters gather, love is never far behind—the festive occasion brings together Daniel Crosbie, tutor to Lucifer Cynster's sons, and Claire Meadows, widow and governess to Gabriel Cynster's daughter. Daniel and Claire have met before and the embers of an unexpected passion smolder between them, but once bitten, twice shy, Claire believes a second marriage is not in her stars. Daniel, however, is determined to press his suit. He's seen the love the Cynsters share, and Claire is the lady with whom he dreams of sharing *his* life. Assisted by a bevy of Cynsters—innate matchmakers every one—Daniel strives to persuade Claire that trusting him with her hand and her heart is her right path to happiness.

Meanwhile, out riding on Christmas Eve, the young adults of the Cynster clan respond to a plea for help. Summoned to a humble dwelling in ruggedly forested mountains, Lucilla is called on to help with the difficult birth of a child, while the others rise to the challenge of helping her. With a violent storm closing in and severely limited options, the next generation of Cynsters face their first collective test—can they save this mother and child? And themselves, too?

Back at the manor, Claire is increasingly drawn to Daniel and despite her misgivings, against the backdrop of the ongoing festivities their relationship deepens. Yet she remains torn—until catastrophe strikes, and by winter's light, she learns that love—true love—is worth any risk, any price.

A tale brimming with all the magical delights of a Scottish festive season. A Cynster Next Generation novel – a classic historical romance of 71,000 words.

THE TEMPTING OF THOMAS CARRICK
Cynster Next Generation Novel #2

Do you believe in fate? Do you believe in passion? What happens when fate and passion collide?
Do you believe in love? What happens when fate, passion, and love combine?
This. This...

#1 New York Times *bestselling author Stephanie Laurens returns to Scotland with a tale of two lovers irrevocably linked by destiny and passion.*

Thomas Carrick is a gentleman driven to control all aspects of his life. As the wealthy owner of Carrick Enterprises, located in bustling Glasgow, he is one of that city's most eligible bachelors and fully intends to select an appropriate wife from the many young ladies paraded before him. He wants to take that necessary next step along his self-determined path, yet no young lady captures his eye, much less his attention...not in the way Lucilla Cynster had, and still did, even though she lives miles away.

For over two years, Thomas has avoided his clan's estate because it borders Lucilla's home, but disturbing reports from his clansmen force him to return to the countryside—only to discover that his uncle, the laird, is ailing, a clan family is desperately ill, and the clan-healer is unconscious and dying. Duty to the clan leaves Thomas no choice but to seek help from the last woman he wants to face.

Strong-willed and passionate, Lucilla has been waiting—increasingly impatiently—for Thomas to return and claim his rightful place by her side. She knows he is hers—her fated lover, husband, protector, and mate. He is the only man for her, just as she is his one true love. And, at last, he's back. Even though his returning wasn't on her account, Lucilla is willing to seize whatever chance Fate hands her.

Thomas can never forget Lucilla, much less the connection that seethes between them, but to marry her would mean embracing a life he's adamant he does not want.

Lucilla sees that Thomas has yet to accept the inevitability of their union and, despite all, he can refuse her and walk away. But how *can* he ignore a bond such as theirs—one so much stronger than reason? Despite several unnerving attacks mounted against them, despite the uncertainty racking his clan, Lucilla remains as determined as only a Cynster can be to fight for the future she knows can be theirs—and while she cannot command him, she has powerful enticements she's willing to wield in the cause of tempting Thomas Carrick.

A neo-Gothic tale of passionate romance laced with mystery, set in the uplands of southwestern Scotland. A Cynster Next Generation Novel – a classic historical romance of 122,000 words.

A MATCH FOR MARCUS CYNSTER
Cynster Next Generation Novel #3

Duty compels her to turn her back on marriage. Fate drives him to protect her come what may. Then love takes a hand in this battle of yearning hearts, stubborn wills, and a match too powerful to deny.

#1 New York Times *bestselling author Stephanie Laurens returns to rugged Scotland with a dramatic tale of passionate desire and unwavering devotion.*

Restless and impatient, Marcus Cynster waits for Fate to come calling. He knows his destiny lies in the lands surrounding his family home, but what will his future be? Equally importantly, with whom will he share it?

Of one fact he feels certain: his fated bride will not be Niniver Carrick. His elusive neighbor attracts him mightily, yet he feels compelled to protect her—even from himself. Fickle Fate, he's sure, would never be so kind as to decree that Niniver should be his. The best he can do for them both is to avoid her.

Niniver has vowed to return her clan to prosperity. The epitome of fragile femininity, her delicate and ethereal exterior cloaks a stubborn will and an unflinching devotion to the people in her care. She accepts that in order to achieve her goal, she cannot risk marrying and losing her grip on the clan's reins to an inevitably controlling husband. Unfortunately, many local men see her as their opportunity.

Soon, she's forced to seek help to get rid of her unwelcome suitors. Powerful and dangerous, Marcus Cynster is perfect for the task. Suppressing her wariness over tangling with a gentleman who so excites her passions, she appeals to him for assistance with her peculiar problem.

Although at first he resists, Marcus discovers that, contrary to his expectations, his fated role *is* to stand by Niniver's side and, ultimately, to claim her hand. Yet in order to convince her to be his bride, they must plunge headlong into a journey full of challenges, unforeseen dangers, passion, and yearning, until Niniver grasps the essential truth—that she is indeed a match for Marcus Cynster.

A neo-Gothic tale of passionate romance set in the uplands of southwestern Scotland. A Cynster Next Generation Novel – a classic historical romance of 114,000 words.

And if you want to discover where the Cynsters began, return to the iconic

DEVIL'S BRIDE

the book that introduced millions of historical romance readers around the globe to the powerful men of the unforgettable Cynster family – aristocrats to the bone, conquerors at heart – and the willful feisty ladies strong enough to be their brides.

ABOUT THE AUTHOR

#1 *New York Times* bestselling author Stephanie Laurens began writing romances as an escape from the dry world of professional science. Her hobby quickly became a career when her first novel was accepted for publication, and with entirely becoming alacrity, she gave up writing about facts in favor of writing fiction.

All Laurens's works to date are historical romances, ranging from medieval times to the mid-1800s, and her settings range from Scotland to India. The majority of her works are set in the period of the British Regency. Laurens has published over 80 works of historical romance, including 40 *New York Times* bestsellers. Laurens has sold more than 20 million print, audio, and e-books globally. All her works are continuously available in print and e-book formats in English worldwide, and have been translated into many other languages. An international bestseller, among other accolades, Laurens has received the Romance Writers of America® prestigious RITA® Award for Best Romance Novella 2008 for *The Fall of Rogue Gerrard.*

Laurens's continuing novels featuring the Cynster family are widely regarded as classics of the historical romance genre. Other series include the *Bastion Club Novels*, the *Black Cobra Quartet*, the *Adventurers Quartet,* and the *Casebook of Barnaby Adair Novels*.

For information on all published novels and on upcoming releases and updates on novels yet to come, visit Stephanie's website: www.stephanielaurens.com

To sign up for Stephanie's Email Newsletter (a private list) for heads-up alerts as new books are released, exclusive sneak peeks into upcoming books, and exclusive sweepstakes contests, follow the prompts at http://www.stephanielaurens.com/newsletter-signup/

To follow Stephanie on BookBub, head to her BookBub Author Page: https://www.bookbub.com/authors/stephanie-laurens

Stephanie lives with her husband and a goofy black labradoodle in the hills outside Melbourne, Australia. When she isn't writing, she's reading, and if she isn't reading, she'll be tending her garden.

www.stephanielaurens.com
stephanie@stephanielaurens.com